*Praise for* **THE WATCH**

PUBLISHERS WEEKLY BEST OF FICTION 2012
SHORTLISTED FOR THE BOEKE PRIZE, SOUTH AFRICA

"[*The Watch*] achieves a subtle balance of dramatic forces—personal morality and public order, duty to God and duty to country—that gives it a philosophical depth and wrenching humanity. . . . Mr. Roy-Bhattacharya brings a rigorous and often disquieting sense of empathy to each of his clashing characters."

—WALL STREET JOURNAL

"The fog of war doesn't begin to describe what awaits the American soldiers in Joydeep Roy-Bhattacharya's novel *The Watch* . . . His description of the firefight in a sandstorm is gripping and terrifying; so are his overlapping accounts of the ethical and military decisions that young men, fatigued, distraught and unsupported, have to make."

—MILWAUKEE JOURNAL SENTINEL

"A heartbreaking and haunting look at the nature and reality of war."

—WICHITA EAGLE

"A powerful reading experience."

—SYDNEY MORNING HERALD

"The quintessential epic tragedy of our times, the ultimate indictment of our human inability to communicate and thus curb our ethnic, religious, cultural, political, and economic extremism. . . . Let's hope our children read the book as a rare and accurate glimpse of combat and the misfortune of what happens when people become disengaged from the policies of the elite."

—PAUL SULLIVAN, VETERANS FOR COMMON SENSE

"A vivid portrait of modern war. . . . By drawing on classical literature, Joydeep Roy-Bhattacharya has fashioned a beautiful and heartfelt lamentation."

—*Irish Times*

"An engaging work of timeless imagination, both vivid and gritty."

—*Fredericksburg Free Lance–Star*

"Roy-Bhattacharya uses a familiar story of loss to examine Afghanistan as it exists today."

—*Poughkeepsie Journal*

"A beautiful re-enactment of [the Antigone] tragedy plays out in the dust of a forlorn outpost in Afghanistan when a young woman parks herself outside a fort and pleads with American soldiers stationed there to give her the body of her brother slain in the conflict. . . . So worthwhile to read this lyrical drama about the horror of war."

—*New Jersey Star-Ledger*

"Must-read fiction. [A] subtle, discomfiting novel, a nonsequential tale that defies conventional storytelling. . . . Given the author's deft arrangement of scenes, readers will dutifully persevere to see what happens, even if the ending is foretold, tragic, and seemingly inevitable."

—*Daily Beast*

"With this book, Joydeep Roy-Bhattacharya has proved himself to be the modern Norman Mailer. *The Watch* is a stunning account of war, of the terrifying range of emotions, the despair and the sheer fatigue which men have to endure in combat. . . . *The Watch* is quite simply superb."

—ABC Brisbane (Australia)

"Sophocles's story of Antigone, who demands her brother's body back after it is decreed that the traitor's corpse be left to rot, is masterfully relocated and updated."

—*THE GUARDIAN* (UK)

"*The Watch* is a story told before—the myth of Antigone. This time it is told in present-day Afghanistan. It is a gripping novel which exposes the futility of this conflict."

—*DURBAN DAILY NEWS* (SOUTH AFRICA)

"Roy-Bhattacharya's powerful, modern take on the Afghanistan armed conflict resonates with the echoes of Joseph Heller, Tim O'Brien, and Robert Stone."

—*PUBLISHERS WEEKLY*, STARRED REVIEW

"Difficult to put down, powerful, eloquent, and even haunting."

—*BOOKLIST*, STARRED REVIEW

"[Roy-Bhattacharya] forces us to face the evil we do to others and to ourselves."

—CHRIS HEDGES, PULITZER PRIZE–WINNING JOURNALIST AND AUTHOR OF NBCC FINALIST *WAR IS A FORCE THAT GIVES US MEANING*

"A poignant and important book about one of the defining events of the start of the twenty-first century; it is devastatingly eloquent and unequivocal about the fact that there is no glory or beauty in war."

—FATIMA BHUTTO, AUTHOR OF *SONGS OF BLOOD AND SWORD: A DAUGHTER'S MEMOIR*

"An ancient tale made modern, passed through different narrators in extraordinary shape-shifting prose that makes this not just an important novel but a remarkable read."

—AMINATTA FORNA, AUTHOR OF ORANGE PRIZE SHORT-LISTED *THE MEMORY OF LOVE*

"Roy-Bhattacharya breathes a 21st-century sensibility into this ancient tale by passing it through different narrators and he dazzles in his ability to inhabit the minds of his characters, particularly those of the soldiers. All in all, it's an extraordinary, shape-shifting telling that exacts a devastating emotional toll."

—THE WEST AUSTRALIAN

"*The Watch* is a tale that illustrates the futility of war at its most basic level."

—BOOKBROWSE

"A carefully and fully realized novel . . . [Joydeep Roy-Bhattacharya] is excellent at presenting the isolation of the Americans in a landscape of desert and foothills, as well as the feelings of isolation inside their heads. . . . Beyond partisan politics or hysterical reactions, Roy-Bhattacharya has given us a brilliant account of the experience of occupiers and occupied."

—TORONTO STAR

"You will remember her voice. . . . What a masterpiece of the art of fiction—proof, if any were needed, that the Muse is real."

—JONATHAN SHAY, MD, PhD, AUTHOR OF
*ACHILLES IN VIETNAM* AND *ODYSSEUS IN AMERICA*

"*The Watch* is a meticulous, gut-wrenching analysis of how we perpetuate violence. It is a reminder that we all—participants and onlookers alike—are complicit in the barbarities of war."

–ANNA BADKHEN, AUTHOR OF
*PEACE MEALS: CANDY-WRAPPED KALASHNIKOVS AND
OTHER WAR STORIES* AND *WAITING FOR THE TALIBAN*

"*The Watch* is a work of beauty and terror, exacting in its realism, breathtaking in the range of its sympathy, devastating in its judgment."

—PETER TRACHTENBERG, AUTHOR OF
*THE BOOK OF CALAMITIES* AND *7 TATTOOS*

# THE
# WATCH

A NOVEL

JOYDEEP ROY-BHATTACHARYA

*Thank you -er reading!*

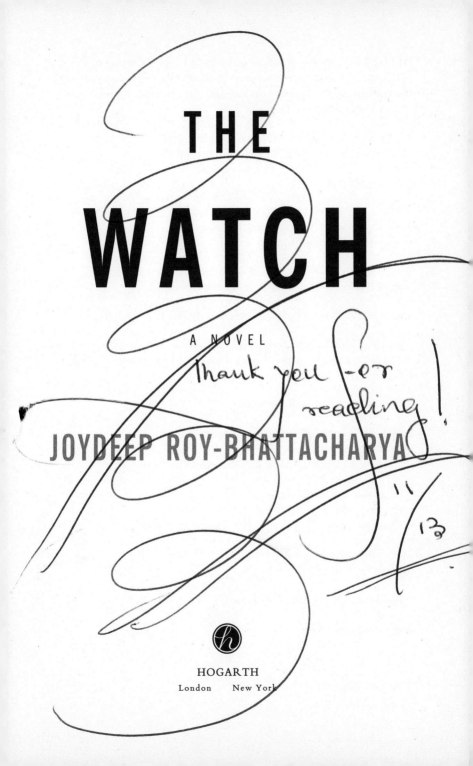

HOGARTH

London    New York

Copyright © 2012, 2013 by Joydeep Roy-Bhattacharya
Reader's Guide copyright © 2013 by Random House, Inc.

All rights reserved.

Published in the United States by Hogarth, an imprint of the Crown Publishing Group, a division of Random House, Inc., New York.
www.crownpublishing.com

HOGARTH is a trademark of the Random House Group Limited, and the H colophon is a trademark of Random House, Inc.

EXTRA LIBRIS and colophon are trademarks of Random House, Inc.

Originally published in hardcover in slightly different form in the United States by Hogarth, an imprint of the Crown Publishing Group, a division of Random House, Inc., New York, in 2012.

Permission credits appear on page 285.

Library of Congress Cataloging-in-Publication Data
Roy-Bhattacharya, Joydeep.
  The watch : a novel / Joydeep Roy-Bhattacharya.—1st ed.
      p.   cm.
  1. Afghan War, 2001—Fiction.  I. Title.
PR9499.3.R596W38    2012
823'.914—dc23                          2011037317

ISBN 978-0-307-95591-3
eISBN 978-0-307-95590-6

Printed in the United States of America

Cover design by Ben Wiseman

10 9 8 7 6 5 4 3 2 1

First Paperback Edition

*This book is dedicated to the people of Afghanistan*

• • •

*And to*
*Chris Hedges,*
*Preceptor, Exemplar*

*Rick Sullivan,*
*Officer, Gentleman*

*&*
*Jonathan Shay*
*Physician, Healer*

θανουμένη γὰρ ἐξῄδη, τί δ᾿ οὔ;

κεἰ μὴ σὺ προυκήρυξας. εἰ δὲ τοῦ χρόνου

πρόσθεν θανοῦμαι, κέρδος αὔτ ἐγὼ λέγω.

ὅστις γὰρ ἐν πολλοῖσιν ὡς ἐγὼ κακοῖς

ζῆ, πῶς ὅδ᾿ Οὐχὶ κατθαὼν κέρδος φέρει;

οὕτως ἔμοιγε τοῦδε τοῦ μόρου τυχεῖν

παρ᾿ οὐδὲν ἄλγος· ἀλλ᾿ ἄν, εἰ τὸν ἐξ ἐμῆς

μητρὸς θανόντ᾿ ἄθαπτον ἠνσχόμην νέκυν,

κείνοις ἂν ἤλγουν· τοῖσδε δ᾿ οὐκ ἀλγύνομαι.

—SOPHOCLES, *Antigone*

*I know that I must die,*

*E'en hadst thou not proclaimed it; and if death*

*Is thereby hastened, I shall count it gain.*

*For death is gain to him whose life, like mine,*

*Is full of misery. Thus my lot appears*

*Not sad, but blissful; for had I endured*

*To leave my mother's son unburied there,*

*I should have grieved with reason, but not now.*

—SOPHOCLES, *Antigone*

# CONTENTS

# COMBAT OUTPOST
# TARSÂNDAN

### Kandahar Province

### Afghanistan

# ANTIGONE

NE.
Two.
Three.
Four. I count the moments and say the Basmala in my head.
*In the Name of God, Most Gracious, Most Merciful . . .*

It's up to me now. I'm scared: my hands are shaking, my mouth is dry. I cast a look back at the mountains where I have spent my life, where I was born, where my family died. All my family, that is, except my brother, Yusuf. I remember what Yusuf said before he set off to storm the fort: There are moments when, in order to be master of a situation, you have to go mad and keep your head at the same time.

I remember this as I turn the wheels of my cart and trundle down the sloping track to the square field and the fort. They've leveled everything here: there are no trees, and there's no vegetation, not a semblance of shade; the earth is dry and cracked and already scorching hot despite the early hour. Dust swirls about me; the sun blazes down on the drab earthworks of the fort. The ground is scored with boot marks and the tracks of many vehicles. Piled up on one side of the fortifications is a jumble of rubbish: discarded oil cans, bent iron posts, and plastic bags and buckets. The only signs of life are occasional metallic glints reflecting the rising sun, and a vertical line of smoke. This arid landscape could not be more different than the fertile green valley I started out from. It's a desolate prospect, and yet I've spent my entire overnight journey across the mountains waiting for this sight.

As I push against the ground with my hands to propel the cart forward, I think of the precarious mountain trails and can hardly believe I've made it here with nothing more than the strength of my puny arms and shoulders. Some of my muscles are raw to the touch, like open wounds; others are dead to all sensation. The stumps of my legs, only recently healed, have begun to bleed; the constant thrusting forward required by my journey has rubbed the sutures raw. I ignore the pain; I ignore everything except the fact of my being here. I tell myself that I am here because my heart is huge and my tenderness real. I am here to bury my brother according to the tenets of my faith. That is all there is to it.

A body covered with buzzing flies bars my path. I feel the bile rising up my throat. With a sense of unreality, I lean out of my cart and turn the body over. It isn't Yusuf, but a youth lying with his face down and a bullet hole through his forehead. Blood has congealed over one eye; the other is closed. I let him go and recite the Janaza over him. Some distance away, another body lies huddled. It's Rehmat, one of Yusuf's men, his black turban unraveling in loops as I raise his head. Rehmat was immensely strong: he could lift an entire felled oak with one hand. Now the lifeless hand rests limply against mine. I let him go and sit back in the cart. A flock of crows wheels impatiently in the air. High overhead a vulture flaps its wings and prepares to land. A flag at one corner of the fort snaps like gunshot in the breeze. Already I feel worn out. My brother was a fool to attack here: behind its multiple barriers of barbed wire, sandbags, and mud-and-stone walls, the fort looks impregnable.

I move forward and approach the third, and last, body lying in the field. It's Bahram Gul, the oldest of Yusuf's companions, who once brought me a posy of mountain daisies when I was a child. His open mouth is unnaturally red, his hennaed beard encrusted with crimson muck. Bahram loved to sing; then the Talib came and he fell silent and tended to his fields. But lately he'd taken up singing again. His voice echoes through my head as I leave him behind. Bahram's daughter Anisa was my closest friend before she died in childbirth. Now they will meet again. I envy them the good fortune of their reunion.

A puff of dust kicks up from the ground to my left. I see it out of the corner of my eye before I smell its burning scent and hear the high-pitched ringing sound. My brain dulled from my recent exertions, I keep pushing myself forward until a second puff kicks up fiercely to my right. That's when it dawns on me that I am being fired at. When the third bullet shrills past, I come to a stop. The silence seems to last a lifetime. The shadow of a solitary cloud drifts across the land.

I reach up and touch the taweez around my neck. Many years ago, Father brought back a written prayer from the shrine of a Sufi Pir near Zareh Sharan, and I've worn it sewn into a leather pouch ever since. Now the leather's softness reassures me. Instead of looking at the fort to see who's firing at me, I look behind at the mountains. They stand like faithful sentinels in the sky, their enormity dwarfing everything. When I turn around again toward the fort, it seems shrunken in contrast and no longer as intimidating. I see it for what it really is: a rudimentary structure slapped together with adobe, sandbags, and drywall. An alien accretion.

I hold up one of Yusuf's white shirts and wave it in the air.

Moments later, a metallic voice echoes across the field and asks me what I want. Tsë ghwâre? it asks. Although it speaks Pashto, the voice has a distinct Tajik ring to it. I am not surprised.

The fort seems very far away. I make my own voice big and answer that I am here to bury my brother, who was killed in the battle yesterday. I am his sister, I call out. My name is Nizam.

There is a lull, and then the voice asks: What is your brother's name?

I tell them. Once again, there is a silence. I try to picture how they must see me from their side: a small, shrouded figure in a wooden cart slung low on the ground. I imagine their surprise. I must take advantage of it.

The voice breaks the silence. I detest its metallic gargle.

It asks: Who told you that you could find him here?

I reply: Those who survived the battle.

What does he look like?

I feel the weight of my answer as intensely as the burden of my brother's death, but I manage to control my emotions and describe Yusuf, taking care to be precise.

After a moment the voice returns:

Your brother is being held for purposes of identification.

I can identify him, I reply.

You must leave. He will be identified by people coming from afar. Experts. Then he will be buried.

When will they arrive?

Soon.

How soon?

In two days.

That cannot be, I answer, trying not to let my emotion choke my voice. Yusuf must be given a proper burial. That's why I'm here. It is my right.

Our business with him is not finished.

He is dead. What business can you possibly have with him?

He was a terrorist, a Talib, and a bad saray.

That isn't true! My brother was a Pashtun hero, a Mujahid, and a freedom fighter. He fought the Taliban. And he died fighting the Amrikâyi invaders. He was a brave man.

You are as misguided as he was, Pashtana. You've no place here. Go away.

I've brought a white shroud, I answer. I will ask you for water to wash him, as is my right. I will dig the grave and place him in it, with his body facing the Quibla. Then I will say a prayer, pour three handfuls of soil over him, and recite: "We created you from it, and return you into it, and from it we will raise you a second time." After that I will leave, I promise. Do not deny me this duty that I must perform.

In the space of silence that follows, I lower my eyes and gaze at the stumps of my legs, wrapped in goatskins held together with puttees and rags. The goatskins have stained red. My legs, usually numb, have begun to burn and sting.

Eventually the voice replies, sounding surprised but also slightly derisive.

You are a woman. You have no role in a Muslim burial. We are many men here. We'll take care of it. I've asked the Amrikâyi captain who commands the fort. He's an honorable man. He gives you his word.

I lower my improvised white flag.

I will not leave, I answer. My voice shakes with fatigue and anger. I'm close to tears.

There's an electric crackle as the megaphone shuts off, and I'm left wondering. A crow flaps across my line of sight and I realize that I am surrounded by carrion birds. Then a shot rings out and a vulture keels across the sky and folds to the ground.

The next time I look up I'm startled to see four men slip out of a gate embedded in the high walls. They come to a standstill behind the barbed wire barrier with their guns pointing in my direction. The only one of them not dressed in a uniform is a wild-eyed, gangling boy, not much older than me. He must be the Tajik interpreter. He's the first to speak.

What are you doing here, you stupid woman? he blurts out in a nervous, indignant voice that's markedly different from its omnipotent metallic incarnation. Didn't you read the signs? You could have been shot!

I am not lettered, I tell him, forcing myself to be calm.

He brushes off my reply with an exasperated wave of his hand. My sense of him is of someone trying to play an adult, manifestly out of his league.

The captain, he says importantly, gesturing at a short, stocky man, would like you to know that he has no quarrel with you. But you've exaggerated your status and you must leave. This is a battle-ground. It isn't a place for women's hysterics.

I decide to ignore him and focus on his companions. I watch them without expression as they stand there, burdened with their guilt and lies.

The officer steps out in front, flanked by two helmeted soldiers. All three wear bulky jackets and dark glasses, and I imagine they must be stifling in this heat. I'm too far away to make out their features, and as the captain turns away from me and addresses the Tajik, the soldiers raise their guns and aim at me. The captain's terse voice, the jittery interpreter, and the two wary soldiers all suggest the cautious bearing of a group of fighting men caught in an unprecedented situation. Clearly, I am a dilemma for them. I am a woman in their man's world, and they do not know how to proceed.

They look at me expectantly, waiting for me to speak, but I remain silent.

The Tajik addresses me again, and it's my turn to be surprised.

Listen to me carefully, Pashtana, he says. The captain says you are free to stay here and rot in the sun. But if you move even a single gaz toward the fort, you'll be shot on the spot.

Can I bury the men lying in the field? I ask.

The Tajik turns to the captain, who speaks irritably, gesturing with both hands.

That's between you and the vultures, the Tajik says. It's none of our business.

They turn and begin walking back toward the fort, but the Tajik calls out to me over his shoulder. Remember the captain's orders, he says. One gaz toward the fort, and it's all over for you.

The dust from their retreating feet ascends slowly into the sky.

Sensing a small but crucial victory, I have a mad desire to laugh, which I manage to suppress. I have not, after all, been killed out of hand, which might easily have happened. I turn my cart around and roll it in the direction of Bahram Gul. The heavy wooden wheels drag over the cracked earth; the metal joints squeak and squeal. The sound must carry up to the fort, but I don't care.

When I reach Bahram Gul, I take out my shovel and chase the crows away. Apart from these accursed birds and the plague of flies, there isn't a living thing in sight. I take a deep breath and, turning my back to the fort, raise the veil of my bughra. It's going to be hard work, and it must be done quickly. My poor dear Bahram kaka is beginning to smell. I remember the flowers he gave me, say a short prayer, and begin to dig. Fortunately, the ground is soft and yields easily to my shovel.

Hours later—how many hours?—my work is done. Three raised humps of freshly dug soil mark the final resting place of my brother's faithful companions. On top of each grave I place a stone. Against the bare ground, the sparseness of the mounds embarrasses me: they should have been marked with gravestones, and poles at the head and foot decorated with green flags, as befits their status as heroes. But I hadn't expected to be doing this work, and the only flag that I've brought is reserved for my Yusuf.

I hobble back to my cart. My back is almost rigid with pain, my hands are scratched and bleeding, but I feel at peace with myself. I put down the shovel and clean my hands with dust. Then I drink some water from my goatskin bag. I'm so exhausted, the water swills out of my mouth. When I lower my veil and turn to face the fort, there is a line of soldiers watching me in silence. Some of them carry guns slung over their shoulders; others point theirs in my direction. One of them takes off his helmet and mops his face with a red handkerchief. He stuffs it into his pocket when he's done and, turning to me quite deliberately so that there can be no mistaking his gesture, makes the sign of a cross. It's a small indication of humanity. And yet, all afternoon, I smell the inhuman scent of their guns.

Dusk comes later on the plains than I am used to in the mountains. Crickets crawl out of the fissures in the ground and trill in the cooling air. The sunset fans across the sky in a play of glorious light. It soaks into the mountains with a crimson glow. Thousands of stars emerge to replace the melting sun. They make up for the absence of the moon. The fort hangs suspended in a swirl of evening fog, its sloping roofs slowly fading into the darkness. The spiderweb of trails I've had to traverse to get here, with their long and precarious stretches studded with mines, already seem part of another life.

In my cart I have a burlap bag filled with food: naan, walnuts, pistachios, dried fruit—enough to last me a couple of days. I eat some of the bread, tearing it into bite-sized pieces, but my mouth is dry and I have to chew for a long time before I can swallow. As I drink some water, lights come on inside the fort, but out here in the field, all is in shadow. Somewhere a hyena sets off on its nocturnal rounds with a mocking cry. I shiver involuntarily. I've never spent a night outdoors on my own, but I'm too tired to dwell on it. Besides, the heavenly garden of stars consoles me. When it's completely dark, I crawl away from the cart and attend to my bodily needs.

Soon the night turns cold and I draw my blanket over my shoulders. I reach for my rebaab, which Father taught me to play after he lost his sight. He was an expert at the lute, and I learned quickly, graduating from simple expositions to more complex melodies until he said I sounded better than him. As I pluck the strings, they vibrate through me and fill up the boundless emptiness all around. The fort seems to fall silent in response, but that must be my imagination. I think of Father as I play, but later on, after I curl up in my cart, it is Yusuf's smile that colors my sleep. I promise him I will not leave this place until I've given him the burial he deserves. I am determined to be implacable.

Suddenly a searchlight switches on and roves around the field before it finds me and pries my eyes open. Its glare is hot and sharp. From time to time it darts away and restlessly probes the ground behind me and the road farther up. Then it darts back to rest on me again. This goes on the entire night until the break of dawn. I summon all the strength that's left in me, pull my blanket over my head, and press my hands between my thighs for warmth.

Morning. Mist rises from the earth. My hair is damp, my blanket covered with dew. As I sit up in the cart, I nearly cry out in pain from my cramped muscles. My neck is stiff, my movements leaden. The chill in the air has crisped visibly; what little I can see of the field glitters like a mirror. The sun crests the horizon, but the mist continues to softly shield me. I cannot see the fort: perhaps this is all a bad dream?

The Tajik is the first to appear, accompanied by two soldiers with drawn guns. They stop just inside the barbed wire fence that encircles the fort. The soldiers go down on their knees with their guns pointed at me, while the Tajik stands between them with a dirty gray shawl wrapped around his shalwar kameez and shouts out a question. It is difficult to make out what he's saying since the lower part of his face is concealed by a scarf. His surly, nervous tones barely reach me, and I have to ask him to speak up. I wonder about this strange habit of yelling from a distance. Perhaps it's the Amrikâyi manner of doing things? Yesterday's exchanges have left me hoarse, and I resent it.

He removes his scarf and repeats his query. Why are you here, really? he asks.

I've told you already. I've come to claim my brother.

It's a man's job. Where are the men of your family?

You've killed them all, men, women, and children. I'm the sole survivor.

He ignores my accusation and asks me what the matter is with my legs.

I lost them to the bomb that decimated my family. It came from the air. We were returning from a wedding.

He turns around and disappears with his escorts, but the blue gleam of guns from the fort warns me that I am being watched. I cast off my blanket as the heat and sunlight intensify. Soon I've gone from shivering in the chill to sweating profusely. I tell myself it's the heat and not my nerves.

The mist dissipates as I wait. The fort emerges into the light of day. The square field is peaceful, the sky tranquil. As the morning wears on, a great tide of humidity rolls across the plain, the fort shimmying in its wake and appearing strangely evanescent. Soon after, the first smoke rises into the air from the fort, and the smell of cooking wafts out. I reach for my own dust-encrusted bag of food and am about to eat when the Tajik returns with a soldier. The Amrikâyi's hands are thrust deep in his pockets; occasionally he touches his collar tenderly. Like the rest of his countrymen, he has a perfectly nondescript face. The interpreter walks with a slouch, his face hidden once again behind his scarf. They come to a halt just outside the fort and speak almost in unison, the Tajik struggling to keep up.

They say: We enjoyed your lute last night. It was soothing.

I don't reply.

They say: It's good that you're able to play music again in this country. Under the Taliban, it was forbidden, but we've made it possible. That's what freedom means.

I say: Under the Taliban, my family was alive. Now they are all dead. What is better? Freedom or life?

My answer discomfits the Amrikâyi. He grows visibly awkward

and constrained. He paces up and down, haughty and uncertain, then says something to the interpreter in a terse voice.

The Tajik shouts: You have displeased the lieutenant!

Why have I displeased him? I speak the truth.

It's hardly that simple. You understand nothing.

What don't I understand?

The Tajik turns to his master, who says: This is war. People die. It's what happens.

I strain to keep calm. I say: You killed my blind father who couldn't fight back. You killed my family from the air. But for you, my mother, my grandmother, my sister Fawzia, my sister-in-law, and my little brother Yunus would all be alive.

They're about to reply, but I carry on speaking.

I say: This isn't war but the slaughter of innocents. I know what war means. We're a land of warrior tribes, of blood feuds that last for generations. But no man here would stoop to deliberately killing women and children. He'd be purged from society and subjected to lifelong contempt.

There's a pause, then the officer gesticulates angrily. Your brother Yusuf wasn't innocent. He was a Taliban leader who murdered my friends and fellow soldiers. He was a dangerous militant.

My brother was a leader of the Pashtun, and a prince among men, but he wasn't a murderer, and I've already told you he wasn't a Talib. He died a hero's death to avenge his family. He struck at you because you struck at us.

Then perhaps you'll understand when I tell you that I myself am here because innocents were killed—thousands of innocents. Do you know what was done in my country? Entire buildings collapsed!

I can assure you that my family had nothing to do with it! I protest. We're simple farmers and shepherds. I don't even know where exactly your country is.

You may not know but I'm sure your brother did, he says.

Speaking quietly and intensely through the Tajik, he continues: Who brought you here?

No one. I came on my own.

Where have you come from?

I mention the name of my valley.

The Amrikâyi spreads out a map on the ground and they study it together. Then he laughs while the Tajik exclaims: That's impossible! It's too far away. Do you think we're fools to believe that you pushed yourself in that cart all the way from the heart of the mountains?

It is the truth. It is up to you whether or not to believe me.

The officer folds away the map and rises to his feet.

But this is a very important matter, he says, and it's important for you to speak the truth. If you don't want to answer, that's your decision, but words can be bridges, and I'm trying to understand your motives.

I feel worn down. I address the Tajik directly: Tell your master that words count less than actions and I'm not prepared to engage in a conversation that impugns my family's honor. Tell him that I am conscious of the passage of the hours, which belong only to God, and all I want to do is to ensure my brother's safe return to Him.

They say: We are waiting for men who will come in a helicopter to take your brother to Kabul. There they will display his corpse on television. Ministers and generals will be interviewed about the battle. He was an important insurgent. That's why we are waiting.

That's sacrilege! I exclaim. You can't rob a dead man of his soul. It's forbidden, and I won't allow it! I have a religious duty toward my brother.

And I have a duty to the state, the Amrikâyi says, which is also your state, by the way. I have a duty to abide by the rule of law, which are now your rules. Without laws, we'd be back to your tribal anarchy.

I turn to the Tajik. You're a believer, aren't you? You know this is wrong.

He shoots me a quick, anxious glance.

I tell him: I thought you said the soldiers would bury him here, that the captain had given his word.

He evades my eyes, while the lieutenant throws up his arms.

He says: It's impossible to talk like this, always shouting.

I say: I agree. Why don't you come closer, or let me approach?

Their answer baffles me: Because we're concerned for our safety.

I feel like laughing. I'm a single, unarmed woman, I tell them, and you're an armed garrison bristling with guns. How can you be concerned for your safety?

The Amrikâyi goes red in the face when my answer is translated.

He snaps at the Tajik, who in turn snaps at me. How do we know you're not a black widow? he says. How do we know you're not carrying a bomb?

How can I be a widow when I'm not even married? As for a bomb, I am here to bury—

Yes, yes, we know, he shouts, cutting me off. But we must check you for explosives. There've been reports. Maybe you have other intentions.

What do you want me to do?

They do not reply but their answer comes later in the day, a little before noon.

The lieutenant reappears, as does the Tajik, but with them is an enormous black man, along with a line of marksmen who lie prone on the ground and aim their guns at me. Others crowd behind them, and they all stare at me as if I'm some strange animal, potentially interesting, yet dangerous enough to maintain a guarded distance. Meanwhile, the black giant lumbers purposefully toward me.

I begin to wheel back my cart in a panic.

Mëyh khudza! the Tajik shouts. Don't move! He won't harm you; he'll just check you for bombs.

Then he says quickly, confidentially: The bomb is in the cart, isn't it? You can tell me. I won't betray you.

I don't even bother to answer, merely glance at him with contempt.

The giant turns authoritatively and says something, after which the Tajik looks embarrassed and speaks to me with less assurance than before, and with lowered eyes.

Lutfan burqa obâsa, he says. Please take off your burqa.

I can't do that! I blurt out, my voice rising.

You must take it off if you want to stay here, he repeats irritably.

Is this the foreigners' sense of honor?

Just do as they say, I tell you.

So I am to be humiliated before an audience of men. I hadn't anticipated this, but I realize I've no choice but to obey. I will not leave this place without burying Yusuf. All the same, I feel ashamed that they will see me with my hair worn loose.

I take off my bughra slowly. My hair hangs down to my knees. As I let the bughra slip to the ground, dust billows from it. I'm sure my shalwar kameez is equally dusty and stained with sweat. I lower my eyes, my naked face burning with shame.

It isn't the end of my ordeal. I'm instructed to move away from the cart. I say a silent prayer as I climb out shakily. The strand of cowrie shells and coins that I wear on my head tangles in my hair. I brush it free and, trembling with mortification, hobble away on my stumps while willing myself not to fall. My goatskin wrappings smudge with dust. I come to a standstill after a few gaz.

Now put your hands on your head and turn around, the Tajik calls. Turn a full circle.

I do as he tells me, my stumps hurting.

When I face him again, the black giant makes a tipping motion with his hand, which the Tajik translates: Please lie down facing the ground with your hands on your head and your legs spread apart.

I refuse! I cry out, scandalized. What you are asking is shameful!

The Tajik ignores my response and says: Once you lie down, the sergeant will approach you and search you for explosives.

Didn't you hear me? I won't do it.

The sooner you comply, he says, his voice turning shrill, the quicker they will resolve your petition for your brother's corpse.

I stare at him for a long moment. He is sweating profusely. I cannot tell if he is lying, but the tone of entreaty in his voice is unmistakable.

I lower myself slowly to the ground and lie down on my stomach. A silence closes over me; all I can hear is my own heart beating.

I turn my head and see that, in the distance, the Tajik has averted his eyes. Closer to me, the giant approaches the cart and prods it with his rifle. He turns it over gingerly and examines it. Putting it down the right side up, he begins walking toward me, all the while speaking in a surprisingly calm and gentle voice. He ignores the bughra lying on the ground, walking past it. He grips my hands and places them wide apart on the ground above my head. When I feel his hands on me, I grow rigid and imagine I've turned into a pillar of stone. Closing my eyes, I sink deep into myself.

When he is done, he helps me get up and once again places my hands on my head before repeating the search. He is discreet, efficient, and all the while he continues speaking and I'm gratified that his voice isn't entirely steady: he's as afraid as I am. I decide to focus on his shoes, which are surprisingly small for a man his size. Somehow, that reassures me.

When he finally steps away, I can sense him relax. He's been holding his breath and now he lets it out in a long sigh. Just as he turns to inspect the bughra, I slump against him. I'm shaking uncontrollably. He holds me gently for a moment. Okay? he says huskily, patting me on the shoulder. Okay?

He takes off his helmet and shouts to his comrades in a relieved voice. He invites me to return to my cart and offers his hand for support, but I ignore him and make my own way back, picking up the bughra as I go. All the marksmen have risen to their feet. The tension in the air dissipates. The Tajik keeps his eyes averted, possibly waiting until I've put on my bughra, but I simply throw it into the cart and collapse in an undignified heap on top of it. A cheer goes up from the line of soldiers, but whether they're cheering me or their comrade, I can't tell. I'm close to tears; I feel utterly spent.

The giant walks away and approaches the lieutenant. They talk for a while, and then they call their men back into the fort. When the lieutenant returns, he crosses the field briskly with a couple of soldiers and walks right up to me, the Tajik trotting at their heels like a dog. The lieutenant's hair is cut so short, I can see right through to his shiny pink scalp. He stands before me and bows in an exaggeratedly humble gesture of greeting, which the Tajik dutifully imitates. I recognize the signs: they want to be chatty after stripping me of my dignity.

Salâm, the officer says. Peace.

He continues speaking, and the Tajik says: Lieutenant Ellison hopes you weren't scared.

I think of how Father taught me not to bend before adversity. I remain silent.

Then the Tajik says: The lieutenant would like me to convey his sincere apologies, but he hopes that you understand he didn't have a choice.

Now the officer smiles and addresses me directly, speaking very slowly and in loud, distinct tones, as if to an imbecile. The Tajik translates: The lieutenant says he hadn't realized how young you were. He says you remind him of his sister—his younger sister—who goes to college. She wants to be a doctor. Maybe she will come and work in Kandahar province.

I think of my younger sister, Fawzia, dead before her time, and remain stone-faced.

The lieutenant says his grandfather took part in building the highways south of Kandahar, after the Second World War.

So what? I think to myself, and look away.

The officer's voice falters for a moment. Then he speaks confidently to the Tajik, who says: The lieutenant would like to ask you a few questions.

The Amrikâyi takes out a ketâb and holds his qalam at the ready. He smiles encouragingly at me. I ignore him and tell the Tajik: I will not answer anything until you have returned my brother's body to me.

The Amrikâyi says: As I have explained to you, we cannot do that. We have rules and regulations governing such matters.

I have no illusions about that, I say with scorn. You are here to impose your rules by force, but they mean nothing to me.

The Tajik interjects hurriedly: Pashtana, you would do well to listen to him.

He turns to the officer, who appears to interrogate him about my response. They go back and forth, and I sense the Tajik defusing the aggressiveness of his master's queries with some well-turned phrases. Eventually he says to me: The lieutenant would like to assure you that if you answer his questions, he will arrange for you to be given a thorough medical examination, especially in terms of the injuries to your legs.

I compose myself but find I have to swallow a few times before I can speak, and even then I barely recognize the whisper that emerges from me. I tell them that all I want is to accomplish the task I've set myself so that I can leave this wretched place. I don't want anything else.

The officer looks disappointed. Still, he wears a conciliatory smile in the hope that I will fall for his ludicrously transparent ruse. I turn away from him and look back at my mountains. Somewhere high up is the narrow patch of emerald green that is my valley. Despite my attempts at stoicism, a tear spills out of my eye and courses down to the kameez that Fawzia had embroidered with flowers. I miss her very much; I miss them all very much. I would like nothing better than to go home now, but I recognize that sometimes there is no going back.

The officer clears his throat, as does his factotum.

He says: We'll leave you now.

Please open the eye of your heart and give me my brother, I reply.

He says: I can't do that. It's not in my hands. I have my orders.

I think of Yusuf rotting inside their fort and watch with cold fury as they leave.

Shortly afterward, I am surprised when the Tajik returns with yet another Amrikâyi, accompanied as usual by gun-toting soldiers. The lieutenant is nowhere to be seen, and I feel distinctly relieved.

The newcomer plants himself before me and, without further ado, hands me a stiff and ragged piece of brown cloth. I fix my gaze warily on him: he has coarse stubble, a hard reddish face, and watery eyes. He addresses me rapidly, his teeth flashing as he belts out the words, his eyes opening wide once he finishes and awaits my response. I turn my face to the Tajik and wait for him to translate. With a peculiar diffidence, he says: Sergeant Schott has cut out this piece of cloth from your brother's kameez.

I glance at the rag with shock and nearly drop it.

At length, in a stranger's voice, I hear myself telling them that my brother's kameez was green in color, while this cloth is brown.

That's dried blood, the sergeant says indifferently.

From his very indifference, I know that he is speaking the truth. I hold the rag; it burns like a red-hot brand.

I ask the Tajik: What am I supposed to do with this?

He replies in an undertone. The Americans would like you to bury this cloth in place of your brother and, in return, give them the information they seek. After that, you can depart in peace.

I close my eyes and bury my face in the rag. Before my shuttered eyelids I see my brave and handsome brother with his ever-present smile—but also the moment of his death. I see him lying broken-backed in the dust, his eyes cast down in shame at my own ordeal. I would give the last of my food and water for a final word from him. I would surrender my own life with a glad smile if I could exchange it for his.

Before I open my eyes, I press the cloth to my face again and breathe in deeply. It retains the scent of our house and the mass of mountains that surround it.

Then I let it drop to the ground.

Addressing the Tajik, I say: Tell your masters that I refuse. I am not going to barter on the basis of these pitiful credits and debits.

Even before he has finished translating, the sergeant takes out a shiny tablet and stabs his fingers into it. Then he nods at the Tajik and begins firing questions at me, the words shooting out as if from the barrel of a gun:

What is your full name? What is your father's name?

What is the name of your tribe? How many men are in it?

How many of these men accompanied your brother in the attack? What are their names? Who will succeed your brother now that he is dead?

How many guns does your village hold? How many villages in your tribe?

How soon . . . ? How much . . . ? How many . . . ? How far . . . ?

I meet all these questions with a dignified silence. I do not budge, even when the sergeant raises his voice and leans his face close enough to mine for his spittle to rain down on me. Finally, he steps back in frustration, his face flushed, and snaps: How is it possible for anyone to be so ignorant? Is it because the women in your tribe are locked indoors and separated from the men as in the rest of your damn country?

No, we are neither locked indoors nor separated from our menfolk, I say calmly.

Then how do you explain your ignorance? Are you a fool?

I have other things to do, I reply, than to eavesdrop on what the men may be talking about.

But you have ears, don't you? You have eyes and all your senses!

When one is busy with work, one does not hear or see.

My determination must show on my face because his voice loses confidence. He gestures to the soldiers behind him and they point their guns threateningly at me. The Tajik implores me to cooperate but I don't respond. He continues pleading but my wall of indifference saps his spirit. He stops abruptly and we're left staring at each other. The sergeant shakes his head, gives his device a few desultory pecks, steps back, and marches off with the rest.

I am left staring at the rag on the ground, this pitiful remnant of my proud Yusuf.

Soon I myself might be forced into silence. Who knows.

Meanwhile, it is clear that they mean to exhaust me with this endless procession of interrogators. They mean to break me, but in this, as in their attempts to persuade me to leave, they will be disappointed. I will not go until I have satisfied my duty.

I gaze at the barbed wire fence and the walls that separate me from Yusuf. If it were up to my heart, I would send those barriers wandering south across the deserts until they disappeared from our lands. If it were up to my will, I would ignore the warnings of these interlopers and breach their fortress with my bare hands. I would dig a deep hole in the ground and, lifting his body, relieve the shame of my mother's son, left to rot as an unburied corpse. But my mind holds me captive. My mind tells me that any hasty action on my part would ensure my death before my brother's burial—and then we would both be left unmourned, unwept, unburied without the rites, an unexpected treasure for the carrion birds. Heart or no heart, I have no choice: my anger and despair must yield to patience, resolution.

So I wait in the dust instead, the silence ringing in my ears.

And many memories. A host of memories crowding around, slipping through the air like specks of dust; slipping through the silence until I hear the voices they carry. Whose whispers? What voices?

In my head, Yusuf laughs. He says:

Nizam, you silly girl, you are talking to yourself.

I know, my brother, I know. I know that it's nothing. It's nothing but the silence—cruel, endless silence whispering in my ears. But what else do I have to keep me company—to console me now that you too are gone, lost remnant of my flesh and blood? My first, my best friend from childhood. My last, my final companion.

How my heart hurts.

The sun is high when a new soldier appears with the Tajik. He carries a steaming bowl of food that he places before my cart. He's young, with a closely shaven head and a martial, erect bearing. He glances at me fleetingly, but other than that, his face shows nothing.

That's for you, the Tajik says. The men in the fort are concerned about your welfare. Maybe you will think better of them after this. There's meat in it, and lentils.

They walk away, and I leave the food untouched.

Soon, the ubiquitous crows congregate. I wheel my cart away and the bowl disappears under a blizzard of black wings. I watch two crows squall over a piece of meat while I chew my dry bread. It's gone stale and crumbles at the touch. I search instead for my figs and nuts.

The same young soldier returns with the Tajik to pick up the bowl. The crows disperse with raucous caws. The Tajik looks pained. His narrow smallish head bobs from side to side.

There was no need to reject the food, he says. They were trying to be kind, that's all. It was a gift. It's against our traditions to refuse a gift. Now you've rejected their overtures and made them angry.

He stands a few paces away from me and says that I should put my bughra back on. My lack of response doesn't seem to bother him. His expression is guarded but also intrigued.

He lights up a cigarette, which he smokes in quick puffs while continuing to stare at me. It's sad, he says finally. We're both Afghânyân, we're much the same age, and yet we're on opposite sides. I work with the Americans because nine years ago the Taliban slaughtered my family. We were prosperous traders in Charikar; my mother was an educated woman. He pauses and draws on his cigarette.

In other words, he says, I can understand how you feel, believe me. But I sincerely think the Americans are here to help us, to make our lives better before they leave. And you—I suppose you believe, with equal sincerity, just the opposite, because they killed your family.

My loyalty is to my brother and the memory of my family, I reply. Yusuf is not carrion for these jackals to tear apart.

He gazes at me without animosity. You're so fierce, so determined, he says with admiration. I've never met a woman like you. I'm sorry I called you stupid earlier. I wonder if my sister would have grown up to be like you had she lived.

What is your name? I ask abruptly.

Masood, he says, and blushes.

Then listen to me, Masood. You are a dog and the servant of your masters. I've seen how you behave around them, without any dignity or self-respect. I've no desire to speak to you. I find your presence distasteful.

He raises his face and squints at the sun, which is directly overhead. He purses his lips and exhales forcefully. It didn't have to be like this, he says, and motions to his armed companion that it's time to go.

There's genuine regret in his voice and it's because of this, perhaps, that I find myself asking, despite everything: Did my brother suffer . . . when he died, I mean . . .

No. He didn't suffer. He was shot through the heart. A clean shot. He died instantly.

My voice breaks. I'm glad.

You should be. He was lucky. But some of the others—they suffered terribly.

Tell your masters I won't leave until Yusuf is returned to me.

He hesitates. His expression shades with regret.

Then you're going to be here for a very long time, he says quietly.

What do you mean?

Didn't you hear what the lieutenant said? Your brother will be taken to Kabul. It was his fate to be transported through the air as a dead man. It was written.

I watch him dully as he walks away with the soldier, scuffing the dust with his slippers.

Then I sit back in the cart, my head pounding.

They haven't even reached the perimeter of barbed wire that surrounds the fort when I let out a sharp cry of grief. The Tajik freezes and glances back wide-eyed as my cry echoes across the plain and soars into the mountains. I follow it up with another cry, which seems to unnerve him completely. He picks up his slippers and sprints toward the fort, while the soldier glares at me with undisguised hostility. I beat my head with my fists and begin to laugh, but in reality I am crying.

The day drags on. The sun beats down relentlessly; the light is blinding. I look around the field with a heavy heart. This is where I'm staying. This is now my final home. How strange life is. I used to have so many wishes, so many dreams.

I steel myself. I raise my face to the sun and it burns into my skin.

All through the afternoon I carry a feeling of extreme sadness. I listen to sounds from the fort. Someone laughs; someone else shouts. The laughter ceases abruptly, as if cut by a knife. There's sporadic singing, whistling. The crackle of a radio swims in and out.

As the sun goes down, a steady wind blows from dark clouds forming over the southern plains. The day's heat had made the mountains hazy. Now they reemerge in the dying light, crowding in on the fort as the air turns cold. But the sunset inspires me with awe, the colors moving me simultaneously to laughter and tears. It lasts much longer than I'm used to in our high valley. There the transition from day to night is instantaneous: bright light one moment, coal-black darkness the next.

The night arrives with a cavalcade of clouds. I'm grateful for the blessed silence and the absence of the searchlight, but when I strum on my lute, a shot rings out, and I stop playing.

Soon the air turns glacial. I put on my bughra and drape my blanket over it. My hand slips inadvertently through the hole my baby brother Yunus had made in the blanket. Mother had given him a hiding for it. My eyes mist with tears as I remember my family. I still find it difficult to believe I'm the only one left.

Without warning, the searchlight switches on. It skitters across the field and comes to rest on me. I shrink away from it and close my eyes. What I desperately need is sleep.

At daybreak, I am awakened by the melodic sound of sheep bells. I sit up and look around. A flock of sheep has entered the field from the same mountain trail that brought me here. Some of them wear blankets. There's an especially plump white animal, not much more than a lamb, with a bright crimson blanket embroidered in black. They scatter over the field, looking for pasture, weaving in and out of strands of mist.

Dawn is cool and silent. The black silhouette of the fort is more like a dream than reality. When I clap my hands for warmth, it attracts the attention of the sheep. Their quest for pasture in this arid plain is proving fruitless. I call out softly to them and they gather around. In the solitude of the plain, I enjoy their inquisitive company. It reminds me of my childhood years shepherding flocks in highland pastures. Soon the white lamb is frolicking by my side: I stroke the fuzz underneath its chin, and rub its muzzle in the manner that sheep like best. A larger animal, no doubt its mother, nuzzles it as we play, and I stroke both of them.

A red sun rises in the gray sky. I watch it with weary eyes and feel as if I've been here for a very long time. Fatigue has lent a touch of the illusory to everything. It's as if I'm living on the sharp edge of a knife. The slightest relaxation in my vigilance threatens an onslaught of held-back tears. At times, I feel feverish, especially now, with the warm, soft lamb in my grasp. So I force myself to attend to the task at hand, mute and exhausted.

Without letting go of the lamb, I draw out the knife concealed in the inner lining of my bughra. Forcefully yanking back its neck, I plunge the knife with brutal swiftness across its throat. It doesn't even have the chance to bleat but simply hammers its hooves against the earth. A stream of blood spurts into the air and indiscriminately sprays the terrified flock. It drenches the mother, who cries out loudly, the whites of her eyes showing. She lurches forward, but I push her away with one hand. Blood continues to spurt from the severed arteries and splashes the sleeves of my bughra and my veil. I hold the lamb down with all my strength until it stops kicking and shudders to stillness. Then I drop the knife and drive the mother away with my fists, leaving bloody marks on her pelt. Still she circles around, calling out in distress, while the rest of the flock scatters. Finally, even she moves away, and I rest my violently shaking hands on the dead animal, my breath coming in bursts. To kill in these circumstances requires nerves of iron, which I do not have. There's blood, blood everywhere.

Only then do I hear the commotion from the fort. There's a gaggle of soldiers clustered behind sandbags, but they're too far away to register what happened. Instead, it is Masood the Tajik who comes racing out, skidding to a stop just inside the barbed wire fence. He looks bewildered.

I point to the lamb and call out: This is in exchange for your masters' gift of food. We Pashtuns also have our traditions of hospitality. Now we're even.

His face lights up in perfect comprehension. He gives an excited laugh.

This was well done! he exclaims. I will certainly convey your message.

He casts an appraising eye on the lamb. We will feast tonight, he adds. Do you want me to take the lamb to them?

No. Tell your captain I would like to give it to him personally.

I will do that. He's meeting with his officers, but I will find a way to tell him.

He turns to leave, then hesitates. Four soldiers are hurrying purposefully toward him, led by the hard-faced sergeant from yesterday. He begins yelling at Masood even before they close in on him. The Tajik points to the lamb and begins to explain something to them in their language, but the sergeant cuts him off angrily and escorts him back to the fortress. Remarkably, in all of this, I am ignored almost as if I were invisible. I watch them leave, and am left to wonder why their wrath was directed at their own interpreter and not at me.

Not knowing what to expect next, I wait in the light of the rising sun. Slowly, the mist clears; the sun begins to blaze down, as always. The heat intensifies. It steams from the circle of blood-drenched earth surrounding the cart. Light touches the stone walls of the fort. It illuminates the dead lamb; the necklace of blood around its throat glitters.

When the Tajik returns, it is with an armed escort. They walk up to the barbed wire. The Tajik looks crestfallen. He flops down on his haunches. The captain has refused your gift, he calls out, gazing in disbelief at the lamb. The soldiers who watched you kill the lamb deemed your act barbaric: they claimed that civilized women do not slaughter animals. I tried to explain it was a gift from you in keeping with our traditions, but they refused to listen to me. They made fun of your sanity. I don't understand it. I simply don't understand it.

He steals a sidelong glance at his escort, who're staring at me with undisguised contempt. I notice that they seem to be keeping watch over the interpreter as much as over me.

The Tajik winces. I don't understand them, he says again. It must have to do with their customs. They've adopted a stray dog, for instance, and treat it as their pet. They give it the choicest morsels as if it were a prize sheep and not a mere dog, that most unclean of animals, and they fuss over it and fondle it in a manner that makes me ill. They're a strange people.

As he speaks, I realize he's inched forward until he's a gaz or so ahead of his companions.

There's more . . . he says, and pauses.

I wait for him to continue.

He clears his throat uncomfortably. They've decided to take you away.

I start and stiffen. Take me away? Where?

He makes a vague gesture southward. Kandahar.

To the city! But why? My place is here!

The captain has decided that you need to be admitted to a hospital. A hospital for people whose minds have been damaged by the war. He says you need treatment.

What rubbish. I'm not deranged. I won't go.

They'll take you by force. They've made up their minds. They're on their way here. What can I say? There's nothing to say.

Suddenly he rises to his feet and looks straight at me.

Listen to me! he says with urgency. You've still time to get away. Turn your cart around and leave this place. I'll convince them you've changed your mind about your brother. They're not bad people. They'll understand.

He leans forward and places both his hands on the wire.

Do as I tell you, please. Go away. Your brother is dead, but you still have a life to live. Soon our country will be free. Our leaders will reach an agreement. Then we'll live as we've always lived, without outside interference.

He pauses and looks at me pleadingly.

Go away. You're wasting your time here. Do you understand?

I sit up very straight. He slumps back and looks at the ground. He appears devastated.

You're not going, are you? he says.

No.

You're making a terrible mistake.

It's my decision.

Can you tell me why?

I remove my veil from my face and gaze at him. Our eyes lock.

I couldn't live with the shame, I answer.

He raises his hand to his face and covers his eyes. Without a word, he turns on his heels and stumbles away, the soldiers following in his wake. Soon I am alone in the sunlight again. I feel a sudden pang of thirst and raise the goatskin to my mouth, but there's no water left.

I take off my blood-soaked bughra and shake my hair free. I examine my blood-spattered hands, my blood-speckled wrists. My callused palms are the color of unfired bricks. The white sleeves of my kameez lie over them like lips of snow.

I turn my head and look back at the mountains as at a lover. The slopes are a serene blue, as if sculpted out of the sky itself. The highest ridges now glow silver in the sunlight, now golden. Such beauty exists only in paradise.

Time begins to pulse in swift fever spasms. The morning air is neither warm nor cool, but of a consistency that is perfection itself, and of which I too am made.

I bow my head and say my father's name, my mother's name.

I say my sister's name, my little brother Yunus's name.

I say my brother Yusuf's name.

When I raise my head, I see the soldiers advancing toward me, with the captain at their head. The black giant is with them, as is Masood the interpreter, which is unfortunate. I recite the Shahada in my head.

*There is no god but God, and Muhammad is His Messenger . . .*

I begin counting the moments. One.

Dwa.

Dré.

Tsalor.

It's up to me now. I'm terrified: my hands are shaking, my mouth is parched.

I wait until their shadows enter the circle of blood.

Then I reach under the blanket covering the lamb with my knife and cut the plaited wire.

# LIEUTENANT

T'S a beautiful day. The temperature's in the upper sixties, the sun's dipping in and out of cottony clouds, the sky's an iridescent blue. I'm canoeing down the Hudson, following the river's slow, wide course as it navigates between gentle slopes. Occasionally, a wooded copse spills right down to the waterline: green, brown, yellow, clad in camouflage colors. I can't see a single house, but a freight train runs parallel to the river, its metallic clangor stopping only when it slips into a tunnel at the neck of a bend. The silence that follows seems even more pronounced—and the great white-headed eagle that wheels over my head, riding thermals, suddenly plunges down to the water and flaps away, dangling the silver ribbon of a fish from its talons.

I'm smoking a cigarette, which surprises me, because I'm not a smoker, but I don't question it. Instead, I glance over my shoulder to where Espinosa is in a bright yellow canoe just like mine, water streaming from his paddle. He's smoking too, and I wonder if it's to overcome the pungent smell of the decaying apples bobbing up and down on the water. There are hundreds of apples, and as many birds— ducks, cormorants, geese—feasting on them, seemingly oblivious to the eagle in the air. Espinosa holds his paddle above the water and waggles it at me. He tucks his cigarette behind his ear and scoops up an apple from the water, throwing it to a duck. I laugh and lean back and let my gaze travel across the crest of a high cliff crowned with pines. I feel grateful at having been able to get away from the ugliness of war. I remind myself to write a letter to thank whoever arranged this day-long excursion.

A thickly wooded island looms ahead, and a black horse with a white star on its forehead lopes down to the river and plants itself knee-deep in the water, nuzzling the apples. I glide my canoe gently past it, water droplets sprinkling my face as I breathe in the smells of the river, the lazy summer day, the strangely silent birds, the float- ing apples. Someone behind me starts singing Country Joe and the Fish's "I-Feel-Like-I'm-Fixin'-to-Die Rag," which I find a little inap- propriate, given the circumstances. Then Folsom slips past me with a beatific look on his face. He's grown his mustache back, I notice. He says: Man, this is fucking *awesome!*

The play of light and shade on the water reminds me of a mosaic pattern I once saw in a mosque in a village near Kandahar. I'm sur- prised I remember it—and so clearly. The mud-daubed domes of the houses in the village were like egg cartons, and the splendor of the mosque stood in jarring contrast to the poverty surrounding it. But that world is somewhere else now. I look around and reckon we must be somewhere between Cold Spring and Garrison, and although I've canoed this stretch more times than I can remember, I don't recog- nize a thing. But I'm not worried. Just before the river narrows into a shadowy corridor, I turn the canoe around momentarily to watch Alpha Company form into a compact group behind me, the knot of yellow, red, and green canoes like a flock of brightly colored birds on the water.

Ahead of me, Folsom slows down and I pull up alongside him. He's sweating profusely and spits a spent wad of chew into the water.

Where are we, Lieutenant? Bear Mountain?

No . . . No, that's farther south.

Then where? I don't remember this part.

It's all right, I tell him. You're not from around here.

That's true. We should've gone to Wisconsin, where I'm from. The White Lakes.

Good fishing, I expect.

The best.

He falls behind and lets me take the lead.

The river contracts into a stream, steep gorges rearing up on either side. I can hardly see the sky overhead but I still feel strangely unconcerned. Then the sides of the canoe begin to scrape against the rocks and I smell the first whiff of scorched earth. The roll of rusting concertina wire that stops me dead in the water is buried just beneath the surface, a litter of rotting weeds concealing it. It's almost dark as the men cluster behind me with no room to turn around.

Folsom says: Lieutenant, with all due respect, this is impassable terrain.

I acknowledge the obvious and tell him to begin backing up.

He attempts to maneuver his canoe back, but bumps against the man behind him. I raise my hand and signal to the last man to reverse, but he's too far away and it's too dark. There's no sound but men panting and the scraping of plastic hulls against rock. Come on, come on . . . Folsom whispers fiercely to the man behind him . . . Frickin' hurry up!

Initially, I only see a single muzzle flash and a bright swift line of explosions puckering through black water. A second later, the slopes light up. The rounds that hit us tear through flesh, canoes, and gear.

I feel thankful for my body armor vest, but then I realize I'm only wearing a thin cotton T-shirt. I struggle to squeeze out of the canoe, but the lower part of my body seems fastened down somehow. Still, I contract my muscles and try to get out, but it's no use—and too late. The blow that hits me on the back of the neck catapults me around and I face Folsom just as a hole opens up where his nose should be. I'm hypnotized by the blood that gushes out of his face. He's screaming, but I don't hear him—I'm already under crimson water struggling to surface, but there's something thrusting inside my mouth and pinning me down. I begin to gag. I strike out with my hands as my vision fades . . .

. . . I can't breathe . . .

. . . Lieutenant . . .

. . . I can't breathe . . .

. . . Lieutenant Frobenius . . . Sir . . .

I make out Whalen through half-closed eyes. He's thrust his head right into my bunk.

I struggle to wake. I'm moving slowly. I shouldn't have taken the sleeping pill last night. I prop myself up groggily on my elbows.

Christ. What time is it?

Just past 0100, Sir. The sandstorm's outta control and the ANA guards want to come inside. You better get up.

How bad is it?

Bad. Visibility's near zero. And the storm's made our detection systems friggin' worthless.

I try to absorb the news that the storm has knocked out our thermal sights. I've never faced a situation where that's happened before.

Gimme a moment, I tell him. I'll be there.

You better tie a cloth around your face, Whalen warns as he goes out.

I lie on my bunk for a moment, listening to the sand grains buffet the flimsy plywood walls that separate me from the storm outside. I've only had three hours of sleep, and the pill has left me stupefied. It's dark and claustrophobic inside the B-hut. I scratch an itch from one of many fleabites on my arm, but it only makes it worse. Cursing, sweaty, I slide out of the bunk and land heavily on my feet. In my haste, I knock my iPod to the ground and step on it. I fling it back on the bunk, hoping nothing's broken, and struggle into my clothes. I'm filthy, unshaven; I haven't showered in two days. Everything is dusty and covered with grit. I lace my boots quickly and shrug on my body armor vest as I head out.

Whalen's waiting for me by the entrance to the hooch with his face wrapped in a bandana that used to be white. The sky overhead is a mottled black, but the rest of the world is an eerie yellow-brown wall of sand. The hurtling grains instantly lacerate my face and hands with a million pinpricks. I follow his lead and wrap my scarf tightly around my face. The air smells of sulfur. The wind whistles fiercely in the darkness, the entire sky a dark cave filled with swirling sand. The acoustics magnify every sound.

I look around. This *is* bad.

We gotta ride it out somehow, Whalen says, but his voice lacks conviction.

Mitchell and Folsom are on guard shift at the Entry Control Point. Mitchell's bleeding from a cut above his eye, although it's probably not as bad as it looks.

He notices me looking at his eye and volunteers: The wind's slinging stones off the ground. It's fucking lethal, Sir, like being in the path of a slingshot!

Mitchell's a cherry, a newcomer to the platoon. Folsom shrugs wryly. I say nothing.

Folsom says: The ANA over there want to go inside. They keep coming over to tell us they're quitting for the duration of the storm.

No way. I'll go talk to them.

I turn to Whalen as we make our way along the Hesco wall that runs around the perimeter of the base, where the Afghan National Army soldiers are crouching miserably. What do you think, First Sarn't? I ask him. Should I let them go?

He squints through his bandana. The Hadjis would be crazy to attack in these conditions—but then again, the Hadjis are crazy! So: no. They better stay.

My thoughts exactly, I say.

Closer to the ANA, we walk backwards to be able to breathe. Already my lips are chapped, my face encased in dusty mold. I grimace and my skin hurts. We've had no letup from the storm these past two days. Now we're feeling its full impact, and we'll have to find ways to deal with the situation without letting the enemy catch us off guard. My men know it, but the ANA troops are a different story altogether.

There are three of them by the Hescos and they run forward even before we reach them. I wave them back, but Fazal Ahmed, the smallest of the three, signals to his companions authoritatively, and they attempt to slip past us. I bar them with outstretched arms, while

Whalen, who's six four, picks up Fazal Ahmed and sets him down by the Hescos. Stay here! he roars.

I drag the other two Afghans back. You're not allowed to leave, I yell.

Ya'll understand? Whalen roars again, shouting above the wind.

They don't reply, but return to crouching sullenly by the Hescos.

We leave them and canter over to the camo nets surrounding the guard tower. I clamber up the staircase, while Whalen stays behind. The raw wind buffets me as I ascend the rickety steps, and I have to grasp the guardrails with all my strength. Sand, stones, and clumps of dust whirl upward and hit me. A loose splinter ricochets off the back of my hand and leaves a bloody smear. Then the platform looms above me, its wooden planks bucking madly in the wind. There's sand streaming off it, and Staff Sergeant Brandon Espinosa, who's on watch, bends down and hauls me up. He's put up a canvas screen with the help of the two ANA who're there with him. The guard tower sways like a ship in the storm. Espinosa looks exhausted, and I don't blame him.

He shouts: I'm going to send my ANA crew down and stay up here by myself. Less trouble that way.

I lean toward him and shout back: Suit yourself.

The relieved ANA slither down.

I watch them go and shake my head: You'd think they weren't in their own country.

Espinosa says: They aren't. They're Uzbek. This is Pashtun land.

I say: No point telling you to keep a look out, but still . . .

He cracks a smile and shoves a wad of chew into his mouth. He's a veteran of Iraq, a man of few words, capable, efficient. I'm not worried about leaving him in the tower by himself.

Back on the ground, I run with Whalen past the brick-and-mortar command post, then follow the Hescos back toward the ECP. We slow down by the shelter of the mortar pit where Manny Ramirez and Pratt have secured the gun with canvas. Pratt has his M-4 tucked inside his poncho liner, while Ramirez stands some distance away, pissing into one of the PVC tubes jammed into the ground for that purpose. He's bending over with his back to the storm, but the wind arcs his urine way past where he's aiming it. He buttons up his fly with a grin as we approach. Whoo! he says. Whoo . . .

Whalen coughs and spits out a mouthful of sand. Motherfucker, he says to no one in particular; then he repeats himself for emphasis.

This is *fun,* First Sarn't! Ramirez shouts. He prances around Whalen with an exaggerated mince.

Pratt doesn't say anything. His dark leathery skin looks gray; his eyes are bloodshot and streaming.

You okay, Pratt? I ask.

M'fine, Suh, he says. This ain't nuthin'. I worked through worse storms in the fishin' fleet.

Snowstorms?

Yeah.

I try to see the analogy, then give up.

Ramirez shouts: You expecting an attack tonight, Sir? I'm sorta goin' crazy doin' nuthin'. I haven't fired a shot in days, I swear to God.

Whalen says: You got gunner's tourette, Ramirez.

No shit, First Sarn't, Ramirez says. Whatever that means. He asks me again: So . . . ?

I say: Maybe. Maybe they'll come for us tonight. I got a feeling.

You gotta respect those feelings, Sir, you know what I'm saying?

Pratt says: Be perfect weather for it—if it happens.

Ramirez laughs happily and slaps his thighs. Finally! he exults. Time to kill some badass motherfuckers. I'm stoked!

A gust of wind whips away his bandana and he spends the next few moments cursing wretchedly while trying to tie it around his face again.

Fuckin' sand in my eye! he yells.

You're an open target, Ramirez, Whalen says calmly, stating fact.

Like hell I am. Aah! Fuck this.

It might help if you put on your wraparounds, I suggest, stating the obvious.

Can't see when I have them on, Sir. No peripheral vision.

Jes' put 'em on, Ram, Pratt says.

Pratt's an Athabascan fisherman from north of Fairbanks, and functionally illiterate. He's also the most lethal fighter in the platoon. Rumor goes, before he joined the army, he once waded into a dock-yard scrim and disemboweled three men as casually as if he were in some barroom brawl. He always carries an ice pick tucked in his belt and rarely speaks; when he does, you have to lean close to catch what he's saying. In contrast, Ramirez rarely shuts up. By his own admission, he used to be a drug runner along the Arizona-Mexico border. Strictly part-time, he's quick to qualify. Strictly part-time, Sir. The rest of the time I worked the night shift at the local 7-Eleven. A bored restlessness is his signature style; he's a deadly shot, a crack poker player, and he seldom sleeps. Together, Pratt and Ramirez make an unpredictable team, and the other men give them a wide berth.

The base is shaped like an oblong, and Whalen and I circle around the entire perimeter one more time, past the sandbagged mortar pits, the burn-shitters, the plywood B-huts, stopping to check each guard position until we return to where we began. And all the while, the banshee wind scourges the base. I glance back at the plastic shitter screens billowing crazily in the storm.

What do you think? I ask Whalen again as we take shelter behind the medical tent.

I don't like it.

Me neither.

We're completely blinded, he says. They can take us out any way they please.

How? If we can't see anything, neither can they.

They could surround us and we wouldn't even know it, he says tersely. It's my nightmare scenario. Three-hundred-sixty-degree catastrafuck.

Whalen's thirty-seven, a career soldier and another veteran of Iraq, like Espinosa, and I listen to everything he has to say because he's always sound. All the same, I rib him now.

You've been watching too many movies, First Sarn't.

He laughs. You asked.

I say: At the same time, I don't know what else we can do in this situation but wait it out. I'm clean out of ideas.

It's all that college learning, Lieutenant, Suh, he says mockingly.

You're prob'ly right, I tell him, thinking for a moment. Then I make up my mind: Wake up Grohl and Spitz and send them out to replace the ANA. I'm pulling the Afghans back. They're useless in a situation like this.

All right. I'm also going to wake the Cap'n.

No. Let him be.

He hesitates. As First Sergeant, he answers directly to Evan Connolly, Alpha Company's Captain, but we both know that Connolly's not the best leader in a crisis, so Whalen's had very good reason to seek me out first, and I've the same good reason to avoid waking Connolly.

Whalen continues to look worried. I'll wake Lieutenant Ellison, then, he says.

Nope. Let him sleep as well. He had the last watch.

Lieutenant Frobenius, he says: I don't know about this.

C'mon, First Sarn't. We can handle this.

Whalen leaves, and I make my way back to the ANA position. As I pass Folsom and Mitchell, I peer out at the swirling murk. I can't see the concertina wire at all, and when I turn my head and run my eyes down the Hescos, I can hardly make out the guard tower. There's something wrong. I can sense it.

I hear a whimper behind me and turn around. Shorty, the platoon's adopted year-old pup, nuzzles my leg, his tail between his legs. Shorty's a misnomer: he's already massive, a cross between a mastiff and some kind of Afghan hound. I can't imagine how big he's going to be full-grown. I bend down and pat him. His bushy coat is matted with sand and dust. He whimpers again, then growls, showing his fangs. He's pointing at the wire perimeter, tail held ramrod straight behind him hound-dog fashion. I feel the hairs on the back of my neck prick up. He growls again and begins to bark nonstop. There's something going on out there all right.

Whalen rejoins me. He's panting. I can't believe how quickly he's made it back. Grohl and Spitz are on their way, and Sergeant Tanner's at the ECP, he says rapidly. I glimpse the whites of his eyes flash behind his bandana. I can tell he's worried. We begin running toward the ANA position. The dog paces alongside, then darts out ahead of us into the maw of the storm. We hear him barking wildly.

The ANA turn and watch us approach. They don't move until we're standing right before them. See anything? Whalen says jerkily, pantomiming the question as he gestures toward the perimeter. Fazal Ahmed removes his face cloth. He looks disgusted. His two companions do the same and stand by with surly expressions. None of them answers Whalen.

A wave of irritation invades me, and I seize Fazal Ahmed's arm and draw him to me so roughly that the others begin to protest. Fazal Ahmed resists, his eyes filling with rage and pain. He continues to remain stubbornly silent, and suddenly he jerks and falls against my shoulder. I hear one of the others shout as I attempt to prop him back up—then let go of him abruptly. His helmet slaps off his head with a neat hole drilled through the back. Bits and pieces of brain slop down the collar of his tunic. The other two ANA swivel in tandem and gawk in the direction of the wire. Initially all I see in the brown darkness is a single muzzle flash. Then a fan of red tracers begins arcing through the haze. Grohl and Spitz come running up just as a turbaned silhouette darts through an inexplicable gap in the wire. Whalen hollers: TAKE COVER! WE'RE BEING BREACHED! He dives behind the sandbag walls that surround the ANA's position. Something shrieks over our heads and detonates against a B-hut: it's

an 88 mm round. The two remaining ANA are still standing in plain
view as if frozen. Then the enemy opens up from about fifty meters
away. I hear AK-47 rounds and rocket-propelled grenades. The ANA
finally hit the ground and begin crawling toward their machine gun,
but Grohl and Spitz beat them to it. We begin returning fire while
enemy bullets rake up the Hescos all around us. There are others
taking up position beside me. Most of them are in gym shorts and
flip-flops: they must have come pelting out from their cots. Someone
detonates the Claymores, and they engulf the man in the turban. As
he disappears in an explosion of dust and smoke, Pfc. Jackson begins
firing meaty M-203 rounds: good man; it's the perfect antidote for
an attack under these conditions. From the guard tower, Espinosa
goes cyclic with an Mk-19 belt-fed automatic launcher grenade—
firing without stopping. Almost immediately I hear the retaliatory
crump of a rocket-propelled grenade, and the guard tower buck-
les and disappears in a black pall. That RPG came from a different
direction from the ones up front pinning us down. We've been taking fire from the north and the west and now someone else begins
firing RPG rounds from the east. I replay Whalen's nightmare scenario in my head: we're surrounded. And we can't retaliate effectively. We're all firing blind.

Shorty zips past, heading for the B-huts. GET AWAY, DOG!
someone shouts. The dog's howling like crazy but the sound merges
with the storm. Tracers light up the darkness. The enemy's aim is so
precise, they have us pinned down. They must have started moving
into position as soon as the storm began. Ahead of me, Grohl and
Spitz are working away methodically with the .50, spitting rounds. I
can hear them swearing. The two ANA flank them, firing away with
M-4s until one of the guns jams. The man spits into the breech of the
gun, trying to clear it, but it's no use. He throws it away, loses his
nerve, and sprints past me for the brick-and-mortars. He doesn't make
it. I take over his position, firing short bursts. Whalen pulls me down
behind the Hescos. You wanna die young? he snarls. His face is red

with exertion; his bandana's fallen off. The other ANA starts, then slumps to his knees. I grab him by the vest and pull him down. The ground is littered with empty shells. Things are happening too fast.

The air clears momentarily, and I glimpse Connolly to my left standing behind Mitchell and Folsom, screaming grid coordinates into his radio. I shout to him and race over through incoming rounds.

He stands up, fires a round, ducks down.

We're in a fucking shooting gallery! he screams. And I can't even call in the birds!

No shit, Sir, I yell back. They'd wipe out in this storm.

Where'd they come from?

They must have used the ratlines down the mountains.

Figures. Okay, I'm going to circle round to the back. See how things are with Ellison.

He flicks a glance at me. You should've woken me the moment you suspected a fucking TIC situation, Lieutenant. We'll talk later.

A mortar shell thuds into the Hescos just as he takes off. He stumbles, catches himself, and runs on. White phosphorus residue from the shell washes over the ground. I watch him disappear from sight, then take up position beside Mitchell and Folsom. I'm seething from his rebuke, partly because he's right. I should've had Whalen wake him.

I glimpse a dark silhouette dart past the wire. Mitchell screams at the same time: THEY'RE PAST THE WIRE!

Folsom starts cursing. Their M-240's jammed up. The barrel's smoking.

Come on, come on . . . he says urgently. Frickin' come on . . .

He manages to get the gun working again.

I aim and empty my M-4. The silhouette staggers back and falls against the wire. I realize I've run through all my ammunition save one magazine.

I hear the distinctive snap of a bullet inches away.

Folsom jerks back, then turns almost lazily and crumples into my arms. There's a hole where his nose used to be. Blood spews out. I try to hold him up, but his head lolls to one side and his eyes slide back in their sockets. He's gone. A gust of sand sweeps over us.

I lay him down and slide in next to Mitchell, feeding him the belt. His hands are raw, sweaty. He stares at Folsom.

Keep going, I tell him. Just keep going.

He steadies the M-240, stolid, workmanlike. For a cherry, he's holding up all right. He glances at me and shouts: This is *nuts!*

I can feel my adrenaline pumping. Don't think about it, I yell, then begin to cough. There's sand between my scarf and my mouth. A thick coating of dust sheathes my face. I'm having difficulty breathing. I clear my throat and spit. I'm slathered in Folsom's blood.

Two more ghostly apparitions cross the wire. The M-240 stutters, then jams again. Mitchell struggles with the breech of the gun. It's coated with sand and grit. I snatch up my M-4 and aim at the enemy. Before I can fire, one falls, claimed by a Claymore, but the other seems to float right through the sandstorm while coolly firing an AK-47 with one hand. A jagged line of bullets rips up the Hescos. Dirt smacks me in the face. Then Mitchell clutches his elbow and yanks back from the M-240. He's hit. Another bullet slams into his chest but his body armor saves him. Even so, he spins around. Blood belches down his arm. He squats on the ground in a stupefied daze. I'm about to yell at him to fall back when our senior medic, Doc Taylor, comes loping up. I empty my last magazine to give him cover, then catch the 9 mil that Doc throws at me. I've lost sight of the other militant, but a fire team sets up beside us and starts blazing away with an LMG. All around, every man in the company is emptying magazines into the darkness. The noise is deafening, the crack of guns somehow amplified by the howl of the storm. Red tracer ribbons stream back and forth, forming an illuminated web overhead. Incoming bullets spark off surfaces. We're taking heavy fire, and it's concentrated, accurate. And it's coming from all directions.

Doc's wrapping a tourniquet around Mitchell's arm, but the sand's making things tricky. Mitchell's in agony: I catch a glimpse of white bone piercing through a tattoo spelling 𝕳𝕰𝕬𝕿𝕳𝕰𝕹. Doc packs the bloody wound cavity with Kerlix, then straps a bandage around it and slides an IV into the other arm. It's a miracle he hasn't been hit yet.

He eyes Folsom. Is he . . . ?

He's gone, I tell him. Now take Mitchell and get out of here!

He ignores me and crouches over Folsom.

I yell at him: Go, go, *GO* . . .

Mitchell gets up on his own and staggers away.

The LMG team start retreating as well.

Doc takes Folsom by the shoulders and drags him past me. At the last moment, he turns to me and yells: You better drop back, Lieutenant! We're being overrun.

Mitchell glances back at me, ashen-faced. He looks astonished, as if he can't believe what's happening.

I pick up his discarded M-4, and something slams me in the back of the neck. I feel my breath explode out of me as I catapult with the force of the blow, and then I'm staring up at the sky, everything around me strangely yellow . . .

. . . I can't breathe . . .

. . . yellow, yellow, hello . . .

. . . I can't breathe . . .

. . . Hello? I can't hear you . . .
. . . Hello? Is anyone there?


. . . Hello . . . Emily?
. . . Nick? I can't hear you . . . You're breaking up . . .


. . . breaking up . . .
. . . We're breaking up . . . I'm sorry, Nick, I'm breaking up . . .


. . . with you . . .
. . . you . . .


Emily?

Hello, Nick.

Emily, I love you, baby. I got your letter. Please don't do this to me! Please.

Why are you calling me, Nick? I asked you not to. It's only going to make this harder.

You send me a letter telling me you're breaking up with me, and I don't even have the right to ask you what the hell is going on?

I'm sorry, Nick, but I can't talk to you. I'm so sorry.

What is this? Is there someone else?

Of course not. I'd have told you if there was.

Em, I've been counting the days. This is fucking crazy! I'm in the middle of nowhere, entirely dependent on a fucking phone for my sanity and . . . I don't believe what's happening. You're my lifeline. Tell me this isn't happening. Tell me everything's going to be all right.

Nick.

What?

It's too late.

Why? For God's sake, *why?*

Because you've changed! You've changed so much. I read your letters and I don't know you anymore. There's so much violence in you. Where does it come from?

Violence. Christ. I'm in a war zone, in the middle of fucking Afghanistan! What do you expect?

You wanted to go to Yale Divinity when we met. Do you remember?

That was a long time ago.

Not so long. Three years ago.

All right, three years. What's your point?

That was the man I fell in love with.

Jesus. People change, Emily.

Not to this extent. I haven't.

What's that supposed to mean?

I'll always love you, Nick, but I can no longer imagine a life with you.

Can't we talk about this when I get back? Please? I'm on my knees. I'll be home in less than seven weeks.

I won't be here when you get back, Nick.


. . . Emily, don't leave me . . .

. . . hello . . .

. . . Emily, don't leave me, baby, please.
. . . I've nowhere else to go.

. . . It's okay, Lieutenant . . .
. . .
Doc . . . ?
Don't try to talk.
What happened?
You took a round . . .

. . . I can't breathe . . .

. . . Try putting some feeling into it, Frobenius . . .
. . .
What . . . ?
JoAnn walks over and looks at me as if I'm waking up.
She says: You gotta *feel* it, Nick. Feel it in your gut. This is Sophoclean tragedy, not Broadway. You're in the presence of the god of Death. Now: *show it*.
I'm sorry, JoAnn. I'm having trouble breathing. It's probably stage fright.

Okay. Calm down. Let's try again. No, wait. Emily, why don't you show him? Read from the Chorus, lines 115 to 120.

Sure thing.

A girl runs up. She's petite, blonde. She offers me her hand.

Hi, I'm Emily. Emily Tronnes.

Nick. Nick Frobenius.

Frobenius. Finnish?

Close. My dad's from Sweden, actually.

Sweden. Cool.

It's the first time I've been on stage, by the way. It's probably why I keep making mistakes. I'm a Classics major.

Classics. That's awesome. I'm a sophomore. I haven't declared yet, but it's going to be Theater.

JoAnn calls out crossly: All right, you two. Enough chitchat already.

Emily laughs. We're just getting to know each other, JoAnn. To emote better.

Emote better, my ass. When you decide to take some time out from flirting, I'd like to get on with the play, please.

I blush furiously. Flirting, wow.

Emily says: Don't mind her. She's all bark and no bite.

She steps back, pauses, runs her hand over her face. When her hand comes down she's a different person. She looks exhausted, and I stare at the tiny wrinkles that have magically appeared at the sides of her mouth and eyes, wondering how she did it. The transformation is breathtaking.

In a voice filled with gravity, she says:

> *Polyneices!*
> *He stood above our city's homes, hovered there,*
> *Spears thirsty for blood,*
> *A black circle of death.*

*And then, before the flames of war could burn our*
    *tower's crown,*
*Before he could slake his jaws' thirst with our blood,*
*He was turned back.*
*The war god screamed at his back.*
*Thebes rose like a dragon before him.*

She stops, and I whisper: Wow.

After an instant, she moves away from me.

Do you want to try it now? she asks.

Sure. You were terrific, by the way.

Thanks.

I mean, really, that was stupendous!

Thanks. Thanks very much.

I start off in a rush and realize I'm reading haphazardly, so I stop.
I turn to look at myself in the mirror, and see that I have gone pale.

Emily says: You need to slow down.

She leans forward and touches my arm, and I tremble as soon as
she lets go. She stares at me, and I stare back at her until she leans
toward me and touches me again. I stop trembling.

JoAnn asks: What's going on?

Then she says: Maybe we should try something else. Let's
see . . . why don't you read from Creon, lines 174 to 180. Nick?

I jump. I'm sorry. What was that again?

JoAnn rolls her eyes. Where are you, Frobenius? Earth to Nick.

I make a vague movement of embarrassment with my hand, and
Emily takes it in midair, squeezing it gently before letting go. Her
palm is slightly damp. My heart thumps; I feel dazed. I look down in
confusion, scroll through the pages, and find the lines.

Emily whispers: You can do it. Be my king.

I glance at her with wonder. I feel disconcerted, then exhilarated.

Still gazing at her, I say: All right.

JoAnn calls out, exasperated: Nick!

*Men of Thebes,* I say suddenly, my voice already gaining in confidence. *No king can expect complete loyalty from his subjects until he
shows his control over government and the law. You cannot know his
mind, his soul.*

*For I truly believe that the man who controls the state must have a
supreme and moral vision for its future. But if he is prone to fear and
locks his tongue in silence, then he is the worst of all who ever led this
country or could lead it now.*

I pause, and Emily begins to laugh.

Why are you laughing? I ask her.

I'm laughing because that was wonderful. You were wonderful.

Are you serious?

Of course I'm serious, dummy.

And she takes my hand in hers.

. . .

. . . Emily . . .

. . . It's okay, Nick . . .

. . .

Captain . . . ?

How do you feel? Connolly asks.

I don't know. Confused.

I bet. Take it easy now.

Where am I?

We held them off, dude. We pulverized them! Fuckin' sand devils. They're all dead.

Sand devils. What?

Relax. It's over. I've called in the birds. They're on their way.

We're having you medevaced out of here, you lucky sonofabitch. You're going to be okay.

What time is it?

He holds up his digital watch before my eyes. The bright green dial's all blurry.

0400, he says. The storm's died down and it's all quiet.

He bends close to my face. He's still wearing his body armor. His face is grimy, sand-caked. It makes me wonder what I look like.

He asks: Can you hear me, by the way?

Of course I can hear you.

Okay, okay, no need to get all het up. Just checking, that's all.

I cough a couple of times; something dribbles out of my mouth. Connolly leans over and wipes it away.

That fucking gave new meaning to "fog of war," I whisper. My voice sounds clotted, unrecognizable.

Yes, it did. It did, Nicko.

I can hear men shuffling around in the background.

Who did we lose, Sir?

His voice drops. Konwicki, Terranova, Folsom, Espinosa.

Jesus. How many wounded?

Four, including yourself.

What about the ANA?

Five casualties. The rest disappeared. They must have hightailed it outta here sometime during the fight.

Fuckers.

No kidding.

Tom Ellison leans over me.

Lieutenant? You okay?

I'm coming around.

They nearly breached us, he says.

But they didn't in the end, Connolly says. It was close, but we won, we fucking totaled them!

There's a boyish triumph in his voice, as if he's talking about a high school football game.

I say: I'm sorry I didn't wake you guys earlier. My call. My bad.

Connolly places his hand on my shoulder. Lieutenant, you're alive. Forget about the rest.

Okay.

It was the perfect ambush, he carries on. They caught us with our fucking pants down. There was none of the usual radio chatter beforehand.

I've never been in a firefight like it.

It was *intense,* he agrees, then adds: We lost the tower.

I know. I saw it fall.

But we speared a big fish. I spoke to Battalion on the telephone. They're pleased.

Oh? Who'd we get?

He's about to tell me when Whalen walks in. His jaw's swollen.

Connolly and Ellison make room for him. Hello, Lieutenant, he says. How you doing?

I always wanted to be an infantryman, I say grimly. I musta been drunk as fuck.

He laughs.

What happened to your face? I ask.

I punched someone. He didn't like it, so he hit me back. Now he's dead.

How many of them were there, First Sarn't, d'you know?

Well, there's seven gents inside the wire, and a few more lying out in the field; it's still too dark to tell. And I don't know how many got away.

The Seven against Thebes, I observe grimly as I tally the enemy's head count.

What was that? Connolly asks.

Doesn't matter.

Tom Ellison says: We're waiting for the survivors to show up and start removing the ones outside.

Someone in the back says: It's strange they haven't turned up yet.

Ellison laughs. They're probably shit scared. Or we wiped them out.

Connolly clears his throat: You were talking to yourself, by the way, Nick.

What was I saying?

I dunno. It sounded like you were reciting something. Something weird about laws and gods. I wasn't paying attention. You were delirious.

Whalen smiles at me. Musta been your Greek shit.

Prob'ly, I reply. Not that you'd know any better, First Sarn't.

He arches an eyebrow. I aced Western Civ. 101, as a matter of fact. I went to Morehouse, remember?

I can't resist ribbing him: How could I forget? Let me see. Class of 1900, right, Pops?

Very funny, Lieutenant.

Feeling punchy, I guess, I tell him.

That isn't unusual postcombat, Doc says. It'll take a while for your adrenaline to come down. Then you'll crash and sleep.

I ask: Doc, what did I take? How bad is it?

Relax, Lieutenant. You're going to be fine. Just fine.

My head feels like it's gonna explode . . .

Concussion. And your neck's in a brace.

Something wet drips on my face from the cot above me.

Whalen leans over and wipes my face. Sorry about that, Lieutenant, he says softly. He calls Doc over.

Who's up there? I ask.

McCall, Whalen replies. He's flying out with you. Chest wound.

How old is he? Twenty?

Nineteen, Doc says. He reaches up to check on McCall. His glasses catch the light and glisten.

Whalen says: You're ancient in comparison, Lieutenant. It's a wonder they let you in. And now look at you.

I try to crack a smile but my jaw hurts, so I whisper instead: Look who's talking. Old Man Methuselah himself.

You want a shiner?

Technically, that would constitute insubordination, wouldn't it?

Doc's fussing with my dressings. He says: So a doctor, a soldier, and a politician walk into a combat zone. Trust me, you haven't heard this one before . . .

Connolly stands up suddenly, interrupting him. I hear birds, he says briskly. All right, they're here. Time to go, Nick.

He walks out talking into his radio.

Whalen helps Doc adjust my stretcher. Good luck, Lieutenant, he says huskily. Ya'll take it easy now.

I say: I'll see you soon, First Sarn't.

Right.

I'm coming back, you know. Pro patria mori and all that.

He says: I bet.

My platoon sergeant, Jim Tanner, accompanies Ramirez and Pratt as they carry out my stretcher to the landing zone. There's a Black Hawk on the ground, and a couple of Apache escorts making slow passes overhead. The Black Hawk's rotors raise an alarmingly familiar cloud of thick brown dust. We duck through it.

Garcia says: Adios, Lieutenant, Sir. Have a safe journey.

Ramirez says: Courtesy Pan American Airlines, First Class. Way to go, Sir. Whoo, whoo . . .

Tanner simply grips my hand hard.

They hoist me onto the bird, and someone straps down the stretcher.

Connolly darts over. He's talking to me, but I can't hear him above the din of the rotors. He waves and backs out, and another stretcher slides in beside me.

A while later, the Black Hawk's filled. We take off with a lurch and bank away from the ground. The rising sun spools through the windows of the bird and slathers the valley red. It lights on the face of the man in the stretcher next to mine. It's Mitchell.

Someone sticks a needle into my arm. I swallow hard.

I'm going home.

# MEDIC

ONE.
Two.
Three.
Four. I watch as Jackson and Grohl count to four and heave the dead Talib to the ground. Grohl lets go early and the dead man hits the ground at an awkward angle, arms flailing. I glance at Schott as the squad's leader to see if he will say anything, but he doesn't seem to notice. Jackson and Grohl pick up the next body and this time it's Jackson who flings the corpse so that it falls heavily on its head.

I can't keep silent anymore and tell the men to slow down.

Why? Jackson asks, somewhat defiantly.

Because they fought honorably and deserve our respect.

Oh come *on,* Doc, Grohl drawls, spitting chew so that it lands right next to the dead man's head.

No, I say firmly.

For Chrissake! Jackson snaps. What are you turnin' into?—some kinda bleedin' heart Judas-goat-towelhead-hugger?

I laugh. I'm as much of a Judas-goat-towelhead-hugger as you guys are a bunch of Heathers, and you know it.

Then I add: How do you think they would have treated us under similar circumstances?

Staff Sergeant Schott clears his throat. I don't even wanna begin to imagine, he says. He runs a bandaged hand over his shaven head.

Exactly, I say, and we're supposed to be better than them, right?

They killed Sergeant Espinosa, Jackson says in a low voice. He shoots me a disgusted look. They killed Konwicki and Folsom and Terry and . . .

I cut him off: Brandon Espinosa was my friend. We were buddies from way back in Iraq. He was a soldier who lived by the soldier's code and died a soldier's death. He'd have been the last person to waste my time with explanations of how the U.S. Army treats dead enemies on the battlefield.

The men stop working. In the half-light of dawn, their dust-caked features are a startling white. Some of them clench their fists; others grow visibly tense.

Schott raises his hands conciliatorily.

All right, all right, Doc, no need to get all pissed off.

I say: I was trying to make a point for a reason, Sergeant.

The boys get what you're saying.

Why are we the ones doing this anyway? Jackson says. It's the fucking ANA that should be on the case.

They skedaddled, man, Grohl drawls. There's no ANA left on base.

Motherfuckers! Jackson says.

That'll do, Jackson, Schott snaps.

I think it's bullshit, personally, Jackson says sullenly, but when they go back to work, they treat the remaining bodies with a bit more consideration.

I take a deep breath and step back and watch the Black Hawk take off from the landing zone on the other side of the base. It banks steeply, gaining elevation as it veers off toward the south with the two Apache helicopters flanking it. I say a mental good-bye to Nick Frobenius and the three injured grunts on board. The day is rising, the night's cold air solidifying into a milky mist. The base and the plain surrounding it grow lighter by the moment, each shaping itself out of the shadows. I watch the three birds until they dwindle into specks in the distance. I stare at the sky, motionless, until I feel an arm on my shoulder.

Doc, I don't want this to sound wrong, Schott says quietly. If I didn't respect you, I wouldn't be saying this, but you gotta understand the boys are hurting—hurting bad—about our losses. You gotta understand these are kids in their teens and twenties. They've come through a lot together . . . and then this happens. They're exhausted and in shock. I don't want others walking all over something that's important to them. You gotta understand. If there's anything we have to respect, surely it's their feelings and not the fuckin' Taliban who killed their buddies.

I turn to face Schott. I have to close my eyes: his youthful features are twisted with pain. I'm a medic, Sergeant, I say gently. These aren't merely bodies to me. You can't take out your anger on dead men. You know what I'm saying?

I know.

I grasp his hand. My eyes are now close to his—which are icy and have a fixed expression. Schott's very close to exploding.

Look there, I say, averting my gaze. That one has a black turban. D'you know what that means?

The question distracts him.

He stares at the body and says: I don't have a fucking clue.

Then he adds: I guess I'm not that much into faggots.

I ignore the barb. That's the one that goes in a body bag and stays inside the base. They're sending out a bird to fly him to Kandahar.

The rest get dumped past the Claymores at the two-hundred-meter line, where their buddies can pick them up. Don't go any farther. Captain's orders.

What about the ones already in the field?

Leave them as they are. They're too far from our lines, and we don't know how many of their friends might be waiting in the slopes to strike back at us. We don't want to tempt them.

Schott smiles without humor. Oh, I'd *love* to tempt them, he says.

He walks over to the corpse with the black turban and nudges him with the toe of his boot. So what's the big deal with this guy?

I asked you.

And I told you I didn't know.

Suddenly inspired, he turns to one of the men:

Hey Duggal. What's the deal with the black turban? What does it say in your holy book?

Mitt Duggal stops what he's doing and stares, his dark eyes guarded. Then: I don't know, Sarn't, he says slowly. I'm California Sikh. Diff'rent religion.

He thinks about it for a moment, then lights up. I bet Nate knows . . .

He hollers to Nate Alizadeh, who's working with the squad repairing the breaches in the concertina. Hey, Nate! Come on over for a second. Sarn't Schott wants to know somethin' . . .

Pfc. Alizadeh, a lean, rangy 203 gunner, walks over with his arms swinging loosely. What up, Sarn't? He nods at me. Hello, Doc.

Schott says: So what does the black turban on this guy mean?

Alizadeh looks at Schott, then at Duggal, then at me. He purses his lips.

Finally, he says: What is this? Some kinda trick question?

Schott says: You're from Eye-ran, aren't you?

Jackson in the back titters inanely, and it ripples around the others.

Alizadeh shakes his head two or three times with a smile of benign bewilderment.

Well? Schott demands.

Alizadeh reddens. Jeez, Sarn't, he says softly. What do I know about turbans? I'm from downtown Dee-troit.

The men begin to gather round, looking warily first at the dead man and then at Alizadeh.

I say: I think the assumption we're making is that you're Moslem.

He laughs awkwardly. I'm Methodist, Doc. My mom's Pennsylvania Dutch. She wouldn't have it any other way. I go to church like ev'one else.

I curse inwardly at the connection I've inadvertently made between Alizadeh and the dead Talib, but before I can speak, he continues: I mean, my granpa arrived from Eye-ran and all, but that was way back in the forties. Both Granpa and Pa worked for Ford. Why, Granpa was in the design team that built the '57 Ford Fairlane, the sweetest car that came out of the line that year.

Jackson—a known aficionado of the classic Detroit years—whistles softly.

No kidding. '57 Fairlane, huh? He crouches next to the dead man and studies his black turban with as much avid attention as if it were the front grille of the Fairlane. Then: I don't know, Nate. I mean, the Fairlane was sweet and all, but in terms of that particular year, I'd go for the Bel Air myself.

It's Alizadeh's turn to crouch on the other side of the dead man.

You gotta be kidding, right? The Chevy Bel Air was nothing! The next time you're in Detroit, I'll take you on a test drive in the Fairlane. You'll see.

You got one?

Damn right, we got one. It fucking lights up the highway.

They go at it back and forth as the tension in the air palpably dissipates.

Then Schott collects himself and says: All right, all right. Cut it out.

He turns to me. So what does the damn turban mean?

The men wait for me to answer, but in a halfhearted manner, their attention clearly still on the car conversation.

I clear my throat, already feeling didactic even before I've spoken.

Well, I remark, the black turban means the man is a Sayyid, a descendant of the Prophet Muhammad.

Schott seems unimpressed: I thought the black turban meant he was Taliban.

Not all black turbans are the same. The Taliban loop theirs differently.

So . . . ?

Grohl says: So is he a mullah, or what?

Alizadeh interjects with a crooked grin. My granpa used to say the only good mullah is a dead one. He fuckin' hated them.

He looks at me sideways. You bin takin' Taliban Turban 101, Doc?

He laughs, delighted with himself, and Jackson laughs with him. Soon they're all roaring with laughter, and Alizadeh laughs the loudest, his nativist credentials safely reestablished.

Schott continues to eye me, genuinely puzzled: I still don't get it, Doc. What's the big deal with this guy? He's Taliban, ain't he?

I give up. It doesn't matter, I say wearily. Just zip him up and carry him to my tent. I'll take it from there.

I watch as Jackson and Grohl pick up one of the charred corpses. The dead man's head is attached to his neck by a mere sliver of cartilage. Grohl directs a stream of tobacco spittle at the ground as he eyes his load with disgust. Stinkin' meat jerky, man, he says disdainfully.

One day we'll all end up like that, I tell him. Skin's just another costume.

He looks at me, surprised, but doesn't say anything.

I run my hand through my hair and realize how tired I am. After the craziness of the battle, I've been attending to injuries nonstop, in addition to helping Connolly and the remaining officers restore some semblance of order to the base. With the departure of Frobenius, First

Platoon's senior Staff Sergeant, Jim Tanner, has taken charge until the lieutenant's replacement arrives. The other platoon's led by Second Lieutenant Tom Ellison and Sergeant First Class Adam Bradford, but both are newbies to the company who took over less than a month ago when Lieutenant Dave Hendricks and Sergeant Brian Castro were killed in an ambush in the mountains. More critically, both platoons are now understaffed, and there's no certainty that we've seen the last of the Taliban.

The stars vanish one by one in the dawn light.

The men finish carrying the last dead Taliban out to the field, where they've been laid out in a straight line. Schott studies the slopes at the other end of the field and announces: Back.

He raises the collar of his jacket and begins walking back toward the base. The men follow him with their heads down. Jackson and Grohl come last, walking backward with their M-4s aimed at the field. Everyone looks done in, their faces grimy and sweaty, their eyes glazed.

They pass me in silence, the mist winding in and out of their ranks. The sky turns scarlet. Drops of dew appear on the ground. The first rays of the sun skirt the mountains and light up the brass shells littering the field so that it seems speckled with gold and blood. The slopes disappear in the mist. Although I have my fleece jacket on, I can't repress a shiver. Already great flocks of crows are flying out of the mountains.

Spcs. Garcia and Lee show up to collect the insurgent leader in his body bag, and I accompany them to the medic's tent. We pass the smoldering ruins of the guard tower.

It ain't fair, Doc, Garcia says suddenly. It just ain't fair. Folsom just got married. Terry's wife's expecting their first child.

No, I say, it isn't fair.

What's today? he asks. Tuesday?

Yes, I reply.

He was going to call his wife today.

Who was?

Terry.

It coulda been me, Doc, Lee says. It shoulda been me. I'm single, I got no dependents.

Garcia says: Fuckin' luck of the draw, man. Fuckin' luck of the draw.

They fall silent. We reach the medical tent. Just as we're about to enter, across the southern horizon a sudden explosion of color spools into the sky. It mushrooms into a giant ball. It turns orange, then red, then bright white. The men stare.

Jackson comes running up. He's panting. What the fuck is that, guys?

Garcia smiles uncertainly. Maybe the Pakis let off one of their nukes.

It's coming from the south, I point out.

From Eye-ran? Jackson says. He laughs dryly. Maybe I should go ask Nate.

Leave him alone, I tell him.

Just kidding, Doc. Trying to get your goat, like.

Well, knock it off and go get some rest. You're all wired up.

Jackson slopes off.

Garcia and Lee enter the medical tent, and I direct them to put down the body bag on a table in the corner. When they leave the tent, I walk out with them. The cloud on the horizon has ballooned into a massive black sphere. A plume of smoke connects it to the ground. I dismiss Lee and Garcia and continue to watch the cloud. From the tent comes a whiff of rotting blood.

The radio telephone operator, Heywood, comes by to tell me that the captain's been stung by a wasp. I decided to walk over to the command post to check on him, just in case.

The C.O.'s inside the hut, standing at the window, staring out at the sky. He turns to look at me as I enter. I hold back instinctively, mindful of the rank differential. I notice that his right hand, which he's holding out at an angle from his body, is swollen.

I heard you were stung by a wasp, Sir?

Yes, can you believe it? I go through a vicious firefight without a scratch, and then I get stung by a fucking wasp.

Do you want me to take a look?

He waves me away. It's only a wasp, Doc.

He turns to look out of the window again. That's when Whalen walks in.

I just called KAF about that smoke in the sky, he tells Connolly. It looks like it's somewhere over the Arghandab River Valley.

And . . . ?

They're investigating. I'm waiting to hear back from them.

The birds went in that direction, I remark.

Connolly looks at me irritably. Thanks, Doc.

I'm sorry, Sir, I reply. That was a stupid thing to say.

I'm gonna call KAF myself, he says suddenly. He walks over to the desk and sits down with a thud. He stares at me. You better turn in for a while. You look like you're about to drop.

So do you, Sir. So do we all. But you're probably right. I feel like I'm moving in slow motion.

He listens to me but seems distracted.

I walk out while he sits at the desk all hunched up.

Back in my hooch I lie down on my bunk and pick up a book. *Habits and Customs of the Native Tribes of Kandahaur Province,* by Lieutenant Colonel Sir Rupert Jollye, Her Majesty's Gordon Highlanders, 1897. I read a page with effort and put it down. I slip on my iPod headphones and scan for something easy to listen to. I click on "Desert Angel," by Stevie Nicks. She sings me to sleep.

I couldn't have been sleeping more than a few minutes when I realize that someone is nestling against me. I turn to my side with a start. It's Sarah. She lies there smiling serenely. Her body feels soft, pliant. I stroke her breast, touch her nipple. She runs her hand through my hair. I press closer to kiss her when I glimpse a man lying on the other side.

I wake up with a gasp, then sit up. My heart is pounding wildly. I'm sweating, my breath coming in gasps. I fold my hands around my knees and force myself to breathe slower. I feel old, spent.

I push back on the bunk and gaze at Sarah's picture on the wall. She's tied back her heavy bronze hair and stares at the camera fixedly. We'd just had an argument, something silly; I don't even remember what it was anymore. I look at her intently, then stretch out on the bunk again. I lie there staring at the ceiling, thinking about how stuffy it is in here, willing myself to fall back to sleep.

It *is* stuffy, Frobenius agrees as he leans past me and opens a window. Outside, the sky has cleared up after the rain. Across the street, a man is shaving at an open window. He's short, squat, his white shirt unbuttoned to his navel. Soapy water runs down his neck; he contorts his face hideously as he shaves.

D'you think you could get a bead on him from here, Dave? Frobenius asks.

Dave Hendricks glances over indifferently. He aims an imaginary sniper rifle at the man. From this distance, easy, he says.

Frobenius says: This town is dead, man.

Hendricks says: It's Vicenza, Nick, not Frankfurt.

Yeah, whatever. It still sucks.

Hendricks suddenly pushes back from the table and stands up.

Ya'll going somewhere, Lieutenant? Whalen asks.

Yup. I'm heading into town. Time to party.

He puts on his jacket and glances at Frobenius. Nick?

Oh, I don't know.

Still not over Emily, eh? Hendricks says, grinning.

Let's not go there, shall we? Frobenius warns, his voice suddenly steely.

Sorry, bro, I was just sayin' . . .

Don't.

Hendricks puts his hands up. No offense. I don't suppose you're in the mood, then?

Frobenius looks at Whalen, then at me.

Whalen avoids his eyes. I nurse my beer silently.

With something like a sigh, Frobenius rises to his feet. He puts on his jacket and cap and glances at us again.

Whalen continues to look away; I stare back at Frobenius without speaking.

Abruptly, he says: Fuck this.

There's always that, Hendricks says deadpan.

Frobenius grimaces.

Well, gentlemen, he says tonelessly, good evening.

We watch them walk out, the barroom doors swinging shut behind them.

Lieutenant Frobenius is going to pieces, Whalen observes. He's drinking too much, whoring too much. I don't like it.

He's his own man, First Sarn't.

That still don't mean I gotta like it.

At their age, what else have they got to do? It's all bars and floozies.

Whalen rubs his hands together so hard they turn a pasty white.

Still, he says, I know he's hurting. I went to their wedding, you know. It was by the water. On the Hudson. They couldn't keep their hands off each other. She's a good kid.

Aww, that's sweet, I say mockingly.

I mean it. It was real.

So she loves him?

More than he thinks.

Then why'd she leave?

Because she loves him.

All right, what is this? A riddle? From everything I've heard, she was frickin' hard on him. And more than a bit judgmental.

Whalen winces. Aren't they all?

He downs his beer, then looks at me. There's a movie playing that I want to see. It's in Greek, with English subtitles. Interested?

I raise my eyebrows. With subtitles . . . jeez, I don't know, First Sarn't.

Aw, c'mon. I don't want to sit in a movie hall all by my lonesome self.

I think for a moment, then: Why not? It isn't like I got a hot date waiting.

We walk down to the movie hall. The cobblestones are still wet from the rain, and slippery. Whalen insists on buying my ticket, so I wait in the lobby and look at the poster with Irene Pappas staring out fiercely at the world. I think she's gorgeous.

The picture's from 1961; the hall's half empty. It's an old print, and white blips and flashes spark across the shadowy screen. I feel my eyes blurring from the combination of too much beer and too much straining to read the subtitles. I begin to regret coming, when, with her voice pitched low, Pappas seems to address me directly:

> *I will bury Polyneices. I will do what I must do*
> *And I will die an honorable death.*
> *I am his family, his kin, and kin will lie by kin.*
> *Mine will be a holy crime.*

She reaches out of the screen and shakes me by the shoulder.

Wake up, Steve, she says urgently. *Wake up!*

I start and sit bolt upright: Pfc. Serrano has his hand on my arm.

He says: I'm sorry, Doc, but the captain wants to see you in the command post. Immediately.

I peer at my watch: I've been asleep for less than twenty minutes.

What's going on? I ask, but Serrano's already on his way out. I'm not sure, he calls out over his shoulder, but I'm on my way to get First Sergeant Whalen and Lieutenant Ellison.

I swing myself off the bunk with a sense of foreboding. I throw on a shirt, pull on a pair of shorts, tie my boots. For a moment I struggle with the laces. Then I run out.

The stars are still out, but they're fading fast. The mountains tower over the landscape. The mist has spread evenly on the ground, and it is damp and thick.

I catch up with Whalen just as he's about to enter the communications hut, which also serves as the base's command post, a fourteen-by-eight-foot space filled with radios, maps, and computers. Inside, it's already crowded. Beside the C.O., Lieutenant Ellison, Sergeant Tanner of First Platoon, Sergeants Bradford and Eric Petrak of Second Platoon, Staff Sergeants Ashworth, Flint, Tribe, and Schott, and the radio telephone operator, Heywood, a number of other NCOs pack the hut. Connolly looks at us as we walk in. He's unusually pale, as if some essential spark has gone out of him. He glances at his watch, then announces in a flat voice, without any preliminaries, that, about thirteen minutes ago, we received the news that the Black Hawk carrying Nick Frobenius and the others crashed about twenty-eight kilometers due southwest of us. All personnel on board are feared lost.

Something like a collective groan escapes from the men. There is no other sound. Not once does Connolly look up. We see nothing but his own and the RTO's bowed heads as he speaks. He says that as yet we have no indication of what might have caused the crash. What's more, one of the two choppers that were sent from Kandahar Airfield to rescue any survivors from the Black Hawk crashed in its turn in the same area, leading to a decision by Battalion to ground all helicopter flights to Alpha Company until there was information on the causes of both accidents.

He goes on to report an attack on the ground troops dispatched to the Black Hawk's crash site. He adds that although there are no signs that that attack was related to the one on our base, we need to remain vigilant.

He pauses for a moment and looks at Whalen and Tanner. He suggests that they get some sleep since Lieutenant Ellison's volunteered for first shift. Whalen turns on his heel and walks out without a word: he's taken the news of the crash hard. Connolly tells Tanner that he'll have him relieve Ellison when his time is up. Bradford and Petrak are next as he divvies up responsibilities. As I listen to him, I find myself comforted by his efficiency and composure. Then I realize that he's talking to me. He pauses and stares at me expectantly. His face is impenetrably calm, but deep lines around his mouth pull it downward.

Is that okay by you, Sergeant? he prompts.

I'm sorry, but what was that again, Sir? I ask, abashed.

You're gonna have to hold on to the corpse until the birds can fly him out of here, he repeats patiently.

That's fine, Sir, I answer.

He nods tiredly and then, after a moment, dismisses us.

The mist is beginning to thin out as I leave the hut. A few rays of sunlight spear through the ragged wisps, but almost at once the sun dips back behind a bank of clouds. The plain around the base retreats into shadows. The mountains merge with the clouds. The air becomes perceptibly colder. The thought crosses my mind that if there is an afterlife, it must look like this.

I head to the medical tent, where a rank and penetrating odor reminds me of the dead Taliban in the body bag. Spc. Chris Svitek, the unit's other medic, is in attendance, and he's wearing a face mask. He pulls it off as I walk in, and his face is gray, disgusted. He stalks out of the tent and clears his throat copiously before reentering.

Can't we park this fucker somewhere else? he says heatedly. Having to breathe his fug is frickin' insane!

Like where else, Specialist?

Over by the motor pool, where the ANA huts used to be, for instance. No one ever goes there. My God, at this rate, I'm gonna need a chemical suit to survive this stint.

It's gonna get worse, I reply. We're holding on to him until they fly the birds out, and they don't know when that's going to be.

Aw, man, that's fuckin' unbelievable!

I'll ask First Sarn't about relocating him, though it's probably going to be a negative.

Why?

Because this guy's high priority, that's why, and we're supposed to watch him like a hawk before the birds come for him.

He's dead, Svitek points out. He ain't going anyplace.

I'll ask the First Sarn't, I repeat. It's going to have to be his call. Or maybe I'll talk to Lieutenant Ellison.

Svitek pulls a face, but doesn't say anything else.

A faint breeze makes the canvas of the tent sway slightly, and at each movement the entire structure creaks. I feel exhausted, dizzy, and realize that I'm no good to anyone in this state. The first order of my day is to catch up on my sleep. I tell Svitek I'm going to be napping in my hooch.

Lucky you, he says with feeling.

I'll be back before you know it.

I pat his shoulder in sympathy as he puts on his face mask again, and then I walk out and take a long, deep breath of fresh air.

I pass the mess tent on the way to my hooch. The men are just finishing up their morning meal. The air smells of cigarette smoke and coffee, but unlike most other mornings, everyone is silent.

I sit down on my bunk and remain there for a while, motionless.

I wonder if I should take a sleeping pill, then decide against it. The hooch feels overheated as always, but I hardly notice as I sink into weary, dreamless sleep.

I wake up when Grohl pokes his head in to report that Svitek wants to know if I've found out about relocating the dead Taliban. Grohl's face is red and puffy; he looks straight ahead as he speaks, avoiding my eyes. Then I recall that Pfc. Spitz, who was on the bird with Frobenius, McCall, and Mitchell, was Grohl's bunkmate.

How you holding up, Grohl? I ask.

Okay, he says inaudibly.

When I ask again, he turns around and leaves.

Outside the hooch, the day is now a dark shade of gray. The sky is cloudy, overcast: there's no sign of the sun. Combat Outpost Tarsândan's all hunkered down in the shadow of the mountains.

I walk over to the Hescos to ask Ellison about the dead insurgent, but Ellison's no longer there. Instead, Whalen paces back and forth between Pratt and Ramirez. He nods at me briefly.

Why are you here? I ask. I thought it was Ellison's shift.

I couldn't sleep.

When I eye him with concern, he says: Don't even go there, okay?

How long do you plan to stick around?

Tanner's relieving me at 1600.

I leave him alone, realizing there's much about grief that can't be put into words. Instead, I gaze out at the deserted field. Past the Claymores, the corpses are still lying in a straight line at the two-hundred-meter marker. Farther beyond, I count three more bodies. A cloud of raucous crows keeps them company.

I'm taken aback that no one's shown up to collect the dead. Soon they're going to be stinking up the entire base. I wonder if the others are thinking the same thing. I observe Pratt, who's leaning against the Hescos and staring at the mountains impassively, but Ramirez, true to form, is fidgety. From past experience, I know him to be notoriously volatile in situations where there's nothing to be done but wait endlessly, and I wonder how much longer he's going to be able to keep still.

Suddenly he walks right up to Whalen and looks into his face, close up. Whalen stares back with an empty glance, as at an inanimate object. From the expression on his face, I can tell that Ramirez is about to say something cocky, when Whalen lifts him physically off his feet and slams him against the Hesco wall. In a quiet, conversational tone, he tells the restive Mexican: The next time you feel the need to scratch that itch to blab, your Mona Lisa face is going to be pulp, d'you get me?

Okay, First Sarn't, okay. No sweat.

Do you *get* me?

Roger, First Sarn't Whalen!

Whalen lets go and Ramirez collapses at his feet.

Whalen turns to me. You still here, Doc? Something the matter?

As a matter of fact, yes. Could we move the dead Af out of the medic's tent to someplace where we don't have to smell him? He's stinking up the tent and it's making it impossible for us to stay inside.

Whalen gazes at me for a moment. He shrugs his shoulders.

Hmm, I don't know. Lemme think about it. Maybe I'll sound out Lieutenant Ellison.

D'you want me to ask the C.O. directly?

Nope, no need to bother him. I'll take care of it. Okay?

Okay, I answer, and walk away as he puts on what I think of as his blind expression. Ramirez is still on the ground, rubbing his neck. Whalen glances at him indifferently and resumes pacing.

Back in the medical tent, I nod at Svitek and tell him to take a break.

Why don't you park your chair outside, I suggest. That way you don't have to smell him at close range.

He agrees gratefully and lugs a chair out.

I wear a face mask and unzip the black body bag.

I stare at the dead man without emotion. He is young, fair, and sparsely bearded, and his staring kohl-lined eyes are a startling shade of gray that reminds me of the light outside—they seem to look at everything and nothing at once. His nose is small and sharp, his forehead wide, his jaw pronounced, but the skin of his face is beginning to lose its tautness and become spongy and discolored. The fatal wound was a clean shot through the heart. I unbutton his shirt and examine it for a good minute or two. Before I zip up the body bag again, I try to picture him as he must have been in life, but here my imagination fails me.

I leave the tent feeling like I've come up for air from a hundred feet underground. Preoccupied, but not sure why, I walk around the base aimlessly. I try not to think of Frobenius and the others, even as I realize that that's a lost cause. And I'm not the only one. Everyone's looking subdued, and when a couple of men ask me to take a look at minor injuries, I oblige instantly, relieved to get my mind off our casualties.

A while later, I find myself passing the C.O.'s hut. His light is on, and he emerges into the open just as I slow down for an instant. His face is bloodless. I wonder if he's had any sleep since the firefight or if, like Whalen, he's gone without. He glances at me interrogatively and raises his eyebrows. Yes? he says sharply. What is it?

On the spur of the moment, I seize my chance and ask: Have we had any word on when they're planning to resume the bird service, Sir? Our dead insurgent is beginning to smell up the medic tent, and we were hoping we could move him somewhere else, like over by the motor pool.

Have you spoken to First Sergeant Whalen about it?

I hesitate. Yes, Sir, I have.

And what did he say?

That he'd think about it and let me know.

His reply is acerbic: Then you'll know when he tells you.

He pauses, and then, as if to make up for his asperity, beckons me into his hut. I hear you've been reading up on the Taliban, he remarks.

Oh, just a few things, Sir, like local customs and such.

I follow him in as he walks behind his desk and turns his laptop in my direction, angling the screen so that I can see it. He nods at me, giving me permission to relax. Take a look at this, he says. Tell me what you think.

The screen displays a photograph shot from the air. It shows a sun-dappled forest clearing with a couple of people in it. Connolly zooms in on the figures, and the picture magnifies to show a woman sitting on a tree stump playing some kind of long-necked lute, and a man at her feet, listening. Intriguingly, the woman isn't clad in a burqa. It's the first time I've seen a young Afghan woman in these regions without a full body shroud, and I study her closely. Her eyes are shut, her expression concentrated: she is engrossed in her playing.

Connolly points to the man: That's the corpse in your tent. After I'd uploaded our headshots of the corpses for Intelligence, they came back with a match in less than thirty minutes. This particular photograph was taken undetected about four months ago by a Predator drone some two kilometers or so above the clearing. Neat, huh? Man versus machine: machine wins every time.

Who is he, Sir?

Connolly tells me his name.

Seems he's known locally as the Prince of the Mountains, he continues. Correction: he *was* known as the Prince of the Mountains. He was some heavy Taliban dude. I don't know the details.

I'm struck again by the incongruity of the photograph.

But if he's Taliban, Sir, I point out, what's he doing in the company of an uncovered woman, and one playing a musical instrument at that?

Connolly gazes at the screen quizzically, then shrugs.

I don't know, Doc. Maybe it's his wife, and the rules don't count. But I'm speculating. I really have no idea. You're the expert. What's your take on it?

You got me there, Sir. I don't have a clue either, I'm sorry to say.

I gaze at the picture, feeling uncomfortably like a voyeur, before angling the screen in Connolly's direction again. He examines the picture some more, then switches off the laptop. Raising his head, he looks me straight in the eye. All of a sudden, he gets up and walks over to a corner of the room.

He returns with an AK-47 enclosed in a grimy blue silk gun cover, with elaborate floral patterns embroidered in red chain stitch, and with the hole for the trigger reinforced with black thread.

We found this on your insurgent, he says.

*My* insurgent? Well . . .

He takes it out from its cloth cover and balances it on his palm.

I examine it without taking it from him. Its surface is pitted, and the weathered plywood stock strapped with duct tape. On the left side of the receiver, which is solid steel, there's a triangular factory stamp with an arrow inside it, followed by the weapon's serial number and date of manufacture: 1955.

Connolly contemplates the gun for a moment.

This is probably from one of the earliest batches of AK-47s, he observes, made when the Soviets were first arming their troops with assault rifles. Then, somewhere down the line in its long history—and who the fuck knows how?—it found its way here, where it's now part of the Taliban's arsenal. Can you think of any mechanical appliance that you've used that's lasted as long?

Me personally, Sir? I think for a moment, then say, hesitantly: Perhaps the old ceramic toilets back at my folk's place, Sir?

Connolly grimaces and falls into a meditative silence. After a while, he sighs and says: This thing is fifty-five years old. What a country.

He glances at me. Alexander the Great was here, you know.

I stare at him, trying to follow his train of thought.

He continues looking at the gun. They say the name Kandahar is a version of Iskander, which is what people called him in these parts; although it's more likely that it comes from some ancient Indian place name.

Indian, Sir?

Gandhara.

I see.

He smiles wanly. I learned that from Lieutenant Frobenius. You know what he was like. Mad about history and geography and stuff.

I don't say anything.

He glances at me again, and I see that his eyes are brimming with tears.

It's all a bunch of bullshit, he says huskily, attempting to conceal his distress with a laugh. Did you know that the small arms fire in his vicinity was so concentrated that the men trying to reach him could only see the sand and dust kicking up?

I refrain from telling him that I was right there, the first to reach Frobenius.

He wipes his eyes hurriedly with the back of his hand. Clearing his throat, he says: He engaged the bulk of the insurgents, taking the fight right to them. It kept the pressure off the rest of us and fucking stymied the enemy's attack. That brave, crazy fuck!

I look down. There's a long interval of silence.

Eventually, he places his hands on either side of the Kalashnikov, straining downward as if attempting to snap it in two. His face turns red, and the veins on his neck stand out. Finally he relaxes and his shoulders slump. He gives a limp smile and strokes the receiver with his hand. Machine wins, he says in a quiet voice.

He pauses and wipes his eyes.

Lieutenant Frobenius majored in the Classics, did you know that? In some boutique northeastern college. Me . . . he pauses. Where I went to college—*state* college—if you were a guy, you had one of two choices: you either majored in Agro Science or Business Admin.

I remain silent while he nods a couple of times as if carrying on an internal dialogue with himself.

Have you heard of the Pingry School? he asks.

The Pingry School? No, Sir.

It's one of the best private schools in the country. I mean, it's *fucking* elite—a *mint* school. Lieutenant Frobenius went there, and then he went to Vassar. Vassar! he repeats softly and shakes his head in disbelief. If he'd wanted, he coulda walked into West Point and come out a ringknocker with a friggin' stellar record. But for some reason he chose a prissy joint like Vassar. Never could figure that out. I asked him about it once, and he only laughed. So I don't know. Maybe some people want to do things the hard way. But with his background, you'd think . . .

I suppose so, Sir. Yes, Sir.

He glances at me and then turns away.

What was most special about Nick was his enthusiasm. He was able to communicate his passions like no one else. I still have one of his books of Greek plays lying around here someplace. Problem is, every time I pick it up, I'm so damn tired I fall asleep.

He holds up the gun and, aiming it past me at some distant point, he continues: In any case, what all this means is that these fuckers . . . these *fuckers* have been around for a long—a *very* long time. And there's probably Macedonian blood in them, which would explain at least some of their disposition.

And some of their features, I add. The dead man in my tent has fair hair and gray eyes. Very European.

I think the technical term is Indo-Aryan.

You're right, Sir. Indo-Aryan.

He extends the AK-47 in my direction.

Here—have you ever held one of these things?

No, Sir, I have not.

I take it from him. It feels rickety compared to our M-4, its closest equivalent. I tell him so.

He grimaces. You could leave that thing under a rock for ten years and still use it when you came back, no problem. It's the ultimate killing machine.

And still the Russians lost, I remind him, handing back the gun.

The Russians lost because they fought bunched up in motorized convoys. They didn't fan out in foot squads like we do. Their tactics were wrong. We've learned from their experience. We're not gonna make the same mistakes.

He puts down the gun and sits at his desk. Carefully folding the blue silk gun cover, he places it next to his laptop. I'm keeping this as a souvenir, he says. Years from now, when I'm shitting away my time in Flyover Zone in bumfuck Indiana or wherever, I want to look at this thing to remind myself that I was really here, in the middle of nowhere, following in Alexander's footsteps.

Alexander never returned home, Sir.

But I intend to, he says grimly, before correcting himself: *We* will go back, Doc. That's a promise. We'll see this through.

It's summer back home, Sir, I say reflectively. The schools are out. Summer camp starts in two weeks in Williamsfield. My kid brother's a counselor this year.

That summer's miles and miles away, he says. He leans his head on his hand.

I'm tired, he says.

Everyone is, Sir.

He looks at me with an unseeing expression. I don't know if they're gonna attack again today, he says, but if they do, we're not taking any prisoners.

I hesitate before asking: What about when they come to collect their dead?

He doesn't answer. I wait for a few moments, but he remains silent. Then he turns his back on me and goes back to studying a map. I realize I've been dismissed.

I leave his hut and pause for a moment, digesting the conversation. I feel dejected and, as I lift up my eyes to the mountains looming over the base, strangely apathetic. With an effort, I pull myself together, and set out to find Whalen. It's just before 1600, and I want to catch him before his shift ends and ask if he's spoken to Ellison about the corpse.

I find him by the ECP, just about to hand over to Sergeant Tanner.

He looks at me bleary-eyed when I ask him.

I'm still thinking about it, he replies.

What about Lieutenant Ellison?

He said he's gonna think about it as well.

He slaps his cheeks. Boy, he says wearily. I can hardly stand. I guess I'm gonna get some rest. And he shambles off.

I look around. Ramirez and Pratt have left as well, and in their place there's Alizadeh as the only relief who's showed up so far. Tanner's in a lather. He's just beginning to flay Alizadeh about the others' whereabouts when Jackson comes running up. Sorry I'm late, Sarn't, he pants. I was trying to bring Grohl, but no luck. He's taken Spitz's death hard. Maybe you should talk to him . . .

Oh, for fuck's sake! Tanner says exasperatedly. Where is he now?

Holed up in his hooch.

I say: I'll go get him.

Thanks, Doc, Tanner says. Tell Grohl I'll have his ass if he isn't here ASAP.

Jackson offers to come with me.

We'll be gone a couple of minutes, I say. That okay?

He better be here or else! Tanner repeats.

We find Grohl in a fetal crouch on his bunk. He's facing the wall, iPod headphones jammed into his ears. I sit down at the foot of his bunk. He doesn't stir.

Jackson leans over him and yanks off his headphones.

What the *fuck?* Grohl yells, spinning around with his hands clenched.

Doc's here, Jackson says equably. You're supposed to be on guard shift, dude. Tanner's fuckin' seething.

Fuck that, man. Leave me alone.

You gotta get a grip, dude, Jackson says.

It's okay, I tell Jackson. I'll take it from here.

Grohl watches me sullenly.

I point to his iPod. What you listening to?

He answers in a reluctant monotone: Gethsemane.

Is that a band?

Yup.

I don't think I've heard of them, I tell him. What kind of music do they play?

Jackson answers in his place: They're kind of progressive rock, but metallic.

Grohl rolls his eyes, but sits up. They're not fucking prog, they're post-prog, he says irritably. And they're not "metallic," whatever the hell that means. They're death metal, but with an aggravated melodic arc. Okay?

All right, man, Jackson says, have it your way. They're like OMG fucking brutal death metal.

Bullshit, Grohl says. Gethsemane is not OMG fucking brutal death metal. Gethsemane is a band that's way beyond that kind of classification. When they write a song, it's not like they're trying to be as satanic and obscure as possible like some cheesy death metal band. They just write from the heart. Some of their songs sound like death metal, some sound post-prog, some have math rock or grind-core influences, while some others are just mellow ballads. And that is what makes Gethsemane a fucking awesome band.

I got news for you, bro, Jackson says. Mellow ballads are the tool of the undereducated.

You're a tool, Grohl snaps.

Whatever, dude, Jackson says. He turns to me. If you've heard of Dream Paranoia, they're a bit like them.

Grohl bends toward me. Don't listen to him, Doc, he doesn't know what the fuck he's talking about. Dream Paranoia completely lost it after *Downhill*. Christ, my dad listens to Dream Paranoia. Then I played him Gethsemane, and he didn't like it because of the singer's growl. So I kicked his face in and buried him alive in the basement. You don't fuck with Gethsemane.

Jackson giggles. No kidding. I did the same with my mom after I got her to listen to Amesoeurs. We're brothers, you and me.

But Grohl is having none of it.

Ameseours! he spits out with contempt. Talk about cheese-eating surrender-monkeys!

So they're French? I venture.

Yup, Jackson says quickly. Then, nettled by the attack on his favorite band, he says: And what about Gethsemane? They're fuckin' Canadian.

Scandinavian, Grohl corrects him. There *is* a difference. Just goes to show how much you know.

Don't you guys listen to any American bands? I say mildly.

This time they both round on me. Like what, Doc?

Jackson says: Like some fuckin' commercial boy band with an aggregate shelf life of ten days?

Grohl adds: Like babbyy babbyy babbyy ooohhhh and I was like babbyy babbyy babbyy ooohhhh?

Oh, I don't know, I reply. What about Pearl Jam?

They stare at me in genuine astonishment. Then Grohl says wonderingly: You gotta be fucking kidding, right?

I'm thirty-one, but I suddenly feel ancient.

Tell you what, Doc, Grohl says kindly, if you lend me your iPod, I'll download some Gethsemane for you. You can start with *Blackwater Daze.* You'll see. They're like no other band. Even the artwork on their albums is sick as hell.

On our way to the Hescos, he adds: I fucking *hate* Gethsemane. I swear, the first time I heard them I 'gasmed all over myself after just two minutes. They make me feel all guilty for not listening to them from birth, and after every song I can't function for, like, two weeks. Awestruck every time!

We reach the ECP, and Tanner marches over to greet us belligerently.

Well? he demands of Grohl.

I can explain, I interject, but Tanner asks me to stay out of it.

Grohl hangs his head. I've been sorta fucked up in my head, Sarn't, what with Spitty and everything . . .

Tanner takes a step back and purses his lips. He looks disgusted.

Tell you what, soldier, he says, I got a good cure for that problem. Double shift.

I begin to protest, but Grohl says softly: It's all right, Doc, I guess I kinda asked for it.

Tanner turns on his heel and stalks back to the ECP, while I linger there uncertainly. Grohl props up his M-4 against a sandbag and gazes at the mountains. You know, Doc, he says contemplatively, going back to what we were talkin' about earlier on, I'm not religious or anything, but every time I look up at those slopes I get these goose bumps all over, and then it's like all I can hear is Jens singing "Death Whispers in My Head." That's when I realize . . . if I had a religion, he would be my god.

I cough. Who's Jens?

Gethsemane's vocalist, he says with reverence. And the ultimate fucking guitar god. Jens Lyhne.

Amen to that, I say.

I pat him on the back and turn to leave just as the C.O. walks over from his hut. He says: I just heard from Battalion. They're gonna resume Black Hawk flights in a couple of days. Which means that's how long you'll have to put up with your friend in the body bag. Sorry about that.

Two more days!

He glances at me sardonically and says: I'm told that there are certain tribes up north who refuse to go through with a burial until a full week has passed, in the belief that anything less is both disrespectful and immoral.

Couldn't we move him to where the ANA huts used to be, Sir? I mean, there's nothing left there after the insurgents blitzed it.

He pauses and thinks about it. I suppose we could do that . . . But you'd still have to watch over him. Tell you what. Why don't you talk to Lieutenant Ellison? See if we can move the damn thing.

Should I tell him that that's what you ordered, Sir?

All right.

Thanks, Sir.

Sure thing.

He climbs the Hescos and eyes the bodies lying in the field.

No one come to pick them up yet, eh? he asks Tanner.

It's very unusual, Sir, Tanner replies.

They're being sensible. They know they'll get mown down if they try.

Still, it hasn't stopped them in the past, Tanner remarks. I don't know what to make of it.

I don't think we have to make anything of it, Sergeant—it's not our place. But I'm certainly not going to stand around having them rot in front of our eyes and smell up the base. I've asked Sergeant Tribe to round up a couple of squads and bury them out beyond the LZ where no one can see them. Out of sight, out of mind.

Tanner asks him if he's intending to have the three men lying at the end of the field buried as well.

Nope. The light's fading fast, and I'm not taking any chances. They're too close to the mountains, and we don't know who else might be holed up there. If they're still around tomorrow, then we'll deal with them.

In a lowered voice, he asks if he can speak to me in private for a second.

We walk out to the wire, and he says: Battalion also informed me that a rescue team searched the site of the Black Hawk crash. He pauses and clears his throat. They accounted for everyone. There were no survivors. I've told all the officers, and I'm going to make a general announcement tomorrow. Right now I think it's more important for the men to get some rest.

Of course, Sir, I tell him. I can't think of anything else to say.

We stare at each other and then, simultaneously, turn to gaze at the mountains. The evening light softens his features, his expression a meld of youth, sadness, and fatigue. He badly needs a shave—as do I—and he seems to have visibly lost weight during the past twenty-four hours. I'm sure I look no better, but I can't resist glancing at his hand where the wasp bit him: the swelling has reduced and it now looks blotchy and inflamed.

Just then, a flock of crows passes over our heads, and we both look up.

Have you seen Shorty since the firefight? he asks suddenly.

The dog? No, not that I can recall, Sir.

Hmm. He's probably still hiding out somewhere.

Spitz usually knows where he is, I say without thinking, then pull up short. I forgot, I say stupidly.

He stands up very straight, but when he glances at me, he seems gentle, resigned, almost defeated. He runs his hand over his face and shakes his head.

Do animals mourn, Doc? No, don't answer, he says. That was a rhetorical question. A slight grimace deforms his mouth. This is war, isn't it? It's what war does. In less than a month, I've lost my two most experienced officers . . .

He lights a cigarette and tosses away the match with a gesture that indicates both helplessness and an excess of fatigue. His hand is trembling, I notice. He takes a single puff and chucks the cigarette away. He nods at me as if from a great distance.

I'm going to get some sleep, he says. You know where to find me if you need me.

About to leave, he catches himself. What are you doing here, by the way?

I was just about to go to the medic tent, Sir.

Tanner walks over at that moment.

Connolly nods at him. How much longer are you here?

Three more hours, Sir.

Don't forget that your next shift is from 0400.

Not a problem, Sir.

The C.O. nods tiredly and walks away.

Pfc. Jackson joins us as he leaves. He asks Tanner: What was that all about, Sarn't?

We're going to be on guard duty again early tomorrow morning, Jackson.

No shit. How early?

Four.

Fuck.

Yes.

All four of us?

All 'cept Grohl, Tanner says, and then smiles crookedly: This ain't a fucking spa, soldier.

Jackson gazes at him blankly for a few seconds before averting his face and returning to his position. I can't tell if he's pleased that Tanner's omitted Grohl, or disheartened by the prospect of yet another night of inadequate sleep. Whatever it is, something about his reaction obviously bothers Tanner, and I reckon he's about to pull him up for it, but then he appears to relent. Turning to me, he says: I have to remind myself that he's only nineteen.

Good call, Sergeant, I say quietly.

We turn to look at the unusually subdued Jackson and catch him trying to disguise a yawn by breathing out through the corners of his mouth.

On my way to the medic tent to relieve Svitek, I stop by Ellison's hooch to talk to him about moving the corpse, but he's sound asleep and dead to the world. I listen to him snoring exhaustedly for a couple of minutes—it's probably his first sleep in days—and resign myself to waiting until the next day.

The fog is thick on the ground when I set out to find him the first thing the following morning. Bradford's passing by the medic tent, and I ask him if he's seen the lieutenant.

He's either at the ECP, Bradford says, or else somewhere along the Hescos.

There's a sharp wind blowing again, and it whistles through the base. The grunts on duty at the ECP tell me that Ellison is checking up on all the men on watch. So I spend the next hour stumbling around the Hesco perimeter in search of the elusive lieutenant, a more difficult task than usual because the fog makes it impossible to see more than two paces ahead. I follow in his tracks, determined to find him. As I go from one guard post to another, it appears to me that most of the men have put the firefight behind them, and yet I can sense a residue of lingering tension as, heads hunched into upturned collars, rifles held at the ready, they squint to see through the uncertain light. Everything seems curiously dreamlike in the dawn light and the dissipating fog. The optics of the fog make it appear as if the men and the huts are all floating above the ground. From time to time, I lose sight of my surroundings completely, and then it's as if I am no longer part of this world but somewhere else altogether. This odd state of mind must be an aftereffect of the events of the past twenty-four hours, some kind of delayed reaction to the battle itself. The feeling of dislocation is extreme, as if my nerves are strained and I'm experiencing at one and the same time all the contradictory stages of a dream. Equally unnerving is the fleeting nature of this sensation, because every time the fog thins and I can see around me again, I am brought back squarely to the present. What heightens the sense of unreality is the absolute silence across the base, as if the mist has dampened all its usual sounds. Instead, everyone seems to wordlessly watch the play of fog on the field and the mantle of clouds that first settles on the mountains and then lifts slightly, though not so much that the sun can break through. There's no trace of life outside—with the exception of the three corpses at the very end of the field, all else is a bleak wasteland—and at this time of morning even the ubiquitous desert crows are missing.

"By and by, though, as a pale pinkish light seeps through the clouds, the slopes are once more visible in the distance. From their foot, a narrow trail ascends slantwise until it bends at a sharp angle, climbing in a fairly steep zigzag between ridges and pine trees until it vanishes behind a scrim of fallen rocks. It continues out of sight through a high valley that extends far into the chain of mountains. It is in this region of sharply alternating light and darkness that Lieutenant Hendricks and Sergeant Castro met their end a few weeks ago in the course of a reconnaissance patrol. Since then, we've refrained from venturing into the mountains, although there've been rumors of Predator drone attacks and Special Ops missions in retaliation for their deaths.

Gradually the sun eases out of the clouds and makes its presence felt on the plains. As it grows warmer, I take off my jacket. The lower slopes begin to light up, and soon the first rays of the sun sweep across the field and illuminate the base. The first birds appear: not crows, but two slow-moving vultures of enormous wingspan. They circle high above the bodies at the far end of the field but for some reason do not land. Two or three crows appear as well, but seem to be intimidated by the presence of the vultures and fly off into the mountains. Moments later, a hawk swoops down from a high peak and drives off the vultures. And yet, despite all of this aerial activity, perhaps because of the remaining strands of mist, over everything there reigns this peculiar, muffled stillness.

Thankfully, the fog has begun to lift by the time I catch up with Ellison. He's back at the ECP and has taken up position next to Pfcs. Alizadeh and Renholder. Relieved, I'm walking up to him when he stiffens and takes a couple of steps forward. Raising his binoculars, he trains them on the field. Alizadeh glances at him and squints through his rifle sight; neither of them notice me.

I'm trying to make out what they're looking at when Ellison whistles softly and Alizadeh exclaims: Shit! Something's coming down the fucking trail.

Then he says rapidly: It's reached the field . . . it appears to be heading in the direction of the bodies.

Renholder, who's also looking through his sight, says: It looks like some kinda giant roach.

I've finally managed to locate what they are talking about. I watch it intently, while Ellison tells Renholder to fetch the C.O. immediately. Already I can feel my stomach turning sour.

Alizadeh's still staring through his rifle sight. You're not going to believe this, Sir, he tells Ellison in a hushed voice, but I think it's a woman in a burqa . . . on some kind of platform on wheels. She's using something to propel it forward.

Ellison looks through his binoculars.

Then Alizadeh says: Holy fuck. She's pushing the thing forward with her bare hands!

He lowers his rifle at the same time as Ellison lowers his binoculars. Ellison notices me standing next to him. Morning, Doc, he says tersely. What is it?

I shake my head. It can wait, I answer.

Alizadeh glances at Ellison uncertainly.

What the fuck is going on, Sir?

Ellison raises his binoculars again and surveys the rest of the field. It's about a thousand meters from where we are to the foot of the slopes. As far as I can see, barring the woman in the cart, it's as deserted as a moonscape.

Ellison clears his throat and says calmly: We'll find out soon enough, won't we?

He turns to me. You better man your tent, Doc. We might need your services, the way things are shaping up . . .

# ISMENE

FROM the moment I enter the huge helicopter in the Kandahar Airfield, I realize that my life is no longer my own. There are four other men on board: the three crew members in front, and an army doctor who spends the entire flight checking oxygen cylinders and assorted medical equipment. No one speaks to me. Their silhouettes make them one with the darkness inside and outside. The helicopter's rotors keep up a deafening drumbeat. Pinpoints of lights illuminate the interior and reflect against shiny panels so that I feel I am inside a black room filled with colored mirrors. As we ascend with a shudder into the heavens, the lights sway back and forth, and I say a silent prayer and close my eyes.

Blood beats in my ears. A constant pressure constricts my neck. If it is curiosity that persuades me to open my eyes again, I regret it instantly, for it makes me sick. Since I am strapped to my seat, my view is restricted to a narrow rectangle over the pilot's shoulder, and

I glimpse disembodied pieces of earth and sky. Boxed in glass, I brace myself as we plunge in and out of clouds the color of soot. Once I see a gray patch of water, probably a lake. The mountains look like serrated shadows rising into the air.

I am about to be sick again when we plunge straight down through a hole in the clouds. I glimpse a small army base straight below, with the landing zone marked by blinking lights. The base grows in size and separates into a jumble of shadowy buildings slightly elevated above a plain. A funnel of dust rises up to meet us, and it is as if we are descending into the underworld. There's a sudden jarring sound, and I feel a rush of panic as my head thrusts back and the restraining straps crush my body against my seat. A gigantic force strikes against my ribs with muffled blows. Then the pilot turns around and gives me a thumbs-up. Apparently we have landed.

I hang my head in relief at my safe arrival. Everyone else is already bustling around, and I unstrap myself from my seat and drag out my pack. As I throw it over my shoulder, the first stretcher is carried inside. An officer runs up and yells something to the man lying on the stretcher, who smiles weakly in response. I squeeze past him and jump out, and am almost knocked off my feet by the helicopter's downwash.

Outside, everything is veiled by dust. There's a line of stretchers waiting to be loaded, their bearers' faces chalky with dust. I run coughing through sheets of sand whipped up by the rotors. As I pass the men carrying the dead and wounded, I am reminded of the djinns who render service to the angel of death. By the time I pass out of the radius of the landing zone, they have finished loading all the stretchers.

I wait for someone to notice my arrival, but I might as well be invisible in the swirling dust. All around me the landscape is the color of dark graphite. A freezing chill attacks me from all sides. My gaze is drawn to the indistinct beehive shapes within the concertina perimeter—more like tombs than the dwellings of living men. My experiences with the coalition forces so far have been at a small outpost in Paktika province and the massive base in Bagram—but I can already tell that things are going to be very different here in the Tarsândan Outpost, as the Americans call it in their jargon.

The helicopter takes off at that moment, a flurry of dust chasing it into the sky. It hovers in midair for an instant. In the darkness, a colorless break in the horizon signals the advent of dawn. The two Apache gunship escorts that have been circling overhead now draw apart to make room for the larger machine, and together they bank steeply into the clouds. One moment I can see their lights blinking through the haze, and the next they have disappeared, and all that betrays their presence is a rumble that grows steadily distant.

I feel feverish with anticipation: a damp cold grips my bare hands as I zip up my jacket. Its fabric is wet, and I cringe at the memory of having thrown up—twice—during the flight. I lower my pack to the ground, take off my jacket—which smells—and stand there with my teeth chattering in the darkness.

One by one the men make their way back from the landing zone. No one speaks: the only sound is the crunch of their boots on the gravel. The air is still thick with the dust whipped up by the rotors, and most of the men hold their heads down and have their collars turned up. Very few look at me. Fewer still acknowledge my presence. One of them slaps his hands together rhythmically as he walks past in order to keep warm. Soon I am the only one left in that deserted plot of land. Although I know it to be unnecessary, I pull out the crumpled sheet of paper from my pocket and confirm the date and place of my arrival. Just as I am beginning to wonder if I've become altogether invisible, a soldier stops in front of me and asks if I am the new interpreter. I cannot see his face because he is muffled behind a scarf, but I smile anyway and extend my hand.

Hello, I say, yes, my name is Masood.

This way, he says, ignoring my hand and walking on ahead.

Although I find his rudeness incomprehensible, I shoulder my pack and follow him. We approach the concertina wire, then a wall of

Hescos and firing positions lined with sandbags. As we walk past the Entry Control Point, I make out the silhouettes of the men on guard duty, but everything is shadowy in the indistinct light. Inside the base, some kind of night bird flaps away overhead. Then a match flutters in front of me as my escort lights a cigarette, holding it between two fingers. He turns to make sure that I am behind him, and his mouth makes a gray whorl of smoke. I notice that he has **GOD** inked on the scarf tied around his helmet.

The farther we penetrate into the base, the more a thick mist seems to rise out of the ground. The air is cold, but also dank. The clouds that veil the sky are unusually low-lying and black. I expect my escort to say something, to point out landmarks and give me some sense of orientation, but he remains silent. Nor can I get any sense of the base, given the mist, except that it appears almost entirely lifeless and deserted. Then I remind myself of the early hour, and that these men have just survived a battle that, by all the accounts that I heard in Kandahar, was truly horrific.

We pass what I assume is the cookhouse from the thin spiral of smoke that rises into the air. Then we make a sharp turn into a narrow lane between two plywood buildings, and my companion ducks in through a door that yawns open in the mist. He switches on a dim light, and I step in after him and am assaulted by the rank odor of stale air, sour feet, and dust. Scrunching up my face, I squeeze into an aisle between two rows of bunks. Ahead of me, my guide pauses, looks around for a moment, and pounces on a slim metal canister. He points it into the air as I watch nonplussed, and proceeds to release a steady stream of white mist that instantly shrouds the interior with a pungent chemical scent somewhat reminiscent of rotting flowers. Apparently satisfied, he lowers the canister and sets it down on the table. Then he takes off his jacket, helmet, and scarf, and I see how slender he is—almost as slender as I am—but with very wide shoulders from which his arms hang loosely like wings. His face is unnaturally pale—I can see the fine blue-green veins running across his forehead—his eyes are turquoise, his mouth bright crimson, and his closely cropped hair a silky blond. I find him very beautiful.

I must have been staring, because he grows even more pale, if that were possible, and turns away. I hear him say in a muffled voice that this is where I am to be housed. With his face still held away from me, he points to a bunk and explains that the rest are empty because their occupants are on guard duty. He says that I must be tired after my journey and suggests that I rest until I am called for by the commander of the base. He doesn't seem to expect me to ask any questions, because he puts on his jacket and helmet once more, wraps his scarf around his face, shoulders past me, and goes out. I am left wondering whether he'd planned to stay longer but for some reason changed his mind. I'm also taken aback that he didn't feel the need to introduce himself, as is form, and, indeed, courtesy. Perhaps he is simply shy? All the same, I feel disappointed. I promise myself that I will seek him out and speak to him again.

I watch the door close behind him and put down my pack on my bunk. The artificially scented mist has made it even more difficult to breathe, and I struggle with the unholy mix of its chemical smell as it combines with the body odors and the rest. Still, I try not to make too much of it and cope by tying a scarf loosely around my face. Taking out the map of the base that I'd been given, I prepare to study it in order to locate where I am. But when I sit down on the bunk, I feel immediately drowsy. Although I feel uneasy at the thought of falling asleep mere moments after my arrival, my fatigue overcomes me, and I put the map aside and stretch out. I lie there for a moment or two, simply listening to the labored sound of my breath as I inhale through the scarf, before my gaze is caught by the photographs of scantily clad women stuck to the roof of the bunk. They smile at me with intimate familiarity and put me in a strange dreamlike state, to which I gradually surrender.

I wake to something warm and furry wrapped around my feet. For an instant, I am thrown back to childhood memories of sleeping

under a sheepskin blanket in the dead of winter. But this particular
blanket gives a low-pitched moan when I move my feet, and I sit up
with a startled shout and draw up my knees. There's an animal the
size of a small bear on my cot. It stretches and yawns as it gazes at me.
From the bunk across from me, a soldier, woken by the noise, extends
his hand sleepily. I'm Alizadeh, he says. You okay?

There's a dog in my bunk, I blurt out.

He nods politely, still half-asleep.

Yup. That's Shorty. It's where he sleeps.

But it's my bunk!

He doesn't seem concerned in the least. Instead, he merely waves
his hand.

Relax, dude. Your bunk used to belong to a member of our
squad who was wounded in yesterday's attack. He left in the bird that
brought you here. That's his dog. Give him a pat. He's the friendliest
mutt.

I'm sorry, I tell him, but the dog can't stay here.

He gives a forced little laugh. Whatever, dude.

He calls to the animal, who doesn't budge. C'mere, Shorty, he
says, it's all right. His voice sounds so calm and gentle that I am
amazed. Finally, he gets up and carries the dog to his bunk. He lies
down with his back to me and wraps his arms around it. I glimpse the
tip of a furiously wagging tail, and then my bunkmate says, See ya
later—and promptly goes back to sleep. I watch him for a moment,
bewildered, and then, for want of a better alternative, follow his
example and close my eyes.

When I open them again, there's a sliver of muted light penetrating a chink in the door. I glance at my watch. It's 8:00 a.m. Since no
one appears to have come for me, I decide to be efficient and seek out
the commander myself. I have the impression of a new chapter in my
life, and I want to begin it on the right note. I take out my shaving
knife and mirror and look around for some water. There's a plastic
water bottle on a small table, and I pour some of it into my shaving

mug. I don't want to wake Alizadeh by switching on the light, so I prop up the mirror next to the door. At that very moment, it's pushed open and a couple of soldiers step in. We almost collide, but I manage to lurch back just in time with my mug.

As they squeeze past, I read their name lapels: Duggal and Lee. They look exhausted, their faces caked with sand and dust. Lee goes down on his knees and begins playing with the dog, which has jumped off the sleeping Alizadeh's bunk, while Duggal takes off his helmet and boots, which he stows in the cot above mine. Don't mind us, he says with a tired smile, we're brain-dead beat. We haven't slept since the firefight.

He climbs into his cot, Lee squeezes into his, and they both screen off their bunks with blankets. The dog stretches out in the aisle and I have no option but to step over it to reach for my shaving things again. With four men and a dog, the interior feels claustrophobic, and I'm dismayed when the door opens once more to reveal yet another soldier—but this time it's a sergeant with my long-awaited summons. Masood? he asks.

My face is half lathered and I'm standing in a distinctly ungainly posture with my legs spread apart on either side of the dog.

I was just about to shave, I tell him, as if it weren't obvious.

That's all right, he says. The captain won't notice. Trust me, he has more important things on his mind.

Reluctantly, I put away my shaving things, wipe my face with a towel, and turn my vomit-stained jacket inside out before putting it on. I reflect guiltily that I haven't said my morning prayers. As I prepare to leave, the dog jumps up on my bunk.

I can see Shorty's taken a liking to you, the sergeant says.

I don't reply but give a brave little smile instead.

The dog butts me playfully with his muzzle as we walk out.

The sergeant offers me his hand. I'm Flint, by the way.

It's overcast outside. It's getting warmer, but there's still a hint of mist in the air, probably because the mountains are so close.

The sergeant seems to read my mind.

We have strange weather here, he says, but we've gotten used to it. It goes from bitter cold in the morning to 115 degrees in the shade by noon.

I heard about the simoom, I remark. Surely it must have made it difficult to fight?

He turns his head. Simoom? What's that?

It's what we call the burning wind that accompanies a sandstorm.

He takes a notebook out of his pocket and writes down the word, but I notice he avoids answering my question.

You talk funny, he says when he has finished writing.

I hesitate, not sure how to respond. I didn't think I had said anything especially humorous, and I tell him that.

No, no, he says, I meant you have a funny accent. Where's it from?

My conversation teacher in Kabul was British, I reply.

Then I feel suddenly anxious and add: I hope it's not going to affect my standing with the captain . . .

Don't worry, kiddo, he says with a grin. You talk better than most people here.

A soldier overtakes us and turns around and looks at me quizzically. Who dat, Sarn't? he says with a grin. Dude walks like a lady! Whoo, whoo . . .

That's enough, Ramirez, the sergeant snaps. Cut it out.

We reach the command post just as a radio operator runs out with a receiver held high in the air. He glances at us. I can't get main base, he says rapidly as he raises the radio's antenna as far as it can go. There's an urgency to his voice that my escort seems to react to. He tells me to wait before hurrying into the hut. Nonplussed, I idle around for a few moments before deciding to disregard his instructions and follow him inside.

It's crowded in the hut. It takes my eyes a moment to adjust to the darkness. There are officers and men lining the walls, but everyone seems distracted, and my intrusion passes unnoticed. An officer sits at a table with his head held down. The radio operator leans over and whispers something to him. From the officer's chest tabs, I surmise that this must be the captain I am supposed to meet, but something is obviously the matter, because a sudden hush falls over the assembly as he begins to speak. He says that the helicopter carrying the dead and wounded men from the base—the same helicopter that had brought me here, in other words—has crashed a few kilometers south of here. Although they are waiting for confirmation, no one on board is thought to have survived.

A subdued groan of dismay greets the announcement. Some of the men cover their faces; others, more stoic, look on with stony expressions. The captain has a word with a couple of men, and then one of them, a veritable giant, walks out of the hut with anguish written all over his face. Meanwhile, Staff Sergeant Flint notices me and storms over. What the fuck are you doing here? he asks in a fierce whisper. You're not allowed inside the command post. I thought I told you to wait out in the open. Now get the fuck out. I don't want you anywhere within a hundred clicks of the CP!

Click, Sir? I ask him, bewildered.

Didn't they teach you anything at Bagram? he snaps. A click is a thousand meters. And I didn't mean that literally, for fuck's sake, or you'd be stationed permanently outside the wire. I just don't want you in the C.O.'s office, that's all.

Yes, Sir, I understand now. It was my mistake.

And don't fucking call me "Sir," all right? I'm a sergeant. I work for a living.

As he grabs my arm, I ask him about my meeting with the captain, but he cuts me short and tells me that he'll rearrange it for some other time.

Chastened, I leave the vicinity of the hut and return to my quarters.

It takes me a while to find my way back. When I open the door, I find Alizadeh and the others gone, but in their place there's a man in an undershirt stretched out on the floor, sobbing like a child. I'm holding the door open uncertainly, wondering whether I should go in, when he turns to look at me and then bursts out almost in a frenzy: Shut the damn door and get the fuck out of here, you frickin' raghead!

I close the door abruptly and stand outside, my legs shaking.

Another soldier passes by and stares fixedly at me with a cold expression.

I light a cigarette with trembling fingers and try to compose myself. Drawing a deep breath, I walk away slowly. After a few minutes of aimless wandering, I find myself at the Hesco wall that marks the base's perimeter. I follow the wall until I come to the Entry Control Point. It's manned by two men and overseen by a lieutenant I had glimpsed in the communications hut. He glances interrogatively at me as I draw abreast. I smile at him with a degree of uncertainty, and he nods and walks over.

I am Masood, the new interpreter, I tell him.

Ellison, Second Platoon, he says briskly as he shakes my hand.

I am sorry about the crash, I remark. I arrived in that helicopter.

Yes, I know, he says. You were lucky.

He stands beside me as I gaze out at the field and take in the bodies lying there. Beyond the field, the mountains tower over everything. A dense mass of ash-colored clouds veils the highest slopes and scarcely admits any light to the plain below.

It's strange that the Taliban haven't collected their dead, I observe.

He gives a humorless laugh. That's because they know we're primed to clean their clocks if they show up again.

Noticing that my cigarette has burned down to a stub, he takes out a packet and offers me one. He waits to light mine first; I find the ease of his gestures very reassuring. For the first time since my arrival here, I begin to feel comfortable.

So where are you from? he asks.

I am originally from Charikar, which is a small town north

of Bagram and south of the Panjshir Valley, but I've been all over Afghanistan.

Your English is very good, he says. The last few interpreters we had could barely string a sentence together.

Thank you, I reply. Then I ask if I can go out and inspect the bodies.

He turns to look at me, and I notice that he has astonishingly light blue eyes. Now why would you want to do that? he asks.

Because I hate the Taliban, and it would be nice to see their dead faces.

He bows his head for a moment and then glances at me with a neutral expression. I can't let you do that, he replies. The perimeter is mined. I wouldn't want you blowing up on my watch.

But someone must have taken the bodies out and arranged them in such a neat row?

Yup, he replies without explaining.

So that's all I am proposing—to go out and look at the bodies and then come back again.

He laughs. Do you know how security SOP works? What was the last base you were at?

I was in Bagram, and before that in a small outpost in Paktika.

Paktika, huh? I've heard it's frickin' wild there.

It is difficult.

He gazes at the row of bodies with squinting eyes. Then, decisively, he says: Nope. No can do, Paco.

Paco?

Forget it. It was a joke.

Maybe I can identify some of the Taliban, I suggest. Wouldn't that be helpful?

He glances at me sharply. Then he looks at the field again and takes a deep drag on his cigarette. All right, he says at length, but you can only examine the row of bodies lined up outside the wire.

The ones at the end of the field are off-limits. They're too close to the slopes, and we don't want any more casualties from snipers who might be lurking there.

I'm about to go when he stops me with a gesture: I'll send someone with you to make sure you don't stray too far.

That's all right, I reply. I can manage on my own. It's only a few meters, after all.

He purses his lips, his eyes cold. If you take one step outside the ECP without my permission, he says casually, I'll shoot you myself.

I stare at him, wondering if he's joking again.

He smiles at me, but somehow he no longer resembles the affable young officer who'd offered me a cigarette.

Surely you cannot mean that, I murmur, bewildered.

Oh, I mean it, he says. I'm dead serious. Now: you just wait here while I find someone to go with you.

He turns his head to scan the Hescos before walking away a couple of steps and calling out to one of the men. Meanwhile I feel myself coloring furiously as I absorb the full extent of his insult. Does he really believe that I would be that irresponsible? For an instant, I wonder if I am being too sensitive, given their paranoid security procedures, then decide that I am not. Here, then, is yet another example of the contempt with which they seem to regard me. I can't tell if it's an attitude they share toward all my countrymen, but since I haven't met any since my arrival here, I cannot tell, in all fairness.

I realize that I have no option but to wait until the officer returns. I seethe in the shadow of the ECP and gaze out at the field. Soon I hear footsteps behind me and turn around, shading my eyes from the sun.

It's the soldier who escorted me from the LZ last night. He stands there cradling a slim, long-barreled rifle, its metal gleaming black.

I read his name lapel. It says: Simonis.

The lieutenant returns and, with a nod at my guide, says: He's gonna take you to the hajjis.

To Simonis, he says: Keep an eye on the slopes.

I follow in Simonis's footsteps as we skirt the concertina and trace a weaving path that leads directly to the dead Taliban. In the time that it takes for us to reach them, I conclude that I've seldom felt more alienated than I have since my arrival in this place.

A flock of crows rises into the air as we approach, while a buzzing cloud of flies loudly protests our intrusion. I take my time as I walk around the bodies. The ground under them is soaked with dark patches of moisture. It's the first time I've seen the enemy at such close quarters, and it feels curiously anticlimactic. I was prepared to hate them, but they seem disappointingly ordinary and nothing along the lines that I had imagined. They're also horribly mangled, and some are barely recognizable as human remains. The corpse nearest me has his head attached to his torso by the merest shred of cartilage. Farther away, two boys who've fared somewhat better are more or less the same age as me. One even wears an embroidered green jacket that's similar to one of mine. Most of them are farmers: I can tell by the calluses on their hands. The only perceptible difference between us is that they all have full-grown, red-dyed beards where I have day-old stubble. I begin to feel a reluctant kinship with them—one that I cannot but help contrast to the way I've been made to feel inside the base.

Then I remind myself that the Americans are here to help, and it is men like these now-supine wretches who slaughtered my family. They killed my father, my mother, my two older brothers, my sister and her husband, my father's two brothers and their families, and both of my grandparents from my father's side. They stole up one Friday afternoon and surrounded our house, which was some distance from the town. My father and his brothers owned the oldest clothing shop in the Charikar bazaar—my grandfather used to say that it dated back to the time of the Mughal emperor Aurangzeb, yet another of those who'd attempted to subjugate the savage Pashtuns and failed.

My mother was a beautiful, educated woman who ran a maktab, a primary school for girls, under the auspices of a secular women's organization. My father was neither educated nor handsome, but he was a good man who doted on my mother and was supportive of her projects. Later I would learn that it was my mother's school that had provoked the Taliban. They gave her two warnings, and when she ignored them, they acted in the only way they knew.

I was the sole survivor of the massacre, but only because I was catching minnows in a nearby pond. My first intimation of what had happened was the black pall of smoke rising from the burning house. I have no memory of what followed, save that two days later I showed up covered in dust at my maternal grandmother's farm, fifty kilometers to the north. I sat without speaking for days. I was six years old. It took me a long time after that to find my voice.

That is why I would have liked to feel hatred toward these corpses lying at my feet, but instead I feel strangely empty. I crouch down next to them and wonder if it might have to do with their condition. Three of them were obviously blown apart by Claymores, because there's nothing left of their legs but shreds of bone and flesh. Two others took direct shots to the head, and their faces are a bloody mess. I have to twist my head to piece together their features. Only one of the boys my age seems unscathed and appears to be merely asleep; but his neighbor's head is bludgeoned in, although his right hand is braced against the ground as if he's just about to get up. What's more, all of them are beginning to show the aftereffects of the simoom: the tips of their noses and ears have turned black, while their skin looks desiccated and paperlike. But the drying up of the bodies has also prevented them from smelling. Or perhaps it would be more accurate to say that they don't smell yet.

A mournful howl interrupts my thoughts.

It's Shorty, the company's dog. I'm surprised to see him at the far end of the field, near the slopes. With all the fuss that's made over him, I would have expected him to be kept within the limits of the base; but who knows, perhaps they allow him to run around. I watch as he runs past the three bodies at the end of the field and darts up a narrow trail. I follow him with my eyes until he disappears behind a screen of trees.

A shadow falls across the ground in front of me.

I look up. It's my guard. He stands there with a watchful eye on the slopes, his hands cradling his gun. Recognize anyone? he asks.

No, they are not familiar to me—the ones that still have faces, that is.

He glances at the bodies without interest. They all look the same to me.

They are not the same, I reply with feeling. Each one has a different history of sin, of pillage and murder.

Figures, he says indifferently. Time to head back, then.

It's strange, I say quietly. I'd expected it to be different. The Taliban killed my family, so I was trying to find some satisfaction.

He's already begun to walk away when he stops abruptly and turns to stare at me. I see, he says. He walks back to the bodies and aims his gun at them.

You want them to be warm and alive so you can hear them scream, he says.

You have had this experience?

Yup, he says.

Was it satisfying?

Absolutely.

Feeling peculiarly breathless, I rise to my feet and straighten my shirt.

His eyes follow me. Have you eaten today?

No, as a matter of fact . . .

Come on then. Let's go get some chow. It's the end of my shift.

We cross the field and walk past the men on guard duty. The lieutenant eyes me quizzically. Well? he says. Recognize any of the fuckers?

No, Sir, I did not.

He turns to Simonis. See any movement on the slopes?

No, Sir. It's dead as a doorknob.

You must mean doornail . . .

Simonis shrugs. I guess I do, he says.

The lieutenant gazes at him with a trace of condescension before dismissing us.

We walk away from the ECP, and when we're at a safe distance, Simonis says quietly: Fucking asshole.

We pick up MRE pouches from the mess tent, and he asks me where I'd like to eat. I explain the situation in my quarters, and he grimaces and suggests going to his B-hut instead. On our way there, he holds up his MRE with a sardonic half-smile. Do you know what we call these things? he asks.

I stare at him. Meals ready to eat? I answer hesitantly.

Nope. Meals rejected by Ethiopians.

His hut is adjacent to a badly damaged guard tower. It's very small, and when we enter I express my surprise at finding only two bunks inside.

I'm a sniper, he says in a flat, decisive tone of voice, as if that explains everything. That's my bunk over there, and the one opposite it used to be Konwicki's—he was Second Platoon's other sharpshooter—but he took a hit yesterday, so the place is mine until his replacement shows up.

That's bad news about your friend . . .

It happens, he says with a shrug, before adding: Ted was married. I got tired of listenin' to him bitch. He used to go on and on. I've no use for talkers.

We sit down across from each other and eat our meals in silence.

When I've finished, he asks me if I would like some tea.

Yes, please, I answer. Thank you for offering!

His mouth twitches. Don't get your hopes up. It tastes like dishwater.

Yes, but still. You must know that it's our custom to offer tea to a guest. It's part of our code of hospitality.

He doesn't reply, but as he boils water over a portable stove, he begins to take off his clothes until he has stripped down to his shorts. He does it casually, without looking at me, and almost as if I am not there, while I sit frozen on my cot. I would like to look away, but I can't. I'm scandalized, but also fascinated.

He hands me my tea and settles down across from me on his cot. Almost in a daze, I notice that he has beautifully formed hands and feet, just like a woman's.

I raise my cup to my mouth and drink the wrong way, spilling it all out.

Is something the matter? he asks when I've recovered.

You are almost naked, I say nervously. We are not used to it in our culture.

He simply sits there, sipping his tea, gazing at me steadily.

The silence grows uncomfortable, and I wonder if I've insulted him.

I didn't want to offend you, I blurt out. I'm simply not used to it, that's all.

Relax, he says. It's no big deal. It's warm in here.

I could open the door . . .

Nope. I like it closed.

Then, quietly, he says: You're not so bad yourself, berâdar.

What did you call me?

Berâdar.

I feel a rush of warmth flood through me as my heart rejoices. I nod my head several times. I'm almost giddy with the feelings of affirmation that race through me. It makes me want to reach out and hug him.

I say: I knew from the moment I set my eyes on you that we'd be brothers. Now I feel satisfied. I am your brother and your friend, am I not?

We'll see, he says. What's the rush?

We are young, I reply fervently. We are supposed to be in a rush.

How old are you?

I'm eighteen, I answer, then correct myself: I'll be nineteen in less than a month's time. In twenty-eight days.

You're just a kid, he scoffs.

Why, how old are you?

Twenty-one.

Then you are young as well. You will be my first and best friend here. We'll walk around as friends do in Afghanistan: hand in hand.

You crazy? he says with a laugh.

Why am I crazy?

Because we'd be lynched, that's why.

Lynched?

Yup. Hung from the rafters. No questions asked.

But why? Is it banned for Americans and Afghans to be friends? You're in my country, and we have an old saying: When in Balkh, do as the Balkhis are prone to do. Balkh was the mother of all cities, and the inhabitants were famous for their friendships. And so over the years we have inherited their ways. It's in our nature.

This isn't Balkh.

Still, it is the same country, is it not?

It ain't that, dude, he says quietly; and then, with an undertone of bitterness, he says: It's because some people don't care for others who may be different from them. They like their own kind.

I hesitate before speaking, trying to decipher his meaning. Finally, I ask him if he is not of their kind.

Nope, he says decisively. I'm not.

What about me? Am I your kind?

He scratches his chest. We'll see, he says.

I feel hurt, but try to cloak it.

If you feel you don't belong with your people, I tell him, then perhaps you can settle in Afghanistan. I'd find you a good woman to be your wife.

My wife?

To have children with.

His mouth twitches again, but he remains silent.

Will you think about it? I prompt.

Sure, I'll think about it.

Then while you think, I continue, feeling elated, I would like to thank you, on behalf of all my countrymen, for coming here and fighting for us. I would like to tell all Americans—and I'm starting with you—that we need you to remain here until there is peace in our lands. Don't abandon us prematurely. You hold the responsibility for an entire people in your hands. You represent democracy, freedom, and the rule of law; your task is truly noble, and the only mistake you've made so far is your support for our present government, which is completely self-serving and corrupt. You must believe me when I say this. When I was in Kabul, I saw with my own eyes how much they stole, and how often. Moreover, they are Pashtun and will make peace with the Taliban the moment you leave, and we all dread to think of what will happen after that. So you need to support someone else—someone like the hero Ahmed Shah Massoud, the commander of the Mujaheddin, who was Tajik, like me, by the way, and whom the Arabs murdered—someone who will be a real leader and not a scoundrel.

I pause and ask: Am I not right?

He shrugs, looking bored.

I don't know, man, he drawls. I don't do politics.

I lean back in confusion and stare at him: his eyes are indifferent.

Then why are you here? I ask.

Before he can answer, I point to the 9/11 tattoo on his arm. Is that why?

This? Nope, he says carelessly. I got that because everyone else did.

Then why?

Maybe because I like being a soldier. It isn't that complicated.

That's it? You like being a soldier?

And seein' the fuckin' hellholes of the world on Uncle Sam's money, he adds with a twisted grin.

I ignore the jibe. So you are a tourist in my country?

A tourist with a gun, sure. They pay me to shoot up the sights. Pow! There goes the pride of Ghazni. Or wherever.

I think you're joking. You are here to protect us from the kind of damage the Talib did to places like Bamiyan.

He grins again. All right, you got a point there. Then how about I'm a big-game hunter? I drill people instead of animals and get a bounty. More fun to shoot people anyways compared to some damn statue or pile o' bricks.

If you are after that kind of bounty, then you would make more money as a private contractor. Trust me, I add bitterly, I know about these things.

Instead of answering, he lights a cigarette and draws on it deeply. When he exhales, the smoke makes rings around his head. He follows them with his eyes as he blows more rings.

I have to point out to him that it's against the rules to smoke inside B-huts.

Oh yeah? he says, but makes no move to stub out his cigarette.

At least that was the way in the other bases I was in . . .

You wanna hang here with me?

Yes, of course, but what if an officer comes in?

Fuck that, okay? If someone comes in, I'll deal with the consequences.

I refrain from pointing out that I'd be in trouble as well, and lapse into silence.

Abruptly, he says: I'm from Sparta, New York . . .

From New York City?

Nope, farther north. Small town in the Catskills. One dead-end main street, eleven broken-down houses. Dirt poor; way ignorant.

That's where I grew up with my stepdaddy. He was really fucked up, and he fucked me over, so now I fight to get my own back.

Even though I don't fully understand his meaning, he seems to be looking for something from me, so at length I say: I see. I'm sorry.

No need to be sorry. I can take care of myself now.

He throws me his lighter and cigarette pack.

I hesitate momentarily, then light a cigarette and lean back on the cot.

When you grew up in Sparta, did you ever think you'd be here one day, in Kandahar province? I ask.

His mouth gives its now-familiar twitch. What do you think?

I feel my throat knotting with emotion.

I think our meeting was fated. It was written.

Oh yeah? he says without conviction, and stretches out on his cot. There's a languor to his movements that reminds me of a leopard.

I have known poverty, I continue quietly, and I am still poor. But I feel a closeness to you that is worth more than all the wealth in the world.

You've got quite the gift of the gab, he says.

You still don't believe me? Then listen to this. When I first saw you, I was reminded of a stone statue that I'd glimpsed in a refugee camp in Quetta. It was a very old statue, very beautiful. It was made when our people were all followers of the Buddha. A thief had smuggled it out of Bamiyan and was trying to sell it.

Oh yeah? And what does that have to do with me?

I will tell you. Have you heard of the Bamiyan Buddhas? The ones that the Talib blew up? Yes? They had some of the same features as this statue, only they were much bigger, of course. Well, I was a boy in Mazar-i-Sharif when I heard about their destruction. At the time, I was working as a porter in a bazaar. It was a hard life, but everywhere I went I took along the only book that I had with me at the time. It used to belong to my mother and was a volume by the famous English poet, Mr. Shelley. And in it there was a poem that reminded me in a strange way of the disaster that had overtaken Bamiyan. Have you heard of Ozymandias, the king of kings?

Nope, he says and yawns, I can't say I have. The only Ozzy I know of is Ozzy Osbourne.

I pause, losing the thread of my story. Ozzy Osbourne?

I guess you haven't watched the TV show.

No.

He thinks, then sits up and reaches for a small plastic case the size of a matchbox.

D'you know what this is?

Yes, of course, it's an iPod.

Then I'll play you something.

He moves over to my cot and sits down next to me. I smell his overwhelming masculinity and feel faint. The backs of his hands are covered with a fine gold down. Small beads of sweat fringe his lips. He moves closer to me and taps repeatedly on the machine. Finally, he says: Here, listen to this.

I put on the headphones and yank them off immediately with a start.

I think there is something wrong with your machine, I tell him.

A thin line creases his forehead. He listens for a moment. Then: Nope. That's the way it's supposed to sound. That's Ozzy singing "War Pigs." Try again.

No thank you. That was terrible! He sounds like the devil himself.

Really? he says sardonically. This song always reminds me of lying on a sunny beach listening to the waves roll in. I'll never get sick of that smooth, sexy voice and the romantic lyrics. It's a wonderful song to relax to with—oh, I don't know—maybe your lover or your family. Real nice 'n' easy, like.

You're not serious, surely? To me it sounds like the sort of noise that might be used to extract information from terrorists. If we played that here, it would attract all the jackals from miles around.

He laughs softly, before tapping me on the chest.

You're a skinny little thing, aren't you? It wouldn't take much to break you.

I'm almost the same height as you are, I point out.

Yes, whatever. Do you wrestle?

I have never wrestled, I confess.

I might take you to the gym sometime. Give you a workout. Toughen you up.

That would be nice, I say, trying not to let my voice quaver. This is what friends do—they find things to do together. I think we will be true friends.

You've told me that already.

Then may I also tell you that I am very unhappy with where they've put me up. There are too many people inside, and also a dog, which is too much.

I don't care much for dawgs either, he drawls.

But you have this bunk free, I say quickly. Perhaps you can let me have it?

You wanna move in?

It would help me considerably.

He runs a finger down my arm, and I shiver.

I'll think about it, he says.

I fall silent, dismayed by his lack of empathy. We watch each other for a moment, and then I observe: It would also help you, I think.

He draws away from me slightly.

Oh yeah? he says, narrowing his eyes. How would it help me?

I think that deep in your heart you are lonely.

He doesn't deny it. Instead, after an interval of silence, he says: You think I give a flying fuck?

I flinch, but I don't want to take offense.

He gazes at me without expression and then suddenly brings his hands down so hard on my shoulders that it jars my spine. When I lean back, startled, a shadow falls across his face. He digs his fingers deep into my arms before letting go. Then he gets up and stumbles over to his cot. He lies down with his back to me. I'm tired, he says in a muffled voice. You talk too much. Jibber jabber, jibber jabber, yak yakety yak . . .

I realize that I am being asked to leave. Coloring fiercely, I get up.

You left your iPod behind, I tell him.

Chuck it on the cot. I'll get it later.

I pause irresolutely and stare at his prone body.

May I go now? I ask.

Yup, he says faintly. Close the door behind you on your way out.

I step out and lean against the door. I feel completely confused, as if I have just had an encounter with a member of an alien race. I am about to walk away when I swivel around unthinkingly and open the door.

He turns slowly on the cot and stares at me.

Do you always fuckin' barge in without knocking? he asks.

I forget what I was about to say and retreat. Without hesitating, I shut the door carefully and stumble away. It's evening already, but I hardly notice. I feel baffled, humiliated, and at the same time he is all that I can think of. A line from a poem crosses my mind: "Dear Friend, did you travel all the way across the ocean only to torment me with your ruthless beauty?" I feel my eyes fill with tears. I thought I had found a companion in this miserable place, but now even that has proved false. I cannot believe the extent to which things are going wrong for me here.

Preoccupied, I turn a corner blindly and walk straight into the giant sergeant from the morning's assembly.

Careful where you're going, soldier, he says sharply, before stepping back and looking me up and down. Wait a minute, he says in a gentler voice. You're our new interpreter, aren't you?

I am Masood, I say with a nod, forcing my mind back to the present.

I've been looking for you, he says. Have you had your orientation?

My orientation? No . . .

Not good, not good, he says wearily. Sorry about that. We've had too much going on. He stops and thinks. Tell you what, he says. Come and see me tomorrow and I'll take you through your paces. Ten a.m. okay? See you then.

He turns to leave, and then halts.

By the way, he says, I heard you took a look at our dead Taliban. Any conclusions?

I gather my thoughts, sensing the need to make a good impression on this man.

I found it very unusual that they went in for a direct confrontation, I say carefully. It isn't their normal method. They're usually much more sly.

He steps back and looks at me again as if seeing me in a different light.

I can see that we're going have an interesting talk tomorrow, he says. I like you already. Ya'll make a fine addition here.

He shakes my hand and moves on.

His words echo through my head as I return to my quarters. It's a fittingly unreal conclusion to the day. I follow the Hesco wall and run my eyes over the field. The sun is low in the sky, and it lights up the mountains with an unearthly red-gold glow. When I reach my quarters, I hesitate before opening the door, and then I grit my teeth and walk in. The tiny room is jammed with soldiers playing cards. One of them looks up: it's the man who yelled at me this morning. Astonishingly, once again his face twists with rage, and he shouts: What the fuck! Who are you? What're you doing here?

Someone else says: Chill out, dude. He's the new interpreter. He has Spitty's bunk.

Are you fucking kidding me? Who told you he could have it?

The soldier named Lee puts down his cards.

No one told us, man, he says calmly. We didn't have anything to do with it. He was assigned Spitty's place, okay? He's just following orders.

I think that's fucking demented! the other man says, almost choking out the words. Are they out of their motherfucking minds?

I'm amazed at his rage: I can actually see the veins on his neck bulging out.

With barely repressed contempt, he turns to Duggal. Maybe you should take him somewhere else, hot stuff, seeing that you're from the same place and all.

Fuck off, Grohl, Duggal growls. You're way outta line. They put him here 'cos there's nothing left of the ANA's hooch. It was totaled.

Grohl throws down his cards and pushes me aside as he storms out of the hut.

I'll fucking own your face if I see you around here again, he yells in parting.

There's a moment of awkward silence, and then another man walks over and introduces himself. Welcome to the Cave, he says. It's what we call our hooch. And how are you today? I'm Specialist Garcia. Ricardo Garcia—that's Rick to you. There are seven of us here, and I think you've met everyone except for Ash Jackson, though I'm sure you'll run into him soon enough. As for Chuck Grohl, don't mind him; he lost his best friend in the bird crash, and it's made him go crazy.

He called me a raghead this morning, I say quietly.

Both Duggal and Lee swivel their heads and stare at me.

There's a pause, and then Lee says: He was just messing with you.

Messing with me?

It means Chuck was kidding around with you, Duggal explains. He didn't mean what he said.

He seemed serious enough, I reply. He stormed out of here. You saw how angry he was.

He wasn't angry, all right? You can take it from us. We know him well. He's hurtin', man—we all are. We just went through hell. It's been tough. Our brothers died.

He's basically okay, Lee says. He's family. You know what I mean?

I don't think he's slept since yesterday, as a matter of fact, Duggal adds.

So what should I do? I ask.

Just let it go, man, Duggal says. Chucky'll come around. Give him some time.

And don't fucking snitch on him, Lee says tersely. Or on any one of us. It ain't a good habit. All right?

He looks away from me in disgust and says to his companions: Fruit's as gay as Father Christmas. Fuckin' loud and queer.

Duggal appears to share my bafflement at this strange comment, because he asks: Santa Claus is gay?

Lee ignores his question. Instead, he says morosely: If jigga starts goin' through the gears here, I'll whack him, I swear.

Garcia intervenes even as Duggal bursts into laughter. Still and all, guys, he says, Grohl isn't the easiest guy to get along with. Even at the best of times he's somewhere south of crazy. He glances at me and smiles. If it's okay with you, we can exchange bunks.

I agree instantly, and in a matter of moments find myself in the bunk that's farthest from Grohl's. I reflect on the additional bonus of not having to share my sleeping space with the dog, who, I've noticed, has returned from his jaunt in the mountains. Still, I feel drained as I lie down and go over the day's events. My already disorganized train of thought is frequently interrupted by muted snatches of conversation from the card players. I hear Garcia talk about a lieutenant who went down with the helicopter and how much they're going to miss his leadership. Duggal says that one of the men killed in the firefight was about to become a father. Then Garcia tells them that his house in Florida has been repossessed. Stacey couldn't keep up with the fucking mortgage payments, he says, and that really, really sucks. Lee asks if they think the Taliban will attack again, but then they start talking over one another, and I stop listening to them. Instead, my mind returns to my afternoon with Simonis, and I find myself wondering about him again.

It's because you missed the point, he says suddenly, letting go of my hand. And that really, really sucks.

I didn't know, I murmur, my eyes on the floor. Small yellow flames flicker in the corners of the room, and I try to move without making a sound, intimidated by the destruction all around. We are walking through the scorched remains of my mother's library, which I can hardly remember, but recognize all the same. The rest of the house is as dark as a mineshaft.

He turns to me with somber, burning eyes. Do you understand?

I am trying, I reply. It's difficult for me to put it into words.

He picks up one of the charred books and asks who destroyed the library.

Who do you think? The Taliban. It's what they do. They burn books and murder women.

I'm sorry you had to go through this, he says abruptly. I truly am.

I don't want you to feel sorry for me. That is not what I want you to feel.

He says: I would like to make it up to you.

I try to keep the beseeching tone out of my voice. Really? How?

I'll show you, he says, and waves his hand.

I watch in astonishment as the room, along with all its books and shelves, reconstitutes itself until it is exactly as it used to be before the catastrophe.

I turn to him open-mouthed. Can this be real? Are you a magician?

I'm a galandat, he says. I'm blessed with baraka. So's the captain, by the way.

The captain? What captain?

Captain Connolly, for fuck's sake. The Commanding Officer.

Someone is shaking me by the shoulder. Wake up, Masood. The captain wants you. Right now.

It's Duggal. He looks tense. Come on, man, he says. Hurry up.

Half-awake, I ask him what time it is. It's seven in the morning, he replies.

What is the matter? I ask as I struggle to put on my boots.

I'll tell you on the way, he says, already out of the door.

I have to run to catch up with him, and by the time I do, the captain has arrived.

How's your Pashto? he asks me without any preliminaries.

Very good . . . I begin, before he cuts me off.

We've a situation here, he says tersely. There's a woman in the field outside . . .

A woman . . . ?

Or at least we think it's a woman, but we can't be sure because of her burqa. Here, come along . . .

He doesn't wait for me but begins to walk briskly toward the ECP.

What I want you to do, he says over his shoulder, is translate my questions to her. Keep it simple. Tell me exactly what she says in reply. Got it?

Yes, Sir, I say hurriedly, even as there's a part of me that wonders if I'm still dreaming. It almost feels as if I no longer know who or where I am. I look up at the sky, which is cloudless in the early morning light. A flock of crows flies soundlessly past, heading for the mountains. Everything feels strange. Everything feels very, very strange. We hurry past Simonis leaning against a pile of sandbags with his sniper rifle trained on the field. The rifle's scope gleams as he adjusts his position and shifts slightly to his right. I glance back, and he looks up, catching my eye. I realize he is aiming straight at me now. Then the captain distracts me by handing me a megaphone. There she is, he says, and points. I raise the megaphone to my mouth. He clears his throat, about to speak, when the sun breaks over the mountains. It floods into the field, blinding me. The captain steps back and shades his eyes. The field glows red, then white, then red again. I can't see a thing, the captain says. I lower the megaphone and wait for my vision to clear.

The field flares fire, then blood, then fire again.

# SECOND LIEUTENANT

NE.

Two.

Three.

Four . . . I count off the meters silently as the rickety cart inches forward across the field toward us. Despite the early hour, there's a considerable amount of dust suspended in the air. Beside me, the sharpshooter, Simonis, stretches out on his stomach on top of the Hescos and aims his sniper's rifle at the shrouded figure in the cart. Without turning my head, I ask him:

How far are we from the slopes, would you reckon?

I'd say about nine hundred meters, Sir.

And what would you say is the maximum possible range of a Taliban sniper?

With one of their better bolt-action rifles, Sir, I'd say up to seven hundred to eight hundred meters—that's on a good day without wind. But he'd have to be shooting with a Lee-Enfield or Mosin-Nagant with a telescopic sight, and those are pretty damn accurate.

In that case, line up your sights on her, I tell him. I want you to fire a warning shot the moment she closes in on our one-hundred-meter line. That's far enough from the slopes for their sniper's range, but close enough to us to drill her if there's something fishy going on.

He pulls on a pair of green Nomex gloves while I crane over his shoulders and repeat my instructions to LaShawn "Wonk" Gaines, who's serving as his spotter. Got that, Wonk?

Yes, Sir.

Simonis rests his finger gently on the trigger and waits for me to clear him to engage. Moments earlier, as soon as I'd sent off Pfc. Renholder to fetch Connolly, I'd instructed Flint, Schott, and Ashworth, as the squad leaders of Second Platoon, to secure the perimeter. I also instructed Spc. Simonis to zero in on the target in the kill zone. Simonis mounted the Hescos with two sniper rifles. He eyed the target and selected his modified Remington hunting rifle over the M-24.

Now he turns to me after looking through his sight and says: She's nearly there.

I raise my binoculars and watch the cart approach the one-hundred-meter marker. In her powder-blue burqa, its occupant looks like a mirage against the dun-colored ground.

D'you see that jagged black stone to her right? I ask. It's about ten meters from the marker at nine o'clock.

Yes, Sir.

Can you hit that?

Sure thing.

Then do it. Now.

With a fluid motion, he shifts the Remington's stock on his shoulder and lines up the reticle on his target. The gun's already chambered. The muzzle rises and falls with each breath he takes. At the bottom of his third exhalation, he squeezes the trigger. I don't need to look through my binoculars to see the stone explode.

Hot damn! Gaines says softly. You don't need me here, bro.

There's no wind about, Simonis says. Piece of cake.

It hasn't stopped her, I point out.

We watch the cart wobble forward over a stretch of uneven ground.

If she keeps movin', she's gonna reach the Claymores, Gaines mutters.

Save us some trouble, I reply.

Just look at her crawl, Gaines says. Danica Patrick she ain't.

Neither Simonis nor I reply. I'm too busy trying to sight another target for Simonis, but the ground looks devoid of defining features.

What about that white stone to her left? Gaines suggests. At two o'clock.

Simonis scans the field. 'Bout five meters from the marker? he asks.

No, closer.

Oblong pebble, speckled with black?

That's the one.

I locate the stone through my binoculars: it's barely the size of a pea.

Go for it, I tell Simonis.

He recycles the bolt and settles into his breathing, looking through the scope's aperture and centering his sights on the target. Making a minute adjustment, he shifts slightly to his left and pauses before squeezing the trigger. I watch through my binoculars as the white pebble disintegrates in a puff of dust.

Bull's-eye, I tell him. Nice work.

We watch the cart waver for a moment before it determinedly begins to advance again, the burqa-clad figure pushing against the ground with her hands to make it move forward.

I turn to Simonis. What was your distance shooting score?

288 out of 300, Sir.

All right, Specialist. Here's your chance to top that. I want you to aim just above her head, but close enough so she can feel the draft from the bullet through her burqa.

Don't hose her, Gaines warns.

Simonis grins. He says: Do you have any money you'd like to lose?

Why? Gaines asks.

Watch, Simonis says.

He recycles the bolt again and relaxes into position. I raise my binoculars. The cart appears to hit a snag in the ground because the wheels lock momentarily before moving again. Simonis waits for a moment and then pulls the trigger.

The shot's in the black. The cart lurches to a stop inches from the seventy-five-meter line. We wait for her to move again, but she remains stationary.

Score, Simonis says below his breath.

C'mon lady, Gaines whispers, one more meter and you're dead meat on a hook . . .

Simonis is still looking through his scope.

She's fingering something around her neck, he says. It looks like a pendant.

Could be a good luck charm, I observe. She's going to need it.

Gaines says: She's waving a white flag, Sir.

Good. She appears to have gotten the message.

She's certainly come equipped with flag and all, Gaines says.

He glances behind his shoulder.

Cap'n's here, Sir.

I jump down from the Hesco and walk up to Connolly. The new interpreter's with him; he's discarded his regulation U.S. Army fatigues for the local outfit of baggy trousers, cotton tunic, cap, and sandals. I wonder why.

The sun floods into the field at that moment. The interpreter raises his megaphone to his mouth and then lowers it again. Connolly takes a step back and shades his eyes.

I look at the field but can't see a thing: the sun's pouring down from the mountaintops. It's like staring into a golden haze.

Perched on the Hesco above us, Simonis says: In the court of the crimson king.

Connolly swivels his neck to look at him. What was that?

The sun, Sir . . . Simonis explains.

Connolly turns to me. Morning, Lieutenant, he says. Perimeter secured?

Yes, Sir.

He nods at the cart in the field. What d'you think? Suicide bomber?

Nope. Too slow, Sir. Too prominent. Too unwieldy. With that getup, in broad daylight, she's practically screaming for attention.

All right. What else could she be?

I'd vote for diversionary tactic.

A distraction?

Why not?

You may be right, he says. Something doesn't smell right about this. How far is she from the wire?

We stopped her at the seventy-five-meter line, Sir.

He makes eye contact with me. Too close, he says. I would've liked more distance between that cart and us. Don't take your eyes off the game, Lieutenant Ellison. You should know the drill by now.

I flush and say: Yes, Sir.

A scorpion edges out from a chink between two sandbags and scuttles with its tail raised right before us. Connolly lifts his boot and slams it down.

I hate these things, he says. He lifts his boot, and the scorpion slips into a crevice in the ground, apparently unscathed.

I'll be darned! Connolly says.

They're tough, Sir, Wonk Gaines pipes up.

Like the whole fucking country, Connolly says.

Sergeant Whalen comes up. Morning, Cap'n. Lieutenant Ellison.

I shake his hand. Morning, First Sarn't.

Whalen's eyes are bloodshot. He's taken Nick Frobenius's death hard.

He squints at the field. So that's our WMD? he says. What in God's name is that thing?

I say: On the face of it, a woman in a cart doing her morning rounds.

Connolly says: What d'you think, First Sarn't? Man or woman underneath the burqa?

Whalen hesitates. You got me there, Sir.

He glances to me. What's your take, Lieutenant?

I don't think it matters, Sir. What does matter is that it's introduced an element of danger and uncertainty into our situation. If there are insurgents on the slopes, they could be using her as a ploy— or for reconnaissance. The Taliban have been known to exploit our restrictive ROE by using women and children as distractions—or as human shields.

Connolly says: Well, let's find out either way, shall we?

He glances at the interpreter. What's your name again, son?

The interpreter presses his right hand to his heart.

Comandan Saab, I am called Masood.

Masood what?

Sir?

What's your full name?

Farid Humayun Masood Attar, Sir, he says, and smiles, before adding helpfully: Attar, as in the famous poet who wrote *The Conference of the Birds*.

I see, Connolly says and pauses, nonplussed. I'll just call you Masood, if that's all right.

As you please, Comandan Saab.

Okay, then, ask her what she fucking wants.

Masood steps forward smartly and raises the megaphone to his mouth. There's an electric crackle as he switches it on.

Starey më she, tsë ghwâre? he calls out. Hello, what do you want?

The high-pitched voice carries back to us as clear as a bell.

Salâmat osëy . . . she says, but I can't understand the rest of her reply.

Masood translates: She says she is here to bury her brother, who was killed in the battle yesterday. She is his sister. Her name is Nizam.

Crap, Connolly says, and spits close to his boots. So they send their women to pick up their dead? The rats.

He glances at me. What d'you make of the voice, Lieutenant? Woman or boy?

Sounds like a woman to me. Young.

First Sarn't?

I'll second that, Sir, Whalen says.

It's a boy, Comandan Saab, Masood interjects, sounding sure of himself.

We look at him together. How d'you know that? Connolly asks.

The name Nizam is a man's name, Comandan Saab.

Connolly purses his lips. He's not very clever, then, is he? he says, but he looks dissatisfied.

He's Pashtun, Masood says dismissively, and taps his head.

A deep voice speaks up from behind us: it's Doc Taylor.

What's your mother tongue, Masood? he asks.

It's Dari, Sir.

That's the Afghan version of Persian, isn't it?

Yes, Sir.

And Nizam is a man's name in Persian, am I not correct?

Yes, Sir.

Are there absolutely no exceptions?

Masood hesitates. That I wouldn't know, Sir.

Connolly interrupts: What's your point, Doc?

Simply this, Sir. Nizam isn't always a man's name. The word means harmony, and refers to the order of pearls and other precious things—which might explain why the twelfth-century Persian sheikh's daughter who inspired Ibn 'Arabi, the most famous Arab poet, was called Nizám. So there you have it. More or less.

I didn't know, Masood says, crestfallen.

Whalen whistles softly. Ya'll taking Intro to Arab Lit., Doc?

I've been doing some reading of my own these past few months, Taylor says with a disarming smile.

He steps forward and stands next to me.

I thought you'd gone to man the medic tent, Sergeant, I remark pointedly.

I've my people there, he replies. Ready and waiting. I thought I'd better come back here in case she blows up.

Let's hope it doesn't come to that, Connolly says grimly, before turning to Masood. Ask her her brother's name, will you?

Masood translates her answer, though with a bit less confidence than he'd displayed before Doc showed him up. Both Doc and Connolly react to her answer with surprise.

Holy smoke, Doc says, she's his sister.

Whose sister? I ask.

The guy rotting in my tent.

The leader of the gang that whacked us? Whalen asks.

Connolly nods. When he speaks, his voice has a new excitement to it.

If we play this right, it could be an amazing opportunity to gather intelligence, he says. We can fucking grill her for information on her brother, on their tribe, on the mountains—on everything!

He instructs Masood to ask her who told her she could find him here.

Masood relays her answer: Those who survived the battle.

So some of the fuckers got away! Wonk Gaines exclaims.

I swivel my head and tell him to shut the fuck up.

Connolly suddenly looks troubled. He raises his binoculars to his eyes and fixes them on the cart. After a considerable interval, he says: Something still stinks in this setup, and I'm not sure what it is.

Both Whalen and I ask him what he's thinking.

I don't know, he says slowly, but does it make sense that, in this country, a single, unaccompanied woman—and one who claims to be the sister of a tribal leader, what's more—would show up in a fucking go-kart to demand the return of his body? It seems culturally way off the mark. Too much freedom of movement and direct involvement for a woman. Somehow it's asking for an inordinate suspension of belief.

Still gazing through the binoculars, he says: Masood, ask her to describe her brother . . . in detail.

She does as instructed, without hesitation, and at length.

She knows him, Doc says after Masood has translated. That's the man in the body bag she's describing. I've examined him. She's accounted for all his VDMs.

He studies her through his binoculars and asks Connolly if she could be the woman in the surveillance photograph taken by the drone.

Both Whalen and I look at each other. There's obviously information here that we haven't been briefed on. For some reason, Doc's query annoys Connolly. Ignoring him, he lowers his binoculars and tells Masood to convey the message that the body is being held for purposes of identification.

Tell her that he'll be buried after he's been identified.

Masood translates; the woman replies.

I can identify him, she says.

To our surprise, Connolly turns on his heels and prepares to leave.

I'm not wasting any more time on this, he says. I'm not going to negotiate with this person, woman or not. She's not coming anywhere near my base. Masood: tell her we're waiting for experts to identify him, and that's that.

Comandan Saab . . .

*Now* what?

She wants to know when they're coming.

Tell her—I don't know—tell her it'll be soon enough.

She wants to know how soon.

Oh, for Christ's sake! I've barely slept in two days and . . .

Masood says quickly: I could tell her the experts will be here in two days.

Fine.

Whalen and I exchange glances: Connolly's acting strangely. Could the lack of sleep be affecting his judgment?

Meanwhile, Masood resumes speaking to the woman. We listen to their exchange; then Masood says nervously: Comandan Saab, she says that her brother must be properly buried. She insists that it is her right to bury him.

Connolly grimaces. He steps away from the interpreter and lowers his voice until only those of us in his immediate vicinity can hear him. With his eyes fixed on the cart, he addresses Whalen and me icily: I'm going to instruct the terp to tell her to fuck off. He's our business now. He was a fucking leader of the Taliban and an insurgent who caused the deaths of good, decent, honorable men. *My* men: under *my* command. And I'm going to have to meet their folks and tell them that their sons and their husbands and their brothers—*their* brothers, mind you—aren't coming home after all, that they died on my watch, and I couldn't do anything to save them. Not one goddamn thing. So she can take her rights and shove them up her righteous ass. And I'm gonna tell the terp to convey that to her.

Before I can speak, Whalen intervenes calmly.

Does she need to hear all of that, Sir? he says.

Connolly opens and then closes his mouth. He goes red in the face. Then his shoulders sag and he says tiredly: No. Of course not. She doesn't.

He suddenly looks decades older than his twenty-seven years.

He walks over to Masood and says: Please convey to her that our business with him is not finished.

She replies: He is dead. What business can you possibly have with him?

Tell her that her brother was a terrorist, a Talib, and a bad man.

That isn't true! My brother was a Pashtun, a Mujahid, and a freedom fighter. He fought the Taliban. And he died fighting the Amrikâyi invaders. He was a man of courage.

Masood looks embarrassed as he translates.

Fucking in-credible . . . Connolly says with amazement. He folds his arms and shakes his head. She won't take no for an answer. Gentlemen, do you think she could have attended Model U.N.?

It's a lame joke, and we smile feebly.

Doc says: What I would like to know is why she won't leave the cart. That's kinda strange, isn't it?

Sergeant Bradford studies her through his binoculars.

She's carrying stuff, he announces after a moment. She's got a spade, a brown paper bag, a folded blanket, I think, and something else . . . it looks like one of those old-fashioned pie-plate machine guns, but with a sawn-off barrel, which doesn't make sense.

Masood says: They use all kinds of weapons, Sir. Some of the Taliban have guns that are more than a hundred years old.

Connolly glances at me. You're very quiet, Lieutenant.

I clear my throat: That's because I don't know what to tell you, Sir. On the one hand, if she's telling the truth, then it's a golden opportunity to debrief her, get her biometrics, and extricate all kinds of information about her brother and their tribe. But we can't do that unless we're dead certain that she isn't a suicide bomber, and we won't know that until we go out to her, which means exposing ourselves to a clear line of fire from the slopes. So it's a Catch-22.

I thought we'd established that she's out of their sniper range, Sir, Simonis calls down to me.

They may have longer-range cannons, soldier, I reply.

Maybe we could try telling her to leave, Whalen says, and see how she reacts.

Oh, you mean like: thanks for dropping by, Connolly says with a smirk, and please do come again? I mean, come on!

Well, Sir, if she's genuinely grieving, she'd stick around.

And if she's a suicide bomber, she wouldn't?

Maybe not an entire day—or at least not when the temperature hits the hundreds. It would take a lot of commitment to just sit there roasting in the sun.

And in the meantime what are we supposed to do? Hole up inside the fucking base until she makes up her mind either way?

Do we have a choice, Sir? If our ANA were here, we would've sent them out to deal with it, but they aren't, and so it's up to us, isn't it? I mean, we're going to have to improvise: there's no SOP for this situation.

Connolly eyes Whalen quizzically.

After a moment, he turns to the interpreter: Why don't you tell her that, Masood? Tell her that she must leave—that she has no place in a combat zone.

Her reply is long and emotional, and her voice breaks in the middle of it.

There's an awkward silence on our side, and then Masood says all of a sudden: Comandan Saab, perhaps I could point out to this insolent woman that she has no role to play in a Muslim burial? What she is suggesting is sacrilegious. This is a fact.

Connolly smiles. His eyes glint as he glances at us, and then he rests his hand on the interpreter's arm. Well done, Masood, he says smoothly. Go ahead and tell her that, and then switch off your megaphone. We're done talking.

Turning to me, he says: Keep your eyes trained on her, Lieutenant. And watch the slopes. Call me if there's any sign of the enemy.

How long do we put up with her, Sir?

I like what the First Sarn't suggested. Let's see how long she sticks around. If she's still here tomorrow morning, we'll reexamine our options.

He touches his helmet as he walks past us. I'll see you later, gentlemen.

We watch through our binoculars as Masood announces his final message. The megaphone crackles loudly as he switches it off. The woman lowers her white flag just as Simonis calls down from his perch on the Hesco.

There's a vulture circling her, Sir. It's been descending for a while, riding the thermals.

Shading my eyes, I study the bird. It's massive.

Keep an eye on it, I tell Simonis, batting away a fly from my face. If it gets too close, kill it.

A moment later, a shot rings out, and the vulture plummets down with the dead weight of a rock. It crashes into the ground with folded wings. A feathery plume of dust rises into the air.

Connolly comes running back. What the fuck was that?

Masood points silently to the bird.

Connolly puts on mirrored sunglasses and beckons to Wonk Gaines and one of the men on guard duty, Derek Serrano. Tapping Masood on the shoulder, he says briskly: Come on. We're going out to palaver.

I thought we were done talking, I say before I can stop myself.

He doesn't bother to reply, but halfway to the wire, he calls back over his shoulder: I changed my mind, Lieutenant. Give us cover.

I clamber up the Hesco wall and crouch beside Simonis.

I'll be your spotter, I tell him. Any false move on her part, and I want you to drill her, no questions asked. All right?

Yes, Sir.

Whalen climbs up beside me and stretches out his massive frame.

I nod in Connolly's direction: Something in this situation has really gotten under his skin. This sorta direct involvement is way below his pay grade.

Whalen gives me a sidelong glance.

He's out for blood, he says calmly. After the casualties we've taken, it's personal.

He picks up Simonis's M-24 and uncases it. This yours, I take it?

Yes, First Sarn't, Simonis answers.

I'm borrowing it for the duration of the captain's visit.

He estimates the range and adjusts the reticle by dialing the scope.

Ya'll keep an eye on her, he tells Simonis, and I'll watch the slopes.

He stretches out next to me with his eyes clamped to the rifle's scope.

Below us, Doc begins setting out his IVs and saline bags and making his own preparations for any eventualities, should they arise.

I call out to a team from my platoon's Weapons Squad, instructing them to hoist an M-240B on top of the Hesco wall and cover the slopes. In the event of a firefight at short notice, it'll be the deciding factor in our favor.

The team sets up the gun and settles down to wait out the outcome of Connolly's sortie.

Under my breath, I ask Whalen: So—d'you think she could be sussing us out?

He measures his words carefully: The Taliban are masters of strategy, as we've learned through experience. I'll bet they're biding their time somewhere on those slopes. Meanwhile, they send this woman out to keep an eye on us. The moment we let our guard down—BOOM!

So their kinetic ops agent is a girl in a makeshift go-kart?

Could be. Either that . . . or she's a decoy, though I've my doubts about that. There's an element of brazenness in all of this that makes me believe she could be a black widow.

They'd have to be counting on a shitload of gullibility on our part. Surely, they're not that irrational?

Can I throw some words of wisdom at you, Lieutenant?

Shoot.

Listen up, then. A wise man once said that nine-tenths of tactics are based on logic, and taught in books: but it's the irrational tenth that is the test of generals. It depends on pure instinct, which is as natural in a crisis as a reflex.

I reflect for a moment, then turn my head and smile. You just helped me make up my mind, I tell him. She's a suicide op.

Why do you say that?

Because she's the perfect Trojan horse in the wake of a firefight that's left every one of us jittery and exhausted. They're aware that our rules of engagement prevent us from hosing her out of hand. So they're counting on us to make just that one critical mistake: believe her story and let her get close enough. As a plan, it's brilliant.

He nods slowly in agreement. She sure has the perfect motive, and revenge is as natural to these people as the air they breathe. She could be the dead man's sister and a suicide op.

From below us, Doc calls out: Guilt by association, First Sarn't?

Whalen looks faintly amused. What's sauce for the goose is sauce for the gander, Doc. They're downright crazy about revenge in these parts; you know that as much as anyone else. I believe—if I can recall a briefing—the Pashtun tribes call it badal.

Sergeant Petrak, who's taken up position next to him, now speaks up.

Fuck the Pashtuns, he says tersely. We have our own ways of getting even. I'm waiting for her to make a single false move in order to settle things. Then we can get our own back—and Lieutenant Frobenius and the others can rest in peace.

*We* don't do revenge, Sergeant, Doc protests.

Speak for yourself, Sergeant.

Doc's about to reply when a man from the weapons team calls out: Movement on the slopes!

I raise my binoculars instantly; Whalen sights through his scope.

I catch my breath: it looks like a dog.

Whalen says: Well, I'll be damned, ya'll. It's Shorty.

How on earth did he sneak out of base? I ask.

Beside me, Simonis drawls: Dawg's been going AWOL, Sir. You're gonna have to dock him points.

I wouldn't tell the C.O. if I were you, Lieutenant, Whalen says. He'd have a fit.

Speaking of the captain, Simónis says, it looks like they're having a pretty intense powwow.

I watch Connolly's broad shoulders go up and down as he gesticulates animatedly. Gaines and Serrano have their guns trained on the woman. The interpreter keeps turning from her to Connolly in the course of his translation. There's something about the picture that makes me uncomfortable, and I'm not sure why. Finally, Connolly gestures with both hands before turning on his heels and marching back toward us. The interpreter has to hurry to keep up with him. Behind them, Gaines and Serrano walk warily backwards with their guns still pointing at the figure in the cart. Just as Connolly reaches the Hescos, the woman turns the cart around and wheels it in the opposite direction.

Is she leaving? I ask no one in particular.

Whalen jumps down from the Hesco and leans the M-24 rifle against a sandbag. He walks over to Connolly, who's slapping dust from his trousers.

She asked if she could bury her brother's cronies, Connolly says irritably. I said fine.

So she's not leaving? Whalen asks.

Nope.

Why won't she leave the cart, Sir, could you tell? Doc asks. Is there something the matter with her legs?

We were too far away, Connolly says. And, quite frankly, it wasn't the first thing on my mind.

He glances up at me. Keep an eye on her, Lieutenant.

He seems composed, almost bored. He leaves with Whalen while I scan the far end of the field where the woman has reached the bodies by this time. I raise my binoculars and watch her take a spade out of the cart. It glitters as it catches the sun. She lowers herself to the ground rather clumsily and appears to drag herself to the nearest body. Then she straightens up and begins digging. I watch lumps of earth fly into the air. Soon she's surrounded by a pall of dust.

I overhear one of the men say: Man, she can wield a spade!

Someone else says: She's kinda short, though . . .

I lower my binoculars, feeling like a voyeur. Beside me, Simonis puts down his rifle. He coughs to attract my attention.

So we're supposed to just sit here and watch her bury those three dudes? he asks. There's an undertone of disbelief in his voice.

That's right, I tell him, feeling inexplicably irritated.

His mouth twitches. Way to go, he says softly. America . . . fuck yeah!

What was that, Specialist?

He looks at me without expression. It's from the movie *Team America,* Sir. From the creators of *South Park,* the TV show.

I know, I say. I know what *South Park* is. I just don't see the relevance of your remark.

He runs his hand over his face. I can't tell if he's hiding a smirk.

You heard the captain, I say, annoyed. His orders were clear.

Yes, Sir. I heard the captain. Orders are orders.

Somehow, I feel the need to explain further: These women are very different from the ones back home, Specialist. They're used to hard work. As a matter of fact, they do all the work. I've even heard it said that the Taliban use them as pack animals to carry their equipment around because, as men, they themselves couldn't be bothered. And when there are no women—or mules—to be found, they simply leave their stuff behind.

Those Taliban are pretty fucked up, Sir, he says blandly.

You got it, Specialist.

His mouth twitches again: I guess we're different.

Yes, I reply in a strained voice.

I turn my head toward the woman again—then turn back to Simonis and dismiss him. He swings down from the Hesco wall without a sound.

See ya later, Doc, he says to Taylor, who's busy putting away his medical gear. I wait for him to take leave of me as well, but he doesn't look up as he shoulders his two sniper rifles and strides off.

Then Taylor leaves as well, and I'm suddenly on my own on top of the Hescos. I realize that I'm still feeling dissatisfied, though I can't put my finger on the reason why. Then I realize it has to do with Connolly. I'm peeved at the way he went marching off for his palaver without giving me adequate time to make the necessary arrangements to cover him. It was a risky move in an ambiguous situation, and it's precisely the kind of hotheadedness we can do without close on the heels of a vicious firefight. Perhaps I am going too much by the book, I conclude, but it was utterly irresponsible on his part.

Why are you so annoyed? a laughing voice asks. Connolly's always been something of a loose cannon, or didn't you know that? It's part of your job as a platoon leader to make up the slack.

I look up to see Nick Frobenius standing before me with his arms folded. I have to squint my eyes against the light to make out his features.

I was under the impression, I say stiffly, that one's thoughts, at least, were private.

Oh come on, Ellison. You sound like you've got a stick up your ass. Nothing in this company is private.

It's not right, I say feebly.

He bursts out laughing. What can I say? Life's a bitch. As for going by the book, he adds, if that's your operational template, then you ought to have taken a desk job at Bagram.

I can't believe he just said that. I protest: So the fact that I follow the rules makes me a fobbit?

Now, whoever is saying that? he counters with a lopsided grin.

You just did! You claimed I was hankering after a desk job.

Do you always take things so personally, Tom?

I stand my ground because I suspect that this, too, is a test.

I was trained to follow the rules, I tell him, trying hard not to shout. I was trained that the rules are there for a reason—and that's why they count. Rules save lives. They make the system foolproof.

Foolproof, eh?

Yes.

Combat soldiers seldom follow the rules, Lieutenant Butterbars, he says with a drawl. Garrison soldiers follow the rules. What I'm sayin'.

I shake my head, speechless. I simply don't know how to react.

He claps a comradely hand on my shoulder. You'll learn, he says.

He gives me a quick smile, like a conspirator.

In the meantime, he says, we've got a job to do.

He springs back and holds the locker room door open for me.

I shoulder past him, wondering how in my very first week with the company I managed to let him talk me into a ridiculous ten-mile run around Kandahar Airfield. Not that I had much of a say in the matter, I reflect bitterly: as a newbie second lieutenant, I'm well aware that I'm being assessed in terms of my potential as compared to the hard-bitten legend I've replaced, David Hendricks, a veteran of Bosnia and Iraq. It's just that I'm a swimmer, not a runner; it's always been a drawback for me in the infantry. I guess I should have joined the Marines. All the same, I decide to pace myself carefully in order to avoid total humiliation.

As we make for the glare outside, my eye catches the digital thermometer on the wall. I flinch and decide to appeal to my companion's rationality one last time, even though I'm aware it will make no difference whatsoever.

Why are we doing this, Lieutenant? I mean, it's ninety-eight degrees in the shade! It's going to be like the fires of hell outside. We'll bake, and then we'll burn.

Immortality, Lieutenant, he says gaily. We're doing this to blazon our mark on fleeting time. Remember Pheidippides at Marathon. He ran one hundred and fifty miles on bad roads all the way to Sparta. Compared to that, ten miles on a flat track is kid's play.

I'm not about to give in to some obscure classical bullshit. I say: He ran in one-hundred-fifteen-degree heat?

It was probably warmer, he says. Greece in summer, the worst time of the year. And he was running under duress. He had to get to the Spartans in time to ask for their help before the Persians attacked.

I suppose I'm not Pheidips, then.

Phei-dip-pides, he says, correcting me.

All right. You know what I mean.

You'll forget how hot it is as soon as you settle into your stride. Besides, we haven't traveled all the way from Tarsândan to chicken out at the last minute. We're already signed up, remember? We'll be a laughing stock if we quit.

He grins and puts on wraparound shades.

All right, tough guy, he says. Let's see you strut your stuff.

I grit my teeth and follow him into the sunlight.

It doesn't work. By the fourth mile, I'm pretty much completely dehydrated and ready to drop. Then I pull my hamstring, and the next thing I know I'm sprawling headfirst onto the ground.

Frobenius slows down and comes to a halt. He turns around and looks at me. Down for the count, huh, Lieutenant?

The amusement in his voice exasperates me.

Really, Lieutenant, what do you expect? I snap back. I've only been in this country nine days. I'm not used to running in hundred-degree heat.

A couple of Marines streak past with long strides. Frobenius gazes after them. I guess I'll have to do this by my own lonesome self, he says.

He flexes his knees and stretches—then breaks into a run again.

Can't let the Marines show us up, he says over his shoulder. See you later, Ellison. Go get yourself checked up.

I'm icing my thigh in the waiting room when he joins me at the end of the race. His face is beet red; he's drenched in sweat.

How're you holding up, Tom? Anything torn?

Nope, just sprained. I'm fine, thanks.

The Marines cleaned the field, he says sourly. There was one Brit SAS and a couple of Special Forces runners in the top ten, but other than that, it was the U.S. bloody Marines all the way. Those guys train hard.

He flops down on the bench and gazes at CNN news on the television screen. The newscaster goes from reporting on a presidential trip to Toronto to a meeting of world business leaders in Spain.

You're taking it too personally, Nick, I say slyly.

Damn right I am! I like to be on the winning side.

I'm sorry for letting you down.

He glances at me but doesn't say anything. A bit later, he nods at the screen. Fucking Creons, man, he says. We're run by a bunch of fucking Creons. His face twists with loathing; he seems genuinely disgusted.

Sorry . . . what?

For the first time since I've known him, he seems embarrassed. He flushes brightly.

Don't mind me. I'm talking to myself. I do that a lot when I'm beat.

It would help if I knew what you were talking about.

Let it go, he says. It's too complicated to explain; and I'm too tired.

Picking up his towel, he begins to wipe his face and arms.

Abruptly, he puts down the towel and says: Creon was the king of Thebes in ancient Greece. He was a tyrant and a dictator, but even he had nothing on these clowns. They're all suit and no soul. I tell you, man, the military is the only institution left in America with any conception of honor—or any of the virtues that once made the good old U.S. of A. the place the whole damn world looked up to. Think courage, endurance, integrity, judgment, justice, loyalty, discipline, knowledge. The rest of them—the civilian leadership, especially— are just a pile of crap. They've absolutely no vision. The politicians are shameless: all they care about is power. And the big businessmen and bankers look after their own, and the rest of the country can go fuck themselves. And these are the people who run us, who dictate what we do and how we can do it, the shitheads. They've saddled us over here with a government that reeks of corruption, they've hand-cuffed us in an operational straitjacket with no clear guidelines, and then they forget about us and expect us to work miracles. It stinks, man; the whole damn show stinks to high heaven. I'm sorry, but I'd like my one and only life to be different. I'd like to be proud of my country and what we represent. Call me a hopeless idealist—I don't care—but that's why I joined the army in the first place. I think of my friends from college in their high-rise air-conditioned offices and with their trophy cars and houses, and I think, there, but for the grace of God, go I.

I stare at him in astonishment, his words echoing in my ears.

I'm not sure I heard you right, I manage to say at last, but did I just hear you call our president a fucker?

What?

I'm trying to remember the exact words . . .

Oh, for Christ's sake, he says in exasperation. Just forget it, okay?

I'm just trying to understand—I mean, he's our commander in chief.

No, really, forget it.

He got elected, Nick.

Let's stop while the going's good, okay?

His voice is curt, dangerous. I pause a moment, checking my words.

Then I say: Our military is constitutionally subservient to the civilian leadership. It's part of a clear chain of command.

He does not answer. He stares at the screen, then glances out of the window. I finish icing my leg but hesitate to say anything more.

Finally he acknowledges me with a look.

So that's me, he says. Now you know why I'm here.

I do, I reply. I used to wonder. I mean, you went to Vassar.

Yes, but I had to drive all the way down to Fordham University in New York City to take Army ROTC classes. It was two hours each way on top of my regular course load at Vassar.

Wow, that's insane!

You'd get along very well with my wife, he says drily, before correcting himself: My ex-wife. She thinks I'm nuts.

I don't think you're nuts!

No?

Of course not, Lieutenant. I respect you—and I've noticed, especially, the way the men respond to you. It says a lot to me. You're a natural leader, and I'm proud to serve alongside. We might have our differences—I don't know, I'm still processing what you said—but that has nothing to do with our roles here.

He turns his entire body to stare at me, his expression charged and at the same time ambivalent. It's a strangely blank look, almost as if he's suddenly become a stranger. I see the perspiration on his face. His jaw is clenched, his eyes locked on me. And yet, I can't tell if he's looking at me or somewhere else.

Tell me, he says quietly. Why did you join the army, Tom?

That's a good question, Tommy, Dad says, one that I've been trying to figure out ever since you told us. What's the army got to do with you?

I put away the Doritos I've been munching and look down at the floor to compose my thoughts. I'm sprawled out on the shag rug, which once used to be bright yellow but has since turned a mottled shade of caramel owing to Mom's liberal use of bleach wherever Wannabe the cat has puked, which is practically all over. Dad's sitting in Grandpa's old rocking chair, looking out of the French windows at the mile-long stretch of meadow and woods sloping down to the bay. My sister, Annie, is sitting at his feet, as she often does, leaning against his knees as she reads a book. Mom's in the kitchen washing up after supper, a Sunday evening rite in which she banishes all of us from "her turf," as she puts it, and gets to work at the sink with an unholy rattling of pots and pans that sends Wannabe racing out of the house and into the fading light where he can have some peace and quiet. The moon's out already: it lights up the pond at the boundary of the meadow and the woods. When Annie was a baby, she'd point to the pond and then to the sky and say: Look, Tommy, up moon, down moon!

I know Dad's waiting for me to speak, and his patience isn't infinite.

You saw the towers go down, Dad, I say at length. People died. Tons of people.

He pushes his glasses back from the tip of his nose.

That was three years ago, Tommy. And we got our own back after that. We bombed the bejeezus out of Iraq and Afghanistan.

I know, but I still feel it inside me. Those terrorists are still around. They haven't gone away.

This is Maine, Tommy. No one's coming after us here. Get real.

That's not the point. The country needs people to sign up.

I'm about to say more when I pause, feeling ridiculously self-important having put it like that, so I add: You must know what I mean.

It isn't why we saved money for your college.

I know. But ROTC can help us out with that too. I've covered all the bases.

I'm not gonna take blood money! Dad protests. I'm not gonna let them buy you! I'm not taking money for my son's life!

They're not buying me, Dad. It doesn't work like that. I want to join up.

You could get killed. Tad Murphy's boy died in Iraq.

I notice that the rattling in the kitchen has stopped. Mom's leaning her elbows on the counter. She doesn't say anything, but I can tell from her face she's listening. Then I notice that Annie isn't reading either but just holding on to her book and waiting for me to answer.

I clear my throat. Something's pricking me inside my gullet; it must be the damn Doritos. I sit up and clasp my arms around my knees.

Someone's got to do it, Dad. Think about it for a moment: I could be an officer if I qualified.

Annie drops her book, then picks it up again.

Tommy, Dad says quietly, it's time we had a little talk.

There's no need, I reply. If you don't want me to do it, I won't.

It isn't that, son, he says, sounding suddenly tired.

What is it, then?

For the first time he looks at me directly.

He says: Who's going to look after the boat? Who's going to take over from me when I retire? I can't do this forever; I'm sixty-nine. I hadn't reckoned on your bailing out on me.

I drop my gaze. I can't meet his eyes. Lobstering's been in the family for generations, passed down as a living from father to son. Dad began by helping out his father from the age of five, as Grandpa had his father before him, and as I myself have been going out on the boat since I was nine. I can see his point even as I want to tell him that his expectation's unfair because it's always been the oldest boy who takes over the boat—but we don't talk about Andy anymore, or, at least, not since he got out of jail and moved into an Airstream in someone's backyard in Bar Harbor. The last we heard of him, he was doing odd jobs and working part-time for some trash removal company, but he no longer stops by, and we don't call. Matter of fact, I don't even think he has a telephone.

I turn my head and look out at the bay, the little that can be seen above the treetops. I love this place; I love its sense of serenity and timelessness. Under different circumstances, I'd have taken over from Dad, no questions asked. But those collapsing towers changed everything for me. I haven't even been to New York City, or Washington, or that field in Pennsylvania. But I do know right from wrong, I know you live life by the rules, and someone broke the rules and hurt us bad, and I'd feel like a failure if I didn't do my bit.

Annie takes Dad's hand and holds it between her own. His fingers are chapped from a lifetime of working with salt water and frayed ropes and rusty lobster traps. Annie's fingers look delicate, almost translucent, against my father's gnarled hand.

Mom enters the room and wanders over distractedly to her favorite Christmas cactus in the corner, next to the porch door. She picks off some of the dead flowers before walking past me and standing behind Dad's chair.

You've made up your mind, haven't you? she asks me.

Before I can reply, Dad nods. He's leaving, he says tersely.

Mom's kneading Dad's shoulders as if they were made of dough.

She says: You're going to be an Awayer, Tommy.

Mom, we'll always be Awayers in Maine, regardless of how long we've lived here.

What I meant was that you've found a reason to leave.

That isn't fair, Mom! I'll come back home, just like Grandpa did. He fought in the war, he saw the world, and then he returned and settled down. Right here.

I stab my finger into the floor for emphasis and repeat: Right here.

He came back a changed man, Mom says. He never talked about the war. It changed him. How could it not? He wasn't the same anymore. Ask your father if you don't believe me.

I won't change, I reply stubbornly.

Suddenly, Annie springs up to her feet and runs out of the room. We hear her door bang shut.

Mom leaves the room to be with her.

Dad and I look at each other. He says: I can hold on for five more years, maybe six. But I don't know if I can carry on after that.

I draw back. I don't say anything.

He picks up Annie's book and flicks absently through it.

Does Linsey know about your plans? he asks.

I was going to . . . no, she doesn't.

What will you tell her?

I'm taken aback. I hadn't expected this question, and I feel my face grow warm.

I'll tell her what I'll tell her, I say brusquely.

Not good enough. Bob and Maggie are like family. We wouldn't want you to mess with their daughter.

Dad, I wouldn't hurt her. Actually, I was going to tell her that.

What?

I was going to tell her to wait for me.

He looks me square in the face.

I care about you, Tommy, he says. I also know that you're still too damn young to have thought this through clearly.

Something in his voice strikes me. He sounds remote.

He turns to gaze out at the bay, and I do the same.

Are you taking the boat out tomorrow? I ask.

Of course I am. Why wouldn't I?

What time do you want me to wake up?

Don't worry about it. You can sleep in.

I look down and realize that at some time during our conversation I've twisted out a clump from the shag rug. I stare at it for a moment, baffled. Then I pat it back into place and hope that Mom won't notice. Or maybe she'll blame it on Wannabe.

Dad rises to his feet. I'm turning in, he says. It's been a long day, and I'm tuckered. Good night, Tom.

Wish Mom good night for me, will you?

I will.

I catch him stealing a last glance at the bay. The moon's gone behind a giant bank of clouds. The field's in shadow; the woods are a dark smudge.

I'm still looking at the bay later that night, but this time it's at the faded picture on the wall across from my bed that was a gift from some painter or other who'd taken a shine to Grandma, or so the story went. Scrolling along the bottom are the words: Penobscot Bay, where the water is pure and the living's easy.

I never did understand that sentiment and long ago concluded that only an Awayer could have written it. Lobstering is one of the hardest trades, and even the water in the bay is increasingly polluted these days.

Those are my thoughts as I tiptoe out of the house early the next morning, hard on the heels of my father, who's on his way to the boat. It's the hour before sunrise, and there's a thick mist. I wait on the porch for Dad to cross the dew-soaked field and enter the woods, and then I make my way down myself, ducking into the overgrown path that winds between the pine and spruce trees and passing the three silver birches that Dad had planted when Andy, Annie, and I were born. I stop by the broken-down cliffside shack that overlooks the bay, and watch him unlock the wooden gate to the dock and then the door to the shed where he stores the lobster traps. He works quickly, efficiently, the habits of years ingrained into his movements, but he appears tired, and I wonder how well he slept last night. He loads the traps into the boat, sorts out the orange buoys, and, with a tug of the motor, he's off into the bay.

· I want to call out to him to tell him to circle back and take me along, but I don't. Instead, I climb down the ladder to the dock and sit by the water's edge while the boat's wake washes up around me. I can't see it anymore, though I can hear the motor chugging through the dark. A faint dark line through the mist hints at the hills on the other side of the bay, but everything else is a milky haze, with a few black-backed gulls gliding in and out. I breathe the salt air, the mist settling damply on my shoulders, but after a while, I get up and make my way back to the house. Maybe I'll spend the morning mowing the lawn . . .

Lieutenant Ellison . . .

I look down from the Hesco. Whalen's standing there, shading his eyes against the sun. It's hotter than hell. I run my tongue over my chapped lips. Dried-up saliva crusts around the corners of my mouth.

What is it, First Sarn't?

It's time for your relief, Lieutenant.

I look down at my watch, confused. What time is it? I ask.

It's time, he says as Sergeant Schott walks up; then: Uh-oh.

What is it?

Looks like she's coming back.

I turn to look out at the field. My vision blurs in the glare. A white band of heat straddles the ground. It's so hot I'm almost dizzy. I shade my eyes and wait for a moment for my vision to clear. Whalen's right. The cart's trundling back. There can be no mistaking it.

Whalen climbs up beside me.

I hear Schott shout to the men as he signals an M-240B machine gun team into place to cover the slopes. With the M-240B's maximum effective range of eleven hundred meters for area targets, they can lacerate the slopes. As they settle into position, a second combat team takes up firing positions with M-4s and a .50-caliber machine gun. They let Schott know that they have her in their sights.

Whalen watches the cart with me until it lurches to a stop near the seventy-five-meter marker. Gusts of wind sweep the field, blowing dust into tight little spirals.

I shake my head in disbelief. This is crazy. What does she want from us?

Whalen says matter-of-factly: Her brother's body.

Then he turns to me and says: Would you have acted any differently in her situation?

For an instant, Annie's face flashes before my eyes. I shudder momentarily before dismissing it. I hardly think it's the same thing, First Sarn't, I say tersely.

Why not? he asks.

I'm saved from having to respond by Connolly's arrival.

He marches down to the ECP and comes to a halt with his arms akimbo. I jump down from the Hesco and walk over to him. He barely glances at me before turning to glare at the cart again.

What the hell is going on, Lieutenant?

She's done burying the men, Sir, I reply calmly.

You shoulda let me know the moment he finished.

*He,* Sir?

Well, of course. Do you seriously expect me to believe that a woman—and one apparently crippled, at that—just buried three large men in graves she dug out of the bare ground? With a frickin' spade? And in this heat?

It did take her a while . . .

Connolly swivels around and sizes me up.

Just how gullible do you think I am?

Sir?

If that's a fucking woman, then I'm a fucking camel.

The women around here are pretty tough, Sir.

You're not married, are you, Lieutenant?

No, I'm not, I answer, and stiffen.

You seem very well informed about the local gals.

Well, on the evidence of it before our eyes . . .

He checks his watch. It's too late now, but if he's still around tomorrow, then we'll settle this once and for all, d'you follow me?

I do, Sir. Absolutely. Then I pause and cough discreetly: But how?

How what?

How are we going to settle it?

We'll come up with something. In the meantime, keep me posted, all right?

Yes, Sir, I answer with composure, while inwardly seething at being expected to serve as his gofer. I want to remind him that I'm a lieutenant, not a fucking messenger, but I manage to restrain myself.

Who's on watch next, First Sarn't? Connolly asks Whalen.

Schott steps up. I am, Sir.

Keep your eyes skinned. I've a feeling it's gonna be a long night.

Connolly leaves, and I pick up my things from the Hesco and nod at Whalen and Schott as I walk away. Whalen lights a cigarette and watches me go with a sympathetic look.

I return to my hut and slowly take off my boots and socks. My feet are white and wrinkled: they look as if they've been poached, and strips of skin peel off with the socks. I collapse on the bunk in exhaustion. My hands and face burn with the daylong exposure to the sun, and there's a tight knot in my stomach that's threatening to turn into a cramp. I realize I haven't eaten the entire day. I lie there willing myself to get up and walk over to the mess tent.

They've been feeding you well, Tommy, Mom says. You've filled out.

Annie feels my biceps. She says: No way!

You happy 'bout your son, Ma'am? I ask.

Ma'am! Mom punches me playfully on the arm. Don't you Ma'am me, young man. I'm Mom to you. None of your southern airs here.

Okay, okay, but what do you think of me in this uniform?

Mom glances at Dad, and then at me again. She looks sad. Do you really think you're going to make a difference, Tommy?

I do, I reply. Do you remember what you said when we were sitting in front of the TV watching those towers go down?

You're obsessed with those towers! It isn't healthy. No, I don't remember. What did I say?

You turned to us and said everyone was going to have to pull together, do their bit. So I'm doing my bit, that's all.

She gives me a wan smile. I guess I'm going to have to watch what I say around you. If I'd known how it was going to turn out, I'd have said something else altogether.

The three of them have come down from Maine for my graduation. To save money, they took a red-eye out of Bangor to Boston's Logan Airport, caught a connection via Philadelphia to Atlanta, then drove down to Fort Benning.

That's a hell of a lot of connections, I remark.

Your father was planning to drive us down, but the round trip would have taken three days, Mom says with a laugh.

Dad says: So Annie went online and found us these cheap tickets on some travel website. It cost less than half as much as it would've to drive. He shakes his head in disbelief.

It'll be better on the way back, Mom says. We just have one changeover in Illadelph, and bigger planes on both legs, not those tiny turboprops.

Illadelph? I ask. Where's that?

That's Philadelphia to you, white boy, Dad replies.

I do a double-take and stare at them: Mom? Dad?

Mom laughs. The Roots crew are in the house, she says. What's yo izm, homeboy?

I jerk my eyes open and lie still for a moment, bewildered.

Then I realize I can hear Wonk Gaines talking a mile a minute on the other side of the plywood partition that separates my hooch from theirs. I must have fallen asleep the moment I lay down on the cot. I grimace and search for my earplugs, but I can't find them in the darkness and continue to lie there half-asleep, with snatches of conversation filtering through the partition.

Wonk says: So I'm in this basement in North Philly, maybe ten feet by ten feet square, and there's forty of us inside, and everyone's doped out of their minds, and ?uestlove, man, he sets down this beat on a shoebox, and the whole crowd's swayin', you know what I'm sayin', and a brother begins to rap. It's Black Thought. He says: Hip-hop, you're the love of my life . . .

The high-pitched voice of Brad Everheart, the company's Christianist, cuts in: Who moved my fucking boots?

Pfc. Serrano says: They're right there, bro . . .

No, they're not! I'd placed them like this . . . at an angle to the cot, see? . . . and now they're here, which is not the same thing . . .

Pfc. Lawson says: What the fuck are you talking about?

They gotta be at this angle, see? It's very precise. What's so difficult to understand?

Why the fuck do they have to be at that angle? Matt Lawson asks. Does it say so in your Bible?

Everheart says: Come on, Matt! That was a cheap shot.

Lawson replies: You're losing it, Brad. I'm worried about you.

No, I'm not losing it. I'm saving lives.

There's a growl from Serrano. What the fuck is that supposed to mean?

Everheart continues: Listen up, you guys. The night before the firefight, I was too tired to place them at this angle, see, and all hell broke loose shortly after. And the time before that, four weeks ago, I'd chucked them under my cot any old how, and Lieutenant Hendricks and Sergeant Castro got hosed the next day. So now I gotta be extra careful, okay? I'm not taking any more chances. This is for all of us.

No shit! Wonk says nervously. Guys, he's got a point.

Lawson drawls: Brad Everheart. Dude. You need to go home and get laid.

Laid?

Yup. Big-time.

Is sex all you can think about?

What else is there to life? Ejaculation, procreation, extinction.

Bro, you need, like, a dozen Valium chased with a shot of chastity.

Not a chance, Lawson counters. Matter of fact, I could use some nymphetamine right about now.

You missing the litter back home, Matt?

Fuck off, douche bag!

God bless, shitface, Everheart says magnanimously. You're just like fucking SpongeBob, d'you know why?

No, why?

Because you live at the bottom of a fucking bikini, that's why.

That's all right by me, dipshit, Lawson says, laughing. I'd go for a bikini over your holy book any time.

Serrano cuts in: Speaking of boots and shit, guys, I smell like a pig. I'm tired of cleaning up with fuckin' baby wipes. I can't hardly wait till the next rotation through Battalion for a shower and a call home.

What the fuck for? Wonk asks, his voice laced with sarcasm.

Don't you like washing with wipes and water bottles left to warm in the sun?

I'm not from Killadelphia, brutha, Serrano says suavely. I like working showers and *laundromats* . . . he draws the word out.

Suddenly Lawson says: What's that noise?

Serrano says: Sounds like someone playing a guitar . . .

Dude, that's no guitar, Lawson replies. And it's coming from somewhere outside the base. Listen . . .

Everheart says: Grab your guns and let's go check it out . . .

I hear boots tramping out of their hooch and sit up on my bunk, straining to listen. Moments later, I find myself outside as well, my hand resting on my 9 mm as I join a steady stream of grunts in various states of undress, all heading in the direction of the music. I make out a row of men ranged along the Hesco wall, their silhouetted forms black against a backdrop of stars. Except for those on guard duty, practically the entire company's here—and everyone's silent, quiet for once. The only sound in that surreal gathering is an unearthly plucking of strings filtering through the night air.

I walk past Staff Sergeant Tribe leaning against a pile of sandbags.

We should just fuckin' whack her, he says sourly. Just as I was fallin' asleep . . .

Bradford makes room for me on top of the Hescos. Whalen's next to him, gazing out at the dark field. I make out Doc, Tanner, Petrak, Ashworth, Flint, Masood. Glowing cigarette ends flicker in the darkness like fireflies.

The air smells of the mountains.

# FIRST SERGEANT

WHEN you're young, you're sleeping.

I swim to the end of the small pool, then turn around and swim back. It's my twentieth lap, and the pink dawn stipples the water. I feel like laughing out loud with pleasure—and maybe I did earlier on—but am content to simply enjoy the sense of well-being that suffuses me. It's good to feel the water stream down my face while its buoyancy cradles my body. The dawn clouds are out of a dream: they turn vermilion, then orange, before the red orb of the sun soars over the horizon. The night's long shadow lifts from the pool. A cool, pale radiance filters through the overhanging branches. The magnolias emerge from the half-light into the mirroring water. Their reflections surround me as I climb out of the pool.

Aunt Thelma's knitting on the back porch. She smiles at me and tells me that my grandfather is up. I can't think of too many moments when I've seen her without those needles and a ball of wool on her lap. Thelma brought me up with the help of my grandparents when my father died. I was twelve. They told us there'd been an accident in an air show in Germany. Dad was one of the spectators. He'd driven there with his buddies from the nearby base at Landstuhl. I remember Mother's strange response to the telephone call—she went ashen-faced, then smiled. She attempted to cover it up by biting her lip. But I'd already noticed, and lying in bed that night, I couldn't figure out what was worse, Dad's death or her reaction.

A week later, she was gone: she'd taken off with runty little Alvin Jones, one of the mechanics at the auto repairs place where Dad serviced his car whenever he was in town. It was left to my grandparents to receive the men from Dad's unit when they came by with his personal effects. As for Mother, we heard that she and Al ended up in Abilene, where he opened an auto shop of his own. I never saw her after that. Rumor went she'd had a kid who didn't survive.

Now my grandfather is sitting at the kitchen table like he does every morning, getting in Grandma's way while she makes breakfast. As I pass them on the way to my room, he asks me to bring my uniform out with me when I return for breakfast.

Not again, James! Grandma protests. Leave the boy alone.

You leave *us* alone! You don't understand.

Oh, I understand all right, Jimmy Whalen. I was an army wife for thirty-nine years, and if I don't understand I don't know who will.

Thirty-nine years? You must mean *fifty*-nine years! I can see you're ready to go plant me in my grave afore my time comes.

You retired twenty years ago, may I remind you?

I can do that math! he barks. They retired me before I was ready to quit. I'd never have left on my own, you know that.

I know, I know, I hear Grandma say patiently as I reach my room. I almost trip when my foot catches on a rip in the carpet, but manage to keep from falling and carry on.

My grandfather's in the study by the time I return. I'm dressed casually, but my uniform on its hanger is crisp from the dry cleaner's. It smells of the plastic wrapper I unspool before handing it to him.

Louise, he calls out, where are my glasses?

She brings them to him and pulls me behind her as she goes back to the kitchen. I catch a glimpse of my grandfather running his hands over my combat ribbons and SFC stripes. He's sitting ramrod straight, but there's a faraway look in his eyes. I know that look well: he's dreaming about his glory days again.

Grandma makes me promise to attend Sunday service at her new church, the Greater King David Baptist, where she's been going ever since the one closer to home burned down.

They have the best gospel music, she says. Just listenin' to that sugar-sweet sound brings you closer to the Lord, though I've yet to be able to persuade your grandfather, that stubborn old man, to come with me. I'm planning to talk to the pastor about setting up your wedding date for when your tour's done. So bring Camille with you: she's going to need to get to know him and all.

Grandma . . .

No, no, Marcus, not a word. I'm not getting any younger, and you can see what your grandfather's like. I want to see you settled before I go. You're thirty-seven. It's time.

She clasps my hands and looks into my eyes. You hear me?

Yes, Ma'am.

Good. Now sit down and tuck into your pancakes and eggs. I've made them just the way you like them. You see, I don't forget, regardless of what your grandfather may tell you about my failing memory and nonsense like that.

Yes, Ma'am.

When I finish eating, I sit with her for a while and talk about Afghanistan and the general direction of the war. She asks me about Tarsândan, and tells me about the book she's taken out from the public library about a woman her own age in Kabul. It's my turn to be interested, and it's no surprise that by the time I leave the house it's nine o'clock, and I'm already running late for my errands.

On my way out, my grandfather asks me how long I'll be gone.

Let's see, today's Sunday, so I'd say Friday or thereabouts.

You takin' your father's car or what?

Yes, Sir, I was planning to.

Your grandma had it serviced last week—or, at least, that's what she says she did, in anticipation of your comin'—so you should be fine. Drive carefully all the same, you hear me? It's an old car, and those great big loons in their SUVs are enough to put the fear of the devil into a law-abidin' man.

Before I can answer, Grandma calls out from the kitchen: James, are you swearing again?

What you talking about, woman? I'm havin' a conversation with my grandson, that's all. Can't a man get any privacy around here?

He shakes his head in disgust. *Women,* you know what I mean?

I repress a smile. Yes, Sir.

Aunt Thelma walks me to the door. Bring Camille home, she says. It's been a while, Boo. It'll do me good to see your sweet gaienne again. She has such a beautiful head of hair, and her eyes!—as blue as the morning sky.

Aunt Thelma's originally from New Orleans, and she still falls into the local patois sometimes, using Boo for child, gaienne for girl-friend, and so on. It used to bother me no end when I was a teenager, but now I find it endearing and give her a hug instead.

She asks me to stand still while she measures the sweater she's knit-ting for me against my back. How cold is it there, anyway? she asks.

Afghanistan? It's cold. I mean, there's entire parts of the country that close down for six to seven months of the year because there's so much snow on the ground.

Good thing you're here, then. No point in getting frostbite. Still and all, I'll make sure I get this done before you go back. Maybe you can wear it next year.

Aunt Thelma, it's still going to be winter when I get back, trust me. Where we're posted, the cold lasts until the end of May.

Holy Mary, Mother of God, I'm glad you told me! I had no idea. I'm turning into a regular vielle fille! I'll have to buy you warm underwear, child. She looks at me over her glasses. I've been using six-ply yarn. Maybe it's not thick enough. What do you think?

It seems fine to me.

I should probably use single-ply worsted weight yarn and start over.

There's really no need to do that! It'll be fine.

I don't know, p'tit boug. Let me think about it. You run along now.

I slide the tarp off the car in the garage. The Chevelle looks like it was born yesterday: Gauguin Red paintwork, glittering chrome grille, spotless tan interior. I open the door, slide into the front seat, and rest my hands on the leather-covered steering wheel made shiny by my father's loving use. I turn on the ignition and sit there for a moment, puzzled that nothing's happening. Then I laugh. I'm so used to the roar of Hummers and Strykers that I've forgotten what it's like to be in a real American car.

It slides as smooth as silk out of the garage and down the short driveway onto the street. The sun's already hot. I'm glad I wore an open-necked cotton shirt and loose slacks. I merge with the traffic headed for Government Street. My first stop is Phil Brady's, one of the best blues establishments in Baton Rouge, where Camille tends bar four nights a week.

I use the back entrance, pausing before the employees' bulletin board to check Camille's schedule for the week. She's taken off till next weekend, which is when I'm flying out. I feel a rush of anticipation as I rest my eyes on her name: Camille Thibodeaux. Just as I'm turning away, Donnie, the day manager, sees me and hurries over.

Welcome back! he says, pressing my hand. Where you at, podna? Good to see you again! How long you staying this time around?

Seven days. Camille told me to come pick up some things . . .

We got 'em ready and waiting for you, Big Boy, the whole nine yards, exactly as ordered. That gal of yours don't stint none, I'll tell you that much. Come along now.

Donnie, please don't call me Big Boy.

He turns to look at me and laughs.

That's big of you, Chief. You're a hero, naw what I'm talkin' about? A genuine, twenty-four-carat American hero. Everybody looks up to you round here. I can't tell you how good it feels to have you back.

Thank you, but I'm no hero. I'm simply doing my job, like you're doing yours.

He slows down and glances at me uncertainly. Then he winks. C'mon now. I know courage when I see it, you know what I'm saying? He leans close to me and drops his voice. I would've joined up too, but I got a family; it makes things difficult. But God, I'd love to be doin' what ya'll do, I imagine, goin' after those terrorists! I saw a report on PBS, and it was sweet, Marcus, sweet. All that action!

He pulls out a couple of giant hampers from the freezer and a carton of booze and motions to one of the busboys.

Careful with those, he says. There's ice at the bottom to keep 'em cool for the ride.

I eye the hampers in astonishment. Lord, Donnie, what's in them?

He puts on his reading glasses and scans a piece of paper.

Let me see now: you got red beans and rice, meatballs in tomato sauce, crawfish fettuccine, ersters, our special hot sausages, wings, and po-boys for lunch; Cajun spiced redfish for grilling in the evenings, fresh-picked mirlitons to have with shrimp butter sauce, crawfish and mynez, alligator pears, strawberries, and boursin cheesecake. For the booze you got champagne, wine, port for you, I imagine, beer, Scotch, bourbon . . . jeez, the gal's thought of everything . . .

He glances at me with a wicked grin.

I burst out laughing. We walk out to the car together.

You coming this weekend or what? he asks. We got hot bands playing.

Who you got?

The best, as always. On Thursday, there's Atlanta Al leading the blues jam, on Friday we got Dexter Lee and the Prophets, and on Saturday there's Muddy Creek playing all the way through midnight.

Probably Saturday, then, I think—it's up to Camille.

You lucky man! You got the greatest gal and the greatest job in the world. You're a lucky son of a gun, if you'll pardon the allusion.

He thumps me on the back as I slide into the car.

See ya'll on the weekend, maybe . . . ?

Maybe . . . I wave at him as I pull out.

I've one more errand to run before I cross the river. I drive a few blocks along Government Street past my old high school and then swing around the corner, on Jefferson. I pull up in front of a record store with wide glass windows papered with posters of concerts and bands, and park behind a battered brown van that has "Rawlings, Sons & Daughter" stenciled on one side and "We Buy Used CDs and Records" on the other. The sign above the store reads: "The Old Man and the CD." I pause before the storefront and look inside. Behind the counter there's a broad-shouldered bald white man in a Harley-Davidson T-shirt and a bright red bandana. I'm already smiling as I open the door, and I stand there for a moment, letting my eyes adjust to the neon-lit interior. Then I say: Sergeant Rawlings, where y'at?

He looks up from the magazine he's reading and hollers so loudly that all the customers turn around.

First Sergeant Marcus fuckin' Whalen! he shouts. Well, shoot me down and stand me up against the wall!

He maneuvers himself adroitly on a pair of crutches down the narrow aisles packed with CDs and records. I meet him halfway. He's grinning from ear to ear. He says: C'mere, ya great big Tahyo, gimme a hug! Wassup wit'cha? You lookin' good, bro. You finally lost some o' that baby fat.

I aim a playful punch at him before looking around the place and taking in the changes. I see you expanded, you knocked down the back wall and all . . . And what's with the fancy new name? What was wrong with "The CD Store"? Plain and simple, just the way I liked it. Since when did you become the Old Man?

He scrunches up his face in embarrassment. Marketing gimmick, bro, he says wryly. It was my daughter's idea. I'm introducing my kids to the bizness, see?—and they got new ways of doin' things.

I gesture dismissively at the nearest CD rack: Like selling gangsta rap and trash like that? You used to be a blues purist, Gene.

You got to run with the pack, bro. Sales were way down, and kids don't listen to the deep blues anymore. Fact is, you and me are prob'ly the only ones left from our generation . . .

Speak for yourself, soldier! You might be getting long in the tooth but I'm only thirty-seven, so don't you go callin' me old.

But seriously, who else d'you know these days that's our age and into old Bluesmen? I got mouths to feed, Marcus. Trash sells.

All right, all right, no need to get your back up.

And I haven't sold out entirely, he adds defensively. I'm helpin' out with the Blues Festival this year.

Oh yes? When's it gonna be?—April again?

Sure thing. That's when you should have taken your leave, bro. You're gonna be missing out. You remember that trip we took up to Oxford to Proud Larry's?

I sure do, bro. There was so much cigarette smoke in that joint, the music tasted of it.

And the hogs too. Hogs and whiskey, guitars and catfish, and the music growin' out from deep under that Marshall County mud. That's the meanest blues there is, bro. Hip-hop's got nothing on it.

Now you're talking, I reply, regarding him affectionately. So how you been in gen'ral? How's the family?

I'm awrite, everyone's awrite. Millie's good, Crissie and Travis are helping me out with the store, Gene got a job . . .

Gene Junior? I thought he was still in school . . .

He's finished up, bro. Time passes. Yessir, he's almost as tall as you now. He passed his GED, and now he's working as an oil rigger out in the gulf. I told him, don't you go getting into trouble now: that there's risky work. But he got all cocky on me—you know how kids are these days—and he says, they got foolproof systems, Pops, foolproof. World class tek-no-logy is what they're about. That's the way he said it: tek-no-logy. So he's earning good money now.

He clasps my arm. I miss ya'll! What are the boys up to? Cleaning up the Tally-ban? Connolly still got a chip on his shoulder about Frobenius? And what about Brandon Espinosa? Where's he at?

The questions come a mile a minute, and I have to ask him to slow down. Connolly's fine, I tell him. And the rest of the boys are doing good.

Does the lieutenant still do Tai Chi in the mornings?

I smile, remembering. He sure does, I reply.

We got the A-team, bro! he says with genuine pride in his voice. I love ya'll. I follow the news every day, and not a day passes when I don't say: damn, I shoulda been there! So I tell all the kids that come in here: you want meaning in life, you want a fucking sense of purpose, you better sign up.

I don't know if it's that simple, Gene. I glance meaningfully at his amputated leg, but he's not paying attention. So I ask: But tell me— how's Joe holdin' up?

His face falls. I guess ya ain't heard. He gone, bro.

Joe Woods? What you talkin' about?

You know how he wanted to buy a shrimp boat after his discharge an' all? He kept goin' on and on about it and makin' all these plans, and all the while he was hitting the jiggalate big-time, naw mean? Anyways, we had conversations. I had him by for dinner a couple of times. Millie was complainin' about it—you know how he got no table manners at all—but I stood my ground and said: He's coming by my house and that's that, 'cuz I don't care 'bout his fuckin' manners, he's my brother! Then I heard he was flippin' tacos at some fast food joint for five-fifty an hour, and I made up my mind to go talk to him again. The next thing I know, I'm reading in the papers: Specialist Joseph Woods, a veteran of Operation Desert Storm, shot himself in the head following a struggle with depression.

It takes me a while to absorb this news. "Happy" Woods was the last person I'd have thought a likely candidate for suicide.

Mechanically, I say: He was a good man.

Damn right, bro. You recall how he got us all laughin' when we was pinned down behind them berms near Bag-dad? Or the time he smuggled that chicken into Folsom's tent? Always cool in a crisis, always got a smile on his face and a new joke coming up. But he changed when he got back; he changed big-time. And that was what I had in mind to tell him. I was gonna tell him to reenlist. I was gonna say: Happy, for guys like you, the army's the best damn life a man can have. You get to see the world, you get respect, you get a reg'lar paycheck. You can even afford a swimming pool in the yard like First Sarn't Whalen's folks. But before I could get to him, he bailed out. The Armed Forces was his home, with the brothers standing shoulder to shoulder; but out here he went back to being homeless, naw mean? He had no one standing by him when the crunch came. And I guess, in the end, he just gave up. Steep slope down—with no traction to check the fall.

He bangs the top of the counter in frustration. It kills me, Marcus! We serve for love of the country, we serve so our brothers don't have to go, we serve so them rich kids don't have to go, but when we get back home . . .

He looks straight ahead, the lines of his mouth pulling down.

Anyways, don't get me started. Millie says I'm becoming a boring old man. All I can say is, Happy musta been really down and out to find suicide an attractive proposition. VA failed him big-time, man. Anyone who volunteers to put his life on the line deserves to be treated better. It's a question of respect, naw mean? Once you've fought and bled with your fellow soldiers, it's something you can't explain to someone who ain't been there. They simply don't understand.

He rolls up his sleeve, balancing precariously on his crutches as he does. On his right arm, he's got a new tattoo that reads: **ONCE A SOLDIER, ALWAYS A SOLDIER**.

Just then, a customer, a young white rasta with dreadlocks, who's probably decided he's heard more than enough of our conversation, storms out of the store, but not before giving us a dirty look.

I glance at Gene apologetically. I think I just lost you a customer.

He shrugs. Who, him? He's soft, bro. He's nothing like you and me.

He gives me a wry smile. You gotta be hard to love the blues.

Speaking of the blues, what you got for me this time?

Good stuff, bro, he says, good stuff. He moves swiftly on his crutches to a low shelf behind the counter. I bin savin' up for you. Take a look at these babies. Rarities, all of 'em. Cost me a fortune, but what the hell: I'm in it for the chase as much as for the bucks.

He reaches down and brings out a stack of CDs and a couple of fragile old shellacs. Look at what I got. This right here is the beating heart of the U.S. o' A.

With the air of a conjurer, he hands me the CDs one at a time:

Here's Lightnin' Hopkins, and Furry Lewis, and Blind Lemon Jefferson, and your favorite, old Mississippi John Hurt, then Johnnie Lee Hooker playin' Henry's Swing Club, Sleepy John Estes, Big Joe Williams, Honeyboy Edwards, Son House, Charley Patton.

I sift through his catch reverently.

These are the real deal, bro, he says. Legally intoxicatin'. He taps the Sleepy John CD. Now there's a rarity. He's a physician, naw mean? He use the blues fer healing . . .

They're all rarities, Gene, I point out. I mean, you got me John Lee Hooker at Henry's Swing Club! How many people got that? You done good, bro. You're the ultimate. Now what about those shellacs?

He chuckles. I tell you, Marcus, the first time I laid my eyes on them, I got a lowdown shakin' chill runnin' up and down my back.

I examine the records and whistle softly. One's a 1930s Paramount pressing of Blind Lemon Jefferson singing "Black Horse Blues." The other's even older: first and second takes of King Solomon Hill's "Down on My Bended Knee."

I place them on the counter with care.

Hot damn, I say quietly. I don't know what to say.

Then my watch catches my eye, and I point to it regretfully. I gotta go, Gene. What do I owe you for these?

Lemme check your account from the last time.

He wets his thumb and pages through a fat ledger.

Then: Seems like I owe you ninety-three cents.

I shake my head and say: That can't be right . . .

He's already counting out the change. That's what it says here, bro.

Fine, if that's the way you want it, but what about these babies here?

They're yours for free. Courtesy of the house.

Excuse me?

Take 'em or leave 'em, Marcus; it's up to you.

He puts the CDs and shellacs in a cardboard box.

I'm short of time right now, I tell him, but I'm gonna be back to pay for what I owe you, and you'd better be reasonable. 'Cuz I'm not acceptin' any freebies.

Where you scurrying off in such a rush?

Where d'you think?

He smiles. Going by the Atchafalaya, huh? How's the houseboat holdin' up?

I say: I guess I'll find out soon enough. I haven't seen it since Camille repainted it, so I'm looking forward.

He grunts in approval. These Acadian gals! They work hard and they play hard. You got lucky, bro. She's a charmer. Don't mess this one up.

He comes with me to the car. You still driving Gracie?

I sure am. She's a part of me.

He insists on closing the door after I get in. Tell Camille I said hello, he says. Millie keeps askin' after her. I'll tell her you stopped by. She prays for ya'll every Sunday in church.

As I put on my Ray-Bans, he says, a trifle wistfully: If I don't get to see you again, say hello to the boys for me.

I sure will, I say with a smile as I swing away from the curb.

On the way to the bridge, I pass under a giant guitar-shaped billboard that reads: "Buddy Guy, Son of Baton Rouge, Home of Delta Blues." I pull up at a traffic light behind a blue Honda Civic hatchback with stickers plastered all over the back. As I wait for the light to change, my eyes run over their slogans: WICCAN WITH ATTITUDE; **War Is NOT the Answer**; **The Saints Kick Ass**; KEEP THE PLANET GREEN; *WHY IS OUR OIL UNDER THEIR SAND?* Proud Mother of an Autistic Child; BE VEGAN, SPARE ANIMALS; **Back Off, I'm a Goddess**; SAVE THE BAYOU; **NO BLOOD FOR OIL**; Tree Hugging Dirt Worshipper; and finally, **Support Our Troops; Bring Them Home!**

On the bridge over the Mississippi, a white pickup truck with a gun rack in the rear window and a Confederate flag over Alabama license plates changes lanes without warning and cuts me off. For an instant, I envisage putting the driver's head in a lock and snapping his neck off his spine. Then I take a deep breath, turn on the radio, and lean back in the soft leather seat. Soon, a distinctively ebullient voice cuts through the traffic noise on I-10. It's Baton Rouge's cult radio DJ, its designated Ambassador of the Blues, Zia Tammami, who was born in Iraq but has been playing blues and jazz programs on local stations for more than thirty years. In fact, it was Zia's legendary show *Spontaneous Combustion* that first hooked me onto the blues when I was a lonely teenager wanting to break away from the hip-hop pack. From there, I followed him to his Sunday morning show, which lasted four hours, and always included an hour-long blues segment, "Cool Cat's Corner." Listening to him now makes me feel like I'm home again in more senses than one. I turn up the volume with a smile as I switch to the fast lane and hum along to Blind Lemon singing "See that My Grave's Kept Clean."

Forty minutes later, I'm pulling off the blacktop onto a mean little dirt road with brush overgrowing its sides. I turn off the ignition and simply sit there for a few minutes, getting the noise and confusion of the city out of my head. It's hot and steamy in the shade. I'm close enough to the bayou to be able to sense Camille's presence. I start the car and drive slowly along the familiar winding road toward the water's edge, about a mile upstream from Camille's houseboat. When I'm halfway there, I have to slow down to a standstill to give an old Cajun returning from his morning's frogging some room to squeeze around the car. He stares suspiciously at the black man in the fancy car, but then, for some reason, he lets down his guard.

Ya bettuh watch aht, he says. Deah's a gran' beedey gapuh lyin' up da road 'baht fiffy feet oh deahabahts rahnd da next ben'. He a mean ole crittuh: lashed aht at me an' woulda gaht me good if Ah hadn't scahmpuhd aht o' da way. Ya toot dat hoahn an' he'll scoot, 'cuz he a capon, naw mean?

I don't see the cottonmouth he warned me about, but I do come across a couple of piggies—harmless hognose snakes—sunning themselves in the middle of the road. They slither into the undergrowth as the car nears.

I park under a giant swamp willow, its trunk and swooning branches dressed in Spanish moss. There's not much Spanish moss left in Baton Rouge or the surrounding areas owing to a plague that hit the region years ago, and I wonder how long it's going to be before it wipes out what's left in the swamps. I run my hands over the damp, soft strands and reflect on how different it is here from where I've been the rest of the year, on a different continent on the other side of the world. Overcome by a sudden sense of dislocation, I unload the car slowly, slide the tarp over it, and make my way with the hampers to the water's edge. Once there, I aim a couple of sticks at the canoe, and a bunch of frogs and a snoozing piggy evacuate in haste. Inside, in a characteristic combination of the romantic and the practical, I find that Camille has tucked a can of bug spray beneath a giant bouquet of magnolias, along with a card that says: "I Can't Wait!" It makes me smile and helps me return to the present. I take my time carrying the hampers into the boat, along with the booze and the CDs. The shellacs I've left behind in the Chevelle.

Untying the canoe, I steer it into the stream. The muck lining the banks is pure Atchafalaya swamp, the consistency of chocolate pudding, neither water nor land. Tupelos hug the banks and march right into the stream while nearly horizontal willows brush the face of the water with low-lying branches. Rafts of water hyacinths surround me, along with duckweed that grows sparser as I move into deeper water. An egret takes off as I glide past and alights on the shaggy crown of an immense bald cypress; elsewhere, a great blue heron eyes me warily from the shadows. Everywhere I look, the vegetation is lush and green. I find the heady scent of the place impossible to define: it fills my lungs. Once more I realize how much I love this place, this wild and secret corner of the world that I was introduced to by my girl.

Just before I reach the bend round which I'll catch my first sight of the houseboat, I hear Camille playing her twelve-string guitar. I rest my oar and sit there with my head bowed, listening to the long notes thrumming over the water. It's the sweetest sound I've ever heard, and it fills my soul. The war falls away, and all the fighting and the dying seem very far off. I hold on to the moments for as long as I can. Eventually, the music stops, but I continue to sit there, lost in its spell. Nothing stirs, and no one seems to want to be the first to break the silence. In all of my years with the company, I've never seen the men remain so still and for such a long period of time. Long moments pass before they begin to drift away one by one without a sound, until I finally look up and realize that I'm the only one left. The bright band of the Milky Way is like a luminous river across the sky. The night is cold and crystalline, and there's a frigid wind blowing down from the mountains. I shiver and pull farther inside the sweater that Aunt Thelma knitted for me. Gazing across the barren moonscape of the plain, which is completely featureless except for the cart, I wonder, as I have innumerable times tonight, about its occupant. Personally, I'm convinced it's a woman beneath the burqa, but who knows, maybe I'm mistaken. This haunted land is so completely different from where I'm from that, even after multiple tours of duty, I'm still not clear about who these people are and what they really want.

I cast another look at the cart before jumping down from the Hesco wall. Except for the keening wind, it's so quiet that I almost feel I'm alone in the world. I look around and glimpse the sentries standing at regular intervals along the Hescos. It's time to make a circuit of the perimeter. I adjust the Velcro straps on my body armor and set off.

Pratt and Barela are the first on my round. They're manning the mortar pit and periodically scanning the slopes with night vision binoculars. Pratt hears me approaching and turns toward me so I see the muted green glow of his night vision goggles. The wind picks up, and the temperature, already bone-chilling, plummets.

'Lo, First Sarn't, Barela says, while Pratt, as usual, says nothing. They return to scanning the field and the smudged backdrop of the mountains.

You boys are awfully quiet tonight, I remark. Everything okay?

Barela clears his throat. That music's still in my head, First Sarn't. It was pretty damn intense. It seemed to be coming out of the earth and the air all at once. Do you know what she was playing?

It was some kinda guitar, I answer. Then I give a low laugh. Earlier on today, Sergeant Bradford mistook it for a sawn-off machine gun.

Pratt shivers suddenly and rubs his hands together. Be nice to build a fire, he remarks.

You'd be a sitting duck for every insurgent for miles around, I reply.

I know, First Sarn't, he says. Jus' fantasizin' . . .

Keep lookin' at those stars, bro, Barela says, and they'll keep you warm. You don't see that back in L.A.

Stars! Pratt scoffs. Where I'm from, they a dime a doz'n. You can pick 'em up at the local convenience store.

Barela grins. That's right. I forget you're from fuckin' Alaska, you big bear.

I turn to go, but Barela stops me. First Sarn't, he says, I got a question.

What is it?

D'you think Playboy Bunnies would look better clothed than naked?

I smile, and Pratt chuckles. I bet them Musselmans be thrilled, he says.

Very funny, ya'll, I remark, I can see where your minds are at. Just keep your focus on the job or you'll soon be sayin' hello to those seventy-two heavenly virgins.

I can't wait, Barela says. I can hardly wait.

'Cept you're prob'ly goin' to hell, Pratt quips.

Not on your life, boyo. I can already see me flying aroun' your fuckin' head playing the harp.

My next stop is with the men manning the ECP. I make out Duggal and Lee, with Jackson asleep in the dugout. All is in order, with two men on watch and one at rest who'll take over later. Neatly lined up on the sandbag barrier in front of them are laser range finders, rifles with night vision scopes, and night observation devices.

Duggal sees me and walks over. 'Lo, First Sarn't, he says. What did you think of her playing? That was good stuff, wasn't it? It sure made it hard to concentrate on the job. It reminded me of the kinda music folks play in the old country.

In California?

He hesitates, and then smiles. Nope, Punjab.

Do you know what she was playing?

I asked Masood, and he told me it's a twelve-stringed instrument, like a lute. You pluck it and it makes that sound we heard tonight . . . like raindrops on water.

Twelve strings, huh? Figures.

First Sarn't . . . ?

Don't mind me. I'm just talkin' to myself. D'you know if it has a name?

Masood called it the rubab.

Rub-ab . . . I try out the word in my mouth. Thanks, I'll try to remember that.

I pick up one of the night vision binoculars and study the cart. I can't see much, and after a while, I put it down again. So how're you getting along with Masood? Things working out?

He glances at me awkwardly and fidgets with his gun.

It's complicated, First Sarn't, he replies. Can you spare a moment to talk about it?

Sure thing. What up?

It's like this, he says in an undertone, and I'd like to keep my voice low 'cos I don't want to wake up Ash. First Sarn't, you need to have a word with Masood. I mean, it's barely been a day since he moved into our hooch, but he's already driving us nuts with his questions about our mission. And he won't listen to us—he just won't accept our answers. We keep telling him: Dude, we didn't sign up to save your country. Most of us signed up to get a regular paycheck and avoid working at the local supermart for the rest of our lives. We're grunts. We're just average Joes doing our jobs. We don't get to make those decisions. Even Cap'n Connolly doesn't get to make those decisions. The president makes those decisions; him, and the generals. We follow their orders and do what they tell us to do. If they ordered us to ship out to Eye-ran tomorrow, we'd go. The trouble is, he just doesn't get it and goes on and on. He keeps saying: Yes, but you're Americans! You went to the moon! You can do anything! If it carries on for much longer, First Sarn't, one of us is going to fucking snap and do something stupid.

He looks at me, and his pleading expression suddenly makes me angry at the interpreter and, by extension, the whole damn mission. Controlling myself, I reach out and pat him on the shoulder. In a calm, firm voice, I say: I'm glad you told me, Mitt. I'll see what I can do. First off, I'll have a talk with Masood. Maybe it would help if I moved him out of your hooch. I know Darren Simonis has some space in his hut. Let me think about it.

His gratitude is palpable; his face lights up immediately.

Thanks a million, First Sarn't. I really appreciate it.

You're welcome, soldier. Anything else?

Nope, First Sarn't. That's it.

All right, I'll let you know how it goes.

As I walk away, I look up at the sky. High above, intersecting the Milky Way, there's a thin gray trail left by a jet's afterburner. The plane seems strangely out of place. Then a leaf blows past my face and rolls along the ground. I lean over and pick it up: it smells of the mountains. I suddenly feel strange as I look out at the field. Instead of solid ground there's a sheet of water between the Hescos and the mountains. I glimpse black reeds, marsh grass, swollen cypress trunks. The wind stirs up ripples. I feel a knife turning inside me and nearly gasp out loud. The air shades to gray. There's a ringing in my ears. I close my eyes and open them again, but there's no change: I can still see water lapping against the Hescos, and the wires are almost completely under. I survey the sky where the jet's trail has thickened and blurred. I slap myself hard on the cheeks before looking down again. The water begins to fade; it glides here and there, shrinking into puddles, seeping into the ground. It shimmers as I drink in the scents of sweet, damp earth.

Then it's gone.

From the darkness behind me, I hear Barela call out: You okay, First Sarn't?

I'm fine, I reply.

I shiver with cold. I let go of the leaf and watch it flutter to the ground.

I need some coffee. The fatigue's weighing me down. I realize I haven't had dinner, and my body would probably be better served if I fed myself. I turn away from the Hescos and make a detour to the mess tent. A strong gust of wind buffets the tent as I duck inside. I grab a cold MRE and tear open the pack, pouring water into the lining to let the chemicals heat the food. When it's warm, I choke it down while trying not to compare it with my meals in the houseboat with Camille. I reach into my shirt to touch the tiny pendant she's given me that I wear on a string around my neck. It's a silver charm from Morocco in the shape of a filigreed Hand of Fatima. She found it in a flea market in New Orleans and knew the moment she set her eyes on it, she had to have it for me. I rest my hand on it for a moment before tucking it back in.

I wash the MRE's taste out of my mouth with my own extreme makeover of Baton Rouge Gris-Gris brew: three packets of instant coffee dissolved in a one-liter mug of steaming water, combined with three creamers, a packet of carob powder, and one crushed No-Doz tablet. I grimace as I swallow half the mug's contents, but the result is an almost instant hyperclarity. I lid the mug and take it with me with the idea of nursing what's left through the rest of my watch. It's a comforting nightly ritual, with the added advantage of giving me the energy that I need to do my job on little to no sleep.

I'm about to step out of the tent when I hear a rustle from behind it and instantly switch to combat mode. Soundlessly placing the coffee mug on top of a carton, I ease out my 9 mm and creep all hunched-up around the corner of the tent. In a narrow space between two stacked pallets of plastic water bottle containers, there's a soldier sitting on the ground with his head held down and his hands around his knees. He raises his face as I lower my gun, and I recognize Garcia from First Squad, his face streaked with tears. He clears his throat and hurriedly wipes his hand across his face.

We stare at each other, each at a bit of a loss.

I'm the first to react. What's going on, Rick? I ask. Ya'll okay?

I'm sorry, First Sarn't . . . I just needed some private time, and I can't get that in our hooch.

He clears his throat again as I kneel beside him.

D'you want to talk?

He gives a strangled sob and begins to weep again while attempting to speak—soft, bitter, choking sounds that make it impossible for me to understand what he's saying.

I place my hand on his shoulder, and that seems to steady him.

Take your time, son, there's no rush.

I'm so sorry, First Sarn't, you must think I'm totally FUBAR . . .

I don't think any such thing. Just tell me what's going on, and let's find out if we can fix it.

I dunno if it can be fixed, First Sarn't—not from here, at least.

This last remark takes on a familiar ring for me. I've heard it from other men before, and it usually means one thing. Making my voice sympathetic, I ask: Woman trouble, huh?

He nods. Well, yes and no. What I mean to say is that that's just part of it.

Gimme the whole picture then.

He hesitates for a moment, and then his shoulders slope down.

My life's fallin' apart, First Sarn't. I've lost my house. Stace—Stacey, my wife—couldn't keep up with the bills. It happened a while ago, but she kept it from me, so I didn't know what was going on. I on'y just found out. She's left our house and moved in with another man . . . and now she wants a divorce. So I'm screwed. My life is over, and there's nothin' I can do about it 'cos I didn't even know until now. She didn't even give me a chance to make things right—just said she was no longer interested in a guy who's never around, and that she has her own needs and they weren't being met.

Any kids?

No, thank God!

Well, that's one thing in your favor. Now: d'you think you could persuade her to agree to a temporary divorce for a year until you can get back and sort things out?

I dunno, First Sarn't. Prob'ly not. Her mind's set on this new guy, and she wants a clean break from me. That's what's fuckin' me up even more: not just knowing that she's goin' down on another man, but that she screwed me over doing it. I mean, what would it have taken for her to at least keep up with the mortgage payments? It wasn't like I wasn't sendin' her the money. Hell, I live like a pig and send her everything!

So where did the money go, d'you think?

He hesitates, and then says reluctantly: Prob'ly on pills, First Sarn't.

Pills? Does she have a history of substance abuse?

She did, before I met her. She was a fucking Rx queen—but she cleaned up when we were together. I made her promise. And I trusted her because I was crazy about her. I guess that was my mistake. All I know is that from the moment I deployed, she went from being Staceydarling to Staceydracula double quick, and the pills are prob'ly where all the money went.

So what are you going to do now?

He strikes his forehead hard with the flat of his hand.

I don't have a fuckin' clue, First Sarn't. It's like I'm cursed . . . He buries his head abruptly in his hands. The problem is, I'm still crazy about her!

Recognizing the signs, I decide to concentrate on practical details to bring him out of his funk. I ask him if he has talked to anyone else about his situation.

Oh, the guys from the squad know about the house, but I haven't been able to tell 'em about Stacey. It's too damn humiliating.

There's nothing humiliating about it, Rick—lots of people go through what you're dealing with.

I don't think so, First Sarn't, he says, shaking his head. I don't mean to disagree with you, but the fact of the matter is that I'm royally screwed. First off, I know I can't go back, so I can't show up for the hearings. Second, I've no money in the bank 'cos she took it all, so I can't afford an attorney. Third, even if I had the money, I can't go lookin' for a lawyer without actually bein' there. And from what I've heard, family court's fuckin' insane. So I'm screwed every way you look at it. If your spouse files for divorce and you're on active duty, you're a dead man walking.

That's where you're wrong, I tell him.

He looks at me, a little taken aback, while I continue: We got your back, brother—everyone at the base. There's a bunch of people here who'll understand what you're going through, 'cuz a lot of us have been in your shoes. You'll be all right, and we'll figure out a way to make sure you don't get screwed. You want to talk to someone else just to clear your mind? How about the chaplain, or the combat stress folks?

Oh, I don't know, First Sarn't.

I pat him on the shoulder, and he relaxes for the first time and smiles halfheartedly. That opens up the space for me to enter and persuade him to take the next step, which would be to seek counseling. He listens to me patiently, but then he counters: I hear you, First Sarn't, except that we've been trained to be strong, like we're war machines or something. Then, when shit like this happens and we're supposed to switch gears straightaway to counseling, it becomes a mind game, and that wigs me out. I don't want to be seen as weak. What's going to be left of me—the real me, whoever that is—at the end of it? I mean, I'm lookin' at ending up one hell of a mindfucked individual.

Instead of answering, I pull out a cigarette and light up. It warms me instantly. I lean back against the pallet and watch the trail of cigarette smoke dissolve into the air. Then I say: Do you think I'm mindfucked, son?

His eyes grow wide. *You,* First Sarn't? 'Course not! You're the steadiest individual I know. You're like a rock.

I take another drag on my cigarette.

D'you smoke, Rick?

No, First Sarn't. Never have, actually. Couldn't afford the habit.

I take in his face: there's something pure and severe about his features.

In a casual tone, I say: Does that mean you would think that I'm not the sort of person who's been to counseling?

He seems to choke on this idea, then breaks out coughing. It takes him a while to stop.

At length, he manages to say: *You've* been to counseling?

Sure I have. Many times, as a matter of fact, over two different periods in my life, 'cuz that's as many divorces as I've been through during my years in the service.

No shit. Get outta here!

It's the truth, soldier.

He seems to have lost his voice, because he simply stares at me. So I rise to my feet and put out my hand to help him get up. I can see that he wasn't expecting this abrupt termination of our conversation, but I'm already brushing the dirt off my camos. He remains quite still, and I can literally hear the wheels turning in his head. Finally, I straighten up.

I take a step toward him and stand him up very straight.

There are no easy solutions to your problems, Rick. If you need help, step up to the plate and get it. Reach out to your friends, and come and talk to me some more first thing in the morning. Maybe we'll set up sessions for you with a counselor at Battalion; they'll have ideas to help you out. How does that sound?

I can't thank you enough, First Sarn't . . .

Don't thank me, soldier. Get a handle on your problems so that you can be there for someone else when he needs your help. That's only fair, wouldn't you agree?

Yes, First Sarn't, for sure.

Band of brothers, right?

He nods fervently.

Good. Now go and get yourself some rest. It's amazing what a sound night's sleep can do for the body and the mind. And don't forget to report to me in the morning. Tomorrow's gonna be a brand new day in your life.

Thank you again, First Sarn't.

He puts on his ACH, and I watch as he moves off in the direction of his hooch. His shoulders still droop a little, but I'm hoping his youth will help him bounce back. As for the Suzy Rottencrotches of the world, to hell with them. They're not worth a fraction of the quietly serving men they choose to betray and abandon.

And on that rather bitter note, I pick up my mug of Gris-Gris brew and resume my nightly round. I return to the Hescos and proceed to complete my circuit of the perimeter. I take it slow, stopping at each position to chat with the men. Eventually I circle back to the ECP manned by Duggal and Lee, except that Jackson has replaced Duggal, who's now asleep in the dugout.

Howdy, First Sarn't, Jackson says in greeting, while Lee looks up from his scope and shivers: It's frickin' cold. Makes me wish I was back in my hooch.

I smile and pick up the sleeping Duggal's night observation device and scan the field outside. What had appeared to the naked eye as a pale, almost featureless plain, now reveals itself as a neon-green expanse, with the cart an isolated black smudge in the middle. I put down the NOD and gaze once more at the field in the steely light of the stars. It almost looks like it's covered with snow.

Jackson sighs audibly. There's somethin' about this place at night that creeps me out, he remarks. He nods at the cart. I don't know how she can bear to be there all by herself, with the mountains loomin' over her like that. I know I couldn't do it.

According to Masood, they're called the Red Mountains, Lee remarks.

Masood says the Pashtuns are downright crazy, Jackson adds.

Masood! Lee says, and snorts, but before he can carry on, I interrupt him with an observation of my own: The mountains' name's sorta interesting to me, given that I'm from Baton Rouge, which means Red Stick.

No kidding! Lee says, and grins suddenly. And I was born in Marrakesh, in Morocco, which is also known as Red City.

Jackson's response to this rather surprising news is characteristically pugnacious: I thought you were fuckin' Korean, dude.

I'm American, fuckface, Lee counters with dignity.

Well, all right, American. So what were you doing in fuckin' Arabia?

Arabia? Where the fuck did you get that? Morocco is in North Africa, dickhead.

Fine, Africa, then. What were you doin' in Africa?

I wasn't doing anything, moron. Haven't you been listening to me? I was born there. I didn't have anything to do with it.

But Jackson isn't one to give up easily. What were your parents doin' in Africa then? I mean, he chuckles, besides fuckin'.

You better watch your mouth, shithead, Lee threatens.

Well . . . ? Jackson demands, determined to get to the bottom of the mystery. What were they doing?

They were just travelin' around, dude. They were kinda into the whole alternate living scene, smokin' pot and seein' the world—and the pot in Marrakesh is supposed to be pretty intense.

Korean hippies? Jackson exclaims, clearly incredulous.

Dude, you really need to check your attitude, Lee says resentfully. I mean, talk about making broad generalizations.

Whatever, Jackson says, and then giggles: So what happened? They were smokin' pot, and you just happened to pop out like a genie?

Fuck you! Lee retorts, while at the same time glancing at me: Beggin' your pardon, First Sarn't.

Turning to Jackson again, he says: I was born a month premature, okay? Right in the middle of a real famous square in Marrakesh called the Jemaa el Fna. You can look it up on a fucking map, if you like, to find out where that is. Jeez, and you thought it was in Arabia! You need some education, dude.

Fuckin' famous square, Jackson scoffs.

At least I was born someplace diff'rent, Lee replies with a mocking smile. I mean, you never even left Embarrass, Minnesota, until you joined the army. If you were to compare the two places on a CDI scale, mine would rate, like, ten outta ten, while yours probably wouldn't even make it past zero.

Utterly vanquished by this low blow, Jackson retreats into silence.

What's a CDI scale? I ask.

Chicks Dig It, First Sarn't, Lee says, while Jackson maintains a sullen silence.

Sensing victory, Lee closes in for the kill. Jackson wouldn't understand, First Sarn't, seeing that he's never known what it's like to be cool.

Jackson stands up and stretches.

Glancing at the short, squat Lee, he yawns rather deliberately. Then: Who the fuck cares, Justin? I mean, just how many chicks have you done it with? And even if you've scored way more babes than I think you have, what does it matter in the end anyway? Maybe a high CDI score will help you land a chick, but does that mean the sex is better because of it? And if one day that chick graduates to become your wife or girlfriend and all of a sudden starts dressin' up like Buffy the Vampire Slayer and flies onto your fuckin' slackerjohnny after swinging in on a trapeze, it's still her. So much for your fuckin' CDI scale.

Slackerjohnny? Lee growls. What the fuck is that?

It's your limp lil' cock, dickhead, Jackson says, before nodding at me: 'Scuse us, First Sarn't.

I don't think I've heard that one before, I comment.

I made it up, he says with a quiet pride. On the fly, like.

He turns his attention to Lee again. Just shows where your

education's at. When it comes down to the important things in life, you know squat. I may not be educated and all, but at least ignorance is skin deep, while stupid goes to the bone.

Don't even go there, Jackson, Lee says. You're such a bonehead that if First Sarn't here were to put a price on air, I'd take away all your money.

I'd rather have sex than money, dude, Jackson replies languidly. Not that you'd know the difference.

You got a girl back home, Jackson? I ask.

He gets all flustered.

In a softer voice, he says: Ah . . . yes, First Sarn't. Her name's Kimberlee. She's an English major, he adds with a touch of awe. She goes to community college an' all. She's aimin' to be a journalist.

English major, Lee mutters. Fuckin' pansy.

Whatever, you retard, Jackson says dismissively. It ain't like you got a patent on intelligence or somethin'.

For some reason, this seems to provoke Lee beyond all limits of tolerance, and he puts down his rifle and rises to his feet as well.

They stand face-to-face, glaring at each other, until I intervene.

That's enough, ya'll, I say sternly. Knock it off.

Given the turn the conversation's taken, I decide it would be wiser not to bring up my own hand-shaped pendant and its Moroccan origins. Instead, I return to scanning the field. There's a fog coming down from the mountains, and it's already screened off the slopes. It rolls toward us in filmy waves. Soon, I can no longer see the cart or anything around it.

Jackson gazes at the advancing wall and picks up his rifle.

This is making me edgy, First Sarn't, he says abruptly. It's kinda like when the sandstorm hit, but different.

It's colder, Lee says, stating the obvious. Then, voicing what's on all our minds, he asks me: Do you think they'll attack us again, First Sarn't?

Before I can reply, Jackson says: I wish they would and just get it over with. This hanging around doin' nothing fucks me up big-time. I'd rather be killin' than chillin', if you know what I mean.

Lee nods. Combat's a fix, man.

'Cept that it ain't a fix for me this time around, Jackson says, his voice suddenly icy. This time it's personal. I can't wait to get back at those bastards for what they did to Spitty. He bends low to spit out a stream of Copenhagen juice. I'm dying to kick some serious ass, First Sarn't. In flames I reside.

I look at them and realize that we're all beginning to react to the same thing: the adrenaline rush that accompanies the anticipation of combat.

Well, I say calmly, our situational awareness is better now than it was before the sandstorm. If they show up tonight, they'll stand out as warm bodies in your thermal sights, fog or no fog. Then ya'll can go to work on them. It'll be like target practice.

It better be, Jackson says tersely. I feel like a fucking venomenon.

I wouldn't want to hit the girl by mistake, though, Lee says. Those tunes she played were sweet.

Tough luck, Jackson says without emotion. She got no business being in a war zone. If she gets hosed, it's collateral damage.

There's a sudden silence; Jackson's voice, without having been raised, seemed unnecessarily cold-blooded. Staring at him, Lee appears to wait for an explanation, but when none is offered, he snaps: You've no appreciation of the finer things in life, Jackson. None at all, nada, zilch. You see that sea of fog rolling through, and all you can think of is a killing field. I see the same thing and think of how it might resemble a dream or something. That's the difference between you and me.

Makes me a better soldier, Jackson says coolly.

Then, with more verve, he dismisses Lee's take on things: Frickin' dream, my ass . . .

But he never gets to finish because Lee suddenly tenses and says: Movement in the field!

I grab the thermal weapons sight and search the fog.

I don't see anything, Jackson whispers. Sure you weren't focusin' on a tumbleweed or something?

'Course not! It was somewhere to our right. One o'clock.

I scan the haze, the suddenly sinister silence roaring in my ears. The cart stands out against the fog as a dark blur. I lean out over the Hesco and do a slow 180 scan. The roaring in my ears subsides, and I can only hear my own feverish breathing. The fog has a damp smell that makes me want to puke.

Jackson says hoarsely: Nothing. There's nothing in the damn field.

He's silent again, and once more I hear only my rapid breathing.

Lee cranes forward and crosses my field of vision. I lower the thermal and see that he is studying the cart. The green glow from his scope illuminates his face. He exhales heavily, and draws back into the darkness.

I don't understand it, he mutters. I could have sworn . . . Wait a minute! What's that?

What are you looking at, Lee?

Two o'clock, First Sarn't . . .

Jackson gives a low laugh. That's a chair, dude. It's standin' on its head. Fuckin' wind musta blown it away from the junk pile.

Fuck, you're right, Lee says. We gotta clean up that pile.

He sounds utterly dejected.

Jackson grunts. Sometimes I think we're in a movie, he says. We know so little about this place, it's unreal. We might as well be the blind men leading each other through the land of the blind. Isn't that how that goes, First Sarn't?

In a manner of speaking, Jackson.

It was in a movie once. A whole city of the blind—cops, politicians, lawyers, doctors, everyone. And each group was blind for its own reasons.

Lee says: You nervous, Jackson?

'Course not. Why?

'Cos you won't stop talking. I'm finding it distracting.

You're an asshole. Do you know that?

You want to go there again? Lee says, surprised.

Jackson falls silent. Then he says: I'm just tired. Anything's better than this waiting around. I'm lookin' for ways to stay awake.

Try thinking for a change, Lee snaps.

Anyway—Jackson says, patting his M-4—havin' this killing machine with me at a time like this certainly gives me a warm an' fuzzy feeling. It's like I'm fucking invincible.

He stands up and flexes his arm exaggeratedly. I'm made of hard rock, my M-4 carbine, and fucking infinity.

You can't be made of fuckin' infinity, dude, Lee counters. It's intangible.

Whatever, Mickey Mouse. Amerika ist wunderbar.

I grin as I caution him: If you've made it this far, you're doing pretty good, Volcano. But don't let it go to your head, because you could very well die the moment you let your guard down.

Lee snickers: No shit. It would be a brutal end to a short and brutal life.

You shut your trap, Mofo, Jackson snaps. You've made it this far 'cos I always got your back. Most people would've been on life support at this point with some other partner.

Most people wouldn't survive with you by their side, dude, Lee says calmly. Which is another way of lookin' at the glass, half empty or half full, is what I'm sayin'. They wouldn't be able to handle your epically epic ego.

It ain't 'bout my ego, fuckwit, it's 'bout my M-4, the most instant cause of death associated with taking me on. Last man who tried it got chopped into two perfectly symmetrical pieces. You saw it happen, so it's a scientific fact.

You got it all wrong, dude. Reason the man exploded was exposure to the deadly Jackson persona. That's why he kept on head banging like he was at a fuckin' Metallica concert after initial contact.

Fine, it's me *and* my M-4. Point is: I must be some kind of god . . .

The words have barely left his lips when Lee curses under his breath: Shit, I see it again! It's a dog . . . he exclaims, peering through his thermals. Fuck, it's probably Shorty!

Not a chance, Jackson says. I know Chuck left him with Cap'n Connolly 'cos he asked for him.

I'm already sighting through my TWS.

Then Lee says: There's more than one! Christ, what are those things?

To my left, I hear Barela exclaim from the mortar pit: Holy fuck! What the hell is goin' on?

I still don't see what they're talking about. All I can see is the damn fog—my high-tech scope filled with fog. Again I search the field, willing the night not to slip out of control.

A groggy Duggal emerges from the dugout. Yo, guys, what's all the commotion? Jerkily, he picks up his rifle.

I straighten up. I've glimpsed eyes gleaming in gray faces. Weaving in and out of the fog are one . . . two . . . three hyenas, with the biggest animal loping up front, followed by two slightly smaller ones on each flank. They're closing in on the cart.

Holy shit, Lee whispers, just look at 'em! They're ugly motherfuckers. Those massive jaws.

D'you want us to holler real loud an' make a racket, First Sarn't? Jackson asks.

Hang on a moment, soldier, let me think. Then I answer: Nope. We've no idea how they'd react. I don't want to provoke them into attacking the woman, and we're too far away to intervene if that happens.

We could gun them down, Duggal suggests.

We can't take that risk either. We might hit her. The fog's made our visuals difficult.

What, then? Jackson says impatiently.

I raise my left hand. Quiet, I whisper.

I make up my mind. Rising to my feet, I say: Hang on a mo, all right?

I run over to the mortar pit. Pratt and Barela look at me expectantly.

Turn on the searchlight and focus on the cart, I order. That'll create a ring of light around her that should scare them off. And if it doesn't, it'll make it easier for us to shoot them.

Pratt complies instantly. A powerful beam of light bathes the cart.

I hope it don't wake the sister up, Barela says.

There's no helping that, I reply.

I look through my thermals and see her stirring inside the cart.

Them critters be leavin', Pratt says, looking through his rifle's scope. That was good thinkin', First Sarn't.

I zoom in to where I last saw the animals. I spot their retreating backs: they're headed in the opposite direction. They glide side by side, their silhouettes overlapping, little spirals of fog coasting in their wake. I keep my thermals focused on them, watching them recede into dots until they disappear.

I feel myself relax and lower the device. Pratt is looking intently at me.

They're gone for now, I announce, but we can't get lazy 'cuz they might be back. Ya'll leave that light on for a bit, and then turn it off.

Couldn't we just leave it on through the night for her, First Sarn't? Pratt asks.

And have some Taliban sniper take it out? Use your head, soldier. I tap his helmet with my knuckles. But keep checking in on her if that makes you feel better. Switch it on periodically in case those critters get it into their heads to pay us a return visit.

Done deal, First Sarn't, Barela says and grins. We'll do the job right. You can depend on us. Fuckin' hyenas!

They remind me of the tundra, Pratt says suddenly. But there we got furies.

Both Barela and I stare at him.

He spreads his hands. It's what we call wolves back where I'm from. I forgot where I was for a moment, he explains with an embarrassed smile. I dunno what came over me.

A moment of madness, Barela says.

No, Pratt replies. He tilts the searchlight and sends it probing through the field and into the lower slopes, and then brings it back to the cart. No, he says again. I ain't gone mad. But I'd like to sometimes. 'Cos I'm not always sure I understand the way things are done.

I look at him with surprise. I don't think I've ever heard him talk as much.

What things? I ask.

Like that girl in the cart, First Sarn't. I'd like to cover that sleepin' girl with a proper blanket an' slide a pillow under her head. It ain't right for her to be there like that. I thought we was here to help these people.

You *have* gone mad, Barela says quickly. He tilts his helmet back a little.

It's jes' my opinion, Pratt says, so I wish you'd stop attachin' madness to it.

You can't say anything about this situation, I observe. Nothing like this has ever happened before. We're still working things out.

We're disrespectin' her, First Sarn't, Pratt says in a low voice. No offense meant, but there are lines that can't be crossed. Even here.

Ramirez had better get here soon, Barela growls. You need some sleep.

So you don't think I have a point? Pratt persists.

Hell, Barela exclaims, I'd do it if that's what First Sarn't thought needed to be done! I'd bring her a blanket and a care package and throw in some TLC free of charge.

I think ya'll had better hunker down and get back to attending to your duties, I say with a smile. I need you to get your game faces on.

They fall silent, and I leave them and return to where Duggal,

Jackson, and Lee are waiting for me. I'm gonna do a quick check of the perimeter, I tell them. And then I'll be back.

Again I walk along the Hescos and then crisscross the base. My footsteps echo in the silence of the fog. I pass the bee huts, the command post, and Connolly's office, then the mess tent and the open lot where the Humvees are parked. I walk rapidly past the ruins of the ANA huts and notice the brown smudges on the whitewashed walls where some of the Afghan troops had rubbed off opium from their fingers. I reach for a cigarette, but find that I'm out. I try to focus, but there's only one thought in my head: the prospect of sleep, of rest, of closing my eyes and waking up at least eight hours later. I come back to myself only when I find I've reached the remains of the watchtower, where I dragged Brandon Espinosa out of the flames—too late to make a difference.

Why's it so dark here? he'd whispered. Then: I'm sorry, so sorry . . . before closing his eyes.

I rest my head against the one remaining beam that rises vertically into the fog. I press myself against it with all my strength until my arms begin to shake and my chest tightens. I feel a scream coming, but choke it back and turn away instead. The fog is so thick, it's like everything is dissolving. I begin to run, blundering over uneven ground. I go fast, past tent ropes and stacked ammo boxes. I try to avoid them but miss a hole and trip. Staggering heavily, I crash into a wall. A small animal, probably a rat, scurries away. I crouch motionless, and the fog encases my head, my chest, my hands. A chill runs through my body. I pick myself up wearily and head over to the ECP. Climbing up on the Hescos, I take up position next to Jackson.

He glances at me and nods to his right. Doc's out there.

I turn my head and glimpse the flicker of a cigarette. Taylor? I call out.

Right here, he replies out of the darkness. I squint my eyes and see him leaning against the Hescos, staring out at the field. I decide to go over and bum a cigarette. He fishes out a pack of American Spirit even before I ask. I pick one out. American Spirit, now that's a real cigarette. Where'd you get these?

Care package, he says.

Lighting up, my head heavy, I ask him what he's looking at.

What do you think? Our WMD out there. What a fucking pile of horseshit we're standing on! It makes me sick.

You gotta hang loose, man, I reply. No point in cutting yourself up. There's nothing you and I can do about that situation. It's out of our hands.

How long have we known each other, First Sarn't?

Too long, I say wearily. Why do you ask?

Because I envy you your ability to take things in your stride.

I wonder if I should tell him about my panic attack from moments ago, but decide against it.

Abruptly, he says: This is my last tour—if I survive, that is. I've decided to quit.

Caught off guard, all I can do is stare at him.

Have you decided what you want to do when you go back? I ask at length.

I'm going to try out for med school. I'll be older than most applicants, but that's what I want to do. I just have to work out the money equation, see if I can handle the debt.

I don't want to rain on your parade, but that's a big *if,* isn't it?

Sure it is, but nothing ventured, nothing gained . . . As his voice trails off, he narrows his eyes at me. So: is that why you keep renewing your tours of duty? Because you don't really believe there's a place in civilian life for vets like us?

His question makes me feel resentful, so I evade it. Instead, I gesture with an outstretched hand toward the darkness of the field. In a tone of mocking sentimentality, I say: What back home could possibly compare to this?

But he's already speaking again: Maybe I'll set up shop in the badlands of Youngstown after I get my degree. Make up for all the killing I've seen.

There's gotta be as much killing there as here, I point out.

He smiles sadly. Still and all, it's my home turf.

You sure 'bout this? I wouldn't want you to be settin' yourself up for a fall.

'Course I'm not sure, he replies. But one thing I do know is that this war's not worth another casualty. That much I *am* sure of.

I watch him as he stands there, hands resting on the Hesco, unmoving and stiff, a slight breeze ruffling his hair. I feel as if I'm seeing a different person than the one I've known all these years.

Congratulations, I murmur. In that case, ya'll got a good plan.

He scrutinizes my face, then returns his gaze to the field.

In a quiet voice, he says: I can't do this anymore. That girl out there is officially my breaking point. I don't want to be part of the SitRep that writes her off as collateral damage.

You're assuming she's innocent, I counter. You're ignoring the fact that it might have to do with their whole religious shtick.

His tone and glance are pointed. No, I'm not assuming her innocence, as a matter of fact, he says. But I do know this much: if she turns out to be a suicide bomber, it won't be because she hates our religion. I mean, I don't even have a fucking religion. It'll be because we whacked her brother and we're in their country. How difficult is that to understand? When you kill people and wipe out their families, strafe their homes and burn down their villages, litter their fields with fragmentation bombs and gun down their livestock, you've lost the whole fucking battle for hearts and minds. I mean, who're we trying to kid? Ourselves? Is it any wonder they're fighting back? We're not winning this war; we're creating lifelong enemies. It's time to admit that our own leadership has ring-fenced us with lies.

I don't reply. I can't altogether say that I hadn't seen this coming.

All the same, I'm left feeling a mixture of understanding and regret. More than anything else, though, his little tirade leaves me feeling even more exhausted than I was before.

No response? he prompts without looking at me.

All I can muster by way of a response is: It sounded like you needed to get that off your chest.

And I'm not done, he says with feeling. I'm tired of playing these boys' games. I'm tired of being surrounded by nineteen- and twenty-year-olds who've been conned into believing they're fighting the good fight. I'm too old to play these games—games with youngsters who lack the maturity to understand the consequences of their actions, for themselves as much as the people they're primed to kill. I'm tired of supplying an endless array of prescription pills to help these kids cope with their fears and their confusion and their guilt. You know what I mean: I'm the fucking gatekeeper to the valley of the dolls, and I can't take it anymore. I've lost my ability to pretend.

He stops all of a sudden and turns toward me.

I don't know about you, he says, but I can't look at myself in the mirror anymore. I've stopped believing—and do you know why? He jabs his cigarette in the direction of the field. *That's* why. Armies don't win wars; people win wars. People feel things like sacrifice, loss, grief. The Pashtuns are in this thing as a people. And that legless girl in her cart is part of that. They know what they're fighting for— they're fighting for their survival, their homes, their beliefs. Okay, fine, those beliefs are fucked up, but what are *we* fighting for? We got kids here whose only option in life is either the army or methland. Sure, we also got the high-tech ordnance and every damn textbook strategy under the sun. It doesn't matter. Their slings and stones are more powerful than our M-203s. Their nation's more powerful than our army.

He drops his cigarette to the ground and stubs it out with his boot.

The moment that girl showed up, I knew it was over for us. If Lieutenant Frobenius's death was the beginning of the end, then she *is* the end. Game, set, and match. I mean, think of all those who started out with us way back in Iraq—Dave Hendricks, Brian Castro, Brandon Espinosa, Bradley Folsom—all gone. And for what? For what? So there it is. I'm done now. I've said my piece.

I put out my cigarette. I feel just so incredibly tired, and somehow the loaded silence that follows Doc's tirade makes it worse. Turning away abruptly from him, I say: Best of luck. I nod a couple of times and climb down from the Hescos. I gotta go, I explain. I can't think of anything else to say. Maybe he was expecting more of a response from me, but he isn't going to get it. I'm simply not up to it—not at this time of the night, at least. And not when I know that my guys are patiently waiting by their guns for me. They might be young, but their exhaustion is as old as time itself. All the same, I'm aware of Doc's eyes boring into me as I walk slowly back to the ECP. The night is clotted with fog.

At 0300 my watch ends, and I head for the NCOs' hut. Dark clouds crouch over the plain; the fog is thicker than ever. Visibility's near zero, and everything's in shades of black and gray. Numb with the cold, I stumble over ground covered with frost. The extremes of heat and cold are beginning to wear me down. Geography isn't my strong point, but I guess the climate must match the altitude and location: landlocked desert thirty-six hundred feet above sea level. I try not to compare it unfavorably with the Atchafalaya and fail miserably, as usual.

I enter the hut and wake my replacement, Tanner, who's sound asleep.

Your watch, Tan. Rise an' shine.

He sits up on his bunk, rubbing his hands together to keep warm while I brief him. It takes him a while to put on his clothes and pack his gear, but after he leaves, I hit the sack and pass out almost instantly.

The alarm rings at 0600, and I rise to the sight of Garcia and Masood waiting outside the hut for their meetings with me. I take Garcia first: he seems much more composed than he was last night, and I tell him that, as a preliminary step, I'll set up a meeting with a counselor at Battalion.

The conversation with Masood is more complicated. Right off the bat I inform him that I've decided to move him in with Spc. Simonis. He looks surprised, and not entirely happy, which is understandable given that he's only just arrived at the base, and I'm already shifting him around. When he asks why he's being moved, I bring up Duggal's complaint, without mentioning any names, and conclude that I've decided it's the best solution all around.

I'll introduce you to Spc. Simonis, I tell him. He's a sniper. A quiet guy, unlike the rowdy fellers you were with. I'll have him walk you around and orient you to how we do things here. I'm sure ya'll will get along fine.

He bites his lip. I have met him, he says, and falls silent.

In that case, you're already ahead of the game, which is good, because it saves me work. I look at him and smile. That's all, unless you've any more questions . . .

He looks disconsolate.

May I have some time to think about this, and then come back and meet with you again? he asks.

Sure thing.

He leaves, and next up is Pratt, which comes as a surprise, given the amount of time I spent with him on the Hescos last night. He stands there with his feet planted characteristically apart, but something about his expression lacks its customary stolidity. I eye him with a vague sense of discomfort myself, not sure what's going on.

Howdy, Specialist. What up?

He thinks for a moment, and says: I dunno if I got any issues, First Sarn't, but there's certain things I'd like to talk about.

Okay, shoot.

What he comes out with transforms what ought to have been a perfectly straightforward meeting into something much more complex.

D'you have any eddication about crows, First Sarn't?

Crows? No. Dogs and cats maybe, but not crows.

He looks to his left, and then to his right, before looking back at me.

A few years back, I was workin' on a farm in Montana, attendin' to sheep, he says. Boy, what can I tell you, First Sarn't. I came to love those animals. I loved their sof'ness an' their kindness, but I hated the carrion crows that made them mis'rable. Each year in lambin' season, the crows would swoop down in great black swarms on the newly borns. They'd peck at 'em an' slash at 'em an' scoop out their eyes— while they was still alive. Crows are bad news. At least vultures wait till you're dead.

He pauses for a moment, gazing at me, while I wait for him to get to the point. I know better than to hurry him. He shifts his weight from one leg to the other and continues to look at me. At length, having received some mysterious signal to resume, he says: So what I'm about to tell happened las' night. After I got done with my shift, which was shortly after you'd left us, I hung aroun' the dugout to keep Barela and Ramirez company. I musta fallen asleep, even tho' I was still standin' on my feet, 'cos the next thing I know I'm havin' this dream.

A dream?

Yup, things that come to you in your sleep.

Go on, Specialist, I say with a guarded calm.

In this dream, see, I was lookin' at birds like I never seen, crows an' suchlike, but bigger, scrawnier. They was attackin' that girl in the cart—an' I knows she was a girl 'cos she had her veil off an' I could see her face an' also that she was cryin' real hard—and the birds kept tryin' to hose her while she kept tryin' to bury her brother. She'd dug a hole in the ground like the ones she'd made earlier, but ev'ry time she tried to ease the body in, those birds attack'd her an' screamed like they was furies or somethin', and it was bad, real bad—it was a terrible scene to watch.

He pauses again as I search through my pockets for a cigarette: I've a feeling I'm going to need it.

Am I goin' too slow for you, First Sarn't? he asks.

Inwardly I'm raging with impatience and raring to get on with the million tasks that I know are waiting for me, but I also know that if I don't give him a hearing now he'll simply turn up somewhere else. So I grit my teeth and say: Just keep talking.

Thanks, First Sarn't. Much appreciated.

He lapses into a moody silence, as if remembering details.

At length, he says: There was patches of blood all over the ground, an' more blood drippin' from the birds and spreadin' all across the base, like.

Why do you think the birds were storming?

I was gettin' to that, First Sarn't, he replies calmly.

Then he says: The meanin' of the dream is clear to me, I think, an' it goes like this. The crows be us, the land be where we're at, the girl be the girl, the blood be from ev'ryone, an' if we keep her from buryin' him, there's gonna be trouble, a whole load o' trouble, 'cos that's what the dream was all about.

He gazes at me with certainty, while I give a tight little smile, which probably comes off as a grimace, while wondering to myself why we need military intelligence when we've a soldier who can interpret dreams.

That's very interesting, Pratt.

I know it must sound nuts to you, First Sarn't, but among my people, when you have a dream like that standin' up, you take it seriously.

I purse my lips. You're from Fairbanks, aren't you?

From way north of Fairbanks, First Sarn't, a tiny settlement called Allakaket, bang smack on the Arctic Circle. That's my home of record. Cold, dark, and isolated. Sorta like this place at night.

I guess I asked because some other people would hold that when you have a dream standing up, it's called daydreaming.

He flushes, a slow tan spreading across his weathered features.

No, First Sarn't, he says, I wasn't daydreamin'. I know what that's like. This dream was real, an' it was diff'rent enough for me to rec'nize it for what it was.

So what do you want me to do, Pratt?

Convince the Cap'n to let her have her brother back. We're killin' the dead a second time round, an' that ain't right. He's a corpse to us, but he mean ev'rything to her, an' we're keepin' 'em both from findin' peace—he in the ground, where he now belong, and she inside hes-self, which is equally importan'. It ain't why we're here. We're makin' a big mistake.

I decide I've given him more than enough time to speak his mind. All right, Specialist, I say briskly. You can go now. Thanks for bring-ing the matter to me.

You gonna talk to the Cap'n? he persists.

I'll see what I can do, Pratt—but I'm not making any promises.

Thanks, First Sarn't. That's a weight off my mind. I knew you'd gimme a fair hearin'.

He nods at me as he leaves.

I stand there for a moment, staring after him, and then I resolve to go and get some coffee to clear my head. On my way to the mess tent, I try to stifle an uneasy feeling, but once I'm there and making the coffee I'm even more distracted than before, and it takes me an embarrassingly long time to realize that Lieutenant Ellison is trying to attract my attention.

Do you have a moment, First Sarn't?

Yes, of course, I murmur absently, while attempting to regain my focus.

You won't believe what I've been dealing with this morning, he says angrily.

Oh, really? I answer as I stir sugar into my coffee. I glance at him. Coffee for you?

Umm . . . sure. I guess I could use it.

You and me both, bro, I think. Aloud, I ask him how he wants it.

Black, with no sugar, please.

Then he says urgently: I need your advice. The shit really hit the fan this morning. A bunch of guys from my platoon want us to return the body in our custody to the creature outside.

He couldn't have gotten my attention faster if he'd slapped me.

With a start, I turn around to face him, almost spilling my coffee in the process. For the first time, I notice that his pallor is even more pronounced than usual. I hand him his cup without a word.

Clearing his throat, he says: At 0630 this morning, I was approached by a group of men from my platoon. They asked that we release the body of the Taliban commander to the woman outside. They claimed that, after her gig last night, they could no longer view her as one of the enemy, and our refusal to surrender her brother's body for burial now struck them as—and I quote—"just not fair." They ended by telling me that if I didn't do something about it, they'd delegate a couple of representatives to talk to the C.O. themselves and try to persuade him to—and I quote again—"do the right thing."

Having said his piece, he looks down at the ground and adds: I can only tell you that I've never faced anything like this before. I feel almost apologetic for sharing this with you. It's fucking outrageous!

What have you decided to do about their petition?

He looks up at me in astonishment. Do? Why, absolutely nothing.

I take in his earnest, indignant face, and wonder if I should envy him his clarity, or chew him out instead for disregarding his men's concerns so casually, however frivolous he may find them.

Just then I hear a cough behind me, and turn around.

It's Heywood, the RTO. He greets us—first Ellison, then me.

Addressing me, he says: Captain wants to see you, First Sarn't.

I turn to Ellison and excuse myself, then walk back with Heywood to Connolly's office.

The C.O. has his feet up on the folding table he uses as his desk.

He looks completely done in, as if he hasn't slept in days—which is probably close to the truth. He eyes me wearily as I enter.

How you doin', First Sarn't?

I can't complain, Sir.

Good. He takes his feet off the desk and leans forward.

I spoke to Battalion about our problem outside, he says. Fortunately, KAF has a drone in the area and they've directed it over the slopes to find out if there are any insurgents hanging around. So we'll find out about that sooner or later, and if they come back with an all clear, then we can go out and take care of Calamity Jane.

Sir . . . ?

The LN outside, he explains.

Any word from Battalion on the corpse?

He massages his brow tiredly.

Oh, they're flying it out tomorrow, as planned, which will come as a fucking relief, quite frankly. It's beginning to stink up the whole base, as I'm sure you've noticed, and the medics have had no option but to be stoic and put up with it.

I wait for more, and he says: If we do get word that there are insurgents on the slopes, then we'll take out the cart, clean and simple. But if the slopes are deserted—and that's a big *if,* I know—then we'll have to eliminate the possibility of a suicide bomber, get as much info as we can, and get rid of her . . . or him. She's in the way.

Get *rid* of her, Sir?

His eyes don't leave my face. We'll have to come up with something, he says.

I begin to ask if it wouldn't be wiser to wait until the new batch of ANA show up and can then be assigned to deal with the task, but he cuts me short: The ANA won't arrive until tomorrow, and I'm not waiting another twenty-four hours while an LN holds an entire U.S. Army base hostage. Not a fucking chance—I'm waiting for word from the drone and then we'll resolve the matter ourselves.

I'm not sure I'm following you, Sir.

This is personal, First Sarn't.

I consider this for a moment without saying anything. Then: What if we don't hear from Battalion about the drone today?

Well . . . then I guess you'll have to send someone out to make sure she isn't strapped with explosives.

And if she's clean?

Sorry—what was that? he says distractedly, flipping his laptop open.

What should we do if she turns out not to be a suicide op?

We'll still need to find a way to get her out of our hair, First Sarn't—after grilling her thoroughly for intelligence, that is.

That's when I ask: Could we not simply give her the body, Sir?

I'm met with an angry exclamation from Connolly, who glares at me.

And what would you suggest I tell Battalion? And what about Brigade, and Bagram, and the clowns in Kabul? Do you want the whole fucking chain of command to come crashing down on our heads?

Couldn't we just send photographs? Why do they need the corpse?

Connolly gazes at me for a long moment as if composing a suitable response. At length, he says: The powers that be in Kabul have made a big deal out of the prospect of displaying the body on television. They don't want people to question its authenticity. Nor do they want to deal with the kinds of questions that have arisen in the past regarding the credibility of their claims about the deaths of key insurgents, who then turn out to have survived after all. The government is weak, and they'll use anything they can to project their strength.

But he's already beginning to rot, Sir, I point out. I doubt he'll be any good for displaying on television in another day.

It isn't up to us to interfere, he says firmly. We have our orders.

He returns to his papers, then pauses abruptly and slams his laptop shut. What's with all these fucking questions, Marcus? You're not a novice, you know how these things work; there are things we can and can't do in this situation. Our freedom of action is strictly circumscribed.

We stare at each other without moving.

Then he sits up very straight with his head tilted back to take me in as I look down at him from a height. Abruptly, he says: You're looking ragged around the edges. It's affecting your judgment, quite obviously. Why don't you get some sleep?

I nod slightly.

Just do it, he urges.

# LIEUTENANT'S JOURNAL

One.

Two.

Three.

Four . . . in five seconds I will have turned twenty-four. Yet another year added to my life. I hold up a mirror to my face. Below the wall of forehead, the eyes crouch warily. Stone-gray gaze, eyelids rimmed with red, lashes bleached by dust, mouth encircled by grime. Taut, thin lips, distant, long gaze. God of memory, god of longings: grant me the gift of rest.

It's night outside, a foggy, dust-smeared darkness. The wind whips the earth into shades, the desert hides in shadows, there's dust, dust everywhere.

Dust clouds, dust moon, dust senses.

In the beginning, I wanted to make a difference. Dreamed we were a force for the good. Believed we could change this world: change it through the power of intention, goodwill, language. That was before survival became paramount. The mere act of staying alive. Alive: that single, most dangerous word. Dangerous, yes. We are never entirely ourselves until we contend with the length of the night, the fact of its finitude, its protean, distinct shades, its inevitable end.

Absent star. When I look at myself in the light of day, I appear very different, even to myself. But in the darkness of the night, this is what I am.

And so the moments pass, dust stirs the plains, the mountains hem in air. Twenty-four years. A window to a view that no longer exists. A calm, peaceful landscape. Sunlit stream winding through green Burlington hills. Graveled driveway, cars parked in front of the house. Dad with his sleeves rolled up, on his way to the tennis court, looking back over his shoulder and waving me good-bye.

I've changed so much, who would've thought it possible? I, who used to believe I'd never change. Look at me now: I'm a stranger to myself. Bearer of the dead. My eyes close, but sleep does not come.

### Day.

Dawn. The silence is absolute. For an instant, the fog parts to reveal the plexus of huts and tents huddled in the half-light. Otherwise everything around me, this translucent, swirling haze, is bathed in tints of violet. Even the barren landscape assumes carmine shades. I've never lost the love of landscape that you planted in me, Dad. It's sustained me in the most extreme situations and places. One day I'd like to pass that on to my children.

So I began writing this journal for you, Dad. You said I would need a place to bury the graveyard that war becomes when the dreams of glory dissipate. I remember clearly when you told me that. We were walking down the long, planked pier, the still waters of the lake on either side of us. The pier seemed to go on and on, the water was an even-tempered blue, the lake sky-colored and sky-shaped. You said: I've never understood your commitment, but I respect you, so I've accepted it. I said: Thanks, Dad. You said: Time is what is left when we decide to start living, Nick. I want you to come back to us alive.

I remember looking up suddenly when you said that. Something had startled me—not what you'd said—and at first I couldn't figure out what it was. Then I noticed: In the clear light, the sky seemed to have no beginning, the lake no end. There was no line on the horizon.

Before we turned around and walked back, you asked me what was going to be the most important thing for me on this deployment.

My answer, the same as it ever was: Winning the war and bringing my men back alive.

You said: Always remember that experience is an arch. That's from Tennyson, by the way.

I remember smiling as I replied: In the army we call it the steep learning curve. You go from innocence to experience. Then from experience to more experience. In other words, from shit hole to shit hole in an endless procession of shit holes, if you'll excuse my French. From one . . .

Problematic situation to another?

Exactly. Yes.

We laughed together at the way you'd deflected the possibility of more profanity by finishing my thought. But when we reached the end of the pier, you held me earnestly by the shoulder and said: This country is broken, Nick. We've been lied to and robbed blind and left to the mercy of swindlers. I can't remember the last time I've felt as depressed. No—not even during the Vietnam years. We're desperately in need of heroes, Nick—of good, honest, hardworking leaders. We need men like you to come back and rebuild what's been destroyed.

I remember the long silence as I looked at you with sadness.

You're looking to us to come back and rescue the country, Dad?

I am. I don't believe war solves anything, Nick—and these wars in particular are like gaping wounds. They're draining us of our life-blood.

**NIGHT.**

So: this journal is where I put down my most private thoughts, Dad. It's like the little compartment the others carry around in their heads where they stow away all their thoughts and emotions until such time as they can bear to safely unpack and dwell on the nightmares, the sadness. Dave Hendricks says it's the first thing he does when he's back Stateside, even before he meets the family. He locks himself up in a dark room and lets go slowly . . . He opens the box.

Me? I prefer the white page. No dark rooms for me. No shut containers in the mind.

No cigar box like the one that Connolly has in his desk drawer that he flips open every time something goes very, very wrong.

I write down my thoughts instead. I live on the page. This is home for me now: my true home. And that St. Louis apartment with the Ikea furniture and Em's collection of quilts and all our books from Vassar and on . . . that's fiction. It's a movie, a different life that featured some other man who shared my name and body for a time. He's gone.

He's been gone for a while now.

**NIGHT.**

The long stare. The eyes that take on a life of their own. Emily remarked on it the last time we were together; she kept telling me to look at her and not past her at some gray distance. Where are you, Nick? What are you thinking of? And then, later, when the shock of our separation finally hit with full force: You chose to break away, Nick. You had a choice. You should've known that this could end.

I tried to explain it to you, but you were always somewhere else. I could see it in your eyes. You were miles away. What happened to you? Do you like the way that sand tastes?

Miles away. I'm twenty-four, but I've aged so much. My eyes are holes where light no longer penetrates. What did she expect? I'm no longer who I used to be. I've seen my core break away.

I close my eyes, just for tonight. The sun still sleeps for me where she wakes.

Why didn't you wait for me, Em? I see your face in the sand everywhere.

Tonight I'll dream of you. Outside there's a sickle moon. A glitter of yellow scales on my bed. Tonight I'll plunge into my labyrinth.


## Day.

In a few days, summer will end. I know why I've become so conscious of time, Dad. I'm afraid of not being able to see my son again. It keeps me up at night, and then in the morning I don't want to get out of bed. Even the relief of having survived another twenty-four hours can seem ephemeral. It's almost easier to walk over to the wire and watch those formidable mountains sweep their shadows over us. Strange how alien the mountains appear, and the desert as well, with its different coldness. Featureless landscapes. Futureless deathscapes. Still, you get used to them after a while.

Although, when I come to think of it, I can't remember the last time I was near a forest.

Or a river, for that matter. A garden, a pond, a park, a lake.

We've heard rumors of orchards hidden deep in the mountains, and groves of mulberries and grapes. Also stands of holly oaks and cedars, giant spruce and cypresses. When I gaze at the wild, jagged rock faces that loom over us, it seems improbable. But then again, fruits are among the main exports of this parched, dust-choked land, especially melons and pomegranates.

And grapes. Fourteen different kinds, can you imagine?

As for melons, our ANA Uzbeks assure us that the best kind are not from Kandahar but from Ashkalon farther north, where, two thousand years ago, the Greeks led by Alexander—whom they call Iskander—is said to have introduced them from Macedonia.

Alexander's spirit still straddles this place like a colossus, by the way. When I think of the armies he led back and forth over the mountains—in winter, no less—in pursuit of the Persians and the local tribes, I am left, quite frankly, speechless. There is such a thing as military genius, I suppose. Sobering to think that we do not— emphatically—have anything to compare by way of leadership.


NIGHT.

What else can I tell you about the nature of this place?

In the desert there are hyenas and jackals. We hear them call at night, but I've never seen them myself. The gray wolf used to be common here—it's the same species as the ones back home—but the Taliban hunted them with Kalashnikovs, and now there are hardly any left.

And then there are the birds. Yesterday I took a picture of a hoopoe, a striped yellow-beige bird the size of a magpie, with a flamboyant black-tipped crest and an attitude to match. And Sergeant Espinosa tells me there's a goshawk scoping out the watchtower with an eye to building a nest. I've seen it once or twice myself, a lean rust-brown female with sharp yellow talons. She swoops down every morning from some high perch in the mountains.

I'd like to get up to the mountains myself sometime. As a matter of fact, we're going to have to do it sooner or later: it's part of our mission to set up a string of outposts. We plan to piggyback from valley to valley, getting to know the local shuras and enlisting their help against the insurgents.

Our Uzbek ANA tell us they've heard that the Pashtun women go unveiled in the mountain valleys. Also that djinns occupy the highest peaks. And that the pillars of dust that race across the plains are devil-possessed. And the foggy evening coolness is the breath of the dead.

For all these reasons and more, when one of the Uzbeks finds a fragment of pottery in the sand, he promptly buries it again because of the black spells it is said to cast. For the rest of the day, he stands shivering with his spade in a corner of his tent. That is the caliber of the men we are working with. The army brass who send them to us claim that they are highly trained. I hope you smile when you read this, Dad: it's meant to make you smile.


N I G H T .

So I was reading the book you sent me, de Vigny's *Servitude and Grandeur of Arms,* and came across this passage you'd underlined (for me?): "Modern men—men of the hour in which I write—are skeptical and ironical about everything else besides. But each becomes serious the moment its name is mentioned. And this is not a theory, but an observation.—The name of Honor moves something in a man which is integral to himself . . . "

And then again, on another page: "This strange, proud virtue is animated by a mysterious vitality, and it stands erect in the midst of all our vices, blending so well with them that it is fed by their energy."

I wish I could tell you that's the sort of war I'm fighting, Dad, but I don't know, I really don't know, and to lie to you in this journal would be like lying to myself—and where would that leave us? We're using unmanned drones to fight against a bunch of illiterate peasants with bolt-action rifles, and that leaves a certain taste in the mouth that's very far from the glory of Alexander's campaigns, if you know what I mean. Or even Napoleon's, for that matter.

**DAY.**

Mother picked up the telephone when I called you today. I called at the usual time, so it took me aback to hear her at the other end. I braced myself for her slurred yet genteel I'm-trying-hard-not-to-sound-drunk voice, but she seemed peculiarly controlled somehow. We'd barely exchanged a few words when she said: Your father would like to speak to you.

You came on the line. You said: Is this St. Catherine of Siena?

I said: Dad? It's me.

You said: I'm sorry, I must have the wrong number. I was trying the hospital.

I said: Dad? What's going on? It's me, Nick.

You said: Forgive me. I misdialed.

Then I heard you say to Mother: Becky, this isn't the hospital.

She took the phone from you.

I said: Mother . . . ?

I'm sorry, Nick. He isn't doing too well.

My voice rose: How long has this been going on?

He's been slipping up for a few months now. He lost his way in the city last week, and I had to drive down and fetch him. We went to the doctor after that. And now it's worse, as you can tell.

I had no idea!

He still seems to recognize a few things, though. Your letters, for instance.

My letters. Really?

Keep writing. The doctor says it might help.

What else does the doctor say? How bad is it?

Well, we have good days and bad days. Yesterday was bad. He couldn't recognize himself in the mirror and was alarmed at this stranger in the house.

Does he know who you are, Mother?

Keep writing to him, Nick. Don't worry about me. I'm okay.

**NIGHT.**

Night brings it all back.

How could I have been so blind? How could I have been so oblivious to my father's decline? Or my mother's alcoholism?

I go online and read up everything I can about Alzheimer's. I don't know if that makes it better or worse. I read for hours without a break. I fall asleep still reading.

You wake me up. I start and stare at you.

Dad . . . ?

You say: Emily stopped by today, Nick. I told her, in no uncertain terms, that she was wrong to leave you.

She came over all the way from St. Louis?

She must have, or, at least, the woman I spoke to looked like her. But maybe it was someone else. I don't know what's happened to people these days, Nick. I don't recognize them. I walk down the street and I don't recognize their faces. I don't recognize faces anymore.

Don't worry about it, Dad. I'll take care of everything as soon as I'm home.

I told her: I have my standards, and maybe I am a bit old-fashioned, but I do not, as a rule, revise my grades. Your paper on *Antigone* was below par. I was disappointed.

Emily didn't study with you, Dad. She went to Vassar. That's where we met, remember? In Vassar, not Bennington.

Then why did she come to me about her grade? I don't understand.

It doesn't matter, Dad. I'll talk to her about it. You just relax.


**DAY.**

Could have. Should have.

I could have spent more time with you the last time I was home. I should have asked you how you were coping with retirement—you, who loved more than anything else to stand before your students and talk about Herodotus, Thucydides, Pericles.

I remember your telling me that my decisions affected everyone. At the time I thought you had Emily in mind; now I wonder if you were trying to warn me about your own condition. You said: Your attention is given too often elsewhere, Nick. I answered: We all walk alone.

It sounds so glib on hindsight. How could I have known?

Who's going to read this journal now, Dad? Who am I going to write to?

Not to Emily, though I still turn toward her in my sleep.

And not to little Jack—though in my dreams I've heard the sounds of a playground fading.

Must I write for myself? Am I well and truly alone now? Is this what you were cautioning me about?

I'll write for myself. I'll walk alone.


NIGHT.

Four swings in a clearing below an old oak tree. Stands of oak and chestnut on all sides. The sky is dark, but I can't tell if it's day or night. Three of the swings are painted white; one is black. The ground below each swing has deep grooves worn into it. A bright cone of light shines through the clearing straight into my eyes. Mist swirls through the trees, blurring their branches. Where it touches the mist, the light appears diffused, as if filtered through a screen of dust. A paper kite drifts through the clearing and draws my attention to the stream on the far side. My family sits on the banks of the stream— Dad, Mother, and my little sister, Eve—but their complexions are yellow, and they're unnaturally still. I want to run up to them, but the searchlight tracks my every movement, and I can't seem to reach them. The mist clings to the stream; the kite glides again through the clearing. My family continues to sit motionless, oblivious of my attempts to get to them. Is this scene a memory from my childhood, or is it an invention of my mind? I can't remember, nor can I understand why I am kept so firmly apart. In the end, my distress at my separation gets the better of me, and I wake up unable to move or speak.


### DAY.

Top guidelines to myself at Tarsândan:

Always attend one hundred percent to the task at hand; always separate personal sentiments from professional decision making; remember never to let my exhaustion show in front of my men; encourage positive and negative feedback throughout the chain of command; use spare time to study and memorize human and physical terrain (i.e., master the local lingo and always carry a map).


### NIGHT.

So here's what I have within reach of my folding table, in no particular order. Laptop, M-4 rifle, M-9 pistol, magazines of 9 mm and 5.56 mm ammo, fleece jacket, first aid kit, GPS receiver, body armor, advanced combat helmet, red lens flashlight, night vision goggles, colored flares, hand grenades, smoke grenades, three radios, four flashlights, a packet of MRE crackers, a jar of Nutella, a buzz saw, an RR82 mm recoilless rifle (a gift from an ANA commander in Kandahar), a samurai sword, a rain jacket, grease pencils, lead pencils, two pairs of gloves, a 1976 Michelin map of Kandahar province, sunglasses, wraparound shades, a black-and-white checkered headscarf, a fleece blanket, battle dressing, a two-liter bottle of water, Styrofoam cups for coffee, booney hat, a set of English-Pashto and English-Dari dictionaries and phrasebooks, earplugs, two digital cameras, a folded American flag, MP3 player, and, finally, a framed picture of Emily with Jack. These are the things that help me carry on from day to day.

I check my watch. It's 11:21 p.m. Kandahar time, which means

1:51 in the afternoon in St. Louis. Emily's going to be taking a break from work to pick up Jack from nursery school and drop him off at the babysitter's. She's got it down to a twenty-minute commute while listening to NPR on the radio. Usually it's All Things Considered at this time of the day, but sometimes they have her favorite gardening programs. She likes to drive fast: she always has. Slow down, Em, slow down, you always drive too fast. What's the rush, girl? You're always on my mind, especially when I'm here. I love you very much, despite everything.

I love you both very much.

In that part of the world, at least, thankfully little has changed.

That's why I'm here, to make sure it stays that way.

And that's why I make it a point to tell everyone back home that I'm at the epicenter of the place where the forces of fascism—of religious fundamentalism, societal repression, and violent hatred—must be contained. When I'm challenged about the consequences of my actions, I ask the person to look me in the eye and ask if he or she truly believes that peace would return and the condition of the women and children, especially, would improve if we decided to leave this place. You see, I can no longer go through the motions of conversation for the sake of conversation, or that of argument for its own sake.

Not when I've been face-to-face with the consequences of unimaginable barbarism.

I may not be a free agent, but I am an agent for freedom, the freedom to assume the responsibility of ensuring that a devastated society is repaired. That's why I can use words like "integrity" and "honor" without cynicism. If we allow this country to slide back into the darkness, we will all be accessories to the genocide that will follow our departure as inevitably as night follows day.

Do you understand?

You who owe your blissful ignorance to our sacrifices.

No one back home gives a damn about us. No one gives a shit. Fact.

## DAY.

The last time I was home, Emily woke me up one night and told me I was grinding my teeth so loudly it had jolted her awake. She said that at first she hadn't known where the noise was coming from, and then she realized I was lying beside her with my body taut and my hands clenched into fists and my jaw working away like a piston. I switched on the light and we sat up together. I was drenched in sweat; the mattress on my side of the bed was soaked. She drew me close and held me in her arms.

She said: Baby, what are they doing to you?

And that was a full week before the night I woke up screaming that we were being overrun by the enemy and began to throttle her, thinking she was about to kill me.

My screams woke Jack, sleeping in his crib at the foot of our bed. Em spent the rest of the night trying to lull him back to sleep. Meanwhile I paced up and down outside the apartment trying to calm down.

## NIGHT.

So. Emily. Exit ex-wife stage left.

I think I've finally come to terms with the pain. I really think I have.

At least I've stopped believing in illusions like love and marriage. I've become a realist—if that is the word I'm looking for—when it comes to these things. I look back at my broken marriage and don't know what to say of this thing that I made with another person—this hope I invested—that suddenly shattered into fucking smithereens. This hope, this bright, beautiful summer dream, transformed overnight into a fucking nightmare, heavy with grief, with silence. Like blood that spills from a body and alters it. The light's corrosion . . .

I don't think I hate her. I'd like to believe that one day I can simply be indifferent.


**NIGHT.**

I don't want to know your reasons for leaving me. Love has no place for logic.

Only, I beg you, don't go, please. Stay with me a little longer until I can come back home and make this work for us again. That's all I ask. Hold on to the rails of our baby's crib—if that's what it takes—and remember that we both created him, believing in our future together as a family.

I'm still the same Nick, Em; I've just been in some very dark places.

So don't go, please. Don't repeat your mother's mistake. Remember your father's grief.

Hold on tight to the home we share, to the memories, to our child, our child . . .

Don't leave me.


**DAY.**

We took our first casualties today. It was a complete catastrophe. It all began a couple of weeks ago when a delegation of tribal elders from one of the nearby mountain valleys visited us. It was our first breakthrough with the locals, so we were thrilled. The elders sat around in a circle explaining their situation while we served them tea. They said they were being harassed by "bad men" who regularly crossed over from sanctuaries on the other side of the border with Pakistan. In desperation, they had decided to reach out to us as the sole representatives of law and order in a region where the Afghan government is nonexistent. Connolly promised to help, and we set up a rendezvous with the elders in the mountains. He called Lieutenant-Colonel Mark

Lautenschlager, the Battalion commander, and they both agreed that this was the perfect opportunity to establish our first foothold in the mountains, a combat outpost manned by a couple of squads stationed within a five-mile radius of Tarsândan. Then Connolly had Lieutenant Hendricks and me, as the two platoon leaders, draw straws to decide whose unit would go, and Hendricks won.

Early this morning, Dave Hendricks led Second Platoon on Humvees up the steep mountain paths as far as they could go, and then they walked the rest of the distance to the rendezvous. It was a trap. The local Taliban had found out about the meeting and, instead of the tribal elders meeting the platoon, there were forty heavily armed insurgents. Hendricks radioed Tarsândan, and Connolly called in air support and dispatched First Platoon. The Apaches and medevacs reached before I arrived with my platoon, but they were held off by sustained fire from RPGs and mortars. I can still hear Hendricks screaming into his radio: We're surrounded! Get something up or we're not gonna make it!

By the time we managed to link up with them, both Lieutenant Hendricks and Sergeant Brian Castro had been hit. Then an F-15 dropped a JDAM where the enemy concentration was thickest, and that effectively ended the battle. The insurgents lost sixteen men before they retreated. The medevacs evacuated Dave and Brian, but neither of them survived surgery. They were our first casualties since our deployment in Kandahar province. In my SitRep I wrote: 16X INS KIA (CONFIRMED) & 24X INS FLEEING NE ACROSS THE BORDER.

Connolly came to my hut this evening and blamed himself for not having sent Second Platoon in with air support. He said: I can't believe Dave's gone. I just don't want to believe they're gone.

I took a walk around the perimeter at 2200. I overheard one of the men on watch—I think it was Pfc. Spitz—telling another: I don't want to be a hero; I just want to make it back home alive. The other man asked: You scared, Spitty? Spitz said: Isn't everyone?

## Night.

I can't sleep tonight. I lie on my cot, then sit up with my hands clasped over my head. I do my best thinking at night, but it's not working right now. My brain is fogged, my thoughts feel borrowed. I try to deal with the solitude that makes my job so different from the solidarity that binds the grunts. Someone once wrote that there are no good/bad dichotomies in combat decisions, only choices between bad alternatives—but that doesn't make my task any easier when I'm attempting to cope with the consequences of mistakes that result in casualties.

Do I feel guilty about not being able to save Dave and Brian? Hell yes, of course I do. In wartime, the already hazy dividing line between brilliant and stupid decision making becomes hazier still—and while I don't want to second-guess Connolly for what's already happened, perhaps he did cross that line in sending a switch-out on foot into the mountains. Hendricks and Castro were both experienced officers, as is Eric Petrak, the platoon forward observer, but maybe Connolly erred in his reading of the mission?

So we're alone with our burdens, he and I: the knowledge that every time we send men outside the wire, it could be to their deaths. Around me lies that dark shadow, and wherever I go, it precedes and trails after me. The only person unaffected by that shadow is my dad: in his amnesia I am protected. I can't say that of anyone else, and especially not of Emily, once the closest to me. I've often wondered about that—wondered if, when I was lying next to Emily, she could sense the shadow, taste its poison, until eventually it all became too much, and she decided to quit . . .

I get up from my cot and drink some water. It's unpleasantly warm, and I feel no better after I've finished drinking. My skin burns, my face itches: I'm covered with bites from sand fleas. It's stifling inside this hut. A cry from some night bird drifts off slowly into the silence. Dave's imaginary presence moves around in the darkness, and

I catch a fleeting glimpse of his face—or perhaps it's Brian's? All night I will hear their voices in my head.

### NIGHT.

So I've been going over the battle over and over in my mind. Could I have done things differently?—maybe moved the platoon through the mountains faster so we could've reached Hendricks and his men earlier on? And even after we reached them, it was touch and go; the enemy seemed everywhere, but maybe I could have deployed the platoon differently? In the end, it was like we were fighting blind. We couldn't save Dave and Brian.

### EARLY MORNING.

No sleep last night. No one slept. We kept expecting an attack on the base, which, fortunately, didn't happen.

### MORNING.

I feel devastated. I can't seem to focus on anything.

I wish there was somewhere I could go and simply scream my lungs out.

Gotta hold it all in, boy, you're a platoon leader.

Yo

    u

       're

          a

             Fir

                    st Lieutenant. Christ, I was pressing down so hard with the pen, I tore right through the paper. That's a first. All right, Nick, get a grip on yourself.

### Noon.

Lunch today was fried chicken, and it smelled better than I could ever recall. I felt guilty eating, but I was famished. I sat at the table staring at my plate and wondering what was the point of it all. Across from me, the place where Hendricks used to sit was, of course, empty. I felt sick with grief and hungry all at once.

In the end, I ate with a gigantic appetite.

But then, on the way back to my hooch, I threw it all up.

### Evening.

I've retreated to my hooch with my iPod. I know exactly what I want to listen to. Mozart's "Requiem" comes on:

> *Requiem aeternam dona eis, Domine:*
> *Et lux perpetua luceat eis. Te decet*
> *Hymnus, Deus, in Sion, et tibi reddetur*
> *Votum in Jerusalem: exaudi orationem*
> *Meam, ad te omnis caro veniet. Requiem*
> *Aeternam dona eis, Domine et*
> *Lux perpetua luceat eis.*

> *Kyrie eleison.*
> *Christe eleison.*
> *Kyrie eleison.*

When the CD ends, I press "play" again.

> *Eternal rest grant to them, O Lord; and*
> *Let perpetual light shine upon them. A*
> *Hymn becometh Thee, O God, in Sion:*

*And a vow shall be paid to Thee in Jerusalem.*
*O hear my prayer: all flesh shall come to Thee.*
*Eternal rest grant to them, O Lord; and perpetual*
*Light shine upon them.*

*Lord have mercy on us.*
*Christ have mercy on us.*
*Lord have mercy on us.*


When the CD ends, I press "play" again . . .

*Agnus Dei, qui tollis peccata mundi:*
*Dona eis requiem.*
*Agnus Dei, qui tollis peccata mundi:*
*Dona eis requiem sempiternam.*

And again . . .

*Lamb of God, who takest away the sins*
*Of the world, grant them rest.*
*Lamb of God, who takest away the sins*
*Of the world, grant them eternal rest.*

And again, when the CD ends, I press "play" . . .
I press "play" again. And again. And again. And again. And again . . .


N**IGHT**.

Oh God, oh God, I know we're all going to go one day, but if it's my fate to die in this strange and hostile land, dear God please make it quick.

### Night.

I swore off writing, but here I am again, and why not, it's a necessary refuge. I write to try to make sense of things before I go completely off the rails. I cannot let myself succumb to the illusion that there is no larger meaning to this war, no essential truths, nothing transcendental that's bigger than the day-to-day. And yet, there's no peace after hard-earned victory, no rest, and no locus of reality—only blank spaces in place of friends; poisoned air; and vast, dark silences.

### Day.

Daybreak begins with little flakes of light. It's already hot, and the sun has barely breached the mountains. The desert takes on its familiar colors: four shades of gray, five of brown, nine each of buff and beige. I squint up at the jagged peaks, their slopes still shadowy with night. Very soon we're going to have to take the fight into those mountains. Either that, or we remain cooped up in here, day after day, stuck on a cramped little desert island. We have to break out and set up those outposts. It's only a matter of time. Of waiting for the right moment.

War is the only real connection we have with the people of this country.

They know it; we know it. We understand each other. We have an agreement.

We each have our code of retaliation; they call theirs badal; we call ours payback.

It's the age-old spiral of attack and revenge.

The only difference between us—and it is significant—is that we're visitors to this place. We don't belong here; we're not trapped by its ragged history, its chronicle of failures, its uncertain future. That makes it all the more critical for us to do what we need to do, do it quickly, and get out. Get out before we become part of the cycle of failure and violence. Get out before we become just another failed tribe.

# DAY.

The men stand silently in full battle dress in the late afternoon sun, their red-rimmed eyes focused on the two pairs of boots and the rifles stuck muzzle-first into the ground. The chaplain from Battalion drones on and on but merely succeeds in adding to the air of unreality. Soon we're drenched with sweat, and our uniforms are encrusted with white salt stains. Connolly stands some distance away from me, his eyes shadowed beneath a booney hat. My own throat is parched, my mouth dry and sticky. When it's my turn to speak, I recall Lieutenant Hendricks and Sergeant Castro from our time together in Khost province, and keep it short. I would have liked to have said more, but I simply don't have it in me.

Connolly speaks at the end, and his voice is strained. He begins by saying that he sees no point in giving the men a canned explanation that will sound lame even to him. He tells them that if it were up to us, we'd straighten out this place in no time at all. The U.S. Army knows how to do its job and do it right. But that isn't the way things have been set up here, and we have an obligation to the Afghan people—the ordinary men and women and children—not to abandon them in their time of need. That is the litmus test, he says, and, even as we grieve for our fallen, we will do well to remember it. It's hardly an adequate summing up for our losses, but it's all that we have to make them bearable. We are a people of honor, sent here to set an example to those looking up to us.

He ends by saying that we've been entrusted with a task and a responsibility, and we'll do what it takes to accomplish it.

As I walk away, I wonder how many of the men from Second Platoon blame us for the deaths of their leaders. It's the cross that every infantry commander has to learn to live with, because it's the one thing in war that doesn't get any easier with experience. I feel sick to the pit of my stomach, and, on my way back to my hut, I overhear Pfc. Lawson speaking to someone, and what he says gives words to my sentiments: It's like I got this wound deep inside me, and it's always hurtin'. Always, always . . .

I decide to stop by Connolly's hut. He's listening on his short-wave radio to the news of the latest efforts by the regime that we are propping up to reconcile with an enemy bent on our extermination. He turns to me and says: It makes me want to puke. Will someone please tell the suits running the show in D.C. that the Taliban and Al Qaeda are not interested in a bite of the pie; they want the whole damn thing? They're committed to an all-or-nothing strategy, and we're the thin red line standing between them and their clearly stated target: Western civilization.

At a certain point in the report, he begins yelling at the radio: For Christ's sake, we're talking about folks who consider beheading their opponents just punishment, not followers of the goddamn Geneva Conventions!

He switches off the radio in disgust while I walk over to the arsenal captured from the insurgents. It's a motley collection of RPG7s, Kalashnikov variants, Chinese machine guns, RR82 mms, American-made M-16s, bolt-action Lee-Enfield and Mosin-Nagant rifles, and even one snub-nosed antiaircraft gun. The pile of weaponry takes up an entire corner of the hut. One of the M-16s has a series of Arabic letters and numerals etched on its plastic handguard. I translate it haltingly. It reads: "Gift to the inspired warriors of the Amir ul Momineen, 1996."

In other words, already in the early years of Taliban rule, their leader, the functionally illiterate one-eyed Mullah Omar, was claiming the mantle of Umar, the seventh-century caliph of the nascent Muslim community and its second leader after the death of the Prophet Mohammed. So much for the modesty of aspirations of the erstwhile preacher of Sanghisar, a small village an hour's drive north of Kandahar.

**NIGHT.**

I'm rereading the de Vigny, which I like very much, and I come across this passage, which I must have glossed over the first time around: "War seemed to us so very natural a state for our country, that when, freed from the classroom, we poured ourselves into the army along the familiar course of the torrent of days, we found ourselves unable to believe in a lasting calm of peace."

When I go over the passage again, it's as if I can hear Emily reading it to me, and I experience a distinctly uncomfortable sensation, almost like guilt.

**NIGHT.**

We crouch next to the road, then sprint across it in single file. There's a thick fog, but I know this place well. We run past the darkened houses, taking cover in the shadow of the trees. By the time I reach the backyard, the platoon's all there. I signal to Tanner, and he leads the charge to the porch door and slams it down with his shoulder. Moments later, the boys are dragging out a bedraggled Emily with my little Jack in tow. I grab my son from her. Tanner spreadeagles her on the ground and ties her wrists behind her back. She whimpers with shock. I plant my revolver on the back of her head. As I pull the trigger, I hear myself yelling: You took a vow. You made a promise!

I wake up choking. My hands are clenched. I feel enervated, displaced.

The hooch is cool from the night. Outside, the sky is black, and all it is, is darkness.

Husband. Promise and commitment. And me—burning inside.

Displaced.

**DAY.**

This afternoon, Spc. Simonis, one of our snipers, asks me if he can examine the cache of captured weapons. He selects one of the heavy, long-barreled Lee-Enfields. Manufactured by the British Crown, it has a stamp from the government rifle factory in Ishapore, India; its date is 1916. In other words, we were attacked with a ninety-four-year-old weapon captured from earlier invaders.

I watch Simonis disassemble the rifle. It's beautifully maintained and oiled, the simplicity of its design ensuring both reliability and ease of use by the conscript soldiers of the Taliban. Simonis also points out how the firing mechanism increases accuracy since the shooter has to work the bolt to unload a used bullet and cycle the next bullet in the internal magazine into place, which allows him to hone in on the target. Coupled with this accuracy is power: each bullet is designed to kill in a single shot at ranges of 500 to 700 meters or more. In comparison, our units seldom engage outside of 350 meters. It just makes me glad the enemy doesn't have the M1, M2, or 03A3, the Springfields used by U.S. snipers in Korea.

**NIGHT.**

I am haunted by the image of one of the Taliban fighters. He was tall and young, and there was an air of the invincible about him. He seemed totally unconcerned about his safety as he strolled—and I use that word deliberately—through the rain of bullets, firing his Kalashnikov at our positions. I recall being baffled, and then awed, by his insouciance. If this was the caliber of the men we were fighting, driven as they were by a hankering for heaven, then all of our vaunted training amounted to nothing. Even I, with my intellect and education, had nothing that matched up to that kind of belief.

Later, when the smoke from the JDAM had cleared, I saw him trying to crawl up a rocky slope with his right arm and leg sheered away by the blast. My men whooped, but I found myself unable to share in their jubilation. Eventually someone shot him through the head and put him out of his misery. It was like killing a young lion in a slaughterhouse, an act without grace or dignity. This is not why I'd signed up to fight this war. The way he died made me feel angry and ashamed.

## DAY.

Shame.

The ancient Greeks lived and died by a code of honor—lived in the sense that the forces sustaining their existence, their most fundamental self-image—depended on being perceived and judged as meeting that code. And shame was honor's polar opposite, so that when a Homeric warrior like Ajax enacted a shameful act, the result was an abrupt and complete collapse of personality.

This reminds me of the Pashtuns. Their codes are alien to me—I loathe their bloodlust and misogyny—but I think I understand, and sympathize with, the clarity of their honor–shame dichotomy.

During our stint in Khost province, I asked a captured Taliban, who couldn't have been more than sixteen, why he had fought with such blatant disregard for self-preservation. I asked him if he wasn't afraid of dying, and I can still remember his reply word for word: Why should I be afraid? One day time will consume you as surely as it will me. It's a question of how long one is willing to wait. Meanwhile, to permit you to terrorize our land is a matter of shame, a dishonor greater than death.

Homer couldn't have put it better.

## NIGHT.

A bizarre thing happened to me today. While cleaning one of the old Victorian-era bolt-action rifles captured from the Taliban, I stuck my ring finger accidentally into a knothole in its wooden stock. The more I tried to free my finger, the more it got wedged there. It was a blazing hot day: I must have spaced out for a moment. I felt myself becoming one with the stock, the gun, the ground, the field outside, the mountains. A branch whipped across my face. Sand spilled out of my knees; the sun scorched my gray stone head. All around me were shards of broken glass.

I freaked out and wrenched my finger free. The nail almost came off. But the joy of returning to reality was enough to overcome the pain. I almost sobbed with relief. I had to go to Doc to borrow a pair of tweezers to take out the splinters. He said my finger looked like a toothbrush. It took me an hour to extricate all the tiny, jagged slivers. The gun smelled of cordite, as did my finger.

DAY.

In response to the news report that's obviously been nagging him ever since he listened to it a week ago, Connolly's printed out a useful list of some of the things forbidden by the Taliban when they were in power. He has copies of the list distributed to every member of the company, along with a handwritten note that reads: I want this to serve as a reminder, if one is needed, of the kind of people we're up against.

1. No woman allowed outside the home unless accompanied by a mahram (close male relative such as a father, brother, or husband).
2. Women not allowed to buy from male shopkeepers.
3. Women must be covered by the burqa at all times.
4. Any woman showing her ankles must be whipped.
5. Women must not talk or shake hands with men. No stranger should hear a woman's voice.
6. Ban on laughing in public.

7. Ban on women wearing shoes with heels, as no stranger should hear a woman's footsteps.

8. Ban on cosmetics. Any woman with painted nails should have her fingers chopped off.

9. No woman allowed to play sports or enter a sports club.

10. Ban on women's clothes in "sexually attracting colors."

11. Ban on women washing clothes in rivers or any public places.

12. Ban on women appearing on the balconies of their houses. All windows to be painted over so that women cannot be seen from the outside.

13. Any street or place bearing a woman's name or any female reference to be changed.

14. No one allowed to listen to music. No television or videos allowed.

15. No playing of cards or chess; no flying of kites.

16. No keeping of birds—any bird-keepers to be imprisoned and the birds killed.

17. Ban on all pictures in books and houses.

18. Anyone carrying un-Islamic books to be executed.

19. All people to have Islamic names.

20. All men, including boys, to wear Islamic clothes and cover their heads with caps or turbans. Shirts with collars banned.

21. Men must not shave or trim their beards, which should grow long enough to protrude from a fist clasped at the point of the chin.

22. Any non-Muslim must wear a yellow cloth stitched onto their clothes to differentiate them from believers.

I consider sending a copy to Emily to remind her why her ex-husband is fighting in Afghanistan, but then I decide against it as so much wasted effort. She's gone, and I have to come to terms with it.

## DAY.

It's Jack's birthday today. My baby's going to be three. I stand on watch on the Hescos and imagine holding him in my arms, pointing out the featureless field and the mountains. Those mountains—every day they cast their long shadows early over our faces: by four we're trapped in their darkness. Every day, they delay the sunrise so that we have to rise in the shadow of the unnaturally extended night. Our guns and grenades seem laughable against their immensity. It makes me wonder if this was what the Achaeans felt gazing from their beachholds at Troy's impregnable fortress, their faith in their gods their only protection. But then again, these mountains are probably older than either Troy or Mycenae.

And what about my protection? Maybe I'll settle for my child.

In my mind, I hold you up in my arms, little Jack. I hold you high up in the air like a candle to give myself the courage to go on. You are my shining light in this dark land.

## DAY.

We're visited this afternoon by the chief of police of the district. It's his first visit to the base, as well as to the district itself, as he himself admits. Appointed more than a year ago, he continues to live in Kabul, this alleged hero of the war of resistance against the Soviets. We pay the government that pays him to pretend to carry out his salaried obligations. This iconic sonofabitch has mastered the secret of how the game is played. Before he leaves, he asks Connolly to sign a stamped piece of paper attesting to his visit, which he terms an inspection. Connolly points to the dirt road leading into the mountains and tells him he'll sign the paper when police outposts have been set up all along the trail. Connolly's dusty serenity catches our guest by surprise. He says the area falls within our sphere of responsibility. I feel proud of the way Connolly handles the situation.

Thirty years ago, he points out, there used to be police outposts in the mountains.

The police chief smiles uncomfortably and says: They now exist only in the realm of memories.

Connolly smiles as well and says: As does your stamped document. Then he adds: The rules have changed since I took over, Humbaba. It's pay to play.

Humbaba? But my name is Sher Ali . . . it means "tiger."

Connolly says: You can call me Clark Kent—and this is Fortress America. Okay?

He walks the chief to his Toyota and tells him not to come back until he's got a plan to police the mountains.

**NIGHT.**

Apparently the Pashtun ruler Abdur Rahman Khan coined the term Yaghestan—Land of the Rebellious—to describe his country. No Pashtun likes to be ruled by another, he said, not even by another tribe or sub-tribe. I thought of the Soviets who'd originally set up this base more than twenty years ago and then left in haste when the mountain tribes united and swept down in a concerted attack. There's still some Russian graffiti on the dried-earth walls next to the mess tent. For instance, one wall carries a scrawl that reads: "Gorkii Park." One of the ANA translated it for me. Some wag—probably someone from our platoon—has scribbled next to it in English: "Linkin' Park."

Another wall records the distance from the base to "Moskva: 5197 km." I make a mental note to find out the distance to Washington, D.C.

**NIGHT.**

I read a passage tonight that helped me understand the locals. It was from *The Germania,* by Tacitus:

"When not engaged in warfare they spend a certain amount
of time in hunting, but much more in idleness, thinking of
nothing else but sleeping and eating. For the boldest and
most warlike men have no regular employment, the care of
house, home, and fields being left to the women, old men,
and weaklings of the family. In thus dawdling away their
time they show a strange inconsistency—at one and the
same time loving indolence and hating peace."

I showed Connolly the passage, and he sent it to Colonel Lautenschlager at Battalion, who got a kick out of it.

Connolly's trying hard to make up for his meltdown the other
night.

I understand, but I can't deny that there've been times when I've
wanted to tell him to take his know-it-all attitude and shove it. Nothing personal.

All the same, I can't resist asking him about the strategy that saw
us moved out in haste from our previous position in Khost province
and reinstalled here in Kandahar in an area far from established lines
of support. His jaw sets in a familiar obstinate expression, and he
insists, rather mulishly, that the generals know what they are doing.

In response, I cite a passage I'd read in Herodotus the other day,
where, writing in the fifth century BCE, he relates how the Egyptian
priests were able to recite the names of the three hundred and thirty
kings who'd reigned since the founding of their society, before going
on to add that none of them had any significant achievements to
their name.

I was reminded of our high command when I read that passage, I
tell Connolly. Once again, with set jaw, he repeats his mantra about
the generals knowing best. I give up and leave him to his own devices.

Evan Connolly is the perfect midlevel officer, cramped but
shipshape—of limited imagination and initiative—whose strategic

thinking goes no further than the Hescos that surround "his" base. His kind carry out their orders blindly, climb the chain of command steadily, and end up perpetuating the mistakes of the generals they replace. Because of them, the rest of us are condemned to be saddled with all of the servitude and none of the grandeur that accompanies the discipline of military service. And these are the men who command us against the Pashtuns, men born to the gun and the sword, Dear Lord.

## DAY.

I had a vision of Dad's hand closing over mine while cleaning my M-4 this afternoon. I was wiping the chamber with a cotton swab when I felt the pressure of his hand. It felt exactly as if he left it there for a moment—while I went very still. I saw the familiar wedding band on his ring finger, the old burn mark on his wrist, the prominent veins on the back of his hand. A rush of warmth flooded through me, and I was a child in his arms again. The sun lighting up the oil-slicked steel was no longer the sun of Kandahar but of the Vermont countryside. I heard blackbirds singing, an old backhoe going off somewhere in the distance, Eve running around in the yard. Pastel New England colors; subtle New England scents. When I went back to cleaning the magazine springs, what was before my eyes was not the dust and grit coating the M-4, but the mud and dust of an American summer. It went deep, this feeling. Dad and I cleaned that rifle together, working hand over hand.

## NIGHT.

A scattering of tall poles stuck into dark ground that turns out, on closer observation, to be water. A sheet of still water with indefinite boundaries, lit up only by a diffused spotlight that forms a backlit circle in place of the sky. It's neither night nor day, so I can't make out the time. An indistinct shape drifts between the poles, but its form is so hazy that it might be a boat or something else altogether. Three or four crows perch on top of the poles, but they are motionless. I wait for something to happen, and sure enough, a dark head rises out of the water. Soon the figure is wading at chest height, and I guess, with a degree of certainty that I cannot explain, that it's Emily. She bends over and fishes an object out of the water. I know it's Jack, but the strangest thing is the way she holds him, by an ankle, with the rest of him dragging underwater. I'm about to call out when she yanks him up and I see—distinctly—a bullet hole in the center of his forehead. There's no blood, but I can see right through the hole to the other side. I attempt to reach them, but something holds me back and I wake up shouting.

I blame the dream on mefloquine. I'd like to stop taking it—and to hell with the ever-present threat of malaria. So I stay up the rest of the night listening to the whine of the mosquitoes, unable to go back to sleep.

### Day.

We got news today of a drone attack a couple of days ago on a group of insurgents who'd crossed over the border. That same night, a joint operation by Special Forces and Afghan auxiliaries wiped out a Taliban stronghold due south of us. Connolly passed on the good news to the company, and the men cheered. Neither engagement was directly related to us, but we count every blow against the enemy as payback for Hendricks and Castro.

Later, Connolly caught Pfc. Gaines walking around in a flat wool pakol cap he'd taken from one of the casualties on the mission into the mountains and told him to take it off. When I asked him about it later on, he said: Unlike the colonial Brits, we're not going native. Not while I'm in command.

**D AY .**

I paid a surprise visit today to the ANA huts on the other side of the motor pool. For once, I decided not to pull them up for infractions. As if in gratitude, one of them gave me a stem of black cumin, with the grains perched at the tips of the sharp, delicate ends. He told me with a smile that if I kept it under my pillow it would perfume my dreams.

Another man asked to recite a poem in my honor. When I agreed, he told me, wistfully, that it was melon season in Kunduz, where he was from, and the poem was dedicated to the sublime taste of the fruit. He said that the Mughal emperor Babur pined for these same melons and once swore that he was willing to renounce his throne and the entirety of his wealth in exchange for a single fragrant melon from Kunduz. But then he started giggling uncontrollably while trying to read the poem to me, and I realized that he was high on hash. I asked him what he did for a living before the war, and he replied that he'd worked in a brick kiln since the age of seven. It seems he was sold by his parents to the owner of the kiln, who was also the ra'is of their village, to pay off an old debt, but I couldn't tell if that was the truth or the hash talking. If the former, then I couldn't help but wonder whether he was conceived by his parents for the express purpose of settling the debt. Once again, that would be entirely within the realm of plausibility, given what I've learned about the country and its people.

**E VENING .**

The first time I saw Tarsândan, I thought I'd arrived at the far ends of the earth. It reminded me of Death Valley, only worse. Now I don't even notice the desolation anymore. Sometimes I'm even moved by the subtlety of the desert palette, or the brilliance of the desert sunrises and sunsets. Tonight, for instance, the Milky Way resembles a glittering freeway across the sky. Doc tells me the locals believe that the Milky Way is the path traced by Buraq, the Prophet's horse, on his way to the heavens. I look up—just as our ANA Uzbeks begin their evening prayers—and see how that could work. The Uzbeks hold up their palms before their faces and chant "Bismillah ir-Rahman ir-Rahim"—"in the Name of God, Most Gracious, Most Compassionate." It used to annoy me at first, but I've since learned to appreciate the rhythm their prayers give to the day. Their kneeling silhouettes flicker against the starry sky.

Some distance from them, in the open area next to the motor pool, I set up to do my evening Tai Chi exercises. To my left, Pfc. Serrano's listening to his MP3 player and waving his arms around like he's at Burning Man. Whalen's in his hooch playing blues guitar. The air smells sweet, and it is damp from the mist. A shooting star arcs across the sky with a brilliance that takes my breath away. I surprise myself with my own sense of contentment. It just goes to show: there's beauty even in the bleakest backwater.

## Night.

It's a beautiful morning. The temperature's in the upper sixties, the sun's dipping in and out of cottony clouds, the sky's an iridescent blue. I'm marrying Emily on the grounds of Mills Mansion, its bright green swathe of lawn sweeping down to the Hudson. She hesitates before slipping the ring on my finger, and I try to contain my impatience, aware that the boys are waiting for me to get it over with and join them. As the minister pronounces her blessings, I look up at the clouds and close my eyes. Then I say a hurried good-bye and shoulder my pack and rifle. I run between the serried ranks of guests down to the river, where my platoon's arrayed in formation. I turn to wave good-bye and stop short when I see the shadows stretching across the sun-drenched lawn. Emily's wedding gown has turned to black.

I want to call out to her, but the words don't come. She gazes at me with an ineffable sadness.

I wake up with my own face streaked with tears. Why is it so difficult to say good-bye?

I'll never stop believing, Em. What's happened will never change the way I feel.

And the words that wouldn't come . . . I remember them now. They are, quite simply:

My love.

## DAY.

One hundred and twenty degrees. The earth bleached to a dry, bone-white crust. No breeze, but dust and grit everywhere. We walk around caked in dust, sinking knee-deep into dust, coughing dust. The slightest movement sends up dust clouds that hang suspended in the air like plumes. We appear and disappear as in a magic trick, swallowed by the dust and then regurgitated as dust-coated creatures. I wear wraparound goggles and swathe my head in my black-and-white checkered scarf; Doc's clad from head to toe in what appears to be a portable tent; Sergeant Tanner's gotten hold of a motorcycle helmet with a visor, and surgical gloves; Whalen's whiter than the rest of us, despite being shrouded in a poncho. For the first time since our arrival here, I can't even see the mountains. The day passes in a white haze of hot sun and burning dust. It's supposed to get even worse the next couple of days. I can't imagine how that could be possible.

## NIGHT.

It's still warm, even at night, but the wind's picked up. It's blowing from the southeast, directly out of the parched southern plains. Everything is suddenly filled with this wind and the dust and sand it brings with it. The dust makes it difficult to breathe, and everyone's retching up lungfuls of the stuff. The sand crackles underfoot, and when I lie down on my cot I can feel it trickling down my back. I try reading, but my book sheds sand: the words seem to slide off the page. I give up and watch the roof of the hut leaking dust instead. The wind buffets the door; there's sand seeping in through cracks in the floor. It's difficult to keep anything else in mind.

When I step outside, all I can see are vast brown clouds sweeping through the darkness. It's as if the wind has finally uprooted something that had never stirred before but has now taken over everything, erasing the familiar world, replacing thoughts from our minds and words from our mouths—and all we can do is watch its assault, bewildered.


DAY.

The entire base has come to a standstill. The dust storm rages on, and it's reduced visibility to nil.

There's dust inside my hut, on my desk, on my bunk—I can't move without raising a cloud of dust. I'm wearing a face mask, but I have to keep taking it off because it's asphyxiating.

I'm dreading the prospect of going another night without sleep.

We're all so tired, we might as well be dead.

# CAPTAIN

**F**UCK this.

I mean, *fuck* this shit!

I'm furious, and I see absolutely no point in beating around the bush.

I summon Whalen to my office and tell him that I've found out about our men feeding the LN outside the wire and that it simply isn't acceptable. Not by a long shot.

You want to tell me what the fuck's going on, First Sarn't? Since when have the men had so much freedom of movement outside the perimeter? What's the fucking terp doing running around like the fucking Energizer Bunny? Who gave him permission to talk to the girl? What's happened to our friggin' security SOP, for Chrissake?

He takes a while to reply, and when he does, his tone is somber.

I suppose you could say that I've been unlike my usual self from the moment I discovered she had no legs, Sir. When I was walking up to her—with the possibility of a bomb at the other end—all I could think of was me, myself, and I. But when she took off her burqa, it stopped me in my tracks. I didn't want to go on with the search, but I did, of course, and I tried to be considerate, but it shook me up. What can I say, Sir? I wasn't expecting to find her with stumps instead of legs. There are things in war that can get to a man. This was one of them.

Jesus. I never thought I'd hear this shit from you. Are you telling me you're using this crap as the reason to compromise the security of the entire fucking base? Jesus Christ, I could have you fired for circumventing me, Marcus!

You left the decision to me, Sir, and I did what I thought best.

Dammit, you know better than anyone else that I don't even have enough troops to carry out half the missions they expect me to, and you just fucking sit there and tell me how your heart's bleeding for some broad without legs, and that that's good enough reason to do away with the most basic security procedures! I mean, why not dismantle the Hescos and take down the wires while you're at it? Put up a fucking sign, First Sergeant, that says: Shooting Gallery, Taliban Welcome Here!

He looks at me with a strained expression, but remains silent.

With an effort, I control myself, and, in a more formal voice, I say: I'm not heartless, First Sarn't, and the extent of her injuries took me aback as well. But it still doesn't excuse what happened. Once outside the wire, the men are at grave risk from shooters in the mountains. It's way outta line.

Where they went is well outside the range of the enemy's snipers, Sir.

Stop throwing technicalities at me, First Sarn't. They could have an entire fucking arsenal of heavy artillery out there, and we wouldn't be any wiser.

He regards me with a distant, intense gaze.

With all due respect, Sir, the girl's been out there in that beat-up cart for one and a half days. She's been sitting all hunched up through blazing sun and frigid night while we're all hunkered down in our B-huts and tents. It doesn't feel right.

Bullshit, I say succinctly. What's the matter with you? Are you asking to be shipped out to the Peace Corps or some fucking daycare center? I can't believe what I'm hearing! Have you gone off the fucking reservation? The next thing you'll be telling me, you've changed the fucking rules of engagement and we're sending her flowers.

He hesitates. I guess there are times when war doesn't exactly make sense, Sir.

I stare at him, outraged. You going soft? Eighteen years in the army, and it's come to this?

This isn't about going soft, Sir, he says quietly. I'm drawing on all my experience to tell you that this isn't a battlefield situation. It's a humanitarian situation. Human terrain. Hearts and minds template.

We're fighting a conventional war, First Sarn't. I don't believe in that COIN bullshit. We don't have the manpower to support it. Where we are, the reality of the physical terrain trumps everything. Which is why every time you look at that girl, I want you to squint past her and look at those slopes, okay? She's doing exactly what she's supposed to do: persuading us to let down our guard so that her folks can wipe us out sooner than you can say Johnny Thunder. She's the decoy, First Sarn't—she's setting us up for failure. She's staring us in the friggin' eyes, for Chrissake, challenging us in black and white every damn moment.

And I'm telling you that you're mistaken, he responds calmly. If you think it through objectively, you'll realize that there's absolutely nothing black and white about this situation: it's all in grays.

Once you start thinking like that, it's time to quit. As for your objective reasoning, quite frankly you know where you can shove it.

That gets his back up. He sits down and leans forward across my desk.

I was in the army when you were in school, Sir, and I've seen

enough to tell you that you're reading this all wrong. Yeah, sure, in
the army we're supposed to think in black and white because we live
in a gray world 24/7 and it simplifies things, but it also leads to mistakes, and that's where leadership comes in. That's where it's up to us
to tell the boys what to do and what to think. And the boys are confused about the girl. She's outside the conventional template, and it's
driving them batshit crazy.

Bullshit. The next thing you'll have them sitting around like pan-
sies picking posies while the enemy overruns us again. They've done
it once—they've sussed us out and come fucking close to finishing
us off. If we let our guard down, they'll do it again. So her situation
sucks? Big deal. Big fucking deal. I need you to go tell the men to
embrace the suck and deal with it.

He gives me that long stare again. Embrace the suck, he says.
Jesus. He shakes his head. So you're gonna have us eat a steady pro-
gression of shit until we get sick? Unbelievable, Sir. We're the U.S.
Army. We're supposed to stand for more than jes' fighting and killing.
We do the right thing.

I slap my hands down on the desk. Don't even go there, Marcus,
I shout. The next thing you'll be asking me is when was the last time
I've looked at the monster in the mirror.

It's always a good idea to check that ragin' impulse now and then,
Sir, he snaps back.

I respond with an infuriated look. I'll ask for your personal opinion when I want it, First Sarn't. You're my right-hand man, for fuck's
sake—my fucking Capo di Capo. You're supposed to be the unit's
rock—its disciplinarian and enforcer. Your number one job is to support me and my decisions. There's work to be done. Get ahold of
yourself.

I lower my voice. There's to be no more contact with the LN, is
that clear?

His eyes meet mine with a brooding discontent. Then, quietly—
so quietly that I can hardly catch the words—he says: Understood, Sir.

I stick an unlit cigarette into my mouth, making an obvious effort to control myself.

That's all, First Sergeant, I say.

I watch him stalk out, and then get up and walk agitatedly over to the Plexiglas strip that makes up the only window in the hut. It's coated in a thin layer of dust. I press my face against it and look outside. Long shadows lie across the base, the late afternoon light tamping down on everything. Although there is no breeze, occasionally the flaps of some of the tents flutter of their own accord. When I turn away, the room seems very dark.

I return to the desk, uncap a small flask, and pour stale coffee into a mug. The old-fashioned clock on the desk ticks away the seconds. Stirring sweetener into the coffee, I drink it in a single gulp and send for Tom Ellison next. When he enters, I hold up the mug with a grimace and say: This is the worst damn coffee I've ever had! I mean, it's not like I'm expecting espresso, but this stuff is rotgut.

I'll treat you to the Screaming Eagle blend at Green Beans the next time we visit KAF, Sir, he says with a smile. It's my favorite kind.

Then: You wanted to see me?

Yes, I did. How you doing, Lieutenant?

It's been here and there, Sir.

I'm not surprised. I've been in a pretty numbed state myself since the firefight. It's difficult not to be, seeing that there are patches of dried blood all over the base.

I'll have it taken care of, Sir.

Well, there's that, of course. But there's also something else.

The LN outside?

Yup.

He nods, looking troubled. It's proving a major distraction.

No kidding, Lieutenant, I say tersely. Has everyone gone out of their fucking minds?

He stares at me like a deer in the headlights, startled by my sudden change of tone. Ah, well, I guess . . . he stumbles a bit before recovering: I guess the men aren't used to having a female suddenly show up in the kill zone after months of isolation, Sir, especially after a battle that's seen us sustain casualties. They're simply not psychologically prepared.

No shit. And I don't suppose I've been blessed with the good fortune of having competent officers who can communicate to their men that we're not here to offer TL fucking C.

He flushes. Don't worry, Sir. I'll read them the riot act.

Yeah? You telling me you didn't know that it was one of your sergeants who was the NCO on duty?

No, Sir. I became aware of it . . . after the fact. He hesitates, before adding: And, in all honesty, I should probably have mentioned that right off and—

And also dealt with your subordinate without waiting for me to bring it up?

Yes, Sir. My apologies, Sir. I suppose I've acted in ways that have surprised me.

Join the club, Lieutenant, Whalen says as he walks back in.

'Lo First Sarn't . . . I greet him curtly. What is it now?

He thinks for a moment. Then, without looking at me, he says: Actually, I dropped by to let you know I'm about to have the girl brought in to the medical tent to have her evaluated. I want Doc to examine her stumps and replace those filthy rags with clean dressings, at the very least.

I say nothing. Instead, I link my fingers together and look at him steadily for a few seconds.

Then I say: Permission denied, if that's what you're asking. We'll wait for the ANA to deal with her when they show up tomorrow. It's their job.

With all due respect, I don't think the ANA are medically competent, Sir.

We're foreigners, and men. She'd be perfectly within her rights to refuse our help. She probably will, by the way, if I know anything about their culture. And if you force things, we'll end up with a perfectly avoidable incident.

It's still worth giving it a shot. We've a legal and ethical obligation to give her care, Sir. I'll try to persuade her to—

Don't sweat it, First Sergeant, I interrupt, suddenly running out of patience. You may *believe* you've a responsibility toward the girl, but I *know* I have the larger responsibility toward everyone in the base.

I turn away from him and address both of them: I think this has gone far enough, don't you? I need you to compartmentalize this thing and park your sentimentality somewhere else. As leaders, you need to keep your cool when everyone else is losing theirs. We can't all of us suddenly go nuts about this girl. We'd have to be perfect suckers to fall for that ploy. I mean, it's only been a coupla days since we lost Lieutenant Frobenius and the others. The least you can do is to remember who killed them and get ahold of yourselves.

They stare at me. The silence in the hut couldn't have been more complete. Then Ellison takes out a handkerchief and blows his nose.

So you still think she's been planted there deliberately, Sir? he says at length.

What else? I reply.

To what end? Whalen asks suddenly.

What end? Oh—I'm convinced that her companions are biding their time on those slopes, just out of our sight. The moment we let down our guard—BANG! And the fact that she'd be in the way wouldn't slow them down. She's a woman: worthless to them.

I don't know, Sir, Ellison says, obviously torn. I mean, wouldn't they have struck when First Sarn't went out of the wire to make sure she was clean, Sir?

That doesn't mean I'm gonna allow her into the base when we've all recognized the distraction she poses for the men. I can't take that chance. We've lost so many men, I'm beginning to feel like we've all got bull's-eyes painted on our foreheads. I no longer have a wide margin for taking chances.

Yes, of course, Sir, he says awkwardly.

But I'll tell you what, I add. I'll show you something that may convince you that there are enough holes in her story to make me continue to believe she's making the whole thing up.

I get up from the desk, walk over to the wall behind me, and take down the map that's pinned up there. Then I walk back and spread it out on the desk.

Take a look at this, I tell them, and they stand up and lean over the map.

I locate Tarsândan and then trace a line with my finger to the valley that she said she'd come from. That's eleven kilometers as the crow flies, I observe, and twenty-three kilometers by a broken-down dirt track that zigzags between three towering mountain ranges. Not to speak of the streams she'd have to ford—here, at the foot of this mountain, and then again at this place.

I straighten up and look at them with a smile.

Now: if you really want to believe her story of crawling those twenty-three clicks all by her lonesome self on that plank on wheels, be my guest. Attend to her medical needs. Do whatever else it takes to make her trek worthwhile, because it would've been a feat without parallel. But if you share my doubts, then I'm going to ask you to wait until the birds get here tomorrow. It's the least we can do to respect the memory of the men we've lost.

But what if her story is true, Sir? Ellison asks.

Which part of it?

All of it.

That her brother and his men weren't part of the Taliban? What the fuck does that matter, given that we were attacked by them and, what's more, sustained severe casualties. You can hardly blame me if I'm not interested in his story. Or hers, for that matter.

No, of course not, Sir . . . But *she* wasn't part of the attack, and if she did make it here on her own to claim her brother's body, wouldn't that constitute grounds for consideration on our part?

Ellison's persistence is beginning to get on my nerves. Making no attempt to hide my annoyance, I snap back: How do you fucking know that she wasn't part of their attack? She could have been a spotter, or a scout, or a hundred other things besides.

To my astonishment, Whalen backs him up. He says: With all due respect, Sir, given her physical condition, it's hardly conceivable that she could have taken an active part . . .

Jesus Kee-rist! I explode. You're talking about a girl who claims she used that two-bit cart to come down here from the mountains!

I'm sure you know what I'm getting at, Sir.

The look in his eyes is so clearly one of petition that I have to look away in disgust. It would have to be my luck, I think bitterly, to have my company staffed by fucking bleeding heart First Sergeants and newbies straight out of training.

Isn't that what makes us different from the enemy? Whalen persists.

I don't need a lecture from you about what makes us different from the enemy.

So there's nothing we can do to help her, Whalen says abruptly. Is that what you're saying, Sir?—that we're no longer making distinctions between unarmed civilians and armed combatants?

For a moment, we stare at each other. I'm about to give him a dressing down, when I have a fleeting vision of the girl kneeling in her cart, her burqa spilling over its confines, her hands raw and bleeding from pushing against the ground. I gaze at my own hands, the fingers thick and powerful from many generations of masons on my father's side. They were uncomplicated men, independent and fierce. Whatever they grasped became theirs.

I hear Ellison shift uncomfortably and glance at him.

I give a thin smile. Tell you what, I remark, as a concession to the two of you and your fucking scruples, I'll speak to Battalion to see if they can check out her backstory. I'm expecting to hear from them anyways regarding the drone that's been scoping out the slopes for signs of the enemy. If they give me an all clear, and if there's even an iota of truth to her tale, I'll let you evaluate her—*and* I'll sound out Colonel Lautenschlager about shipping her to a field hospital.

Obviously taken aback, Ellison opens his mouth, but then closes it again.

Whalen clears his throat. If you feel that strongly about it, I'll hold off, he says with reluctance. But I'll despise myself every minute of it.

He must have thought that the concessions needed to be mutual and appears taken aback when I suggest otherwise. You've waited a day and a half, I say dismissively. We've no idea how long it's been since she lost her legs—probably months, if not longer. A few more hours won't make a difference.

He nods stiffly, turns without a word, and walks out of the hut.

I stare after him, glower at Ellison, and address him while putting away the map.

Now it's your turn, Lieutenant. Give me the lowdown on exactly what happened with this whole damn business of carrying food out to her.

He looks chagrined.

I guess it all began when the men came up with the idea of a contest modeled on the movie *Fight Club,* Sir, to decide who was going to be the one to go out to her.

Did they beat each other to a pulp?

Sort of, Sir.

Who won?

Spc. Simonis, Sir.

Whose ass did he whup?

Pfc. Grohl, Sir.

So it was Simonis who took the food to her?

Yes, Sir, accompanied by the terp.

Well, that's a relief. I'd hate to imagine Grohl face-to-face with her. That boy hates the locals. We're gonna have to keep an eye on him.

Yes, Sir.

What kind of food did Simonis bring her? Fucking turkey and apple pie?

The men warmed up some MRE stew, Sir, and Pfc. Ramirez made one of his trademark Philly cheesesteaks.

And she turned it down?

Yes, Sir, she did.

I shake my head in disbelief—and then I begin to chuckle.

You gotta hand it to her! Jesus, if I had her in the company instead of a bunch of wet-nosed snots, we coulda overrun those slopes quicker than you can say motherfucker. In any case, now we know how she'd respond to a medical examination. She'd send us packing.

You think?

I know. I hate to be such a hard-ass, Lieutenant, but when you've been in this game for as long as I have, it becomes second nature to look beneath the surface of things. Your survival—and the survival of your men—depends on it.

You're probably right, Sir, he says, and pauses. This war isn't turning out to be what I'd expected, Sir, but that's probably my lack of experience.

I rivet my gaze on him. It's not what Lieutenant Frobenius expected either. And he had plenty of experience.

He flushes, and his pale blue eyes grow paler still.

Luck of the draw, I say bleakly. You gotta go when your time comes.

No room for second chances, Sir?

Very little, Lieutenant. This whole country is like one massive IED for us—and once you step on one of those things, you're lucky if your legs are all you lose.

What about the girl, Sir? What kind of luck does she have?

We've been looking each other in the eye, but now we simultaneously turn away. After a while, I say: I must admit I'd expected
to find a boy behind that ghostlike shroud. In fact, I was convinced
it was a boy—something about the voice reminded me of a fucked-
up creature I'd once encountered by a river near Baghdad. His voice
was pitched high with trauma, yet he had this strange composure, an
unnerving coldness.

He looks discouraged.

She's affecting the men, Sir: I can see it.

I'm not surprised, I reply. Hell, she's affected me. It's impossible
not to be affected; we're only human. Something like that eats away
at you from the inside. But as you can tell, I gotta draw the line somewhere, and with good reason. We're not here on a fucking humanitarian mission. I need the men to transition back from tea and sympathy
to combat mode—and the sooner we can get the girl out of here, the
sooner that will happen. It's important for us to feel normal again. It's
very important.

Yes, Sir.

It's all that matters, in fact. We gotta stay at the top of the food
chain. It's the law of the jungle, Lieutenant.

He nods wordlessly, and I reach for my laptop, signaling the end
of our conversation.

After he leaves, however, the first thing I do is to put in a call to
Battalion as I'd promised Whalen. I feel a curious satisfaction in getting that out of the way.


## 1800.

I decide to walk out to the wire at sundown.

Dusk has come with broad strokes of color that reflect off the
mountains. The air cools rapidly, and the stars appear one by one. I
glance at my watch and think of Jenna dressing the twins for school
and feel a lump form in my throat. I want to gather them in my arms

and hold them there. May God protect those He loves. May He protect them until the wandering warriors come home.

I hear the sound of footsteps behind me and turn around. It's Pfc. Ramirez, one of the mortar crews, his T-shirt dark with sweat. Good evening, Sir, he says.

Evening, soldier.

Don't mind me, Sir. I'm just setting up markers for my sights.

He nods at the mountains. When are we going to take the fight to them, Sir?

Soon, soldier, soon. And if they swarm us before we do, I want it to be the final experience of their lives.

He tugs reflexively at his M-4 rifle.

I'm rarin' to go, Sir, he says. Ready to eat nails.

Only a matter of time, soldier, I reply, and watch as he walks slowly back to his position by the Hescos.

A strong wind has begun to blow across the plain. It puffs up the loose, knee-length shirt and baggy trousers of the Tajik interpreter as he passes Ramirez. They don't greet each other.

The interpreter approaches me and raises his hand to his heart.

Salâm, Comandan Saab, he says.

Salâm, Masood, I reply. Che hâl dâred?

He starts, and his face breaks into a delighted grin. You speak Dari! I would never have imagined! I hadn't heard you speak it earlier.

I know a few words. Just enough to get by.

But I am forgetting my manners, he says quickly, mortified. You asked me a question about how I was, and I am fine, Comandan Saab, thank you. Khub astom, tashakor. Then he says: Mêbakhshêd, Comandan Saab, excuse me for my rudeness, but you took me by surprise. Not one of the other American soldiers speaks the language. Not a single one.

Oh yes? Well, that's a shame, isn't it?

He misses my sarcasm, but, in the meantime, a flock of birds wheeling overhead distracts my attention.

Do you know what those birds are, Masood? Are they warblers?

I don't know their name, Comandan Saab, but they are good for shekâr kardan.

They're a tad on the small side for hunting, aren't they?

No, Comandan Saab, they are very tasty, especially the young. These birds make their nests on the ground on hillsides, and we harvest the chicks by the hundreds and snack on them.

I look up at the darting birds again. They're a bright yellow and green. Their wings catch the dying light.

I don't suppose you've any laws to protect birds and suchlike, eh?

Oh, there are laws, he says with a rueful smile, but these days they are on paper only. When we have a new government, we will enforce them. But first we have to get rid of the topak salaran.

Well, I'll do my part to help you get rid of the gun rulers if that's what it'll take to protect the wildlife. I happen to believe that animals have as much of a right to the land as men.

He looks at me sideways. Are you fond of birds, Comandan Saab?

I sure am. I grew up in the prairies, which are wide tracts of grassland. We've many unusual birds. The prairie chicken, for instance.

To show him, I puff up my chest and strut about with my hands held out stiffly by my sides in imitation of the mating dance of the male bird.

You are a real Afghan! he says excitedly. All Afghan men love birds and flowers. We love beauty in all its forms.

Beautiful women?

Women, not so much. Only genuinely beautiful things.

You don't say, I remark dryly. I point to the girl in the field.

What d'you make of her?

I went out to talk to her this afternoon, Comandan Saab. I wanted to ask her why she rejected our food. She's very stubborn, very proud. She wouldn't speak to me. I said we should be friends. She sent me away.

She didn't say anything at all?

Only that she had no interest in anything other than burying her brother's body.

Do you think that's true? Is that really why she's here?

He shoots me a darting glance. If you want to know the truth, Comandan Saab, I will tell you. I think the girl has been placed here to deliberately divert your attention. She is the property of the black-hearted Taliban. As soon as you relax your guard, they will attack under the velvet cover of darkness.

So you think she's the bait for their trap?

His answer is swift and unambiguous. Besyêr balê, he says. Yes, absolutely. There is no other explanation for her presence.

Then he adds: We are in the heart of Kandahar province, where the Taliban have their stronghold. I have no doubt about the girl. All these people have the same poison running through their veins.

In the quiet that follows, I grow aware of the vultures high overhead, and the wind sending dust devils racing through the field.

I raise my binoculars and scan the slopes.

All right, Masood, thank you, I tell him. I'll see you later. Ba'dan mêbinêm.

Sabâ mêbinametân, Comandan Saab! See you later, as the Americans like to say.

He turns to leave, but I stop him.

Lowering the binoculars and facing him, I say casually:

Oh, and by the way, before you go, I heard that she was wailing like a banshee when you left her this afternoon. What happened?

Oh, that was nothing. I told her about her brother, Comandan Saab, and that she wasn't going to get him back.

Now why would you do that?

Because it is the truth, Comandan Saab.

I feel the color mount to my face. Controlling myself, I say firmly: Hold your horses. You're not to make those decisions, okay? Those are mine to make, at a time of my choosing. She'd have found out tomorrow, in any case. There was no need to cause her suffering.

I don't want to cause trouble, Comandan Saab, I'm just trying to understand. Would it cause her to suffer more if she found out the truth now or if we let her live in ignorance for one more day?

I glare at him.

That's exactly the sort of question that causes trouble, I tell him. What's there not to understand? Your job here is to translate for us and respond to specific queries. Anything outside of that, you need to ask permission from Lieutenant Ellison, First Sergeant Whalen, or any of the other officers. Is that clear?

Yes, Sir, he says, completely subdued.

Good. You can go now.


**1900.**

I run into Ellison and Whalen in the mess tent. We're all there for the same reason: coffee. All around us, men are drifting in little groups toward the Hescos. I watch them for a moment, and then ask Whalen: What's going on? Are we having a fucking concert again tonight?

They look at me warily, and then at each other.

Whalen says: I think some of the men are hopin' she'll play . . .

And I'm hoping she's gonna be out of our hair from tomorrow, I interject, glancing at my watch. Last night she started playing at eight, and it's only seven o'clock now. So what's biting these guys?

They're probably going early to get good seats, Sir, Ellison offers.

It just goes to show how much there is to do around here, I grouse. Which reminds me, I go on, tomorrow's going to be a big day. The birds are flying in at noon. They'll be bringing replacements for the men we've lost, so we'll be back to our full complement. We're also getting vehicles driven up from KAF to replace the Hummers shot up in the firefight. Brand new M-ATVs, straight off the shop floor. We're gonna use them to piggyback into the mountains. And then, later on in the week, there'll be contractors showing up to rebuild the guard tower and install plumbing so we can finally have working showers.

Do you want me to draw up work parties, Sir? Whalen asks.

That'll depend on the situation with the contractors. But before we can deal with any of that, we need to clear the deck of pending tasks, starting with the girl. Once we get her out of the way, I want a proper memorial service for the men we've lost. And while I realize that no memorial is going to be adequate, we'll be remembering our brothers, and I don't want any fucking distractions.

Even as I'm speaking, I feel a tension constricting my throat, and have to stop short. I half-expect Nick to walk around the corner.

I see Whalen's eyes tearing up as well. Ellison coughs and looks away. I forget about getting coffee and, excusing myself, leave the mess tent abruptly. I knock against a soldier on my way out but don't stop.

Entering the blessed silence of my hut, I lurch over to my desk, knocking over a stack of folders in my haste. My heart is pounding like a hammer. I sit down and rest my forehead on the desk. I feel a sort of panic, and then, almost immediately, an overpowering fatigue. My tiredness is so extreme, it's as if it's devouring me alive.

I drop off into an exhausted sleep seconds later.

## 2000.

A familiar music penetrates my sleep, followed, almost instantly, by a gunshot.

The music stops.

I hear the sound of raised voices, and snap awake.

I run out with my 9 mm and see a crowd gathering outside one of the B-huts.

I shoulder my way through the men and enter the hut to find Doc and Whalen and Staff Sergeant Schott already there. Whalen's holding a soldier in his arms. Doc's attaching an IV to a saline bag. Then I notice the pistol on the floor and pick it up. It's hot to the touch. I place it on the nearest bunk.

Schott draws me aside. He lowers his voice. Attempted suicide, Sir, he says.

Who is it?

Specialist Garcia, Sir.

How bad is it?

Bullet creased his skull. He'll survive.

I look around the cramped hooch. It reeks of sweat and body odor. I don't know what to say. At length, I nod and tell him to ask Whalen to report to me with Doc when they have the situation under control. I glance at Garcia one more time and leave the hut.

I emerge into the silent and expectant crowd.

I pause for a moment to address the men. My mouth feels dry and gummy, and I'm still bleary-eyed from sleep. He's going to be okay, I tell them.

A tent flap snaps in the darkness somewhere.

Is he hurt bad, Sir? someone asks.

Not as far as I could tell, I reply gently. I feel fiercely protective of them.

One of the soldiers closest to me—Alizadeh, I think—gasps with relief and covers his face with his hands. I pat his shoulder and make my way back to my hut.

I'm writing up a report on the incident when Whalen and Doc show up. I look at their tight, grim faces. He's fine, Doc says somberly. Sedated and under observation.

Good, I reply. I'd like your report ASAP. I'm shipping him out tomorrow. He needs psychiatric attention, quite obviously. I pause and run my eyes over them. What about you guys? How're you holding up?

I'm too worn out to think clearly, Sir, Doc admits.

I'm all right, Whalen says.

Good man, I reply. It's just one more fucking complication that's gonna take up our time, but we'll have to deal with it. We can't have it dominating the day—or discouraging the men. There's too much else to be done.

I'll take care of it, Whalen says. I'll round up the NCOs and have them sit down with their boys. It's a first for most of them, so it's going to take them some time to get over it. He pauses and runs his hand wearily across his face. Anything else?

It's a big deal, First Sarn't, I emphasize. We can't afford to have it trip us up. We gotta make sure it remains an isolated case.

He shakes his head. It won't trip us up. I'll make sure each one of my soldiers is okay.

They're probably not gonna be able to sleep tonight, that's for sure.

They'll have to figure out how to deal with it, Doc says, but, just in case, I'll check in on the boys in Garcia's hooch.

Do we have any idea why?

His wife dumped him, Whalen answers.

He shoulda come to us.

He did. I was going to set him up with counseling.

The stupid, stupid fuck! I burst out. It had to happen now. It had to be us.

Whalen's tired gaze is replaced by an expression of resignation.

I lean back on my chair and compose myself. I reflect that when I signed up to fight wars, I could never have imagined they'd include a mental health component. I feel played out, ready to throw in the towel. At length, I merely shrug my shoulders and break the heavy silence. Put that in your report, I tell Doc. I don't want the word to get out that we're out to lunch when it comes to looking after our men.

After they leave, I continue to sit motionless for a while.

The night air comes in at the door—air filled with the smell of the desert, a dusty mineral smell so sharp it's almost cruel in its potency.

## 0045.

I've been lying in bed trying to go back to sleep ever since I woke up. I toss and turn in the hollow that my body has molded in the mattress. My sweat-soaked pillow squelches unpleasantly against my head. Finally, a fly buzzing around the hut puts an end to any more thought of rest. I give up and get up wearily from the bunk. I switch on the light, and the first thing that catches my eye is the damn book by Sophocles that Frobenius lent me. As I pick it up and flip through the pages, I hear his voice going off in my head: You have to read this. It's about as cogent an analysis as anything you'll find about where we are today.

And where are we, according to you?

We're in Kalyug, Captain. It's the age of Creon. 'Cept that he's here, there, and everywhere. He's the government and the corporations and everything else that matters, and he's totally faceless. He's a machine, a system, he has his own logic, and once you're part of that, it really doesn't matter if you're a grunt or a general: you're trapped in a conveyor belt of death and destruction. And that's the saddest thing. The saddest thing is that we're part of Creon. We're all compromised and there's nothing we can do about it. It's like losing your virginity. You can't get it back once it's gone.

That's gotta be the most friggin' paranoid thing I've ever heard, Lieutenant.

I'd have to be morally dead if I weren't paranoid under these circumstances, Captain. I kid you not.

I put down the book impatiently and start pacing. In a corner of the hut, Shorty stirs to his feet as well, woken up by my restlessness. We pace together. Then I smear some Nutella on a couple of MRE crackers. I give him a cracker as well, but without the Nutella, and ignore his protests: the dog has a sweet tooth. I've decided to take him back with me when I go home. An army base is no place for a dog. Besides, Jenna has a thing for animals, and it's time the twins got their first dog. But I'll keep it a surprise: I won't tell them until it's time to collect him at the airport. I grin in anticipation at the thought of it, but then my mind shifts back from future pleasures to the hellish present.

I sit down at my dust-covered desk and lean forward on my knees. The ground beneath me is clay seamed with fissures, while here and there are bowl-shaped depressions kneaded from the heels and soles of countless boots. A bat flicks against the Plexiglas window; at intervals, the call of an owl echoes down from the mountains. I dab at the sweat on my throat with a handkerchief and ineffectively swat the huge black flies that torment Shorty. All day long there are flies, and at night the mosquitoes join them. As I fight the inertia that threatens to overtake me, I feel a familiar dull rage at the thought of yet another sleepless night leading to the blinding heat waves of another day. I pick up the book again, hesitate, and then chuck it away.

You really ought to read it . . . Frobenius counters in my head before I cut him off: Go somewhere else, Nicko. I've no time to chat. Maybe I got the wrong fucking kind of education, but for me, to act is all.

But don't you see, it's precisely because of the inbuilt oppressiveness of this place that the locals came up with war as a solution? It's a vast release from the heat and the dust and the flies.

Oh, yeah? Well, tell that to the broad squatting outside in the heat and the dust. She seems pretty content.

The broad outside . . . ? Do you mean Antigone?

Whatever, Lieutenant. I'm not interested.

A high-pitched whine from Shorty interrupts my train of thought, and I smile at him with relief and say: Good dog.

I decide to go out to the Hescos, check the perimeter security, and breathe some fresh air. Maybe that'll help me sleep. I put on my boots, throw on my fleece jacket and a bandana, and escape the hut. Shorty slips out with me, trotting at my heels. Past the flaps of the tent, the cold hits us with force. Shorty barks in anticipation, while

I hunch deep into my jacket. Together, we walk past the company's colors fluttering high on a pole. We used to fly Old Glory too, but Battalion had us pull that down because "we weren't in the country as an occupying force." I wince at the memory and think: Yeah, right.

My first stop is the mortar pit, with Pratt, Barela, and Ramirez on duty.

Ramirez is looking through the thermals attached to his M-4. He glances at me as I crouch down beside him.

How's the imaging? I ask.

It's a sex toy, Sir, he says with a grin.

Glad to hear it, I say dryly. As long as something's keeping you awake . . .

I ask him for his rifle and look through the TWS. I press my face against the rubber cup encircling the eyepiece to activate the display and cooling mechanism. Then I zoom in on the cart in the field. The cart glows as a diffused white oval against a black background. There's no movement: she must be asleep. I look for a few seconds and then hand the rifle back to Ramirez.

Pratt says: When I look through the TWS at the cart, Sir, I see a giant eye, and she's in the middle of it.

Is that so?

I'm a' tellin' you, Sir, I can feel her heart beatin' in the darkness and reachin' right out to me. It make me sad. Real sad.

I see. Well . . .

I get up and begin to walk away, then suddenly feel a spurt of irritation and turn around. I don't mind your feeling sympathetic toward her, I say abruptly, but you need to keep it under control. Eyes on the ball, eh? There's no place in war for a sentimental soldier.

Are we wagin' war on a disabled girl, Sir? Ramirez unexpectedly pipes up. Is that what we're doin' now?

No, I reply, taken aback. No, of course not! You must know what I mean.

I guess it's been heavy, Barela says, our havin' to sit here and look out at her. It ain't like she's some badass terrorist, with all due respect, Sir. She's just doing what any of us would have done in her place. Most of us, at least.

It'll be heavier still if you let your guard down and we're attacked in the middle of the night, I respond. Remember what happened two days ago. You don't want to end up as a casualty in a CQB you coulda prevented, soldier.

I . . . I suppose we just have a feelin' she's different, Sir.

How do you know that? I say sharply.

Nothing tangible, Sir.

Then park that feeling.

Yes, Sir.

We're pretty much worn out, Sir, Pratt interjects quietly, and it's prob'ly affectin' our judgment. Sometimes it's like I can't feel my body at all.

Stand up and stretch when that happens, I say without sympathy.

An' this waitin' aroun' is tellin' on our nerves an' all, he carries on, almost as if I hadn't spoken. 'Specially if you got to do it from here. Ev'thing looks like a threat through a scope at night. It's like havin' tunnel vision.

I glare at him for a moment before walking off. Seconds later, I catch myself wondering why I'm so annoyed. As I pause in the shadow of the Hescos to tie a bootlace, I hear Ramirez saying: What's up with the old man? He was gonna eat our faces in a minnit! Whoo . . . whoo . . . I'd give a hundred grand to know what's buggin' him.

If you had a hundred grand you wouldn't be here, dude, Barela says.

I still can't b'lieve she turned down my Philly cheesesteak, though, Ramirez says, abruptly changing tack. I mean, I used hot sauce an' all.

These people are fickle, man, Barela says.

No, it ain't that, Pratt says firmly. They jes' don' wan' us here.

That's not what the terp says, Ramirez insists.

Masood? Barela says. He's all right.

I don't know, man, I just don't know, Ramirez continues. I don't want to be close-minded or anything, but I don't trust the Afs. I mean, think of the way the ANA fuckin' left us high and dry during the firefight. That ain't right, man. If I see one of those suckers again, he's dead.

He's not going to stick around long enough for you to get to him, Barela points out quite reasonably. Or even if you do, he's gonna be yellin' up a storm, calling on his hadji buddies for rescue.

It's hard to yell when you got a barrel in your mouth, Ramirez says tersely. Besides, our Afs were Uzbek, and I don't know if you can technically call them hadjis, or if that's only reserved for the Taliban, who're mostly Pashtun.

You're probably right, Barela admits.

And the Pashtun wouldn't run from a fight, Ramirez continues. That's why they fuckin' own the country. I mean, just thinkin' about that fuckin' sandstorm attack makes my neck go sore. They've been doing this crazy shit for so long, it's prolly the only way they know to be.

An' I agree, Pratt says. As I was sayin' befo' I was so rudely inn'erupted, the Pashtun feel diff'rently. This be their land, see, an' the girl out there be communicatin' that message to us loud an' clear. I think that's what's gettin' the Cap'n's goat.

She's a real insurgente, man, Barela says with admiration. I mean, she ain't like the other squirters. She must have crawled her fuckin' knees off to get here. She just don't give up.

She give the place a face, Pratt observes. Before she come, this was a dump.

What can I say, you guys? Ramirez laughs. I got ninety-nine problems, and the bitch ain't one, you know what I'm sayin'?

She ain't no bitch, jerkoff, Pratt says quickly.

Whatever, dude, Ramirez says. I'm so tired of this place, I can't wait to go home.

What you plan to do when you get back? Barela asks.

I'm gonna open a bodypaint shop.

Auto body an' paint?

Naw, that's boring. Bodypaint and tattoos. Like on chicks and stuff. I got the idea when I seen that pitcher of Demi Moore in Lawson's hooch. She wasn't wearin' no clothes, but you wouldn't know that from the way they done her up. So I thought to myself: that's what I wanna do. And I'm gonna learn Japanese kanji to do the tattoos right. I'm done with guns and violence, man: I'm turnin' to art.

So you not gonna ride the white pony again when you're back in the barrio, Ram? Barela asks.

Naw, I'm done with all that.

They're gonna miss you at the shooting gallery.

Like I tole you, I'm goin' clean. That bitch don't fly for me no more.

What 'bout you? Pratt asks Barela.

I'm gonna join the L.A.P.D., man, I need the adrenaline fix.

Who knows if we gonna be able to go back at all, Pratt says glumly. We been extended again and again.

Maybe that's why Garcia tried to whack himself, Ramirez suggests.

Naw, Pratt replies. I heard it was girl trouble.

There's a pregnant pause, and then Barela asks: Girlfriend?

Wife.

Bitch!

What about the Cap'n? Ramirez asks. What d'you guys think he's gonna do when his time's up?

From the way he's been fuckin' up lately, Barela says, gettin' people killed and all, they're prob'ly goin' to kick him upstairs and make him into a general.

I miss Lieutenant Frobenius, man, Ramirez says. He was the coolest dude. Best damn officer I've ever served under.

We still got Ellison, though, Pratt says.

Ellison's a prick, Ramirez says. It's like he always got a stick up his ass.

That's 'cos he new, Pratt says. They all be like that the first few months before they settle down.

He's still a tightass. Like he's wearin' boots a size too small.

You gotta have patience, Barela says. That's the first thing you learn in the barrio. That's the way the Cap'n used to be, but he's gettin' old. He's like, what, thirty or something? I mean, that's way old! You start losin' your facilities and ev'rything.

I grimace in the shadows. Thank you very much! I swear silently. I'm twenty-seven, you fuckheads!

They're still talking about me in low voices when I decide that I've heard enough and move on. Next up on my beat is the firing position facing the LZ, on the other side of the base. Everheart, Scanlon, and Pietrafesa from Second Platoon are on watch. I'm still smarting from my last meeting, and am curt with my greetings.

How're you doing, Everheart? I ask. And please don't go quoting the Scripture at me when you answer.

No, Sir, he says hurriedly, rising to his feet. I won't, Sir. I'm all right, Sir. It's been a quiet night.

Quiet doesn't always mean that nothing's happening out there.

Pietrafesa's looking up at the sky. He glances at me with a smile.

Sky reminds me of home, Sir.

We didn't train you to look at the fucking sky, soldier.

He snaps to attention. No, Sir. I won't look again, Sir.

I relent and gaze momentarily at the sky as well.

Home's Hawaii, right? I ask. Same stars?

No, Sir, not actually. But I was looking at the Milky Way. It reminded me of soapsuds draping across the paintwork of a sharp black car in a wash. I used to be an attendant.

Hmm. I can see what you mean. I wouldn't have thought of it myself. You're from a military family, aren't you?

I am, Sir, he says. My dad fought in 'Nam, and my grandad was in Inchon.

They must be proud of you, right?

No, Sir, as a matter of fact.

Oh? Why not?

My dad has PTSD big-time, Sir. He didn't want me to sign up. He was, like, don't do it, Tim, if you know what's good for you, and I was, like, Oh, I don't know, Dad. So I signed up.

I see . . . That's a bummer. I hesitate for a moment, nonplussed, before turning to Scanlon. And what about you? How're you holding up?

I'm totally pissed off at myself, Sir. I lost my wedding band this evening. I'm going to catch it when I get back home.

Gold band?

Fake gold, Sir. Out of a Cracker Jack box. Still and all, it's got major sentimental value for Deedee, seeing that she got it for me, like, when she was nine. We'd been dating for a while before we got married.

Maybe we can help you out with a search party tomorrow. Tell Lieutenant Ellison I suggested that, will you?

I will, Sir. Thank you, Sir.

As I walk away, I feel myself finally hit a wall of fatigue. Relieved, I hurry back to my hut. I'm already drowsy by the time I take off my boots, and I don't bother with anything else as I slide under the blanket. I pass out even before my head hits the pillow.


**0425.**

I'm woken up by a call from Battalion. Lautenschlager is on the other end of the line. He sounds wide awake this early in the morning. I know how much he prides himself on his ability to function on an hour's sleep. Blurry-eyed and still half-asleep, I try to focus on his words against the white noise of static on the line.

When I hang up some twenty minutes later, I sit still for a few moments, and then reach for my boots. As I put them on, Shorty trots over for his morning rubdown. I run a comb through his coat and feel myself relax even as he does. By the time I'm done combing him, my mind has cleared. We leave the hut together and are instantly enveloped by a thick gray mist.

I feel my way through the damp, cottony stuff and am quickly soaked with dew. I reach the Hescos and hoist myself up to look out past the concertina.

An entire layer of cloud has spooled down in pillars that reach to the ground. When the haze clears a little, I catch a glimpse of the ghostlike figure in the darkness of the field and feel a twinge of doubt. As I climb down from my perch, I think of Whalen's words about war not making sense sometimes and wonder if he could be right in this particular instance. Then I dismiss the thought.

I make a pit stop at the mess tent to get some coffee. I cradle the Styrofoam cup as I make my way between the B-huts listening to the sounds of men stirring. Somewhere, a boyish tenor begins to sing U2's "Beautiful Day." A flock of tiny birds dips in and out of the mist trilling in high-pitched voices. The company's pennant snaps in the breeze. The base is coming to life. It's going to be an eventful day. I can already sense it.

## 0545.

A little before 0600, I summon the officers for a meeting.

Whalen's first in, followed by Ellison, then Bradford and Tanner, and, finally, Petrak as the last entrant. I begin by telling them about the new officers who'll be arriving today. Lieutenant Dan Lafayette will be the unit's newly appointed Executive Officer, Lieutenant Stuart Sutherland will be Lieutenant Frobenius's replacement as

First Platoon's leader, with Staff Sergeant Randy Mejia in for Staff Sergeant Espinosa, and Corporal Marty Holmstrom taking over the motor pool.

I pause for questions, then continue:

But that isn't the only reason I called you here this bright and early. Following up on my promise to the First Sarn't yesterday, I put in a call to Battalion to ask for more information on our dead insurgent, and Lieutenant-Colonel Lautenschlager got back to me this morning. We've learned two things. First, she spoke the truth about her brother not being allied with the Taliban. Turns out they come from one of the few Pashtun mountain tribes who hate the hadjis and were able to keep them at bay during their glory days. So that part of her story holds up. However, our local intelligence contacts could come up with nothing to support her story about whether she did indeed make the trip to Tarsândan on her own, as she claims, or was brought here by other parties. What we do know, as a result of the drone that's been assessing the area, is that there are no—repeat, no—Anti-Afghan Forces visible on the slopes facing us. Based on that evidence, it would appear that the girl really is on her own.

There's a rush of exhaled air around the circle.

So we can bring her in for a medical examination, Sir? Whalen asks.

Yes, we can. Have Doc set it up.

Suddenly Ellison leans forward: Is there anything to support her claims about the drone strike that took out her family?

Not exactly, I reply. There is a report of a Predator strike in one of the mountain valleys about six months ago, but we've no information that it struck a wedding party. As far as we're concerned, we targeted, and successfully eliminated, a band of insurgents.

Who were our informants in the Predator attack? Whalen asks.

Locals in the Arghandab River Valley with tribal connections to the governor of Kandahar province. They're part of our extended intelligence network run out of KAF.

You must mean our big black hole in the sky, Sir, Tanner wise-cracks.

I'll ask you for your opinion when I want it, Sergeant, I say curtly.

Wasn't there a report some time ago about a running feud between the governor and the mountain tribes? Whalen asks.

There might have been. I don't remember, and I don't think it particularly matters. If there is a feud, it's business as usual, because they're always fighting each other. They're all as crazy as fuck.

But it might be important in this case, Sir.

I clear my throat. What is this, First Sarn't? Fucking CSI Kandahar?

I'm just asking, Sir.

Yeah? You going somewhere with your questions?

I'm trying to find out if the governor might have set us up to conveniently remove an important local rival. It's been known to happen.

Bradford gives a low whistle. Ellison leans back and bites his lip.

In other words, we might have got played, Bradford says.

No, we didn't get played, I say sharply. Our actions are determined by the intelligence we have on hand, not on wild fucking surmises—and that intelligence was provided by the governor who's part of the present regime. The regime that we support, I might add.

My answer seems to satisfy no one. I notice Bradford avoiding my eyes. Then Tanner says dolefully: Will someone please tell me who the good guys are?

I look at him with narrowed eyes for a moment before leaning abruptly over my desk and letting them all have it. What is this, I explode, a pity party? What the hell is eating you guys? May I remind you that, Taliban or not Taliban, the fucker attacked us, and that's the bottom line!

But don't you think he might have attacked us precisely because his people got whacked, Sir? Ellison persists.

I don't know, Lieutenant. I think that's a pointless question.

I only ask because that's what the girl alleged, Sir . . .

Suddenly, Sergeant Petrak asks: What's the nearest U.S. base to her tribe?

We are, Ellison replies before I can.

His answer hangs heavily in the air. No one else says anything. The silence in the hut is awkward and prolonged.

Then Whalen says pensively, almost as if he's speaking to himself: If the guy isn't Taliban, does that mean we can give her back his body?

I fold my arms over my chest. What d'you mean?

Surely, now that we know she's here on her own, Sir, there's no doubting the genuineness of her claim. I mean, all she wants to do is to bury the damn body. Couldn't we just send Battalion some photographs and be done with it?

I look at him with exasperation. Battalion isn't calling the shots on this one, I reply. It goes much higher up the chain of command. Nor is the issue whether or not the guy's Taliban. What matters is that he's an insurgent who led an attack on a U.S. Army base. That's why the regime wants to display the body: they want to send a clear message of potency to both their constituents and their opponents. They're saying to the Taliban: You fuck with us and you end up like this poor bastard—and we won't be making any more mistaken claims based on fraudulent photographs from this point on.

But the facts themselves in this case are fraudulent if he isn't Taliban! Ellison protests.

It doesn't fucking matter, I answer. Besides, for the regime to cancel at this stage would mean a loss of face. The details are irrelevant to them.

But are they irrelevant to us? Ellison exclaims. I mean, where's *our* integrity? Who the fuck are we working for?

Lieutenant! I look at him in surprise.

With all due respect, Sir, he carries on, is the U.S. Army an independent entity, or are we simply handmaids to a government that everybody and their mother knows has compromised our mission from the get-go?

This guy attacked us! I reply heatedly. His people killed our people. I could hardly care less about what they do with his fucking corpse!

So we're following the enemy's playbook where that's concerned, Sir?

I open my mouth and close it again. At length, all I can say is: I'm going to pretend I didn't hear you, Lieutenant.

Bradford clears his throat and eyes me uneasily.

Sorry, Sir, but I'm with the lieutenant on this, he says.

Let me repeat myself, I say coldly. He's not our problem. He's dead.

So we're letting the regime's SOP trump ours, Sir?

In this case, it doesn't fucking matter, okay?

I'm not sure I understand why, Sir.

Petrak cuts in: I agree. I don't understand either.

Then he addresses me directly: Why are we here, Sir?

Whalen speaks up in my stead. His voice is curiously flat.

He says: We're here because we have a mission to carry out.

All right, Ellison says. What's the mission?

To support the government in Kabul, I reply.

But we know they're crooks! They stole the election. And they're as fucked up as the Taliban!

Maybe, but if the Taliban return to power, you can be damn sure they'll make the present bunch seem like a fucking school of philosophers.

So that's the standard we're using now, Sir? The Taliban?

We don't make those judgments, Lieutenant, I say icily. They're made for us. That's why we have diplomats. Our job is to fight the enemy, clean up, and clear out. I thought that was pretty clear. Apparently, I was mistaken. We don't do politics, and, beyond a certain point, we don't get involved in these people's lives. The boundaries of our actions are clearly defined.

Ellison swivels his entire body in disagreement as he remarks:

With all due respect, Sir, the boundaries of our actions are leading to our losing good men to save the asses of a bunch of mofos in Kabul who're making out like they're on Wall Street.

I'm about to respond angrily, when Masood, the interpreter, bursts in.

I look at him in surprise.

Comandan Saab, he blurts out, Nizam has killed a lamb in your honor! She would like you to have it. Please come out to the field to accept it from her.

I try to check myself, but it's no use. What the fuck? I snap. You can't just barge in like this!

He seems to physically shrivel into himself, but before I can tell him to clear out, Ellison says calmly, as if there had been no interruption: If we can't return the body, then what are we to do with the girl?

What . . . ? I say, still glaring at Masood.

I was wondering if you had a plan concerning the girl, Sir.

I turn away from the interpreter and force myself to answer the question calmly: Battalion's received permission from Brigade to move her out of here. They're gonna shift her to a sanatorium in Kandahar—

At this point, there's a wordless exclamation from Masood, but Whalen, to his credit, grasps him firmly by the arm and escorts him out of the hut. We hear him going ballistic at Masood, and before long he returns without the interpreter.

What the hell's the matter with him? I ask furiously. Has he totally lost it? What makes him think he has unfettered access to my office? And what was that crap about sheep anyway?

I can explain, Sir, Petrak volunteers. The field is covered with sheep. They seem to have wandered down from the mountains— we're keeping an eye out, but I didn't know the girl had killed a lamb.

What am I supposed to do with a fucking lamb? And how did she kill it? With her bare teeth?

I don't know, Sir.

I glare at Whalen accusingly. I thought you'd checked her thoroughly.

I thought I did too, Sir, he says.

I'm glad she's going to get medical attention, Ellison interjects quietly.

You better be, given that after she's evaluated at Kandahar, she's headed for Bagram, where they'll give her a thorough examination before sending her on to Landstuhl.

To Germany!

Damn right. We're gonna make her a textbook example of trauma rehabilitation. She's going to be fitted with the latest state-of-the-art prostheses. By the time they're done with her, she'll be able to compete in the fucking Olympics. What do you gents think of that?

The murmur of surprise that goes around the circle is succeeded by approval. Even Whalen's features relax. I savor the moment by drawing it out.

Are we shipping her out on the same bird as her brother? Whalen asks.

I'd assume so. Why? What does that matter?

I was thinking of the stench, Sir.

Oh, for Chrissake, the CH-47 is a pretty big bird! I reply. Besides, she won't know where it's from.

We could have him towed behind the bird, Tanner jokes. He's probably so bloated with gas by this time, he'll float like a balloon.

'Cept he might get tangled in the rotors, and then they'd be left with bubble gum for their TV show, Bradford ripostes.

All right, that's enough, I say brusquely. Any more questions?

You appear to have covered all the bases, Sir, Petrak says with admiration.

You can thank the colonel. I had very little to do with it.

All the same, Petrak says loyally, he wouldn't have known about her if you hadn't brought it to his notice, Sir.

Well, I suppose there is that, I admit, running a caustic eye over my subordinates, before adding: Although there's still one thing that I haven't figured out.

What's that, Sir?

Where am I gonna get the white robes and angel wings with which to dress up you namby-pambies before sending you out into the mountains to explain to the dead man's tribe how sorry you are for what became of him.

I interrupt the smattering of chagrined laughter by suggesting that we go and get some coffee and take a look at the field.

And then we can have some breakfast before heading out to fetch her, I add.

Whalen pauses in midstride and stares at me. We're not all going, are we?

Oh, I don't see why not. After all the fuss you've made, don't you guys want to give her a fucking parade?

There's still a thick fog outside, Sir, he says. We may have to wait a bit until it clears.

The birds will be here at 1100, so we're gonna need to have her ready to go before then, I reply. Shall we say 0900? And if we have to go out under cover of the fog, that's fine.

You're in a good mood, Captain, Whalen says with a wan smile.

Should I not be, First Sarn't? I'm pleased with the resolution we've come up with for her. It's good to belong to an organization that cares about the finer points.

I turn to Ellison.

You see, Lieutenant? Never jump to conclusions where the U.S. Army is concerned. We do have a sense of honor, we respect courage, and we do things right.

He turns crimson. On behalf of the men, Sir, he says haltingly, may I give you our thanks?

Don't sweat it, Lieutenant, I say crisply. You'll learn. What's more, we're going to get a whole lot of feel-good PR from this story. It's just the kind of thing that gets written up—heroes with hearts, or something along those lines. Maybe I'll suggest it to the colonel the next time we talk. Who knows?—we may even make it to the front page of *Stars and Stripes*. Or maybe we'll get *really* lucky and they'll put her on the cover of *Time* magazine like that gal who got her nose cut off.

Ellison raises his eyebrows, but doesn't say anything.

Whalen's the last one to file out. He catches my eye and says in an undertone: Are you absolutely sure we should all go out to get her, Sir?

I tense up. Yes, I am.

May I disagree with that decision, Sir?

Jesus Christ, not again, First Sarn't! I whisper furiously. It's obvious we're gonna need to have a chat. See me as soon as we've dealt with her, do you understand?

Yes, Sir, he says quietly, before lapsing into silence.


## 0630.

Sunrise.

The mist shades to gold and then red.

I warm my hands holding my second cup of coffee of the day and walk with the others toward the Hescos. The mountain peaks are crimson; the slopes long shadows of gray. Once again, I marvel, as I do almost every day, at the immensity of this landscape, and feel puny in comparison.

We walk right up to the wire. What I see before me is truly surreal. In the middle of the field made black by the shadows cast by the mountains, a flock of sheep mills about in confusion, while the girl sits motionless in their midst. There's something almost statuelike in her stillness. Unable to hold her gaze, I look away. Every feature of the landscape stands out in black and white. An electric current seems to run through the air. I'm about to steal a glance at her again, when a ray of sunlight falls on the dew-dappled ground and carves out a shape like a scimitar.

I clear my throat and look sideways at Ellison, who's gone very pale.

I can't wait to put up an observation post on the spur of that mountain, I remark conversationally. It's our biggest frickin' vulnerability in this place. It'll be our first task once she's outta here. Then we can stop worrying about shooters, and those razor-teeth slopes are gonna look a lot less intimidating. We're gonna fix this problem once and for all.

I hear you, Sir, he says.

I turn toward the field once more and study it closely. Kinda funny there's all these sheep and no one looking after them, don't you think?

He stiffens as he follows my gaze, but doesn't reply. Clearly, it hadn't occurred to him. His eyes don't leave the field.

Did we find out how she killed the lamb? I query him.

She used a knife, Sir. Some of the men saw her do it.

I aim a baleful glance at Whalen, but he's staring somewhere else. There's a moment's awkward silence. Ellison stands ramrod straight beside me, looking glum.

And what are those things covering some of the sheep? I ask him irritably.

He raises his binoculars to his eyes. They look like blankets folded in half, Sir. Probably to protect them from the cold.

Probably? You're speculating, Lieutenant. I don't like it when my officers can't give me answers to simple questions. Do you follow me?

Yes, Sir.

I look through my binoculars as well. Do you know if we've checked them out?

I don't believe we have, Sir.

Jesus. Fucking sheep in the killing zone. I hate imponderables.

I could send a team out right now.

No, let it be. There's no point in spooking her. You can deal with it after we've brought her in.

We'll chase the whole damn flock back up the slopes, Sir, Petrak says smartly.

Break the terp's heart, Tanner says with a laugh, but stops short when I stare coldly at him.

All right then, I tell the others. I've seen enough. We'll assemble here at 0900, fog or no fog. First Sergeant Whalen: I want you to assemble a team from First and Second Platoons to be her escort. Call it her guard of honor, if you like. You can ask for volunteers.

Whalen hesitates. So you really mean it, Sir?

You bet I fucking mean it.

I turn to Bradford. You better round up Masood. We're gonna need him to translate.

Yes, Sir.

Great. Let's go and get some breakfast. I can smell those scrambled eggs and hash browns all the way from here.


## 0845.

I tie Shorty's leash to my bunk. He's not used to being confined, and it seems to make him restless. To reassure him, I pet him and tell him I'll set him free as soon as I get back.

Good dog, I tell him. Good boy.

He wags his tail uncertainly and whimpers. As I walk away, he strains to free himself. He starts barking as soon as I leave the hut.


## 0905.

I watch the men lining up by the Hescos. There's Duggal, Lee, Jackson, Ramirez, and Pratt from First Platoon, and Everheart, Pietrafesa, Scanlon, Lawson, and Wonk Gaines from Second Platoon. With their zinc-covered noses and sun-blackened faces, they look intimidating, even to me. I shake my head. Don't you guys ever sleep? I remark.

I walk up to Scanlon. Don't forget to talk to Lieutenant Ellison about your wedding band.

I won't, Sir. Thank you, Sir.

I turn to Pratt. Glad to be doing this, soldier?

Yessir, he says. Then his forehead furrows. But something don't feel right. An' I can't figure out what that be. He reaches down to touch the desert floor. Snakeskin ground, he says. It's givin' me bad vibes.

Maybe you're worried because she's armed, soldier, I say tongue-in-cheek. Don't forget she has a knife.

One of the men snickers, but shuts up as soon as I scowl at him.

Masood runs up, panting. He glances at me apprehensively. I was wrong about her, Comandan Saab, he says in a stricken voice. She's a parvaneh. A butterfly.

You're gonna have to learn not to talk out of turn, I tell him irritably.

Doc arrives with his medic bag and a couple of blankets. He opens the bag and shows me extra dressings and gauze.

I'm good to go, Sir, he says, snapping the bag shut.

I turn to Schott and Ashworth. To Schott, I say: Once we bring her in, I want you to get her biometrics, okay? No ifs, ands, or buts, just get them—and I don't care how you do it.

I watch as soldiers climb up on the Hescos and set up machine gun positions to cover the field and the slopes. Turning to Ashworth, I ask: D'you have your men on overwatch positions?

Yes, Sir.

And you've got all approaches covered?

Yes, Sir.

Why all the fuss, Sir? Ellison asks quietly. I thought the drone gave us the all clear.

Contingency planning, Lieutenant. When you've been here long enough, it becomes second nature.

Behind us, the men arrayed along the Hescos in the overwatch position scan the field and the shadowy slopes. A weapons team from Second Platoon moves an M-240B machine gun from their fighting hole and places it on a tripod. One of the men slings belts of ammunition over his shoulders.

I walk over to Simonis, who's settling down on his perch on top of the Hescos. The mountains tower over us. With my gaze fixed on the slopes, I say: If you see anything happen out of the ordinary, take the shot. Don't hesitate. That's a standing order.

Roger, Sir, he says tersely. Wilco.

I watch him uncase his sniper's rifle and run his eyes over the field and the mountains' faces. Binoculars and another rifle, an M-24, lie next to him. He stretches out on a bed of sandbags, one leg crooked, eyes pressed to the rifle's sight. He's my ultimate lethal weapon, with a kill ratio of almost one hundred percent, and that reassures me.

I climb down from the Hescos and walk back to where everyone's waiting.

A raven flies low overhead and circles the field twice before heading east toward the mountains.

That's frickin' bad luck, someone mutters.

Whalen turns to glare at the speaker.

I address the men: Any questions?

I wait for a moment, and then say with a tight smile: All right, then. Let's go.

We troop out past the concertina. Whalen takes point.

I pause to absorb the breathless feeling I get whenever I step outside the wire.

I turn to the men and say in a calm voice: Now remember, this is going to be a Zen operation. We're not going to use any force on her. We're going to respect her dignity and treat her with the honor she deserves.

Her eyes stare watchfully at us as we advance, bulky in our body armor.

I can see her bangles glinting in the sun.

Our knees click like castanets as we march in unison.

Scorpions scuttle out of our way.

We're almost there, when she turns suddenly and reaches for the dead lamb. Her knife flashes at the same time as I spot a movement on the slopes. Get down! I scream, even as everyone around me is hitting the ground. A cloud of dust rises from our falling bodies, and it distracts me momentarily from the shot that rings out. We hear the bullet whistle past, and then the girl's falling backward with a bright red explosion where her heart used to be.

In the pin-drop silence, a voice cuts through the air from behind us.

It's Simonis. He says: Score.

I'm breathing in gasps. I feel helpless and disoriented.

Masood's the only one standing. I glance past him with disbelief at the slope where Shorty is darting between rocks. How the fuck did that dog get free?

Masood lurches toward the cart. He moves jerkily, as if someone's pulling his strings. When he reaches the girl, he falls to his knees. Her wide open eyes stare at him. She attempts to speak, but only blood wells out of her mouth. She's pointing at the lamb, and he gently moves her outstretched arm out of the way. The knife slips out of her nerveless fingers. He frees the bright red blanket from the animal and discards it along with the plaited-wire harness that she'd cut. Apart from the portion of its fleece covered by the blanket, the rest of the lamb is drenched in blood. Picking it up, he rises to his feet and begins to walk shakily toward me. When he reaches me, he bends down and places it on the ground. His eyes brimming with tears, he says in the voice of a young boy: Why did you kill her, Comandan Saab? The lamb was her gift to you. We were to feast on it tonight. It is a part of our culture.

I watch my hands reach slowly forward. They sink deep into the fleece of the lamb. It feels absurdly soft to the touch.

ἀλλ᾽ ὃν πόλις στήσειε τοῦδε χρὴ κλύειν

καὶ σμικρὰ καὶ δίκαια καὶ τἀναντία.

καὶ τοῦτον ἂν τὸν ἄνδρα θαρσοίην ἐγὼ

καλῶς μὲν ἄρχειν, εὖ δ᾽ ἂν ἄρχεσθαι θέλειν,

δορός τ᾽ ἂν ἐν χειμῶνι προστεταγμένον

μένειν δίκαιον κἀγαθὸν παραστάτην.

ἀναρχίας δὲ μεῖζον οὐκ ἔστιν κακόν.

αὕτη πόλεις ὄλλυσιν, ἥδ᾽ ἀναστάτους

οἴκους τίθησιν, ἥδε συμμάχου δορὸς

τροπὰς καταρρήγνυσι: τῶν δ᾽ ὀρθουμένων

σώζει τὰ πολλὰ σώμαθ᾽ ἡ πειθαρχία.

οὕτως ἀμυντέ᾽ ἐστὶ τοῖς κοσμουμένοις,

κοὔτοι γυναικὸς οὐδαμῶς ἡσσητέα.

κρεῖσσον γάρ, εἴπερ δεῖ, πρὸς ἀνδρὸς ἐκπεσεῖν,

κοὐκ ἂν γυναικῶν ἥσσονες καλοίμεθ᾽ ἄν.

—SOPHOCLES, *Antigone*

*Whome'er the State*

*Appoints, must be obeyed in everything,*

*Both small and great, just and unjust alike.*

*I warrant such an one in either case*

*Would shine, as King or subject; such a man*

*Would in the storm of battle stand his ground,*

*A comrade leal and true; but Anarchy—*

*What evils are not wrought by Anarchy!*

*She ruins States, and overthrows the home,*

*She dissipates and routs the embattled host;*

*While discipline preserves the ordered ranks.*

*Therefore we must maintain authority*

*And yield no title to a woman's will.*

*Better, if needs be, men should cast us out*

*Than hear it said, a woman proved his match.*

—Sophocles, *Antigone*

# Acknowledgments

My dear friends Lana Cable and Eshi Motahar redefined the meaning of what it means to believe in the literary enterprise. Thank you above all for your integrity.

If I possessed half the idealism and candor of my friend and first reader, Captain Richard Fitzgerald Sullivan of the U.S. Army, I would consider myself fortunate. You're one of a kind, Rick.

My friends Tyler Bourdeau of the U.S. Marines and Jeff Fenlason of the 101st Airborne read and commented extensively on the manuscript. I can't thank you enough.

To the U.S. Army officers in Afghanistan who befriended me and technically foolproofed the book—you know who you are—I have no words to adequately express my thanks. I remain in awe of your objectivity, in gratitude for your unwavering enthusiasm, and in your permanent debt for your gift of friendship.

My grateful thanks to Becky Hardie, my lead editor at Chatto & Windus and Hogarth UK, to Lindsay Sagnette, my editor at Crown and Hogarth USA, and to Louise Dennys at Knopf Canada and Meredith Curnow at Random House and Hogarth Australia. Your collective faith in the book proved inspirational.

Thanks as well for their full-throated support to Molly Stern and Maya Mavjee at Crown and Hogarth USA, Clara Farmer and Parisa

Ebrahimi at Chatto & Windus and Hogarth UK, and Anna Govender at Random House Australia. My humble thanks to Susan Traxel at Vintage Canada and Christine Kopprasch at Hogarth US.

For the paperback edition, Meagan Stacey edited for Hogarth US and Victoria Murray-Browne for Vintage UK.

Finally, *The Watch* owes its existence to the single-minded efforts of one person, my guardian angel, muse, and agent of dreams, Nicole Aragi, who shepherded it from its inception through its final stages with characteristic determination and panache.

NOTES AND REFERENCES

xii, xiii: Epigraph    Sophocles, *Antigone,* trans. F. Storr (Cambridge, MA: Harvard University Press, 1956), 349.

22: Nizam    "relieve the shame of my mother's son, left to rot as an unburied corpse" Adapted from Sophocles, *Antigone,* trans. Robert Fagles (New York: Penguin Classics, 1984), 82.

22: Nizam    "and then we would both be left unmourned, unwept, unburied without the rites, an unexpected treasure for the carrion birds" Adapted from Sophocles, Ibid., 60.

49–50: Emily    Sophocles, *Antigone,* trans. Nicholas Rudall (Chicago: Ivan R. Dee, 1998), 15.

51: Frobenius    Ibid., 17.

68: Irene Pappas    Ibid., 13.

127–28: Medic    Ibn Arabi, *Stations of Desire,* trans. Michael A. Sells (Jerusalem: Ibis Editions, 2000), 147.

134: the wise man   Adapted from T. E. Lawrence, *Seven Pillars of Wisdom* (New York: Anchor Books, 1991), 193: "Nine-tenths of tactics were certain enough to be teachable in schools; but the irrational tenth was like the kingfisher flashing across the pool, and in it lay the test of generals. It could be ensued only by instinct (sharpened by a thought practising the stroke) until at the crisis it came naturally, a reflex."

209: de Vigny   Alfred de Vigny, *Servitude and Grandeur of Arms,* trans. Roger Gard (London: Penguin Classics, 1996), 162.

225: de Vigny   Ibid., 9.

227: on Shame   Adapted from John Jones, *On Aristotle and Greek Tragedy* (New York: Oxford University Press, 1962), 179.

228–29: Taliban edicts   Adapted from Christina Lamb, *The Sewing Circles of Herat* (New York: Harper Perennial), 16–17.

232: Tacitus   Tacitus, *The Agricola and the Germania,* trans. Harold Mattingly, rev. trans. by S. A. Handford (London: Penguin Classics, 1948; rev. 1970), 114.

280, 281: Coda   Sophocles, *Antigone,* trans. Storr, 367.

# Glossary of Military Terms

| | |
|---|---|
| 1 Alpha | First Platoon, Alpha Company. |
| 2 Alpha | Second Platoon, Alpha Company. |
| ACH | Advanced combat helmet. |
| AK-47 | A selective-fire, gas-operated 7.62 × 39 mm assault rifle, first developed after World War II in the USSR by Mikhail Kalashnikov. It is officially known as Avtomat Kalashnikova (Russian: Автомат Калашникова). It is more commonly known as a Kalashnikov. |
| ANA | Afghan National Army. |
| Apache | The Boeing AH-64 Apache is a four-blade, twin-engine attack helicopter with a tailwheel-type landing-gear arrangement, and a tandem cockpit for a two-man crew. |
| AWOL | Absent Without Leave, or Absent Without Official Leave. |

B-hut                Bee hut; Barracks Hut; B-hut refers to a
                     semi-permanent wooden structure, used as a
                     temporary billet for troops.

Bird                 Army slang for helicopter.

Blackhawk            The Sikorsky UH-60 Black Hawk is a four-
                     bladed, twin-engine, medium-lift utility
                     tactical operations helicopter.

ECP                  Entry Control Point.

C.O.                 Commanding Officer.

C-wire               Concertina wire.

Camo                 Camouflage.

Chinook              The Boeing CH-47 Chinook is a twin-engine,
                     tandem rotor heavy-lift helicopter.

Chopper              Helicopter.

Claymore             The M18A1 Claymore is a directional anti-
                     personnel mine, named after the large Scottish
                     sword by its inventor, Norman A. MacLeod.
                     Unlike a conventional land mine, the Claymore
                     is fired by remote-control, shooting a pattern of
                     metal balls like a shotgun.

COIN                 Counterinsurgency doctrine.

CP                   Command Post, a command-and-control center
                     used by a military unit in a deployed location.

| | |
|---|---|
| Fobbit | A pejorative term used to describe soldiers who rarely if ever leave the relative safety of the Forward Operating Base (FOB). |
| FUBAR | Fucked Up Beyond All Repair. |
| Hesco | Hesco barriers are retaining wall blocks and protective containers, for military use including perimeter security and civil use including flood control. |
| Hooch | A military hut. |
| IED | Improvised Explosive Device, also known as a roadside bomb. |
| INS | Insurgent. |
| JDAM | The Joint Direct Attack Munition is a guidance kit that converts unguided bombs into all-weather "smart" munitions. |
| KAF | Kandahar Airfield. |
| Kerlix | Kerlix gauze antimicrobial bandage dressing. |
| Kevlar | A ballistic vest, bulletproof vest, or bullet-resistant vest. |
| KIA | Killed in Action. |
| LMG | Light Machine Gun, designed to be employed by an individual soldier, with or without an |

assistant, as an infantry support weapon.
The M249 light machine gun was previously
designated the M249 Squad Automatic Weapon
(SAW).

LN                  Local National.

LZ                  Landing Zone.

M-ATV               Derived from the Medium Tactical Vehicle
                    Replacement (MTVR) platform, the Oshkosh
                    M-ATV is a Mine Resistant Ambush Protected
                    (MRAP) vehicle.

MRE                 Meals Ready to Eat.

M-1                 The M-1 Garand United States Rifle, Caliber
                    .30.

M-2                 The M-2 machine gun has also been used as a
                    long-range sniper rifle, when equipped with a
                    telescopic sight.

M-4                 The M-4 carbine is a gas-operated, magazine-
                    fed, selective-fire weapon with a telescoping
                    stock. A shortened variant of the M-16A2 rifle,
                    the M-4 allows its user to better operate in
                    close-quarters combat.

M-9                 The Beretta M-9, formally Pistol,
                    Semiautomatic, 9 mm, M-9, is a 9×19 mm
                    Parabellum pistol of the United States military
                    adopted in 1985.

M-16            The M-16 Caliber 5.56 mm rifle is the U.S.
                military designation for the AR-15 rifle
                adapted for semi-automatic, three-
                round burst and full-automatic fire.

M-19            The M-19 Mortar is a light, smoothbore,
                muzzle loading, high-angle-of-fire weapon for
                light infantry support.

M-24            The M-24 Sniper Weapon System (SWS) is the
                military and police version of the Remington
                700 rifle, M-24 being the model name assigned
                by the U.S. Army after adoption as their
                standard sniper rifle in 1988. The M-24 is
                referred to as a "weapons system" because it
                consists of not only a rifle but also a detachable
                telescopic sight and other accessories.

M-203           The M-203 is a single-shot 40 mm underbarrel
                grenade launcher designed to attach to a rifle.

M-240B          The M-240B is the standard infantry medium
                machine gun of the U.S. Army.

M-249           The M-249 Light Machine Gun (LMG),
                previously designated the M-249 Squad
                Automatic Weapon (SAW).

MEDEVAC         Medical evacuation of wounded personnel from
                the battlefield.

MWR             Army Morale, Welfare, and Recreation
                Program.

NCO                Non-Commissioned Officer.

NOD                Night Observation Device.

Pfc.               Private First Class.

Predator           The General Atomics MQ-1 Predator is an
                   unmanned aerial vehicle used primarily by
                   the U.S. Air Force and Central Intelligence
                   Agency. Initially used in the early 1990s for
                   reconnaissance and forward observation roles,
                   the Predator has been modified and upgraded to
                   carry and fire missiles or other munitions.

PTSD               Post-traumatic Stress Disorder.

ROE                Rules of Engagement define the actions that
                   military forces may employ to achieve their
                   objectives.

ROTC               The Reserve Officers' Training Corps
                   is a college-based program for training
                   commissioned officers of the U.S. armed forces.

RPG                Rocket-Propelled Grenade, a shoulder-fired
                   weapon system that fires rockets equipped with
                   an explosive warhead.

RTO                Radio/Telephone Operator.

SAS                Special Air Service, a special forces unit of the
                   British Army.

| | |
|---|---|
| SAW | The M249 Squad Automatic Weapon, now designated as the M249 Light Machine Gun (LMG). |
| SFC | Sergeant First Class. |
| Sitrep | Situation report. |
| SOP | Standard Operating Procedure. |
| Spc. | Specialist. |
| Special Ops | Special forces, or special operations forces, are military units trained to perform unconventional, often high-risk missions. |
| Terp | Interpreter. |
| TIC | Troops in Combat. |
| TOC | Tactical Operations Center. |
| TWS | Thermal Weapons Sight. |
| VDM | Visually Distinguishing Mark. |
| WMD | Weapon of Mass Destruction. |
| Wire | Concertina wire. |

# Afghan Glossary

Afghânyân        Afghans refer to themselves as Afghânyân.

Amrikâyi         American.

Bad              Bad.

Ba'dan mêbinêm   See you later.

Baraka           Divine benediction.

Basmala          A phrase invoked at the beginning of an action:
(Bismillah)      *Bismillah ir-Rahman ir-Rahim* ("In the name
                 of God, most Gracious, most Merciful").

Besyêr balê      Yes, absolutely.

Burqa            Locally known as the Bughra or Chadri, the
                 trademark blue garment worn by women, with
                 its square of mesh in front of the eyes.

Che hâl dâred?   How are you?

| | |
|---|---|
| Comandan | Commandant. |
| Dre | Three. |
| Dwa | Two. |
| Galandat | Dervish. |
| Gaz | Yard (distance). |
| Humbaba | From the *Epic of Gilgamesh*: Humbaba the Terrible was a monster who was the guardian of the Cedar Forest, where the gods lived. |
| Kameez, Kamis | Shirt. |
| Ketâb | Book; notebook. |
| Khum astom, tashakor | Fine, thank you. |
| Luftan burqa obâsa | Please take off your burqa. |
| Maktab | School. |
| Mêbakhshêd | Sorry; forgive me. |
| Mëyh khudza | Don't move. |
| Mujahid | Freedom fighter. |
| Parvaneh | Butterfly. |

| | |
|---|---|
| Pashtana | Female Pashtun. |
| Patlun | Trousers. |
| Peri | Benevolent, winged fairies who dwell in the realm between angels and demons. They sometimes visit the mortal realm. |
| Pir | Spiritual leader. |
| Puttee | Bandage. |
| Qalam | Pen. |
| Qibla | Direction to Mecca, where a Muslim must face during prayers. |
| Ra'is | Headman, leader. |
| Rebaab, rubab | Lute. |
| Saab (Sahib) | Master. |
| Sabâ mêbinametân | See you tomorrow. |
| Salâm | Hello. |
| Salâmat osëy | Hello (to a group of people). |
| Saray | Man. |
| Shahada | "There is no god but God, and Muhammad is His Messenger." |

| | |
|---|---|
| Sayyid | Descendant of the Prophet Muhammad. |
| Shalwar | Voluminous pajama-style trousers. |
| Tarsândan | Frightening; fearsome. |
| Taweez | Amulet. |
| Topak salaran | Gun rulers; warlords. |
| Tsalor | Four. |
| Tsë ghwâre? | What do you want? |
| Yaghestan | Land of the Rebellious. |

# The Watch

# A Reader's Guide

*For additional features, visit:*
www.joydeeproybhattacharya.com

## Introduction

In order to provide reading groups with the most informed and thought-provoking questions possible, it is necessary to reveal important aspects of the plot of this novel. If you have not finished reading *The Watch*, we respectfully suggest that you wait before reviewing this guide.

Just as *The Things They Carried* transformed our understanding of America's war in Vietnam, *The Watch* is a gripping, eye-opening novel of Operation Enduring Freedom—the war against Afghanistan's Taliban that has lasted for more than a decade and claimed the lives of over 2,000 U.S. troops. Unfolding in a series of captivating scenes, *The Watch* opens with the voice of an unlikely narrator—a lone Afghan woman who arrives at an isolated army base in Kandahar and demands the return of her brother's body. Is she truly a grieving family member, or is she a suicide bomber? As individual soldiers and their translator tell the rest of the story, the answer becomes a haunting revelation that gives voice to all sides in this heartbreaking, history-steeped conflict. Taking us deep inside the tense, claustrophobic atmosphere of the camp, where military personnel struggle with the constant threat of terror and undefined battle lines, *The Watch* delivers a powerful portrait of modern warfare.

Bringing readers much-needed clarity about a conflict marked by complex tribal divisions and an elusive mission, *The Watch* fosters important dialogues, putting a human face on the many perspectives that have taken Afghanistan—and U.S. troops—to this pivotal moment in history. We hope this guide will enrich your reading group's discussion.

## Questions and Topics for Discussion

1.  In ancient Greek lore, Antigone (pronounced *anne-TIH-guh-nee*) is a defiant young woman willing to risk her life so that her brother's body can receive proper burial rites. Their uncle, King Creon (*KREE-on*), has become blinded by power, decreeing that no one will honor the remains of this nephew, whom Creon considers to be a traitor. Anyone defying the king's order is to be executed.

    As Nizam confronts the army, what timeless questions of religious faith versus secular power is she raising? What gives women like Antigone and Nizam, living in male-dominated cultures, the strength to wage wars of conscience?

2.  What were your initial theories about Nizam? How

did your opinion of her, and of the U.S. soldiers, shift throughout the novel?

3.  As with Antigone's brother, the guilt or innocence of Nizam's brother makes for a provocative debate. The motivations of Nizam's brother are probed in-depth in "Captain," at 0545, a scene in which Tanner asks, "Will someone please tell me who the good guys are?" What's the best answer to his question?

4.  In "Lieutenant" and "Lieutenant's Journal," we see Nick Frobenius struggle with his memories of home, particularly his relationship with his former wife, Emily. What is at the heart of his struggle? How does his story capture the chasm between a tour of duty and the requirements of civilian life?

5.  What healing power does Doc Taylor have beyond medical treatments? What other wounds—psychological, social—does he attempt to treat?

6.  Ismene (*is-MAY-nay*) is Antigone's less-daring sister in the play by Sophocles, who fears the wrath of their uncle but also fears the gods. How does this parallel Masood's role? How did you react to his naïve assumptions that the U.S. soldiers would see themselves as his rescuers, and that Simonis might become his best friend? What aspects of his situation were especially hard for him to interpret?

7.  As Second Lieutenant Tom Ellison recalls his father, what dialogues about America's involvement in Afghanistan overall is he bringing to light? Did you side with Tom or with his father in those discussions?

8.  How did First Sergeant Jimmy Whalen's aunt help to strengthen his psyche? On page 196, what do we dis-

cover about his leadership style as he listens to the description of Pratt's disturbing dream (which echoes a premonition in the Antigone saga)?

9. As you witnessed the chain of command within each chapter, what did you notice about the characters' use of authority? What distinctions did you observe between officers and enlisted men?

10. Ultimately, what leads to the transformation of Captain Evan Connolly (whom Masood calls "Comandan Saab")? How would you respond to the question Masood asks the captain in the closing lines of the book? What broader answers about war can be delivered in response to the "Why?" of Masood?

11. Reread passages from the first chapter. What does this exercise reveal about perception and interpretation, from the word "wire" to the soldiers' attempts to protect Nizam?

12. Before reading *The Watch,* how deep was your understanding of Afghanistan's history? What can a novel reveal about history that a memoir or history book cannot?

13. The coda is spoken by Creon in Sophocles's play *Antigone.* In that scene, Creon is justifying his actions to his son, who is in love with Antigone. What are your reactions to Creon's defense? How does it resonate in global politics today?

14. Which aspects of *The Watch* echoed themes of mystery and identity in previous Roy-Bhattacharya books you have read?

*Guide written by Amy Clement*

# A Conversation with
# Joydeep Roy-Bhattacharya

**Q. What drew you to Afghanistan?**

A. I'll paraphrase something by the poet Iqbal by way of an answer: Afghanistan is the heart of Asia, and when Afghanistan suffers, Asia bleeds.

It's a wildly beautiful country, with a wildly beautiful people, and one of the last places in the world that appears to have successfully held its own against outside influences. What's not to love?

I live in the countryside because my soul needs it. And I wrote about Afghanistan because I needed to dwell, if only for a while, in one of the world's last truly remote places.

**Q. Western readers are going to be especially interested in your relationship with U.S. Army officers who helped you during the course of writing *The Watch*. Can you expand a little on how the relationships came to be? What aspects of the book did the officers really identify with? And what were some of the bloopers they helped you correct?**

A. The writer Chris Hedges introduced me to the officers who worked with me, and they, in turn, introduced me to colleagues. What I was looking for was input from line officers in Afghanistan, not desk officers back at the forward bases or in the States. The war in Afghanistan, I found out, is very different from that in Iraq, in the paucity of closed encounters and conventional fighting. Rather, the widespread use of IEDs by the Taliban has led to a situation where the comparative certainties of conventional warfare have been replaced by what one officer termed "fencing with ghosts." Given this, I based the battle scene in the book on extensive research on what happened at Wanat, in the Waygal province in Nuristan, where an American position was besieged and nearly overrun, leading to extensive casualties, including nine killed and twenty-seven wounded, the most in a single battle since U.S. operations in Afghanistan commenced in 2001. The sandstorm was my idea; the officers helped me logistically work out how it could interfere with detection systems.

Where their input was crucial was in my understanding of the working relationships within the company between the officers and the men, and the commissioned officers and NCOs. I'd assumed a more rigid vertical hierarchy as in forward bases, but refined my approach given the peculiar imperatives of a combat base situation. For instance, the relationship between the leader of the company, the Captain, and the First Sergeant, was much more vertical in the early drafts.

The aspect of the book the soldiers most identified with was my determination to describe the officers and the men as whole individuals, with three-dimensional personal lives, rather than as testosterone-driven killing machines. They loved the humanity of the book, and especially the attempt to incorporate the point of view of the Other, represented in this case by the Antigone figure and the interpreter, an aspect usually lost in most journalistic depictions of the "enemy."

As for bloopers, ironically the one that took the most work had nothing to do with the officers or the army per se. I was determined to get the Acadian accent right and did quite a bit of research on the local dialects in and around Baton Rouge. Ironically, both my agent and my editor thought that read a bit too much like an *Amos and Andy* parody, and the only bit that survives in the book is that spoken by the old fisherman in the swamp; the rest was briskly deleted.

**Q. You're fulsome in your praise of the soldiers' efforts in your Acknowledgments.**
A. I'm an anchorite. I keep to myself. And I keep people away. But my friends in the U.S. Army—and they are friends, in the true sense—surprised me. Their openness astonished me; their modesty humbled me. Any corporate institution the size of the U.S. Army is, by nature, impersonal, but these were some of the finest individuals I've ever met. They're part of my life now. I feel an intense loyalty to them. I'd rather give them pride of place in my book tours than stand behind a lectern, because it's their rightful place; I've only borrowed it.

**Q. What made you decide to buttress your novel with the ancient Greek tragedy *Antigone*?**
A. *Antigone* for me transcends time and place, quite literally. I first read *Antigone* when I was a teenager, and I've measured all the women I've met since against that yardstick, to our mutual detriment. But I've also taught the play and was fascinated by her hold on my students. I needed a protagonist who could serve as a moral yardstick of the degree of injury done to the Afghans by outside powers. A woman who simply has no interest in compromising with the folks who've slaughtered her family and devastated her country. She rejects their over-

tures in their entirety and, in that, becomes a microcosm of the rejection by the Pashtuns, especially, of all the material temptations offered by Western civilization—in her specific case, both physiological and therapeutic rehabilitation; and, in the case of her people, all the material detritus that will be left behind by the Americans following their inevitable (and increasingly precipitate) withdrawal.

Q. "Slaughtered," "devastated." These are strong words. It would imply a taking of sides. And yet, in the novel, you are remarkably evenhanded in your depiction of the viewpoints of both the Afghan and the American characters.

A. I'm a novelist and I don't believe in taking sides as I write: that's the task of the propagandist. My personal beliefs and private opinions do not matter within the covers of the book. I've no interest in either betraying my characters or holding the reader's hand and telling him or her how to think.

Q. What made you decide to write through the first-person viewpoints of seven different characters?

A. First of all, I needed to get myself out of the picture altogether, and I realized that a good way to do this would be to let each character speak in order to enable the reader to see through their eyes, as it were. It gave the characters their necessary autonomy and made my own work easier. That's the terrific thing about writing fiction; it allows me the freedom to do this. It's entirely subjective; it engages the heart of the reader as much as the head.

Q. Are any of the characters based on real people?

A. Nick Frobenius is a composite of a marine captain and an

army captain, both of whom are fabulous writers—and intensely intellectual. The rest are invented out of whole cloth.

**Q. I assume you did quite a bit of research in the course of writing the novel. Can you tell us about your research? How long did it take?**

A. It would be difficult to give you an exact time span, given that I've been following these wars ever since they began years ago. I suppose I've always been fascinated by military culture. But I wrote the first draft in ten weeks, sending each completed chapter to my agent, Nicole Aragi, who is also my first reader. As for my conversations with the army officers, that commenced after the book was complete, and it helped that I knew exactly what I wanted from them so as not to waste their time.

**Q. What specifically did you want from them?**

A. Getting my logistics right: for instance, gun types and variations, ammunition and ranges, topography, superior-subordinate relationships.

**Q. What was the most memorable experience you had as part of your research?**

A. Innumerable heart-to-heart sessions with my army mates. More specifically, there was the time I went to see how a halal animal had its throat slit, and I came away repulsed and physically drained, though the episode did find its way into my book.

**Q. Did anything in your research overturn your expectations or force you to reassess what you thought you knew? Did anything you discovered shock you?**

A. I'd had an idea about the degradation of women in Pashtun culture, but the magnitude and degree shocked me. I must say that this, more than anything else, influenced my decision to have a strong Pashtun woman as the protagonist—both as a standing rebuke and as an aspirational ideal.

**Q. Finally, what do you hope readers will take from the book?**
A. Greater empathy and comprehension—for both those who fight these wars and for the victims—than when they began the book.

# Recommended Reading
from Joydeep Roy-Bhattacharya

On Afghanistan:

Ahmad, Aisha, and Roger Boase, *Pashtun Tales from the Pak-istan-Afghan Frontier* (Saqi, 2008).

Barfield, Thomas, *Afghanistan: A Cultural and Political History* (Princeton, 2010).

Brodsky, Anna, *With All Our Strength: The Revolutionary Association of the Women of Afghanistan* (Routledge, 2003).

Chaffetz, David, *A Journey Through Afghanistan: A Memorial* (Regnery Gateway, 1981).

Elliot, Jason, *An Unexpected Light: Travels in Afghanistan* (Picador USA, 1999).

Girardet, Edward, *Killing the Cranes: A Reporter's Journey Through Three Decades of War in Afghanistan* (Chelsea Green, 2011).

Kargar, Zarghuna, *Dear Zari: Hidden Stories from the Women of Afghanistan* (Chatto & Windus, 2011).

Lamb, Christina, *Sewing Circles of Heart* (HarperCollins, 2002).

Loewen, Arley, and Josette McMichael, Eds., *Images of Afghanistan: Exploring Afghanistan Through Art and Culture* (Oxford, 2010).

Majrouh, Sayd Bahodine, *Songs of Love and War: Afghan Women's Poetry* (Other Press, 2003).

Newby, Eric, *A Short Walk in the Hindu Kush* (Secker & Warburg, 1958).

Omrani, Bijan, and Matthew Leeming, *Afghanistan: A Companion and Guide*, 2nd ed. (Airphoto International, 2011).


## The Soviet Occupation:

Braithewaite, Rodric, *Afgantsy: The Russians in Afghanistan 1979 – 89* (Oxford, 2011).

Kalinovsky, Artemy, *A Long Goodbye: The Soviet Withdrawal from Afghanistan* (Harvard, 2011).


## The American Occupation:

Amnesty International, *As If Hell Fell on Me: The Human Rights Crisis in Northwest Pakistan* (Amnesty International Publications, 2010).

Anderson, Ben, *No Worse Enemy: The Inside Story of the Chaotic Struggle for Afghanistan* (Oneworld, 2011).

Badkhen, Anna, *Afghanistan by Donkey: One Year in a War Zone* (Foreign Policy, 2012).

Bird, Tim, and Alex Marshall, *Afghanistan: How the West Lost Its Way* (Yale, 2011).

Chayes, Sarah, *The Punishment of Virtue: Inside Afghanistan After the Taliban* (Penguin, 2006).

Johnson, Robert, *The Afghan Way of War: How and Why They Fight* (Oxford, 2012).

Luttrell, Marcus, *Lone Survivor* (Little, Brown, 2007).

Parnell, Sean, *Outlaw Platoon* (William Morrow, 2012).

Rashid, Ahmed, *Taliban: Militant Islam, Oil and Fundamentalism in Central Asia, 2nd ed.* (Yale, 2010).

Tupper, Benjamin, *Greetings from Afghanistan, Send More Ammo* (New American Library Caliber, 2010).

# Meet the Author

**Joydeep Roy-Bhattacharya** was born in Jamshedpur, India, and educated in philosophy and politics at Presidency College, Calcutta, and the University of Pennsylvania. While at Penn, he traveled to Eastern Europe in 1989 and 1990 and witnessed the Velvet Revolutions. He returned to East-Central Europe for the next four years, traveling in Poland, Hungary, the Czech Republic, and Romania, visits that resulted in his first novel, *The Gabriel Club,* set in Budapest and Vienna. Following its publication, Roy-Bhattacharya left academia in 1998 and became a full-time novelist. He spent the next seven years researching and writing what became a 2,400-page manuscript set in Germany between the wars. That project is ongoing and supported by brief teaching stints at Bard College (2005–2006) and the University at Albany (2007). Meanwhile, in 2008, he set out to write a cycle of three discrete novels set in the Islamic world, both to redress the gross simplifications accorded that culture in the West and to highlight aspects of the contemporary world's Muslim inheritance. The first novel in this cycle, *The Storyteller of Marrakesh,* was published by W.W. Norton in 2011. At the same time, in order to directly address the ongoing conflict between the West and the Muslim world, he wrote *The Watch,* set in Kandahar province, Afghanistan, and based on Sophocles's *Antigone. The Watch* featured in the inaugural list of Random House's summer 2012 relaunch of Virginia and Leonard Woolf's Hogarth imprint, and was simultaneously published in Australia, Canada, the United Kingdom, and the United States.

For additional
Extra Libris content and more
on your favorite authors and books, visit

**ReadItForward.com.**

Discover fabulous book giveaways,
sneak peeks at great reads, downloadable
reader's guides, and behind-the-scenes
insights from authors, editors,
booksellers & more.